THE K STREET AFFAIR

THE K STREET AFFAIR

A NOVEL

MARI PASSANANTI

This book is a work of fiction, and the events, incidents and characters are the product of the author's imagination or are used fictitiously. Any resemblance to actual persons or events, living or dead, is entirely coincidental.

Copyright 2012 Mari Passananti

All rights reserved. No part of this book may be used or reproduced in any manner whatsoever without the written permission of the Publisher.
For information address
Rutland Square Press, 58 West Rutland Square, Boston, Massachusetts 02118.

First Rutland Square Press trade paperback edition October 2012.

Designed by Regina Starace

Manufactured in the United States of America

The Library of Congress has assigned the following catalog number (LCCN) to the first edition: 2012904563

ISBN 978-0-985-89460-3 (pbk)

FOR MY PARENTS

JANUARY

1

Every soul employed in the fancy glass office building at 1050 Connecticut Avenue swarms the exits well before the alarm system finishes blaring its robotic instructions. We march slowly and deliberately down a stairwell plunged into blackness, illuminated only by emergency bulbs at each landing. I'm grateful nobody has panicked, but I can't help silently urging my colleagues to pick up the pace. The alarm shrieks deep inside my head, even with my hands pressed over my ears.

How many minutes since the floor rocked under our feet? Can aftershocks take down buildings? Crush the people in them?

I try to estimate our progress, but lose count of the steps before we reach the pavement. I pause and blink at the shock of sunlight before realizing that every person who stops for a moment to regroup slows the evacuation. A detail cop yells at us to move north along Connecticut Avenue. Good. Shorter buildings up there.

On the sidewalk the news barrels over us: Not an earthquake. A bomb. A massive one. The kind that can change everything.

The phones crash as I'm breathlessly relating my escape from Rutledge & Smerth to Damien. My husband listens without comment for several minutes.

I pause to look at the screen. No signal. I wonder how long I've been talking to dead air. Sirens wail, both in the distance and down the block. Conversation ceases while hundreds of my shell-shocked co-workers study their unresponsive phones. There's a bizarre but absolute absence of hysteria.

A vaguely familiar man touches my arm. "Lena, are you okay?"

I nod absently and turn away from this guy I now recognize as a paralegal from my floor. I can't muster any conversation. I just want to go home. Hide under the covers. Erase the past thirty minutes from memory.

Firemen in full hazmat gear herd us further from the smoking crater that used to be the K to L Street block of Connecticut Avenue. They string up yellow police tape several yards back from the crumbling pavement, and plead with the most aggressive gawkers to back off so rescue teams can do their jobs. News vans start to arrive and soon outnumber ambulances. An officer with a bullhorn yells at the crowd to disperse. I pick my way through the crowd of faces, some familiar, many not. I finally reach M Street and turn north on 19th.

The walk takes twice as long as it should, because pedestrians, most underdressed for the January cold, clog the streets. My naked ears and fingers ache, but I feel guilty for wishing I had my coat. I should feel thankful to be alive and unscathed. By the time I arrive at our doorstep on T Street, it takes me three tries to maneuver the key into the lock with my numb hands.

I crank the heat, glad for the first time ever that Damien insisted we keep our landline. I knock a pile of magazines and catalogs out of the way so I can see its caller ID box, which has recorded more traffic this afternoon than during the entirety of the last two years. I try Damien at work. His steady voice on the outgoing message explains he has left for the day. He recites his temporarily useless mobile number and email address.

I talk to my mother, insist I'm shell-shocked but physically fine. I urge her to refrain from taking any of the prescription sedatives one of her book club ladies recommended. We hang up. I scroll back through the missed calls. My friend Hannah is the only member of our inner circle who hasn't checked in. Her office is a block from mine, a few hundred yards further removed from the crater on Connecticut. I saw, through the swirling ash and smoke, that her building withstood the jolt. Maybe Hannah will think to walk over here. We're much closer than her place across the river. I try to check Facebook, but our Internet isn't working. The router's insolent red light blinks under the desk.

On TV, NBC's anchorman reports, "At 12:13 p.m. in the nation's capital, at least six explosive devices detonated on different Metrorail trains. The explosions appear to have been simultaneous. The Secret Service, along with agents from both the FBI and the

Department of Homeland Security, are trying to determine who or what triggered the blasts."

Blasts, plural.

Six of them? I grab the arm of the couch for support. Tell myself the blasts can't all have been as bad as the one under my building.

The screen shows a map of DC's Metro system. In addition to the bomb right outside my building, there are explosion icons at Capitol South Station, between Chevy Chase and Bethesda Stations, at Foggy Bottom, downtown at Metro Center, and across the river, at Pentagon City Station.

The anchorman says, "Initial estimates put the death toll over 700, and rising." I feel the world tilt under my feet. 700? "Many area roads have collapsed from the force of the underground explosions. We have no solid figures on the number of wounded, but police estimate that over a thousand people await treatment at area hospitals. Search and rescue teams from around the country have started to arrive in the DC area to aid overwhelmed first responders. Time is of the essence. If anyone is alive under the rubble, they will be unlikely to survive overnight. Record lows are forecast throughout the region. Elsewhere around the nation, police are on high alert. The FAA has ordered all U.S. airports closed at this hour."

The local affiliate runs a list of road closures across the bottom of the screen. I'll be amazed if Damien makes it home from his office in Virginia, even if he started walking as soon as he heard. When they pause, unbelievably, for a commercial, I fish a tank top and yoga pants out of the dryer and change out of my suit. I wriggle out of my itchy bra of last resort, unpin my hair from its twist and brush out the crackly remnants of hairspray.

I haul the rest of the clean laundry into the living room to fold in front of the TV, because it's sat for five days and a mindless task could help me burn off nervous energy. I wish Damien was here.

The buzzer rings as the newscast resumes.

Good. Probably Hannah.

I pad over to the intercom in my leopard slippers. "Hello?"

An unfamiliar male voice crackles through the speaker. "Henry Redwell. United States Federal Bureau of Investigation, ma'am. We'd like a word with you, please."

What?

I buzz him in, because I don't know what else to do. Heavy footsteps barrel up the stairs. I peer through the peephole. Two men in dark suits blink back at me, their faces and features distorted by the one-way lens. My first, ridiculous thought is that my insane boss has sent the metaphorical men in shiny black shoes to drag me into the office.

I open the door as far as the security chain allows. "Can I ask what this is about?"

"Federal investigation, ma'am. May we come in?"

I chew my bottom lip and consider. Henry Redwell looks nothing like the kind of "bumbling idiot federal bozo" my boss always rails about. He has a full head of salt and pepper hair and a rugged, sun-damaged complexion. He wears stylish rectangular frameless glasses. He reminds me of someone. I realize he looks a bit like Harrison Ford.

"Could I please see some ID?"

Both agents hold out FBI ID's for my examination. *Redwell, Henry* and *von Buren, Maxwell*.

Maxwell von Buren shakes my hand with a finger crushing grip. He's way younger than Redwell, thirty-five to the senior agent's sixty-seven, if I read their ID's right. Agent von Buren removes his Ray Ban aviators to reveal unreadable steel gray eyes and prominent cheekbones. He has a strong chin, an exceptionally fortunate jaw line and the slightest hint of a tan. His dark hair is cropped close, as if recently trimmed by a ten-dollar barber. But even with his underwhelming haircut, if he relaxed a little, he'd be gorgeous.

He catches me sizing him up. I feel my ears burn.

Agent Redwell clears his throat. "Ma'am, the door?"

I shut the door in their faces to undo the chain. I open it again. The agents' big frames fill our narrow hallway in a way that's more than a little unnerving. I wish I'd dressed for the afternoon in something other than slippers, tank top and yoga pants. I point them towards the sofa and mute the television. I fold my arms across my chest and sit on the edge of Damien's beat up leather armchair, a relic from his bachelor days.

"Ma'am, you're the Lena Mancuso employed by Rutledge & Smerth, correct?"

"Yes, but could you please explain why you're here?"

"Ma'am, we'd appreciate it if you would answer a few basic questions. It's a matter of some urgency," Agent Redwell says. "You work on William Acheson's defense team, correct?"

"Yes," I say, warily.

William Acheson is a disgraced lobbyist formerly employed by my firm.

He stands accused of bribing several members of Congress, filing fraudulent tax returns, and a host of other white collar crimes. My aforementioned insane boss, legendary litigator Q. Randolph Smerth, made the unusual decision to keep Acheson's case at R&S in order to prevent any rival attorney from accessing our files.

I scan von Buren's face for clues as to why the FBI is wasting its time visiting me. He gives me nothing. He looks bored, or perhaps resentful of this peculiar assignment. I'm sure he'd rather be doing something sexier than questioning the most junior lawyer on a K Street insider's defense team.

Redwell presses onward, "In your role, you would have access to information about Acheson's financial dealings, correct?"

I fight to keep my nerves out of my voice. Alarm bells ring in my head. This isn't normal. It's nowhere in the vicinity of normal. Not on an ordinary day, and certainly not on the heels of today's bombings. "Maybe I should consult an attorney before saying any more, since whatever I know from my work on Acheson's behalf is privileged. As you would know."

I reach into the laundry pile and grab an ancient URI sweatshirt. It's blue and well worn, and does nothing to make me appear either more adult or professional, but at least it covers my bralessness. A sickening thought hits me as I pull it over my head.

The FBI would have all its resources on the bombing. And even if we weren't two hours from the biggest attack since 9/11, they would never tamper with a suspect's defense. Smerth would barge into court, hollering for a mistrial if he heard the government was trolling his staff for inside info. And he'd get one.

Oh, God. Maybe these men aren't agents.

My breath catches in my throat.

But then who are they?

I fight to keep my voice firm and level. "I still don't understand why you're here."

"To request your cooperation as an informant for an investigation authorized under the USA Patriot Act of 2001. Due to the sensitive nature of the matter, our protocol requires a background check," Redwell explains, as if this should be both expected and obvious.

Even if he's telling the truth, I don't understand why they would want *me*. I'm an inconsequential third year associate in a stuffy law firm. They're the FBI. If they wanted to jeopardize the federal case against my firm's client by consorting with his defense, wouldn't they aim higher than *me*? I feel out of my depth. Not to mention my comfort zone. Besides, all I know about the Patriot Act is what I've heard in the news. It has something to do with counter-terrorism and wire tapping. I should Google it as soon as our Internet comes back.

Henry slaps a file onto the only corner of my coffee table not occupied by laundry. "We suspect Smerth and Acheson knew today's attacks were going to happen."

"You're not serious," I practically laugh. "Smerth may have an explosive temper, but he's no terrorist."

Redwell and von Buren stare at me with the most serious expressions imaginable.

I struggle to process. "What makes you think he is?"

"A number of things," Redwell says. "First, three of Smerth's clients, Acheson, Volodya Korov and Prince Abdullah al Sultan bin Aziz are major players in Clearwater Partners. I'm sure you read the papers, Ms. Mancuso, so you'd know Clearwater has fallen under suspicion due to alleged payments to foreign extremists made by its subsidiary Burtonhall Corporation. Which your firm also represents. Why would one attorney represent clients whose interests could diverge at any time?"

"I'm sure everyone signed conflicts waivers. These are very sophisticated people."

"Of course they're sophisticated businessmen," Redwell says, amiably. "But six months ago we learned through a reliable source that Acheson, Aziz and Smerth established a company in Bermuda called the Lotus Group."

"It's probably one of Clearwater's blocker companies," I say.

Judging by the looks on the agents' faces, the FBI has already considered and dismissed this possibility. Clearwater, one of the largest companies on the planet, has an enormous private equity arm. Like many major PE firms, it maintains offshore "blocker" companies, so that its partners can avoid paying the IRS.

The Vice President of the United States, Jack Prescott, never paid a penny of taxes on hundreds of millions of dollars he made during his days as CEO of Clearwater's private equity division, because he socked the cash away in various offshore blocker companies. I'm sure Aziz and Korov do the same thing.

Which might make them all tax evaders. And quite conceivably money launderers.

But not terrorists.

I've learned working for Smerth that blockers are a legal loophole the mega-rich use to get richer, not only by avoiding taxes in the first place, but by repeatedly re-investing cash they would have otherwise forked over to the IRS. Prescott survived public scrutiny before the election by arguing that he had no role in managing his investments in the blocker companies. A "blind trust," transferred into his horse-crazy wife's name during the campaign, did so for him.

"Lotus is different. It's a blocker company on steroids," von Buren says. "It manages investments through its alleged hedge fund, but it claims those investments, always held in blind trust accounts, exist for the benefit of charity. Its investors repatriate hundreds of millions of dollars annually in the form of falsely secured loans made to Lotus' charitable beneficiaries."

Redwell clears his throat. "We think they also donate hundreds of millions to groups with which the principals would prefer not to become associated."

My head tilts to the right as I try to picture the Lotus Group's corporate flow chart. I glance around the room for a stray legal pad or even a Post-It to make a sketch. We've got nothing. *This is too cryptic. Circumstantial. I wish they'd get to the point.*

Redwell says, "Another remarkable thing about Lotus is that its directors include such financial heavy weights as Acheson's personal trainer and Smerth's nanny. Which leads us to believe that the 'blind' investments are— and you'll pardon my French, ma'am—bullshit."

Smerth has represented Clearwater and its power players for two decades. It's no wonder he's grown to share his clients' disdain for taxes. I'm only surprised that Smerth, with his legendary legal mind, would get caught. "How do you know this?" I ask. The whole point of offshore blockers is that they're secretive and out of range of the authorities.

"I said we have a reliable source," Redwell says.

"So, your source alleges that Acheson and Aziz, and perhaps Smerth, are using Lotus to write off questionable charitable contributions, based on the advice of their supposed fund managers? Who happen to be household employees?"

The agents nod. Redwell shoots me an earnest, encouraging look.

I shake my head. "No. I don't buy it. Wouldn't they get caught on the back end?" It's too brazen, too simple, too plain *wrong* to work. "And if their chosen charities are funneling big money to terrorists, doesn't that present a larger problem for you than chasing down some chronic tax evaders?"

Redwell's unruly eyebrows ease up his forehead. "We believe the two criminal enterprises, the finances and the operations, if you will, are so entangled that we can't apprehend one without the other."

"I still don't understand why you're telling me any of this. If you have probable cause, then start making arrests. Or at least get the IRS to audit the charities in question."

Max von Buren leans forward in his seat. "We came to you because we need someone inside the firm. If we make arrests too soon, we cut off our likeliest sources of further evidence. And auditing bullshit foundations is like playing Whack-a-Mole. One so-called charity shuts down, another springs up."

"Quite frankly, we're pressed for time, and not interested in discussing the many avenues we've already explored." Redwell looks me in the eye and starts to nod slightly, a technique I congratulate myself for recalling from a law school negotiation seminar. "We think you're smart and inclined to do the right thing."

I stall. "I need to talk this over with my husband. He'll be home any time now." I glance in the direction of the door, willing Damien to step through it.

"I'm sorry. There's no time for that." Redwell's tone makes it clear he lacks interest in further discussion. "Almost a thousand people lost their lives today. We think your boss knew it was about to happen. He did nothing to stop it. We need to know if we can count on you to help prevent another atrocity, because we believe today was just the beginning."

Just the beginning? Is Redwell suggesting that someone will blow away several more blocks? Imminently? It's unimaginable. Why would anyone in my law firm want to instigate such devastation? Smerth could have been killed or maimed, just like any other Washingtonian who happened to be standing in the wrong place at 12:13 p.m.

Except Smerth spent the day in our New York Office.

All my concerns for protecting my career and my employer evaporate. Maybe I should have never become a lawyer, because if my boss and his clients knew about today's attacks and did nothing, I wouldn't have it in me to defend them. The corners of Redwell's mouth turn up ever so slightly when I say, "I suppose it doesn't hurt to listen to whatever you have to say."

He cuts me off. "Sign here and we'll explain what we know so far."

I'm behaving completely out of character as I sign the confidentiality agreement Redwell shoves at me, but I don't care. My hand doesn't waver as I scrawl my name on the line. If Smerth has even a remote connection to today's devastation, I'm going to do whatever I can to make sure he pays.

Redwell nods approvingly. "Good. Now we can speak freely. Lena. Sorry, ma'am. May we call you Lena?"

"That's fine."

"Lena, we've wanted to recruit a source inside R&S for at least twelve months," Max explains. "At first we focused on a Charles Winthrop, but our research led us to believe he's determined to make partner at the firm. He's a loyal dog."

I ignore the not-so-subtle slight. While it's no secret to my friends that I don't plan to spend my life in the service of R&S, I bristle when strangers imply I lack the right stuff to hack it in the firm's senior ranks.

Charlie, on the other hand, has no life outside his eighty-plus hour work week, but he's a good guy. He showed me the ropes when I started and ran interference with Smerth until I got my bearings. That may not sound like much, but such kindness rarely exists in major law firms.

Max says, "Next to Charlie, you have the most access. Which makes you our best bet." He hauls a laptop out of his briefcase and shoves some of my laundry back to clear space on the table. He pulls up a map of the Caucasus, Turkey and the Mediterranean. He clicks to the next slide and a bright yellow line lights up on the map. I at least partially understand why we're looking at this part of the world. The yellow line represents a major new oil pipeline, owned mostly by Clearwater Partners. The line, nicknamed K4, pumps millions of barrels of crude oil from Kazakhstan through some former Soviet republics, to Turkish refineries.

K4's construction was financed through an enormous aid package from the United States. Congress sent billions of taxpayers' dollars to the various foreign governments, who paid it all right back to Clearwater Partners. Their subsidiary, the Burtonhall Corporation, built the entire project, supposedly for far less than the amount paid by the taxpayers.

Acheson helped steer K4 through Congress by persuading enough members that the United States would rather have Kazakhstan's oil refined and distributed by a NATO country than by Russia.

K4 was also the beginning of Acheson's major legal problems.

The prosecutors claim he purchased the pivotal votes, a charge that seems almost quaint now that corporations can make unlimited political contributions. At the time, it was a serious offense for a lobbyist to attach *quid pro quos* to campaign donations.

Which is why my life now revolves around his defense. Though the government would have had a slam dunk case against Acheson a few short years ago, Smerth plans to argue that the new, laxer rules allow lobbyists, like Acheson, to act as extensions of their clients.

Charlie calls the argument a Hail Mary pass, but Smerth seems confident. Which is good news for R&S, since Acheson runs his lobbying operation from under the firm's roof—not an uncommon scenario in Washington. Though the arrangement might strike outsiders as ethically dubious.

K4 has wildly exceeded analysts' expectations. Though operational for only a year, it supplies enough of the world's crude to wield considerable sway over price.

Max clicks to the next slide. A purple line springs up on the topographic map, running south to join the yellow line in Turkey. "I trust you know what we're looking at?"

"Yes." It's a Russian pipeline Clearwater wants to build. The plan includes eight or nine new refineries, which would make it the biggest construction project on the planet. By far. And the most expensive. I know this because Clearwater has promised all the potential legal work to Rutledge & Smerth. The deal would create a windfall of billable hours, enough to keep dozens of associates busy for years. If not decades. Which would be welcome news for many R&S lawyers spooked by persistent layoff rumors that will undoubtedly gain steam from today's tragedy.

The way Smerth explains it, Volodya Korov, a Russian oil and casino billionaire and longtime lobbying client of Acheson, controls the Russian oil fields in question. Korov has pledged a substantial percentage of his fortune to the project, on the condition that Burtonhall wins the work instead of a rival contractor controlled by the Russian government.

But there's a rub: a significant number of Congressmen believe Korov wants the refineries so he can do business with Iran, which produces far more oil than it can refine domestically.

At the time of his arrest, Acheson was collecting millions in retainers from both Korov and Clearwater to persuade Congress that the U.S. should help the Russians build their refineries. He disowned his earlier security concerns and appealed to economic pragmatism: The project would move forward, like it or not. Obstructionism by Congress would cost American jobs and profits.

All of which is no doubt fascinating to the board of Clearwater Partners and the management committee of my law firm. And perhaps certain Beltway policy wonks.

When nothing else is going on.

DC just suffered a devastating attack.

Why do I have federal agents in my living room discussing global oil politics?

Henry interrupts my train of thought. "Korov believes that if he secures American financing for the biggest public works project in post-Soviet Russian history, he can make a viable bid for the Russian presidency. But he put too many eggs in Acheson's basket.

With Acheson in disgrace, his clients find themselves *personae non grati* on the Hill."

Tell me something I don't know. Or something that actually matters. I glance at my grandmother's antique clock on the wall by our bay window. Its brass pendulum has ticked off three hours since the attacks.

I wonder how far away Damien is.

Henry says, "We've received a tip that Acheson masterminded a plan, to be financed by his international associates, to sabotage the existing pipeline, K4. The drop in supply would cause a sudden spike in energy prices, which would make the need for a back up line crystal clear to the American public."

"Which would spur Congress to act," Max adds.

"Sabotage?" I ask.

"Blow it to pieces," says Henry.

"I understand that would be an unwelcome development, and forgive me for sounding blasé, but doesn't some vague threat to an oil pipeline in the middle of nowhere pale in comparison to what happened *right here* this afternoon? Have you been downtown? Whole blocks are gone. Lives destroyed. Buildings in ruins. People missing in the rubble." My voice catches in my throat.

"Of course it pales in comparison until it happens."

"I'm sorry. You've lost me," I say.

Henry lowers his voice and leans in so close that I can feel his breath on my face. "We think today's attack was the opening strike in a war started, financed and prosecuted by a corporation. Your firm's clients seek to destabilize the world economy, incite public panic and ultimately orchestrate a takeover of the U.S. government."

"Don't look so shocked," Max says. "The stock market is in free fall. Flags are selling out from coast to coast. People in backwaters are stockpiling canned goods and guns. Once gas prices hit eight bucks a gallon, the masses will fall in line with whoever promises relief. Even if their saviors happen to be terrorists dressed up as good flag-waving captains of industry."

2

The agents watch for my reaction.

I hope my icy stare conveys disbelief, spiked with disgust for their gratuitous dramatization of an awful situation. "Every firm in Washington represents someone unsavory. It doesn't make the lawyers terrorists. And why would these alleged corporate warriors risk destabilizing the entire economy? I doubt their shareholders would approve."

I may sound patronizing, but I don't care. I wish they'd leave. I'm starting to feel faint, a likely result of failing to eat anything all day but a yogurt smoothie some nine hours ago, as much as from shock.

Henry adopts a professorial tone. "Clearwater has major shareholders and operations all over the globe. They don't base their actions on America's best interests. Not since the Cold War ended."

My eyes boggle at him. He's clearly off his rocker.

Of course Clearwater is greedy and socially irresponsible. But I can't imagine they'd bomb Washington to make a buck.

Or stage some stuff-of-Hollywood private war for similar reasons.

"Besides, and I don't know how to say this without sounding rude, don't you watch the news?" I motion at the silenced TV. "All the talking heads, including your boss, seem to believe some unknown Al Qaeda wannabes set off the bombs. Which sounds far more plausible than what you're suggesting."

Henry's eyebrows shoot towards his hairline. Max stares at me over his laptop. I take another stab at explaining myself. "You're making a huge leap. Let's say for the sake of argument that the Burtonhall Corporation gave money to some bad people. It doesn't follow that Smerth or Acheson had anything to do with it. And if Aziz did, he's got diplomatic immunity, which makes him a big waste of your time."

I want to believe Smerth has some scruples, in spite of his unsavory client roster and legendarily vicious temper. "Smerth cares too deeply about his reputation to venture into the criminal underworld. The man is on the short list for the Supreme Court."

"Fair enough," says Henry. "It's a major leap, but that doesn't make it impossible, does it?"

"Not impossible, but certainly improbable." I feel like a witness under cross-examination.

Acheson is more of a wildcard, but only because of his lifelong connection to Vice President Prescott.

Prescott, Acheson's childhood friend, Yale roommate and fellow Bonesman, is the conniving, calculating one. He hides it under a raffish façade, but rumors of his quiet, evil genius circulate continuously inside the Beltway. In fact, if the agents were standing here accusing Prescott of masterminding a deadly power grab, I might believe them.

But Acheson?

He's too flashy and too fly-by-the-seat-of-his-expensive-pants to orchestrate the underhanded things these agents are suggesting. He's a one-trick pony: he trades cash for influence. I doubt there's much else to him.

Max jumps in. "Let's put all this foreign oil stuff aside for a second. What we really need you to do is read files. Help us understand how Clearwater's key people moved their money around."

Henry pointedly consults his watch. "Let's focus on what you should watch for. I assume you have access to Acheson's client files?"

"Right now I do nothing but the massive document review for Acheson's bribery case."

"That's good news for us," Max says.

I can think of nothing less "good" than several consecutive eighty-hour work weeks, spent among boxes of Acheson's mostly everyday correspondence.

Max addresses Henry as if I've left the room. "I was skeptical, but you might be right. She's too junior to attract anyone's notice. If someone catches her flipping through suspicious documents, they'll assume she's a harmless baby associate, off on the wrong track."

"And how would I identify something as suspicious? You obviously have no idea how much irrelevant paper is involved. We're talking about several large rooms, packed floor to ceiling with documents." It's a game that all big firm litigators play—everyone knows neither side can possibly analyze every piece of paper. I think of the times I've glanced only at the top few pages of a file to determine whether the contents deserved a thorough read. When we're under time pressure even sticklers like Charlie joke that there's a reason the firm carries tons of malpractice insurance.

Henry starts ticking off points on his fingers. "We're interested in all contributions to lobbying efforts on behalf of Clearwater or Burtonhall, especially if the funds moved through Lotus. We're obviously interested in any payments through conduits to religious extremists, possibly via a network of obscure charities. We suspect Clearwater subbed out their dirtiest work to willing fanatics. Also, and this should be easier to come by, we want to see all documents concerning the proposed Russian pipeline."

"Say I find what you're looking for. I can't email files out of the firm without anyone noticing. I can't even use a copy machine without it recording a client and matter number."

When I glance his way, Max grins, far too broadly considering the mood of the city. He has a dazzling white smile and perfectly aligned teeth, likely the result of expensive orthodontics inflicted during his junior high years. The man could be in a toothpaste commercial.

Henry clears his throat again. He produces a BlackBerry from his coat pocket and offers it to me.

"I already have one. The firm makes sure they can reach every associate, day and night."

"You don't have one like this. Its satellite phone has special security. Your conversations can't be intercepted by other cellular users, police scanners or nosy neighbors. The device includes a high resolution camera similar to those used by CIA field agents. If you photograph a sheet of paper, even from several feet away, we'll be able to read it. Also, the flash is so fast it's imperceptible to the human eye."

"Wow." I wonder if it's too late to tell them I lack the nerve to help them out. God, I wish Damien would come through that door.

"This BlackBerry supports multiple networks," Max says. "One will go out over Rutledge & Smerth's servers. You can use it for business as usual. Another will connect to us through a secure server."

"You want to read *all* my work email? I could get disbarred for that."

Henry must sense that I'm ready to use this excuse to back out. "You won't be disbarred. We have the proper warrants and authorization from the highest level." He pauses to check he hasn't lost my attention. "This brilliant little device has about a hundred times more memory space than your regular BlackBerry. If you'd be so kind as to hand over your existing device, we'll get everything configured."

I hesitate. I've worked so hard, slogged through law school, billed thousands of hours, given up my daily workouts and much of my social life, all to rack up enough time at a top firm to write my own ticket when I leave, hopefully sometime within the next three years. Damien and I have it all planned out. If I leave R&S for a nice government job before I turn thirty-three, we'll have plenty of time to start a family before I'm thirty-five.

I can't gamble my entire life plan away on the word of two glorified cops.

"I know this is difficult," Henry says. "But think: *Your* clients may have murdered all those innocent people. Can you live with that?"

I hand over R&S's BlackBerry.

"We'll be back. Tomorrow, if not sooner." Henry hoists himself out of our sunken in sofa. He clearly wants to leave before I change my mind.

On the way out the door, Max turns back and looks me in the eye. "Don't worry. You're going to be great."

For a second I feel reassured. I can do this. And since I can't convince myself that the agents are lying, I *should* do this. So why is my whole body shaking?

Maybe because I'm still not convinced that Agents Redwell and von Buren are for real.

3

I try to Google the agents' contact info, but we still have no Internet service. I call information instead. After six or seven tries, I get through to a harried switchboard operator who connects me to Henry Redwell's secretary's voicemail. A female assistant recites the outgoing message. *"You've reached the office of Deputy Director Henry Redwell."* My pulse quickens. *Acheson and Smerth merit the deputy director's time? In the midst of a national crisis?* I hang up at the beep. My mind swims. It takes a dozen tries to get through again. When Max von Buren's voice comes through, clear and unmistakable, I let myself exhale.

I pace tight circles around the living room until the late afternoon sky turns purple and then gray. The news coverage cycles a long loop of short pieces, but I can't turn away. My dad calls, as does my college roommate. Around five, I make a cup of tea. I still feel queasy and light headed, but too shocked to eat.

At five-fifteen Damien finally bursts through our front door in his suit and overcoat. His nose and ears shine bright red from the cold. He has someone else's mountain bike balanced on one arm.

Damien sets the bike down, removes his gloves and runs his fingers through his sandy blond hair. "Everything is closed. I've never seen so many people walking."

I dive across the room and launch myself into my husband's arms. I knew he was nowhere near the explosions, but I'm still relieved he's home. "A whole block of Connecticut Avenue is gone," I snuffle into his shoulder. "I was in the ABP next door fifteen minutes before the blast. All the windows were blown out. The whole store front is gone."

"I know," he says and strokes my hair.

"What if buildings start collapsing? What if there are more bombs hidden under our feet, waiting to explode?" All the bottled up trauma of the day starts to pour out of me. I feel as if my whole body might crumble from the effort of containing my emotions all afternoon.

"Shhh. You're alright," Damien says. "We're alright."

I lean into his chest thinking, *this is why I married him.* Sure he's fun, smart and blessed with classic good looks, but he's a rock in a crisis. When others get exercised over some calamity, Damien remains calm, though never in the maddening manner of the perpetually oblivious. He possesses a cool confidence that says, stick with me, I won't steer you wrong. Which explains why he's a successful money manager, even in a sluggish economy. I also know him well enough to know that his quiet reaction is largely for my benefit. He's as freaked as anyone else.

Wait until he hears about my afternoon visitors.

I disentangle myself from his arms to turn down the TV. I'm about to tell him everything when Damien rubs his temples and says, "Nobody's heard from Hannah."

I'm worried about her, too, but hearing Damien say it makes her absence feel more real, more offensive somehow. "How do you know? Cell service is down. Her building is fine. I saw it with my own eyes." What I don't concede is that Damien might have better information. He and Hannah's fiancé, John, work at the same investment company.

"That's not it," Damien says, and my stomach crunches as I realize he's struggling to choose his words. "John said she went to Alexandria at lunch, to look at a veil in some bridal shop."

He doesn't need to tell me that to reach Old Town, she'd take the blue line, which passes through the site of the Pentagon City bombing.

"She would've taken a cab," I say, without much conviction. Hannah spends ninety hours a week defending one of those too-big-to-fail banks against a mortgage fraud lawsuit. She could bill the time if she brought a file to read on the train.

"John's frantic. I've never seen him so unhinged." Damien kicks off his shoes. "He kept saying that he *knows* she was on the metro. His fiancée thinks nothing of dropping a grand on a piece of white tulle, but she gets cheap about taxi rides. He was obsessively listing the few times she's taken a cab in daylight hours over the years he's known her. Working backwards. Counting on his hands like a first grader." He shakes his head as if to clear the unsettling image of his normally cool and self-possessed friend and colleague.

The tears I've held at bay since he burst through the door start to stream down my face. Damien scoops me up in his arms. He turns my chin up so I'm looking into his deep blue eyes. "She's going to be fine."

"You can't promise that." I cry into his chest. Mascara stains appear on his shirt.

"She will be fine," he repeats, but he doesn't sound particularly convinced. He waits a moment, then kisses me before disentangling himself and heading for the kitchen. I hear him rummaging in the wine fridge, a wedding present from his parents. A cork pops and he returns with two glasses of red. "I think we could both use a drink."

My encounter with the FBI is on the tip of my tongue when I realize that maybe I'm not supposed to tell *anyone*. I tuck my legs underneath myself on the sofa and swirl my wine, unsure of what to do. Damien snuggles up close behind me. "I know you've had this on all day, but I've been in a news outage." He reaches for the clicker, turns up the volume.

The anchor starts with a recap of the casualty report I saw ten minutes ago.

I pick up my unresponsive phone and scroll through the photos for a good one of Hannah. "We should make a flier."

I find a picture of me and Hannah on New Year's Eve and crop myself out on Damien's laptop. I add her details and print copies until the color cartridge gives out.

I'm rummaging around for more ink when the doorbell buzzes. "Hannah?" I almost whisper, not wanting to jinx anything.

Diana, my friend since the third grade, our neighbor since last September, and ranking staffer to the senior senator from Illinois since his last chief of staff quit in disgrace after texting photos of his privates to an intern, breezes into our apartment. She's wearing a huge fake fur hat with a green cashmere coat that most people couldn't carry off. It brings out her eyes, which today are their natural color. If my eyes were like Diana's instead of boring brown, I'd never share her enthusiasm for colored contacts.

I jump up to hug her. "They sent us home," she says, as she unwinds herself from several feet of scarf. "They said the building could be unstable. I can't believe it."

Damien gets off the sofa to kiss Diana hello and offer her a glass of wine, which she accepts after arranging her hair into a twist secured with those sticks that geishas use. If I did my hair that way it would look messy, but on her, it's gorgeous. Diana possesses a God-given gift for accessories and a siren-like charm that causes men to fall all over themselves in their attempts to impress her. Even Damien, who never flirts with my friends, says Diana is phenomenal.

Diana, Hannah and I had plans to meet tonight for margaritas and dinner at Lauriol Plaza, one of our favorite neighborhood haunts. Obviously those plans are canceled, so I'm a little confused about why she's here. Diana lives down the block. It's not like she can't reach her apartment.

She finishes her glass of wine in two gulps and holds it out for a refill, before announcing, "I can't go home."

"I know," I say, and instantly feel like a heel for not recognizing the obvious—nobody, not even brash, fearless Diana—wants to be alone and scared in a crisis. "It's awful. I can't stop thinking about Hannah. I wouldn't want to be alone waiting to hear, either."

"Stop. What do you mean, *waiting to hear*?" she says.

"Nobody has heard from Hannah. John thinks she was on the blue line."

"Oh God. Are you sure? The blue line casualty report will be the last to come in. The senator had me request one. A major donor's son is missing. But the Virginia State Police are useless. They wasted an entire hour debating whether they needed hazmat suits to respond to the scene."

Diana's face turns pale. Damien says, "Let's not panic. It won't help."

We watch the news in silence for a moment. "Wait. If you didn't know Hannah was missing, why did you say you can't go home?" I ask.

Diana sighs. "Paolo is moving out as we speak. Not that I care anymore. I suppose there's nothing like an act of war to give you perspective." She attempts a weak smile.

I'd forgotten about Diana's latest break up. She tends towards intense, short lived affairs. For the past six weeks she's let a starving artist called Paolo—just Paolo, no last name—crash at her apartment. A month ago she called him a misunderstood genius. Last week she decided he's actually a freeloading twit, one with limited talent and nonexistent drive. The final stroke came yesterday when Paolo unveiled an oil on canvas nude of Diana. She claimed he painted her thighs enormous. He argued that fat thighs "aroused the male spirit and drew the eye upward to the *locus of fecundity*." Emphasis presumably added by Diana.

Their final fight seemed worthy of extensive discussion twelve hours ago, when Diana related the details by phone on her way to work. She told me she threw Paolo's palette at the canvas, wrecked the painting and ordered the "amateurish loser" out of her apartment. He called her every filthy name imaginable before storming out.

"Of course I went home tonight thinking I would let the fucker put off moving his stuff for a day. But the self-absorbed asshat was there, boxing up his precious bong and a bunch of other crap, oblivious to everyone but himself. As usual."

I shake my head in commiseration and assure Diana she's better off. The news report cuts to footage of body bags lined up outside the Metro Center blast site. We watch in funereal silence. A lump hardens in my throat. I don't dare mention Hannah, as if articulating the possibility she's hurt or worse could increase the chances of that being true.

Eventually Damien, wearing his ski jacket and a frayed 49ers hat he'd never sport in public, goes out the kitchen window to throw some frozen burgers on the tailgate grill we keep on the fire escape.

He eats riveted to the television. Diana and I nibble, our appetites suppressed by nerves and fresh grief. We all jump when the landline shrills to life.

"Hannah!" I shriek, and dive for the phone.

Damien gets there first and scowls. "It's Rutledge & Smerth's New York office," he says, incredulously. My face falls. I was certain it would be Hannah.

"I wonder what Q. Randolph wants," Diana says.

"He's probably out of paperclips," Damien grumbles. "Go ahead, answer it. You know he'll keep calling if you don't."

"Why the hell have you not checked your voice mail?" my boss's familiar voice booms through the phone. "Just because we've been *inconvenienced* by these Goddamned terrorists does not mean we fucking shut down. We *never* shut down. Never! Are you listening to me?" Before I can formulate an answer, he demands, "And you retrieved your laptop before leaving, right? Because I am not interested in you having a paid fucking vacation tomorrow, even if the Goddamned police won't let us in the fucking building." His voice crescendos. I bet spit flies out of his mouth with each expletive.

Of course I didn't return to my office, four flights up from the conference room where I spend almost every working hour. Like everyone else, I was terrified the building would crash down on my head. I wanted to get out of that dark, crowded stairwell as soon as possible, not fight my way back up it like some kind of deranged urban lemming.

Q. Randolph Smerth continues his tirade. Something about the bastards at the U.S. Attorney's office dumping a warehouse full of documents on us, which I will need to review before the Acheson hearing next week. The thing is, Smerth knows as well as I do, that the chances of the hearing happening on schedule are about the same as the chances of me becoming Miss America *and* the first woman on Mars.

I hate that Damien and Diana can hear every word he shouts at me. I feel my face go red and wonder why I'm the only Italian-American I know who blushes bright pink. "Do you or do you not have your laptop?" Smerth hollers again.

He's an abusive, egomaniacal jerk, but that's all. The FBI must be mistaken.

"Randolph, I'm sorry." I struggle to keep my voice level. "I wasn't able to retrieve anything before leaving the building."

He smashes the receiver down with a final gratuitous string of obscenity.

I've developed rather thick skin working at R&S, but when I turn back to Diana and Damien, I'm shaking all over.

Diana reaches out to touch my arm. "Is that place worth it? I mean, look around, Lena. Life is short. Do you want to spend any more of yours working for that lunatic?"

"Sometimes I feel like quitting on the spot." I swallow the lump in my throat. Smerth is not going to make me cry.

Damien refills my wine. "Then that bastard wins. Suck it up and leave on your own terms when the time is right." He's diplomatic enough not to add, *when we've paid your loans.*

"Or you could luxuriate in a euphoric moment of telling Smerth where he can stick it," says Diana.

Damien shoots her a stink eye, but drops the subject because the president is about to speak.

A grainy address streams from Air Force One, thirty-five-thousand feet over the Pacific Ocean. The Commander-in-Chief reassures the nation that the attacks will not go unanswered, that America is stronger than her enemies. Immediately afterward, Vice President Jack Prescott steps to the White House podium. He struggles to stop an unseemly grin spreading across his ruddy face as he reminds the citizenry that the president cannot take questions because he's flying home from an economic summit in Beijing. Prescott repeats his boss's promise to hunt down the terrorists. He straightens his serious red tie and takes questions, the first batch of which yield no new information.

A reporter frequently seen on *60 Minutes* says, "We've obtained internal memos from your former firm, Clearwater Partners, suggesting that its subsidiary, the Burtonhall Corporation, knowingly contributed to a variety of charities that funnel money to terrorist groups. Is this true?"

"That's a preposterous and unpatriotic suggestion. I know Clearwater Partners. And Clearwater Partners is a great American company, one that provides jobs to hundreds of thousands of Americans." Prescott makes a resolute face at the camera.

The reporter presses onward. "Mr. Vice President, can you rule out the possibility that you ever served on the board of any company that financed attacks on U.S. citizens? Or any company that profited, even tangentially, from terrorist activities?"

"Ballsy question," Diana says, as the reporter pushes his point. "How can you be sure that your offshore interests aren't funding enemies of the United States, either directly or indirectly?"

A blaze of red anger flashes across Prescott's face but the Vice President manages to maintain his composure. "Tonight I believe the American people want to know how we're going to respond to these brutal attacks on our homeland," he says, through clenched teeth. He calls on a friendlier correspondent, assures her that next week's second term inauguration will go on as scheduled, with added security and muted festivities.

I hold my breath and brace for another apoplectic phone call from my boss.

4

When Diana leaves, sometime after ten, I tell Damien about the FBI. Not telling feels like an enormous breach of trust, one I'm not willing to make. He listens, eyes incredulous, but without comment, until I get to the part about snooping inside the firm.

By the time I'm done explaining everything, the tenor of Damien's voice has changed, from curiosity to alarm. "Why would your law firm want to get mixed up with terrorists? And why would they want to blow up K4 when they helped build it? And don't take this the wrong way, but don't they have better sources than you?"

"I have no idea if they are mixed up with terrorists. The idea is to find out. As for K4, that's easier. A major client of the firm wants a rival pipeline built. If someone knocks out K4, it puts the need for an alternate in focus."

Damien's eyes narrow in skepticism. "Right. Because that's how most big time lawyers go about making rain for themselves."

"I'm just telling you what they told me."

"Are you sure you want to get involved? I mean, besides the fact you can kiss your career goodbye if you're caught, it sounds dangerous. I know I'm not a lawyer, but it seems simple to me: the cops have enough for a warrant or they don't. The FBI shouldn't use you to do their dirty work. They want Acheson's files? Subpoena them."

"It's not that easy. R&S would spend months or years contesting a subpoena. What if the agents are right? What if the firm had a hand in today? What if they murdered Hannah? I need to know." My voice catches at the top of my throat and I squeeze my eyelids shut to fight back fresh tears.

Damien rubs his scalp in frustration. Before I can think of anything else to say he tries a softer tack. "Fine. If you agree to help them, can you at least promise we won't get stuck in the witness protection program? I like our life. I don't want to move to Iowa to raise pigs."

"That's not going to happen. I'm not testifying against a mobster. I'll be looking at documents – which I do every day anyway."

Damien's eyebrows shoot up. "But you don't pass along clients' secrets every day."

"I should do the right thing." Right? The agents didn't seem to doubt the safety of their surveillance project. They probably snoop on citizens like this routinely. It sounds like a big deal to me, but to them it's another day at the office.

I'll sleep better knowing I am doing everything possible to help solve the worst crime since 9/11. Damien and I will not end up hiding from the wrath of Q. Randolph Smerth in swine country.

I pass a fitful, sleepless night with no word from Hannah. I check my phone at least every half hour. When Wednesday morning dawns, it's brilliant and sunny, wholly at odds with the mood of the entire city. Damien leans across me and grabs the remote from my nightstand. I settle into the nook under his arm.

We learn that search and rescue teams have recovered evidence suggesting a team of suicide bombers triggered the blasts. The grim-faced head of the FBI says his investigators believe the perpetrators underwent "significant training." Two of the bombers have been identified as thirty-year-old U.S. citizens. The others remain unknown. Both taught math at a community college in Buffalo. One was married with two-year-old twin boys, his companion recently divorced, no children. Clean records, not so much as a traffic violation between them. Last year, both traveled to the Horn of Africa as part of a humanitarian trip sponsored by their congregation. They show the suspects' imam, an ordinary, western looking man with small glasses and droopy cheeks, whose face shows bewilderment, grief and in his eyes, disgust. The banner below his image reads, somewhat curiously: BREAKING NEWS: BUFFALO MOSQUE NOT RADICALIZED.

The president, who irritates me not only because he's too conservative, but also for non-political reasons –he would never be leader of the free world if he was a hefty woman instead of a 350-pound man – delivers an Oval Office address at 6:45 a.m. He reminds the citizenry to remain at the highest level of alert. He calls the attacks "the work of homegrown Islamic militants" even as the banner proclaiming the moderation of the suspects' congregation continues to scroll onscreen beneath his desk.

Damien tears himself away from the news, makes a pot of coffee and holes up in our miniscule home office, the existence of which qualifies our 800-square-foot apartment as a two bedroom. Damien would prefer to spend the morning glued to the television like everyone else, but his clients are rich people. Whenever tragedy strikes, rich people grow anxious about their investments. Damien's phone rings off the hook with clients seeking reassurance that the market won't tank.

This afternoon, they will call back to scream at him because the market has, predictably, tanked.

I alternate between watching the rehashed coverage and dialing Hannah's number. Cell service returns. Still no answer. I swallow the lump in my throat. I'm not going to let myself think about her increasingly likely fate. If she isn't accounted for by noon, I'll go out and post the fliers.

The images on the screen cause my whole body to ache. I should turn off the TV. I can't help Hannah by gawking. My hand moves for the clicker several times, but I can't bring myself to push the power button. I call her fiancé, John, tell him I made fliers. When we hang up, I feel worse, and angry at myself for my inability to offer him any magic words of comfort.

The market drops over a thousand points in its first hour. Both the New York Stock Exchange and NASDAQ halt trading. Damien says he needs an espresso to combat his stress headache and proposes a Starbucks run. I bring along my stack of fliers and a roll of tape. *They're insurance. Like an umbrella to ward off rain. Not really necessary, but nice to have.*

I spend much of the morning posting my missing person fliers up and down Connecticut Avenue. The police turn me back at P Street. All afternoon, I wait for the phone to ring with good news that feels increasingly unlikely as the hours slip away, watch the news and stare out the front window. Twenty-nine hours since the bombings. No word from Hannah. I'm too sick with worry to eat. My head feels light from subsisting on water and coffee. I scrunch my eyes shut but can't purge the image of all those thousands of futile fliers flapping in the streets after 9/11.

Max von Buren reappears when the last pink and orange remnants of sunlight are fading from the sky.

I stand in the doorway, blocking his way in. He hands me the BlackBerry. "All set. Do you need me to review its features?"

"No, I've got it."

Max asks if he can come inside. I usher him back to his post on the sofa. I palm the remote but decide against muting the TV as I resume my perch on the edge of the armchair. Damien is tied up on a conference call. Without background noise his conversation might carry from our home office. The news reruns a report about overwhelmed hospitals. The death toll stands at 988. The number of injured, many times that. I feel teary again.

"What's wrong?" Max asks.

"Are you serious?" My voice is stuffed up but testy.

"I'm sorry. I suppose everyone processes tragedy at their own pace." He looks worried. He's probably concerned they've recruited an emotional lightweight. He studies my face, his steely eyes expectant.

"It's Hannah. My friend. I think she may have been traveling by metro yesterday." Fat tears start to roll. "She was going to look at a veil," I explain. My nose stuffs up.

"What?"

I try to compose myself. "A veil. She's getting married. She was going to some store in Old Town at lunch. Her fiancé thinks she took the metro." What I leave unsaid, because I haven't even confessed this to Damien or Diana: I had planned to accompany her, until Smerth paged me with yet another client "emergency." We would have taken a taxi. Avoided the metro explosion. Every time I think about it my chest tightens. As it does now.

Max produces a handkerchief, a real cloth one, from his pocket and hands it to me over the coffee table. I dab at my eyes. Black mascara stains the bleached white cloth. I probably have raccoon face.

"Are you certain nobody has heard from her?" Max asks when I finish wiping my eyes.

I shake my head no and sniff loudly. I haven't asked why Max wanted to come inside. Part of me doesn't want to know. I've agreed to risk my job. Unfathomable numbers of innocent people are dead or maimed. Hannah is missing. Is it wrong that I feel unable to deal with anything else?

Max frowns. I can't tell whether he's assuming the worst about Hannah or trying to figure out a way to help. In case it's the latter, I feel obligated to ask about his relatives and friends. "Is there anyone you're worried about?"

"No. My family is up in Boston. I'm new to DC. Most of my limited number of friends are guys at the Bureau. All accounted for," he says, almost apologetically.

I seize the distraction of small talk like an overboard sailor grabbing a lifeline in rough surf. "Where in New England? Because I'm from Rhode Island. My parents still live there, near Green Hill Beach. It's great, especially in August when the water warms up. Except some years hordes of jellyfish invade." I realize I sound like a babbling idiot and stop myself.

"Yeah, I know all about it." Max flashes me one of his toothpaste ad-worthy smiles. "Except the jellyfish. That's new and critical information."

I answer his attempt to lighten the mood with a frown. Even though I have nothing to hide, I feel violated by the FBI's mucking about in my life, not to mention angry and hurt that he's making jokes at a time like this.

Max wipes the smile from his face. He leans towards me and tents his fingers. "I know you're preoccupied with your missing friend, but I'm here because it's crucial that we get you back inside Rutledge & Smerth. Tonight. Evidence could vanish by tomorrow."

Is he nuts? The building could be unstable. Structurally sound or not, it's on the edge of a murder scene. The firm is closed. They never close. Not even on Christmas.

Instead of appealing to reason, I say, "In case you haven't processed this, one of my best friends is *missing*. I am not going anywhere until she's found." As if my living room vigil is vital to the rescue effort.

"I'm sorry, but you need to understand this is a matter of national security. You need to do the job you agreed to do." His voice sounds unaccustomed to backtalk.

"I agreed to keep my eyes open for you *during* work, not to sneak in while the building's shut down."

Max fixes an indulgent expression on his face. "How I love working with lawyers. Maybe we didn't explain the scope of the assignment well enough." He looks me right in the eye. "We need you to do this. I will do everything I can to help find your friend. I promise. But you can't help her sitting by the phone. You *can* help us by getting back into the office."

My eyes narrow but I'm listening.

"Like we said this morning, we suspect the Lotus Group is a conduit for funds someone wants off the radar. We need you, with your insider access, to figure out the truth." His grey eyes search my face, pleading silently for agreement.

I still think the Lotus Group sounds more like an aggressive tax shelter than a terror front. I bet the FBI has over reached. I take a second to weigh my options.

"Fine," I agree finally. "We can go to R&S. Not that I think you'll find anything."

"I'm not going in. You are."

"Excuse me?"

"I can't go in with you. That would be what we call a black bag job, and it's illegal. FBI personnel can't physically break into a premises, even to look for evidence. You work there. It's different."

"Sounds like semantics to me. Henry said you had the necessary warrants. Why don't you just serve one and seize the files yourself?"

Max adopts the tone of an exasperated adult explaining something simple to a slow child. "Because then they will know, not merely suspect, that we're onto them. They'll shut down their entire network of shell companies and resurface somewhere else before we're ready."

"This sounds more involved than I thought." I wonder whether I should ask Max to leave, whether he'd pick up and go, and whether I could forget he and Henry ever walked into my apartment. My left eyeball pricks with the first stab of a migraine.

Max waits for me to speak. When I don't he says, "Why don't you give me a description of your friend?"

Maybe he is human after all, and not some bionic, unemotional alien. I rub at the pain in my eye. It doesn't help.

"Her name is Hannah Smith. She's 29 years old. She's got long, light blonde hair, blue eyes, and she's about 5'5" and very thin. Hannah's built like a ballerina. She was probably wearing a blue cashmere coat over her suit and carrying a brown Fendi tote bag. She has a slight southern accent that gets more pronounced when she's excited or stressed." I pause. "Is that enough?"

"For starters." Max whips out his phone. He dials, waits, repeats Hannah's description to whoever answers. He holds. "He's checking," he tells me. Who is this mystery person on the other end of the line, who has access to information nobody else does?

The other person comes back on. Max smiles, then frowns.

"What? What is it?"

"Triage at Pentagon City Hospital has a woman matching the physical description, with minor cuts and bruises and a compound fracture to the left leg. She was injured in a thirty-car pile up by the Pentagon City explosion site."

Relief floods over me and I feel my face break out in an enormous smile. Max listens to the person on the line and frowns. "But her name is Joann Oberlin. She's a secretary at the patent office."

"They're sure?" I feel crushed all over again.

Max says they're positive. She came in conscious, clutching her wallet and screaming for pain meds in a New York accent. I listen as he instructs the person on the other end to alert him if Hannah surfaces. When he hangs up he tells me he's sorry. Really sorry. He omits any polite assurances that there's still hope. Any survivors trapped under the rubble could freeze to death tonight.

I nod and mouth "thank you" because I'm momentarily mute. The lump in my throat feels like it's grown to the size of a large apple. I'm going to cry in front of Max again and I don't care. He steps into the hall and lets me pull myself together.

I sit straight up and stare out our bay window at the bare tree tops, illuminated from below by the streetlights. I listen to my grandmother's clock tick off the minutes and struggle to absorb this latest blow.

It should be rush hour, but the streets are empty. Many businesses, like Rutledge & Smerth, had no choice but to heed the government's call to close. The engineers have yet to pronounce the building structurally sound, but Max expects their announcement soon. That's why it's so important to go in tonight. My reservations about helping the FBI fade as the crater, illuminated by floodlights, comes into view. I can't wait to unearth any answers lurking in Acheson's files.

The awful smell assaults us through the air vents of Max's government SUV as we exit Dupont Circle and merge onto Connecticut Avenue, which in its deserted state resembles a grand boulevard. I breathe into my sleeve to try to mask the chemical stench of burnt plastic and metal. Burnt bodies. Max grimaces and clears his throat. I fight the impulse to gag.

The crime scene remains chaotic. The crowds of bystanders south of L Street have dispersed, but their numbers have been replaced by various rescue workers, many sporting out-of-town uniforms and gas masks. Throngs of reporters swarm each regiment of searchers. A firefighter barks at one of the correspondents to back off. The reporter, dragging her cameraman behind her, ignores the order and pushes forward towards the crater, from which a steady stream of black smoke continues to rise. The stench is overpowering, but the cloud of ash and steam that hung in the air yesterday has dissipated. Because the blast happened underground, the scene is nothing like the images from Lower Manhattan in the days after 9/11. Most of the devastation remains out of public view.

A uniformed DC cop wearing a mask over his nose and mouth intercepts us by the entrance to my building. Max waves his badge and warns him not to interfere with the federal investigation. The cop backs off.

Max leans in close to me and whispers, "Anything at all that connects the Lotus Group to Clearwater Partners. Call me every half hour at least, alright?"

"Where are you going?" The deserted office building looks threatening. I wish Max would bend the rules and come upstairs.

As if reading my mind, he says, "We talked about this. I'll be right out here."

I swallow hard and step forward with more confidence than I feel. My card key grants immediate access through the revolving doors. I march with a purpose through the deserted marble lobby to the elevators, and try not to worry about the fact that the key leaves a record of my entry. I'm glad Max requested I change into business casual attire. My navy pantsuit makes me feel less like an intruder. Or an imposter.

Inside the marble lobby it's eerily silent. Surprisingly, most of the floor to ceiling windows survived the blast. The card key lets me up the elevator and through the glass doors to Acheson's old floor. I thought this through on the way over here. I can look at the documents Smerth assigned me to review anytime, but I won't get another chance to peruse Acheson's personal papers. I'm sure he has files parked in his office. He resigned months ago in disgrace, but his possessions remain more or less intact while we fight the government's stream of subpoenas.

The overhead lights are dimmed, but screen savers flash from every secretarial station. Most people neglected to shut down before dashing out of the building. The firm's generators must have kicked in fast enough to avoid a computer crash when the power cut out. I call Damien from the deserted corridor. I feel guilty about slipping out before he finished his conference call. "Where are you?" he demands. "I tried to call you three or four times."

"I went into work. Did you see the note I slid under your door?" I cringe at my cowardice. Yes, he was on the phone with a client when I left, but I could have put the note under his nose.

"Are you sure about all this?"

"Not really. But it's important."

"Alright, but call me when you're heading home."

"I will. I'll call you soon. I love you."

I snap my phone shut. It's too quiet. Law firms aren't ever boisterous places but I've never noticed how soothing the dull hum of activity can be. It's so silent I can hear my heart pound as I approach the door that reads, Mr. Acheson. I try the knob. Locked.

I try again, knowing it won't work. I call Max. He answers on the first ring. "Lena? That was quick. Successful already?"

"Not exactly. The room is locked."

"Can't you use your key?"

"No, it's not electronic. It's a regular door knob lock."

"Is there a deadbolt?"

I study the door. "I don't think so."

"Do you have a credit card?"

"Yes, why?"

"Get your card out. It's going to open the door for you." He sounds certain and utterly unruffled. Of course he's only coaching a breaking and entering. Not committing one.

My heart feels ready to leap right out of my chest. I cradle the phone awkwardly between my shoulder and ear, and pull my rarely used Neiman's card from my wallet.

Max instructs me to slide the card in between the door and the frame, then use it to push the catch of the lock back. I doubt this method will work, but I try anyway. The card pushes at the lock, which gives a little, but then snaps back into place. I curse under my breath and try again. After four or five attempts, I tell Max he'll have to engage a locksmith if he wants to invade Acheson's office tonight.

Without warning the lock clicks. I turn the knob and triumphantly announce, "I'm in." For a split second my fear evaporates.

"Excellent. Remember to keep the lights to a minimum. Let's not attract attention. Call me if you find anything good."

He's gone.

Without Max's voice, it's quiet as an old tomb again. Normally at eight, the office would buzz with activity. Associates would be dining at their desks on take-out from Smith & Wollensky or Morton's, because rich food soothes the dull pain of tedious work. The smokers among the night shift secretaries would be flocking in and out for cigarette breaks, and the janitors would be arriving with their carts and vacuums.

I've never before set foot in Acheson's office, or rather, former office. Years before my time, Smerth had the foresight to bring DC's most celebrated lobbyist into R&S as a partner. He convinced the firm that their new golden boy deserved a generous office budget. He argued that the decorating expenses would be a steal when balanced against the massive retainers Acheson would generate.

Acheson obviously shared Smerth's confidence in his ability to perform, and spared no expense from his decorating allotment. In the dusky light, bamboo floors gleam underneath an antique carpet. Acheson collects Oriental art. His treasures include several Ming vases. The collection remains intact, a monument to its owner's confidence in his eventual vindication. Boxes of files cover most of the floor.

I close the curtains, switch on the desk lamp and try to triage the boxes. It would take weeks to read through them all. I have, at best, eight to ten hours.

And that's pushing it. If anyone in DC attempts a return to work tomorrow, R&S will have its share of hyper-ambitious lawyers coming in before dawn to try to recapture lost time.

Acheson's boxes display names of prominent energy companies, most longstanding clients of the firm, many subsidiaries of each other. Several bear the label VKOS, Volodya Korov's company. All these are flagged with hot pink Post Its, an interoffice sign that they're included in a contested subpoena. Charlie says paper files, color coded by sticky notes, will be a footnote from the past by the time our contemporaries make partner. I'm not so sure. R&S usually manages to adopt technology without embracing it.

My eyes land on a large box, taped shut and shoved halfway underneath the monstrous mahogany desk. A naked, Post It free label: Lotus Group, Ltd.

My shoulders relax a little. This spy work slash civic duty is easy. I type with my thumbs: "See attached list of files. Please note last sealed. Nothing labeled Clearwater or Burtonhall." Almost instantly the BlackBerry beeps with a response: "Open Lotus box first."

I borrow a silver letter opener from Acheson's desk to slice open the Lotus box. Like everything else in his orbit, the letter opener looks pricey. It has a Chinese dragon engraved in the handle, with stones that might be garnets but sparkle suspiciously like rubies, for eyes.

Acheson's and Smerth's names feature prominently all over the Lotus Group's paperwork. Another name has been repeatedly redacted with thick black magic marker. That's unusual but not unheard of, since law firms tend to be paranoid places. If Lotus is really a charity, it's conceivable that a donor would wish to remain anonymous. I start snapping photos of each page.

The Lotus Group's records don't show money coming in, but they list funds going out to various non-profit entities, none of which sound sinister. The dollar amounts seem negligible by big law firm standards. Twelve pages of disbursements show no transaction exceeding ten thousand dollars. Which shouldn't be enough to arouse the interest of the FBI, nor to justify my late night breaking and entering.

I'm beginning to wonder whether this whole exercise constitutes a colossal waste of time as I turn the page. The name BXE flies up at me. On December 31, the Lotus Group made a $55 million donation to them, earmarked "to underwrite educational endeavors."

BXE is a sister company of the Burtonhall Construction Corp., and another of Acheson's longtime lobbying clients. A government contractor that provides security services in some of the dodgiest parts of the world, they're known for hiring salty, weekend warrior types—the kind who fail to thrive in normal 9 to 5 situations. To their critics, they're purveyors of mercenaries. The government hires BXE to provide men with guns in lieu of deploying military units. I doubt they do much in the way of charitable giving. The file yields no further detail.

I replace the Lotus Group folders inside their box, taking care to maintain the original order and not to leave anything sticking out. I grab the only other sealed box in the office. BXE, the label reads, when I flip the pink sticky note out of the way. I stab it open with Acheson's bejeweled letter opener.

The first folder contains what corporate lawyers would call a closing binder for a deal in which Clearwater's private equity arm purchased fifty-one per cent of a Bahamian outfit called the Titan Import/Export Group. I leaf through. Evidently they specialize in worldwide shipments of farming equipment manufactured all over the former USSR. Not exactly riveting stuff.

Although it must be somewhat lucrative, since Korov, Acheson's Russian oil baron client, serves as Titan's chairman.

The next few over-stuffed folders contain nothing but public information, news clips and press releases. I set them aside and pick up a skinny file that lacks the BXE client tab affixed to every other file in this box. The folder holds only a red and blue electoral map, whose color coding doesn't remotely resemble the results of any election in recent history. Each state has a 0, 1 or 2 penciled on it. I'm sitting on the floor, facing the windows, surrounded by Acheson's files, studying the map, when I hear the door open.

My heart pounds so hard it hurts, but my body feels stuck to the floor.

"I'll take that." A familiar male voice pierces the silence.

My heart skips another beat, not figuratively, like people say all the time, but literally. A terrifying, pinching sensation grips my chest. It feels almost like someone is pouring cement between each of my ribs. My mind goes blank, but I feel my legs propel me to jump up and face the doorway, where William Acheson stands glowering. He looks taller than usual, maybe because of the shadow cast by the dim overhead lighting.

The BlackBerry, lying face up at my feet, flashes with a message from Max: "GET OUT NOW!"

5

For a moment neither of us moves. Acheson and I stare at each other like wild animals, standing our ground. I swear he actually sniffs the recycled office air as he scans the BXE files strewn on the floor. He doesn't advance further into the room, nor does he remove his hand from the doorknob. He's dressed more casually than I've ever seen him, in khakis, a blue North Face fleece jacket and leather Ferragamo trainers. I crumple the map to my chest and try to stop shaking. I have no idea what's about to happen but I instinctively know I shouldn't blink first.

Acheson draws a deep breath through his teeth and breaks the silent standoff. "What do you think you're doing?"

I try to meet his gaze, even though every fiber of my being urges me to lower my eyes to the floor and make a mad dash past him. I settle for looking in the general direction of his chest and focusing on the familiar logo on his jacket.

"I could ask you the same thing. I was under the impression you don't work here anymore." The words are bold but I barely croak them out.

"And I was under the impression that you weren't nearly devoted enough to this firm to come to work during a national catastrophe."

As I frantically search my brain for a serviceable reply, he takes four brisk steps to close the gap between us. He snatches the map. "I was also under the impression that your present duties do not extend to breaking and entering my office."

I screw up a little gumption. "You mean former office. How did you even get in here?"

As the words come out, I realize that I'm not even trying to deny breaking and entering. If Acheson is here tonight, it's because he expected solitude. At least he'll need to explain his own unauthorized presence if he wants to rat me out.

The corners of his mouth twitch upwards. "This firm has never been scrupulous about removing former employees from the security system." He holds up a white card key, identical to the one in my purse.

My mind goes blank. My feet feel bolted to the carpet.

He breaks the silence. "I doubt Smerth would be happy to learn about your clandestine research project."

He stands way too close and looks down at me. I am a full foot shorter than he is. He's a handsome man with a rower's build, but his face bears hints of jowls to come. Maybe he'll end up resembling an English bulldog. I silently snap at myself to focus. "Smerth wouldn't be thrilled to hear you were snooping tonight, either. It's not the typical behavior of an innocent man," I say, with a shaky voice.

My BlackBerry beeps again.

My eyes divert to the screen for a split second, but it's too long. Acheson grabs me by both arms and pushes me backward several feet so I'm wedged up against the front of his desk. My heart races harder, flat out. He pins my hands behind me. He gets in my face, his upper lip curled in a menacing snarl.

"Cut the crap. Why the fuck are you here?" He spits the words out through clenched teeth.

"Firm business."

"Bullshit." He wrenches my shoulder harder. I silence a gasp of pain halfway out my mouth.

"Who sent you?" he demands. "Was it that little creep Charlie? I'll castrate that dickless mother fucker."

"No! Charlie has no idea I'm here."

Acheson shoves me backwards over the desk so that my back screams in pain. "Who sent you?"

"Nobody. Smerth was angry I didn't bring my computer home. I talked my way past the cops downstairs."

For a split second, Acheson's cruel leer is replaced by something resembling amazement. He eases his grip enough to release the worst of the strain on my spine.

I decide to build on my story. "I cried. I told the officer I'd get fired if I couldn't get inside." Acheson's head cocks like a confused dog's. I gamble. "We need some of these files for the motion to quash the latest subpoena. You know the courts can't stay closed beyond this week. So really, I'm doing my job." I force myself to look him straight in the eye. "Trying to keep you out of jail."

I hold my breath and watch him try to process my defense. I twist my head away from his face but he leans in closer. I catch a whiff of alcohol. Or it could be stale cologne.

"Listen to me. You were never here. You never saw me, or the inside of this office. You will not tell a living soul that you came anywhere near this Goddamn building tonight. And trust me, because I will check your story. God help you if you fucking lied to me." He pauses and scans my face for clues. It takes a phenomenal effort to keep from shaking. "Are we clear?" He twists my arms further behind me. They start to throb. I bet he can hear my heart pounding. I start to shake all over. Miraculously I am not crying.

"Uh-huh." I'm too scared to say anything else.

Acheson seems satisfied. He releases his grip on my arms and backs away a few paces. "Now get the fuck out of here."

I scramble to the floor, fling the BlackBerry into my purse, and shuffle backwards to the door on unsteady legs. Acheson stalks after me like an untrustworthy watch dog. When I step into the hallway, he slams the door in my face. I turn and jog down the deserted corridor.

At least it was deserted when I came in. As I round the turn into the elevator bank, a raven haired, waiflike woman I've never seen before steps out of the farthest elevator car. My breath catches. She gasps, clearly stunned to see another person. Something deep in my gut spurs me to hold it together. She could be another hastily recruited FBI spy like me. Or one of the bad guys. Or just a perversely dedicated employee from another department of our 600-lawyer firm.

The elevator I rode up remains on the floor, closer to me than her. I dive inside and lunge for the L button, then pound the door close button as if my life depends on it. The doors shut as her gloved hand tries to push inside. Evidently she's not a frantic first-year desperate to get back to work.

I sprint across the cavernous marble lobby. Only when I burst through the revolving doors onto the sidewalk do I realize that my ankle boots are back on Acheson's Oriental carpet. I kicked them off, thinking I'd be encamped there for hours.

The headlights of a lone black SUV parked inside the police tape flip on. Max rolls down his window and yells, "Get in."

I sink into the leather bucket seat and fight the waterworks so hard my jaw twitches. I'm not sure whether I feel more relieved that my small role in law enforcement has concluded, or terrified that Acheson will come after me to perpetrate some act of retribution on my person. Probably the latter.

Alright, definitely the latter. I rock back and forth in the passenger seat like an abandoned child.

"It's okay. You're okay," Max says.

The cops move a temporary barrier so we can pass. Max points us towards Capitol Hill.

I wipe away a renegade tear with the back of my hand. "Where are we going?"

"4th Street, our DC regional office. I don't rate space at HQ," Max says. "Tell me exactly what happened."

I relate my encounter with Acheson with remarkable clarity, considering I've just been assaulted. I explain that he took a strange electoral map from me and I ran out without my boots. I tell him there was a woman who tried to follow me into the elevator. "She looked surprised to see me. Did you people recruit more than one of us to do your dirty work?"

Max's eyes widen but he ignores my question. He glances at my stocking feet and grimaces. My mind races again. What kind of worthless informant leaves her footwear behind on a covert fact-finding mission? I fight the urge to hyperventilate. Or to collapse into a quivering puddle of fear.

"Look," he says, after I've traveled several blocks in anxiety-ridden silence. "My piece of this investigation is tiny. I don't know what Henry has other agents or sources doing, and if I did, I couldn't tell you. He keeps everyone on a need-to-know basis. Our theory, at the moment, and it can change any time, is that Acheson serves as the conduit between Vice President Prescott and Clearwater's various enterprises around the globe."

"There's nothing so unusual about a politician bestowing favors on his former company."

"Right. But what if Prescott, who's a heartbeat from the presidency, maintains a huge secret stake in Clearwater? And what if he's using his influence at Clearwater to stoke conflict for the purpose of war profiteering?"

"Do you really think your best shot at proving it lies in Acheson's files?"

"I do. Acheson isn't nearly as smart as his old friend Prescott. Our profilers agree he's a classic narcissist. He's got a hyper-inflated sense of his own power and importance. He gets off on supplying money and access, but he has no head for policy. He lacks empathy for others, yet suffers from a profound need for approval from people he sees as prestigious, like the vice president."

"You don't need to waste taxpayers' money on experts to decide that Acheson is one big walking, talking personality disorder, who got carried away by his wildly successful lobbying career. I still think it's a huge leap to implicate anyone else. You'll see for yourself. Prescott's name wasn't in any of his files."

"We'll see." Max flips the radio to a classic rock station and turns up the volume, effectively closing the conversation.

Maybe everything will be alright. Acheson won't find anything missing from his files, so he should have no need to admit our encounter. Whenever Max is done debriefing me or whatever he has to do, I will go home and put tonight's misadventure out of my head.

I'll resume worrying about things that actually matter.

Such as my missing friend. I glance at the dashboard thermometer. Outside temperature: 27 degrees. A new pang of grief stings me in the gut. I try to banish images of burning bodies tangled in twisted metal from my mind's eye. No success.

Max's building is plain, worn and functional. Class B, all the way. I follow him across the ice cold, grungy tiles of the unwelcoming lobby. We ride a noisy elevator to the 6th floor.

Max works in a fishbowl. Glass walls separate and presumably soundproof the generic workspaces, but any passersby can see who's doing what. In the middle of the fishbowl, secretarial stations dot the floor. A few women sit typing, oblivious to our arrival.

Max must be important, because he has a corner fishbowl, with views in two directions. The furniture is crap – particle board surfaced to look like wood and chairs with metal frames. He tells me to have a seat at the small conference table. In the far corner of the office, a printer spews out paper.

"Your photography." He collects the spoils of my aborted expedition and flips through the pages with neither comment nor change of expression. The phone rings.

"Deputy Director Redwell for you. He said not to put him on hold," announces a weary female voice through the speaker phone.

"Put him through." Max picks up the handset. "Henry. We have a problem."

I strain to hear Henry's end of the conversation, but Max mashes the receiver to his ear. "She's compromised... Acheson caught her in the office... Some other woman was in the building... I wasn't about to send her packing..."

Something about Max's tone must aggravate Henry. The deputy director starts berating his subordinate with the ferocity of a cranky high school football coach armed with a brand new bullhorn. Max jerks the phone away from his ear and holds it at arm's length, before shrugging and switching to speaker.

"Is the whole bloody mission back to square one?" Henry demands.

"At first I thought so." Max avoids my questioning gaze.

We hear Henry suck in a huge breath.

Max hastily adds, "But after chewing on it a bit, I doubt Acheson will risk letting anyone know he was in the building himself. Even if we technically broke in, Lena works inside that firm and Acheson doesn't. He's also the subject of a major criminal investigation, whereas she's a lowly lawyer."

I wince at his dismissive, albeit accurate description of me.

Henry continues his dressing down of Max. "An inauspicious start, von Buren. How could you *not* have eyes on the building? Do I need to manage every move personally?" Henry's fury is palpable, even through the phone.

"No, you don't need to micromanage me," Max snaps back. "We had three details watching the doors."

Perhaps because it's obvious to me that Acheson wouldn't have used the main lobby, I add my two cents' worth. "Were your agents watching the 18th Street side? The garage entrance?"

"The DC police had that covered," Max says.

"Wait," I say. "You're saying you didn't know Acheson was in the building? You texted me to get out."

"I knew someone was riding the elevator up, but I didn't know it was Acheson until you got to the car."

"Why," Henry yells, "Was nobody watching the garage?"

Evidently he feels the DC police are nobody.

"Because 18th is closed," Max says. "And unlike you, Henry, I'm used to working on a miniscule budget."

"So, let me try to understand," Henry says. "You thought someone could waltz in the front doors, with the FBI, the federal marshals and the Capitol Police on the scene. Yet you neglected to watch the back doors, where there was one pair of DC cops clocking overtime?"

"Yes," Max says, miserably.

"Max, I like you. But you screw up like this again and you'll be interviewing street walkers in Jersey City for the next twenty years. Understand?"

"Yes," Max says, even more miserably. He rubs the bridge of his nose with his thumb and first two fingers.

"Glad to hear it." Henry slams down the phone.

Max holds his head in his hands. His assistant, an impossibly skinny woman with strawberry blonde hair and tired blue eyes, appears in the doorway. She compensates for her diminutive stature by wearing black stilettos that distort her foot into nearly vertical flexion. Her blouse is undone at least two buttons further than would fly at R&S. A large gold locket dangles between her breasts, which resemble honeydew melons under the greenish glow of the fluorescent lighting.

"Thanks, Audrey," Max says, without glancing up, as she hands him a single piece of paper. He looks at his watch. It's after eleven. "Go home already." Audrey's gaze lingers on her boss a moment longer than necessary before she turns to leave.

Max hands me the paper, a grainy picture, but undeniably the woman from the elevator bank. "That's her. Who is she?"

"Smerth's nanny." He punches the table and crumples the photo in his fist before catching himself and smoothing it out. "Damn it!" He swings at the table again, but stops his fist in mid-air.

Of course it's strange that Smerth's *nanny* would be at R&S, especially while the firm is closed, but Max doesn't seem inclined to enlighten me about how her presence makes anything *worse*.

"Smerth's sort of a lunatic. Maybe he dispatched the nanny on some silly errand," I say, though that doesn't explain her attempt to intercept my dash to the elevators. Nor does it prevent her from informing her boss of my presence. Assuming she figures out who I am. I rub my pounding temples. My small role is proving far more intense than the agents originally suggested. I feel baited, switched and stuck.

Max gets Henry back on the line, confirms that I've identified the nanny, whom they evidently use as an informant, and gets to work calling in teams of agents to watch over me in shifts. I'm to have a 24/7 security detail. "Only for a few days," he says.

My stomach rises into my throat and settles there uncomfortably. I try to swallow but my mouth is too dry. My tiny role in their investigation isn't over. I have to speak up, tell them I'm not cut out for this kind of thing. I'm an idiot for agreeing in the first place.

I try to dispel nervous energy by bouncing my feet up and down under my chair. I catch myself starting to chew my fingernails—a gross, juvenile habit I quit in high school—and wonder whether Damien and I could end up in the witness protection program after all. Maybe we won't have to be pig farmers. Perhaps they could arrange something less rural.

Max finally says we can go.

In the lobby, he hands me off to a pair of agents who look younger than me and annoyed at having their evening redirected. I cross the frozen sidewalk in my stocking feet. As I slide into the back seat of their sedan, Max attempts to reassure me, "It's going to be fine. When you go to work tomorrow, carry on as usual, but see if you can find the papers we talked about."

I have to tell him to find someone else.

I open my mouth but nothing comes out.

"Acheson's probably more scared than you are," Max says.

He shuts the car door behind me.

One agent stays in the car while the other escorts me to my apartment door. I thank him awkwardly. He assures me he'll stay in the hall all night.

I find Damien pacing anxious circles around the living room. He's more worked up than I've ever seen him. He's gripping an open Sam Adams Winter Ale, but it's mostly full. "You have a lot of explaining to do," he says, as I walk through the door. He focuses on my lost boots. "I guess you could start there."

"I left them at the firm," I say. It's technically true. "I left in a huge hurry." Also technically correct. "It's been a long night," I start to explain, and immediately realize I've chosen my words poorly.

Damien, who's usually as laid back as a college senior in a pass-fail seminar, explodes at me. He's waving his arms, turning red in the face and spilling beer on the hardwood. "*You've* had a long night!? What about everyone else? No. Wait. What about me? You go off on some crazy fucking *corporate espionage mission* when you know I hate the idea, and your mother has called four times tonight and I had to *lie* and tell her you went to check the Arlington hospitals for Hannah. Which is *pretty fucking impossible*, since both the bridge and metro are still shut down, and none of the Virginia hospitals have any Jane Does, but she bought it, I think. Jesus, Lena, you haven't even tried to call in hours!"

"Yes, I have," I lie.

I've never lied to him before. I'm shocked by how it just flies out. "No you fucking haven't. Caller ID, remember?"

I don't bother to argue. He's right. I should have called. We always check in with each other. Several times a day. I am a poor excuse for a wife. I've been so caught up in my own drama that I haven't paused to consider Damien's feelings. For that matter, my mother has probably worked herself into a lather pacing her kitchen in her bathrobe and slippers, waiting for me to call with breaking news that I am still okay, and that Hannah is not.

"Damien, I'm sorry. Really sorry. I'm overwhelmed. You were right. This is more than I bargained for."

Damien takes a deep breath and softens. His rare meltdowns never last long. "I'm sorry, too," he says, although he has no reason to be. "But I was so worried. I need you to promise me you're done helping them."

"I will, as soon as you stop screaming at me. I love you, Damien."

"I love you too." His tone reverts to normal. It's one of the many things I love about him – Damien never stews over anything. Plus he's calm in a crisis and his laid back California dude demeanor masks a whip smart brain. He pulls me to him and kisses my neck. "You know, I've never been to bed with a spy before," he whispers in my ear. "It's sexy. Like you're a Bond girl or something."

"Does that do it for you?" I ask, relieved that we're done fighting and hopeful that his playful mood might distract me from the nightmare, however briefly.

"Absolutely. Now that I know it's over."

I rest my head against his chest. I close my exhausted eyes and breathe in his familiar scent. Then I force myself to pull away, sit him down and tell him about the agents guarding our front door.

9

Sunrise is a relief when you can't sleep. I rub my eyes and squint at the clock. Six-thirty. No need to toss and turn anymore.

The firm expects "those employees who can make it" back at work today. This is code for "support staff may take an extra day, but lawyers need to get their butts into the office." I haul myself to a seated position and reach for the remote. Damien groans and starts to stir. No survivors found overnight. I silence the television and somehow find the will to leave the relative sanctuary of our bed. I gaze out the front window and wait for the coffee to brew.

A black car with government plates sits across the street with two men inside. Max said they would watch me, and I should be grateful they stayed out there all night, but their presence still feels invasive and creepy.

When I voice this to Damien he says, "No. William Acheson roughing you up in his office is invasive and creepy." He motions towards the street and musters a weak smile. "This circus is a result of your hyper-developed sense of civic duty."

My stomach heaves with anxiety, and the fact that I slept only a couple of hours makes everything feel even worse. Maybe I should focus on getting back to work. I've lost two days, which doesn't sound like much. Except I have to bill nine hours every day and work at least ten or eleven to hit that target. Two days' labor lost seems like a big deficit to make up. And how am I supposed to go back to representing Acheson as if nothing happened?

On a normal morning, Damien might suggest going for a run. I usually set out with him, struggle a pace behind for the first mile, but return exhilarated and pleased with myself for keeping up for the four mile loop. Today, I'd give anything for a run. Working up a sweat might burn off some of my nervousness, if only for a few precious minutes.

I don't need to look out the window again to know that elective outdoor exercise isn't part of today's program.

Damien emerges from the bedroom in sweatpants and a Stanford cap. He contemplates the sputtering coffee maker. "You think I could sneak in a jog?"

"You're not the one in federal lock down."

"I'm sorry about the circus crack. I would have helped the FBI, too, if I were in your position. You did a good thing."

He hands me a cup of coffee, plants a kiss on my forehead and laces up his sneakers. When he returns half an hour later, red faced and sweaty, he heads straight for the shower.

My phone buzzes on the counter. Max tells me that I need to take my protection seriously while they "assess the continuing threat." He says he should have been informed that my husband runs in the mornings.

I hiss into the phone that they didn't describe the risks accurately when they showed up out of nowhere. He doesn't cut me off until I explain that I never would have agreed to help, if they hadn't approached me in the immediate aftermath of the most cataclysmic event of my life. He strains to keep his voice at a normal conversational tone while he tells me that I don't get it, that the security breach changes things, whether I like it or not. He reminds me that we're dealing with extremely dangerous people. He's duty bound to keep an eye on me for the foreseeable future, and his protocol includes knowing about the routine comings and goings of everyone in my household.

I feel the blood leave my face as we hang up.

Damien emerges from the bathroom, freshly shaved and wrapped in a towel. "Jeez, Lena, who died?" He catches himself, winces, murmurs that he's sorry, and asks in a tentative voice if there's been news about Hannah.

When I tell him about the call from Max, his face turns ghostly white.

Two agents, both square-shouldered and silent, escort me to work.

Downtown is quiet, subdued. People walk with their heads down, hunkered into themselves. The metro remains closed, but most shops have reopened. Inside Rutledge & Smerth everything looks like business as usual, but for the crater on Connecticut Avenue, clearly visible through the huge windows in reception.

The managing partner, Evelyn Peabody, is on my voicemail, demanding I call her. That's unusual. We've never spoken beyond a quick hello at the Christmas party.

Evelyn Peabody is fifty years old and looks sixty. She has devoted her life to R&S. No husbands, no children, no hobbies. She lives with her widowed mother in an unpretentious colonial in Bethesda. Unfortunately, while Evelyn is a Harvard graduate (*summa cum laude*, even) and an excellent appellate lawyer, she's never managed to score a client of her own, which renders her powerless in the firm, despite her years of service and impressive title. The rumor mill suggests that she's biding her time, waiting to inherit millions in annual billings when one of the many geezers who occupy the twelfth floor appellate department eventually croaks. Unfortunately for Evelyn, the firm's geriatric heavy-hitters enjoy robust physical health.

They're also a bunch of conservative wing nuts who like to pretend the firm is some kind of academic dinner club for white men. It's embarrassing yet economically rewarding for me to be associated with them. For the most part, I do the cowardly thing and pretend they don't exist, since working here allows me to build my resume and pay my loans at a good clip. Which maybe makes me not so different from Evelyn. Back when she started as an associate, it would have been a massive coup for any woman to make partner. No one can take that from her.

Approximately eighteen months ago, a white, male, Dartmouth-educated "diversity consultant" determined that R&S needed more women and minorities in positions of authority. As there were no minorities available, the partnership gamely installed Evelyn as managing partner. But only after amending R&S's partnership agreement to render the office largely ceremonial.

Because Evelyn has never factored in my planning, and she must have important things to do, like reassure people the building isn't going to collapse into that crater outside, I'm surprised to hear from her. I have to dig out the phone list to find her extension. When she answers, I launch into an explanation of who I am.

She cuts me off. For ten minutes, our ostensibly powerless managing partner chews me out, because the building records indicate I used my keycard to get inside while the police had banned all access. I briefly consider telling her that Smerth ordered me to retrieve my laptop, but decide that could turn a brief telephonic tongue-lashing into a lengthier ordeal. I apologize profusely and assure her I will never transgress again. As she hangs up, I wonder whether she will muster the chops to call Acheson with a similar tirade. I doubt it. He'd probably tell Evelyn to screw herself.

When I finally arrive at my home away from home, Interior Conference Room C, I'm surprised to see Charlie, sleeves rolled up, tie undone, and settled in to work. He's carved out a spit of territory at the huge table papered with the past six months of my efforts. He's scrawling illegible notes on his legal pad.

"What are you doing here?" Charlie's participation in a lowly task like document review is unusual. As soon as the question leaves my lips I chide myself for not inquiring about how he's doing, or more importantly, whether anyone he knows is among the dead or missing.

"Randolph called me last night. He was disappointed that you hadn't made any effort to work from home during the shutdown. He said you've been flaky lately." Charlie winces apologetically. "So he wants me on this document review."

"Smerth's taking me off the case?" The case has been my life for months. I have no hope of hitting my billing target without it. More importantly, I need time alone to do more digging. As much for myself as for the FBI. I want to know what that bastard Acheson has to hide.

"You're not that lucky," Charlie says, with a slight smile. "But you'll have me for company for a while."

Normally I'd welcome such a development. A boring task like document review goes faster when tackled with a colleague. Big companies and law firms keep everything. We have mountains of paperwork to sift through. We'll be lucky to find anything Smerth can use, or that the prosecutors could deploy against our client.

I keep my phone on the table in front of me, my small way of clinging to hope that Hannah will defy bleak odds. I chant my new mantra under my breath: *Focus on work, worrying won't help.*

After two hours of fruitless tedium, I flip open a skinny file stamped confidential. It contains details of a $90 million donation by Clearwater Partners to the Lotus Group. Tiny alarm bells sound in my head. If Clearwater Partners wanted to make an eye popping charitable donation they would surely choose a marquee cause and make the gift amid a hurricane of PR.

Unless they're avoiding taxes by pretending to donate funds. Several of Acheson's casino clients got in trouble for a similar scheme two or three years ago. They were giving enormous checks to a bullshit urban kids' sports charity Acheson founded. Almost ninety-eight per cent of the funds were spent on such items as golf trips and spa escapes for Congressmen (back waxes in paradise, the *Post* reported at the time), and a new ski chalet in Aspen for Acheson's brother-in-law, who served briefly as the charity's executive director.

In eight years, the foundation sent a grand total of three kids to two weeks of soccer camp.

Acheson disingenuously but successfully claimed he didn't manage the charity's day to day affairs. His by then ex-brother-in-law went to prison for five years for lying to the IRS. Smerth got all four casino CEO's off with fines.

I suspect Clearwater is indulging in a similar exercise, though on a far grander scale. When and if they get caught, they'll ask Smerth to orchestrate a plea deal for their brass as well.

When Charlie gets up to go to the men's room, I dive for my BlackBerry camera. I shoot the first few pages before deciding to fold the sheets in half and ram them into my purse.

I don't find anything else remotely interesting, either to R&S or the FBI, for the rest of the morning. At 12:45, Charlie suggests we go out for sushi. "Didn't you hear what the mayor said this morning? He wants everyone back to work and spending money in the city."

My face must show indecision, because he adds, "My treat."

I agree, telling myself that I am doing a good deed. This is the closest the poor man gets to a social life. More selfishly, I'm less than eager to be left alone with my imagination. I text the agents downstairs that I'm stepping out for lunch.

Charlie and I walk out the back way to 18th Street, the same entrance Acheson must have used last night. As we head north, I am about to protest that I don't want the all-you-can-eat buffet on M Street, next to the strip joint, when Charlie leads me down some stairs to the basement of what looks like a medical building. We pass through an unmarked door into a Japanese restaurant I never knew existed.

In three years of working together, Charlie and I have never sat down for a meal in a real restaurant. Should I worry? He must be about to tell me he's leaving the firm. I'll have nobody to run interference with Smerth. It'll be awful. That is, if I still have a future here. I reach into my bag and finger the Clearwater documents.

When I glance back at Charlie, he looks squirmy, anxious. Maybe he's going to tell me he's in love with me.

It happened to Hannah once, right after she announced her engagement. This unassuming senior associate took her for a drink, sucked down five martinis, and ended up slurring his declaration of love while listing precariously on the edge of a barstool in Morton's on a slow Tuesday night. Poor Hannah had to explain that his feelings weren't reciprocated – a difficult thing to convey to someone senior to you at work, let alone sloshed. I whip out my phone to check, yet again, if there's any word from Hannah. Nothing. "Keep busy," I mutter my new mantra under my breath, for the thousandth time today. "Sitting and sobbing does not help."

Charlie, oblivious to both my unfounded neuroses concerning his intentions and my justified distress over Hannah, holds the door for me. "It's my stealth sushi place. It's usually packed, but I've never seen anyone from the firm here."

Today the restaurant is quiet. The few occupied tables are filled with Asian businessmen. We settle into a booth with doors and Charlie orders us two Sapporos.

"You drink at lunch?"

"Only when stuck on document reviews. Let's order." We make our selections. The waitress retreats, closing the doors to seal us in the little bamboo and glass capsule, but not before I glimpse the agents who drove me this morning, being shown to a table in the main dining room, not twenty feet away from us.

The vaguely defined threat to my person transforms into something intensely real. Those agents are shadowing me because the FBI doubts Acheson's rough behavior was a one-off event. I fight the urge to dash to the ladies' room to hyperventilate while my brain scrambles to wrap itself around my new reality. Acheson might be under indictment, but in a way that makes him more dangerous — with his reputation wrecked he has less to lose. Why was I such a fool yesterday? To feel useful? Self-important? *Patriotic?*

I have screwed myself.

Damien will never forgive me.

The normally inoffensive smell of soy sauce and raw fish settles in my throat. Sweat percolates on the back of my neck as I realize I might lose my breakfast.

Charlie fails to register my panic. He pours his Sapporo too quickly and foam fills the top two-thirds of his glass. He emits a muffled grunt and takes a big sip anyway, before asking, "Can you keep a secret, Lena?" He pushes his glasses up the bridge of his nose. They slip right back down. He doesn't bother to fix them a second time.

"Sure." I pour my own beer with practiced expertise, producing only a tiny bit of foam at the top, only to spill because my hands are shaking. Funny that now of all times, Charlie wants to share secrets. I've had my fill of secrets for the foreseeable future. I wonder whether the agents can hear our conversation, whether my new phone has a microphone.

"No, seriously," Charlie says.

"Of course. My lips are sealed. What's up?"

He exhales loudly. "I think Acheson has started dabbling in election rigging."

I breathe a sigh of relief. Election fraud is serious, but it's not terrorism. "What makes you say that?" I take a large sip of my Sapporo.

"I found the records for a new SuperPAC in his subpoenaed files. A hundred per cent funded by various Clearwater subsidiaries."

"So? That's par for the course, isn't it?"

"Yes and no. This group is spending a fortune on opposition research against several famous liberals with pretty safe seats. Most of them aren't even up for re-election this time around. Why would Clearwater dump tens of millions into races that aren't even races yet? And then there's this strange map that was in the same file."

"Map?" My voice sounds weak. The world falls away from under me, as if my chair is on one of those awful tilt-a-whirl carnival rides.

The doors slide open and the waitress presents our lunch, a dazzling display of raw fish. The colorful, celebratory presentation feels all wrong. We're in crisis and mourning. I'm too nervous to eat and deliriously over tired to boot. Why are we even here?

I try to see what the agents are doing, but the waitress blocks my line of sight. I resist the urge to jump out of my chair to peer around her.

When she retreats, Charlie reaches into his breast pocket and produces a map, which he unfolds and smoothes out on our table. I can't be sure, but it looks a lot like the one Acheson snatched out of my hands last night. "Do you think we should show it to Smerth? Or do I wait and see if the other side has seen it, and if they think it's significant?"

I have no idea. And frankly, I'm having a tough time caring about the specifics of the map or our clients' stupid SuperPAC. Acheson could have some goon watching my every move, waiting to see if I'll be foolish enough to snoop again.

Charlie clears his throat and searches my face expectantly.

"Maybe this map is aspirational. This is how Acheson would like the electoral college to look."

Of course that's implausible. States like Massachusetts and my own home state of Rhode Island are colored red, while Georgia and Colorado, for example, are blue. Any idiot can tell the map doesn't represent a wishful scenario for either party.

Charlie looks unconvinced.

Then it hits me. "It's gubernatorial."

Charlie gives me the sheepish look of a kid caught cheating on a really easy test.

The map seems important, since it cropped up in multiple confidential files, but the rational side of my brain doubts it's anything but reference material. Acheson's clientele skews towards elderly. In my professional experience, the silverback set tends to print out everything. Their emails. Their travel itineraries. Even basic facts you can find in two clicks on the Internet.

But Acheson was incensed when he saw me holding it. I squint at the page, desperate to see some unusual detail that will explain anything. The map looks nothing but ordinary.

"Well?" Charlie says. "Your thoughts?"

I force a laugh. "You're so removed from the drudgery of document review that you're finding intrigue where none exists."

He passes a second sheet of paper over the sushi. "This was in the file with the map. It looks like a list, organized by times of day. Weird, right?"

The list is in Russian. "It must be one of Korov's papers, probably misfiled. It happens."

My eyes scan the list. I remember next to nothing from one ill-advised semester of Russian in college. The words on the page might as well be Ancient Greek. "It does look like a timeline or record, though. Kept by someone extremely uptight." The times noted run chronologically from 9:15 to 23:22. I frown at the sheet of paper before passing it back to Charlie. "Maybe it's shorthand minutes from some marathon meeting. I doubt it has anything to do with the governors' map."

We return to the office by 18th Street, which bears no mark of the devastation on the other side of our building. I find a FedEx envelope on my chair. It's marked personal and confidential, sent from a FedEx store on Capitol Hill. I tear the envelope open and pull out a small packet that looks like chewing gum, wrapped in a small typed note: "Please place on Smerth's desk. Shred this." I pop one of the blister packets and a tiny metal chip, smaller than my pinky fingernail, drops into my hand. I wonder what they expect to overhear. I doubt Smerth would hold forth about anything illicit, even in the sanctuary of his office. He knows the firm records all phone calls.

The red light on my phone flashes insistently, which normally means more work. Smerth wants to see me in his office, yesterday. He actually says yesterday. I grab a fresh legal pad. I always memorialize Smerth's instructions, so I can defend myself when he inevitably accuses me of botching the assignment when he changes it without telling me.

I trudge down the hall. "He said you could go on in. He's walking someone out and will be right with you," says Janet, Smerth's matronly secretary, and the only member of the firm's administrative staff I've seen all day.

I step behind Smerth's imposing desk, squeeze the chewing gum bug between my palm and index finger, and study my options.

The safest thing would be to toss the FBI's device in the trash. Let the feds do their own damn dirty work. On the other hand, it would feel good to get even with Acheson for last night – even indirectly. I glance into the hallway. Janet is on the phone. No sign of Smerth. Luckily he's almost always yelling, which is handy, in that he almost always announces his arrival.

At least a dozen picture frames adorn Smerth's imposing desk. Most are made of wood and my racing heart sinks a little as I hold the chip next to a few of them. No good. Too obvious. There's one five by seven sterling silver frame of two kids I've never seen before. It's tucked halfway behind a larger red one containing a portrait of Smerth's older sons in their lacrosse uniforms.

Smerth might have known about the bombing and he did nothing to stop it.

I press the bug onto the side of the silver frame as Smerth barrels through the door.

"Making yourself at home?" he asks in a jocular voice, which throws me for a second. Then I see he has Abdul bin Aziz in tow and almost jump out of my skin. By which I mean every muscle in my body lurches so fast that the skin gets left behind. I'm not sure why this happens. Maybe some subconscious corner of my mind expected to see Acheson march into the room with them.

"Janet said I could wait in here," I splutter. "And I was admiring your gorgeous family." I pick up an eight by ten of Smerth with his wife and four kids. One situated clear across the desk from the newly planted bug. "You must be so proud." This last comment is nothing more than nervous chatter. Flattery gets me nowhere with my boss.

Smerth answers in his client voice, "Indeed. I'm a fortunate man."

I'm stunned. Smerth never dignifies small talk from his associates. Maybe he drank at lunch today, too. Maybe everyone's self-medicating, due to stress from the bombings. He herds us towards his large conference table by the window onto Connecticut. I try my best not to look outside.

Aziz looks me up and down like some old letch appraising a school girl. He's wearing an impeccably tailored suit, accented with enormous gold cuff links. He smoothes his bushy mustache with his index finger as his rat-like eyes, too small and round for his face, settle on my chest. I raise my legal pad to cover myself and try hard not to scowl at him. I can't believe this creep is a heartbeat away from running a major country. Unless he steps in front of a bus, he's going to be the next Saudi king. Their current king, Aziz's oldest brother Fahd, suffers from stage four lung cancer. Their second brother died in a plane crash six months ago. That puts Abdul, as Aziz brother number three, on deck.

"Mr. Aziz, this is my associate, Lena Mancuso." Smerth continues to speak in his charming voice.

I offer my hand to Aziz, who takes his seat and sniffs dismissively. I sit down as quickly as possible. Smerth ignores the whole awkward exchange and keeps talking. "This morning, as he was having breakfast at his Kalorama townhouse, Mr. Aziz was served with a lawsuit alleging his involvement, in his capacity as an investor in Clearwater Partners, in a plot to finance attacks on U.S. citizens. The plaintiffs include three Americans who lost relatives in last year's sniper attack in Cairo Airport. Charlie is already drafting a motion to dismiss, but we should prepare for the judge to deny it."

I speak before thinking. It's a major flaw that I need to work on. "If we already represent Mr. Acheson in Clearwater-related litigation, can we also represent Mr. Aziz?"

The blood vessel on Smerth's left temple enlarges and throbs. When he speaks, it's not in the charming client voice. "Last time I checked, Lena, I was the partner and you were the *junior* associate. So don't you dare presume to second-guess me."

My face burns, but I know better than to try to defend myself. It would only further enrage him.

Smerth clears his throat. "The crux of the complaint against Mr. Aziz is that his $350 million investment in Clearwater Partners was contingent upon Clearwater buying into certain companies with ties to insurgent groups. Whereas the complaint against Acheson *alleges* that he offered money to various Congressmen in exchange for favorable votes on legislation important to Clearwater. So any drooling idiot with a law degree they bought online for $99.99 could see the cases bear no relationship to each other."

I feel like adding that any first year law student with a room temperature IQ could find multiple conflicts of interest within this fact pattern. Chief among them: Clearwater will end up adverse to Aziz if this new law suit moves forward.

My eyes scan the complaint Smerth slides across the table. He explains to Aziz, "The plaintiffs are represented by a sole practitioner known for soliciting sexy cases that ultimately lack merit. He's a stupid kid. Self trained. Over promises and under delivers. He has an office in Tenleytown." Smerth says 'Tenleytown' in a voice implying that the fly-by-night shop couldn't be less credible if it maintained its principal office in a cave in Tibet.

Smerth pauses, regroups and resumes his charming client voice. "But frivolous or not, we will deal with this complaint against you with the utmost zeal." He turns to me, waits for me to stop reading. "We will assert that because Mr. Aziz enjoys diplomatic immunity, the plaintiffs have no standing to sue. Obviously we will argue that since Mr. Aziz will assume the Saudi throne in the short to medium term future, and he's spent his entire adult life cultivating good relations with the West, it would make no sense for him to make even a passive investment in terrorism. Quite the contrary. Mr. Aziz has every incentive to keep extremists out of his political and economic affairs."

Aziz nods his approval of Smerth's narrative.

Smerth continues, "I've directed Charlie to draft a counter claim, alleging defamation against our client and seeking damages in the original amount of plaintiff's claim: $350 million, plus punitives." Smerth licks his upper lip, as if tasting the punitive damages.

Smerth has to know that such a counterclaim will go nowhere, but I lack the gumption to argue. "Makes sense to me."

"Good," Smerth says. "You will support Charlie by getting started on a comprehensive review of Mr. Aziz's financial relationship with Clearwater Partners. We have to kill this thing before the media gives it traction, and we can't expect the courts to uphold his immunity indefinitely." He shoots Aziz a sober look, but I know Smerth would love to defend a case that would make headlines worldwide.

"This is top priority. Drop everything. Do not eat, sleep or piss until you're done," Smerth adds for the client's benefit. He knows I get it.

Aziz, my new top priority, doesn't bother to look my way while they wait for me to leave. Janet tells me the files are still in transit from off-site storage. Smerth's order to drop everything was theater for a VIP client.

Fuming, I head back to Interior Conference Room C. Halfway there, my BlackBerry lights up with a one-line message from Henry:

"Excellent job! We hear him loud and clear!" His enthusiastic positive reinforcement tempers my annoyance with Smerth.

The afternoon passes with no word on the whereabouts of the new Aziz files. I check my voice mail diligently. The last thing I need is for Smerth to decide I'm ignoring him. We plow through more papers and by six-thirty I'm completely frustrated because I haven't found anything useful. Just pages and pages of legitimate deals, painstakingly memorized for posterity by an army of lawyers not unlike Charlie and myself.

Charlie and I call in dinner from Smith & Wollensky around 7:30. Charlie offers to stretch his legs and pick up our order. He hasn't been gone two minutes when Smerth summons me to his office. I trot upstairs, legal pad in hand. He intercepts me outside his office in his overcoat. He's toting his briefcase, clearly on his way out for the night. "Walk with me."

What on earth does he want now? I grab my coat and gloves from my own office, two doors down. Smerth has never invited me to walk with him anywhere. He's never struck me as the kind of person who needs to move his body to get his brain in gear.

We ride down the elevator and he makes small talk about snow in the weekend forecast. We step outside into a chilly evening that smells nothing like snow to my New England nose. We walk down L Street in the direction of Foggy Bottom at a stroll. One of my evening agents falls into step a half a block behind us. "You've done great work on this case, Lena," Smerth says.

My jaw drops. Smerth has never complimented my work. R&S legend maintains he's never complimented any associate's work. "Thank you," I manage to stammer.

"But I sometimes wonder if you might be happier in one of our other offices, in a more happening town. New York maybe. Or Chicago?"

"I'm sorry. I thought you said I was doing a good job. Why would you want to send me away?" On its face, a transfer away from my mercurial boss sounds divine. But from a career perspective, working in the home office with the biggest name in the whole litigation department is worth a great deal of pain and suffering. Working for any other partner at R&S after Smerth would be a demotion, however subtly packaged. He knows that. He knows I know that. I say, "I'm happy where I am. Besides, my husband and I have a nice life here in Washington."

Smerth ducks into an ATM vestibule and holds the door for me to follow. My agent loiters outside a few yards away and lights a cigarette. Smerth puts his bank card in the machine. "Acheson is paranoid. He thinks you're too nosy."

"I'm sorry to hear that." I don't know what else to say. Apologizing feels like a safe default.

"Cut the crap, Lena," Smerth says under his breath, without looking up from his banking. Perspiration has started to bead along the back of his neck even though it's cold in here. "He's dangerous. You seem like a nice young lady. I advise you to put as much distance between yourself and Acheson as possible, and I'm offering you an easy way to do so."

The filthy floor spins under my feet. "If you're concerned, shouldn't you go to the police?"

Smerth turns away from the screen and guffaws in my face. I see the metal fillings in his molars. "I've made a fortune representing well dressed, smooth talking, Ivy educated gangsters and their corporate interests. What do you think would happen to me and my family if I suddenly turned on these people?"

I feel the color drain from my face. He folds his cash into his wallet, chucks his receipt and ushers us back outdoors.

"Just consider my offer. Talk it over with your husband. And let me know soon."

I wish I could, but Damien's most important client summoned him to New York this afternoon. His train won't get into Union Station until after midnight.

We start walking back towards the office. Smerth curses the weather again and I know the window for discussion has closed. We part ways in the lobby of our building. He rides the elevator down to the garage to his Mercedes; I ride back up to Interior Conference Room C, cold crab cakes and a whole new level of angst.

At a few minutes to ten, Charlie says we should call it a night. He's one of those associates who pulls all-nighters with pride, but he finds document review beneath him, and refuses to act like a slave with regard to this particular assignment. I decide I need to walk home. I feel like an agitated caged animal. Maybe a mile and a half in the winter air will clear my brain. I type a message asking the agents for permission.

As soon as I reach the end of the first block, I know walking was a stupid idea. By the time I reach Dupont Circle, I'm shaking with fear, completely confused about how to proceed. I glance over my shoulder and sure enough, there's a new plainclothes agent—their shift changed—marching ten paces behind me. I give him a little wave and he nods back, but makes no attempt to catch up to me.

I spend the last half mile alternately reminding myself to breathe, and attempting to convince myself that Smerth's offer stems more from annoyance than true concern for my safety.

When we arrive at my apartment, I find a handwritten note taped to my mailbox. In black block letters it reads: "I know what you did. You will pay."

The ground shifts under my feet.

I hold the yellow piece of paper for a moment, unable to convince myself that the note must be intended for someone else. Maybe one of my neighbors caught their significant other cheating. Such domestic dramas unfold all the time. Right?

I hand the note to my security detail. I tell them I found it on the heels of Smerth's warning, which itself came with all the subtlety of a sledge hammer. They remind me that I need to share "important developments" more promptly and promise to look into the origins of the note. Whatever that means. I can't imagine they'll have much luck tracing an anonymous letter, since brick row houses like mine don't feature security cameras.

Unlike last night, the agent enters the apartment before me. Only when he's convinced of its emptiness does he permit me inside. I deadbolt the door and check all the window locks. I spend a restless evening hyper-aware of every little noise our old building makes. I lie awake imagining that Acheson will discover the bug on Smerth's desk and trace it to me. I try to decide how to broach the idea of a move with Damien. I whisper a little prayer for Hannah, feeling embarrassed that I didn't think of it as soon as I fell into bed.

I'm ashamed at how easily I forget my friend because I'm scared for my own skin.

7

The FBI questions my neighbors. The married couple who occupy the penthouse are seventeen months into a thorny divorce. She visits an Argentinean polo star twenty-five years her junior every afternoon. He squanders their savings on internet poker. Each party refuses to leave the apartment, as it constitutes the major remaining asset from thirty years of marriage. While neither admits to penning the note, by the wee hours of the morning, the agents are convinced one of them did. Our mailboxes are adjacent. I tell myself the note was stuck on the crack between them, even though I'm not sure that's how it was.

Because things are never as frightening during daylight hours, and because I doubt any client of my firm would trek to my neighborhood to leave me an anonymous message of menace, I accept their hypothesis and try to put the unpleasant incident out of my head.

The marital meltdown upstairs reassures me. Everything isn't about me. Even though it's Saturday, I get dressed and head to the office before Damien stirs. I feel sheepish slipping out but promise myself I'll tell him everything tonight. Charlie and I have to put in full days today and tomorrow, because of the billable hours lost due to the tragedy. Why ruin my whole day by picking a fight?

I take Damien's temperature about leaving Washington over takeout sushi. I've decided not to share the drama with the threatening note for now. He'd blow a bizarre coincidence way out of proportion. Make me more freaked out. Or so I tell myself. I know I'm a big wuss, but I lack the stamina to argue with him right now.

"You're the one who loves it here." Damien scoops up a spicy tuna roll with his chopsticks. "I'd go back to San Francisco in a heartbeat."

"The firm doesn't have an office there. But do you think we should try New York for a while? It's one of the greatest cities on earth. Plus it's closer to my family."

"We'd have to make over a million dollars a year to live a middle class life in Manhattan. And why do you care where R&S has offices?"

"In case you haven't noticed, the economy isn't exactly robust. It would be nice to avoid the stress of a job search."

Damien takes a sip of his beer and searches my face. He's probably looking for clues as to my level of seriousness. My remaining best friend lives in Washington. I work for one of the most prestigious firms and while the hours feel endless, my cases aren't dull. I've always wanted to apply for a litigation job in the federal government once I've made enough money to leave R&S. I'm firmly on the Washington career track. A move makes no sense.

He puts down his drink and his chopsticks and leans across the table. His green eyes seem somehow cold all of a sudden. "Why don't you tell me what this is really about?"

"Maybe I have a seven year itch with this city," I say, without meeting his gaze. I fumble with a slice of yellowtail and soy sauce splashes onto the table.

"Maybe you shouldn't be snooping where you have no business. Just because you've jeopardized your career doesn't mean we run away and start over. If they fire you, you're going to have to look for a new gig like anyone else." He puts down his chopsticks and pushes away from the table. I understand that Damien isn't enthusiastic about moving, but I'm surprised he's so angry. Especially after saying he would have helped the FBI, too.

"It's not that," I say.

"Guess what? I don't believe you. And I'm not moving to New York." He grabs his coat and storms out.

I clean up the remains of our dinner, pack the leftovers in the refrigerator and load the dishwasher. I top off my glass of wine, get into my pink flannel pajamas and turn on the television. The news is the same as it was when I last checked an hour ago: No survivors found today.

Damien resurfaces ninety minutes later. "Sorry. I needed a walk."

"It's alright. I'm sorry I blindsided you."

"If you really have a seven year itch, we can talk about Chicago," he says. "And you know I'd go to California in two seconds." He sits down next to me on the couch, wraps his arm around me, and pulls me to him so my head rests on his chest. "For you, I'd even brave Boston, though it's awfully close to your mother. But New York? I'm afraid we'd have to scale down too much to make it work, and that would feel like going backwards. At least to me."

"I'm not saying we have to move. Smerth made this offer. I doubt he wants to fire me. I think he wants to put some distance between me and Acheson. He's still mad he caught me in his office. I felt I should at least discuss the offer with you."

"If you and Smerth agree that Acheson's an unhinged nut job, maybe you should call the cops."

"And say what? My client is mad at me and I'm scared of his temper? Besides, what can the cops do that the FBI's not already doing?"

Damien jerks away from me. His eyes flash with anger. "I think you say your client is the subject of a major investigation, he knows you've stumbled onto something incriminating and you're scared for your life. You tell them you think the feds are more interested in using you than protecting you."

"Don't over dramatize. The truth is bad enough."

"Don't underestimate these people. Do you really think Smerth is afraid for you?"

"No. I think I'm less important to him than Acheson is. It would be convenient for him to ship me out of his line of sight."

I'm sure Damien knows I'm spooked. But I hope my anxiety will pass. I don't want to leave our life here. Maybe someday we'll both tire of the city's transient feel, but for now Washington is our home. I maneuver myself back into Damien's lap and drape my arms around his neck. "Let's not change anything. Our life is great. This storm will pass."

He looks at me dubiously but the ice in his stare has melted.

I lean down and kiss my gorgeous husband, the one I'm certain would put aside his objections and move anywhere, even next door to my parents, if I really wanted to. Not that I'd ever propose such lunacy.

Damien kisses me back and his hand slides up my top. I lean into his caress. Our life is great the way it is. I'm going to make sure it stays that way. As soon as the Acheson document review ends, I'll tell the FBI there's nothing more I can do for them. Smerth will assign a new matter and go back to berating me for having only twenty-four hours in my day.

Damien reaches for the remote and silences the television. "I can think of a better way to spend our evening," he whispers into my ear. He undoes the top two buttons on my pajama top and slides it over my head. He nudges me onto my back and kisses a path down my neck to my chest. His fingers tease one breast while he sucks and nibbles on the other. My back arches up to meet his touch. I push his pants over his hips. Damien draws heavier breaths as I nudge him off me, lean over and let him watch himself disappear into my mouth. He rests his head against the back of the couch and strokes the tender part of my neck. "I want to be inside you," he tells me, in a gruff whisper.

I wriggle out of my pajama pants and straddle my gorgeous husband. His hands reach around, cup my buttocks, and rest on my hips. I grind against him. I re-position myself so I can rock against him at just the right angle—the one we discovered several months ago when we finally splurged on curtains for the massive bay window behind the sofa. Damien's hands leave my hips to tug at my nipples. My whole body shakes and quivers. I scream when I come, then collapse onto his chest, spent and sensitive.

"Now that the neighbors are awake, it's my turn," Damien laughs. He scoops me up, rolls on top of me. Every nerve ending tingles and for a moment it feels too intense, but I lift my hips towards him and he loses himself, thrusting hard and deep until he lets out a kind of primal groan and I feel his climax explode inside me.

"God, I love you, Lena," he says, as he rolls back to a slouchy sitting position on the couch, wraps me in his arms, and turns my face towards his for a soft kiss. "I love you, too." I stretch and yawn, sated and sleepy for the first time in recent memory. I've learned, in recent days, that exhaustion and the ability to sleep have very little to do with each other.

I still feel all gooey and glowy when we wake the next morning. I nestle into the nook under Damien's arm. My fingers trace little swirls along his bare chest. "Do you feel guilty?" I ask. "About feeling good while so many people are suffering? When Hannah is probably, almost definitely, dead?"

I surprise myself by saying the words out loud for the first time, since my mind still feels mired in the denial stage of grief. My hand stops its carefree tour of Damien's upper body.

"If anything, the bombs were a gruesome reminder to live life to its fullest, because you never know."

I turn that over in my head for a moment. "I guess you're right."

He grins. "I'm right a lot, you know."

I lift my head from its spot in the nook and smile back. "Is that so?"

"It is indeed. For example, we have twenty minutes before we absolutely need to start our day. I have big plans for that time."

He disappears under the sheets and makes us both late to work.

On the second Monday morning after the attacks, Smerth's assistant Janet announces that Smerth wants Charlie and me to spend the day at a pro bono workshop. All associates attend such "learning opportunities" once or twice a year, but they're usually scheduled months in advance. When the pre-determined date arrives, Smerth complains bitterly about the inconvenience. Janet assures us that she understood her boss correctly. I can't help thinking Smerth wants Interior Conference Room C to himself for a day. I should feel angry, or at least suspicious, but mostly I'm relieved. If Smerth removes any inflammatory files, Acheson will be less driven to get me out of his way.

Charlie and I pack ourselves into a taxi bound for the Whitman Walker Clinic. We pass an uneventful day in a small auditorium, learning about HIV discrimination. It would feel like a holiday if I weren't so spent and anxious. My security detail sits in the back row. The agents blend by taking notes like everyone else. I wonder how much longer they'll shadow me.

I excuse myself before the end of the final Q&A session to attend a vigil and service at Georgetown Law, for the dozen alumni missing and presumed dead in the attacks. Damien can't make it because he's on his way back from yet another day trip to New York. Diana promised to meet me at the security desk in the McDonough Building so we can find seats together in the enormous main auditorium. Diana was glad when I first mentioned the service. We cleared our calendars for tonight months ago to celebrate Hannah's thirtieth birthday. Diana and I agreed we needed to keep the date to do *something*. I was thankful when my *alma mater* obliged by providing a suitable occasion. Especially since we've been doing our best to deny the fact that she's gone. Neither of us can bring ourselves to say the words "Hannah is dead." We always say she's "lost" or "missing."

Maybe a service will help us start to grieve in a healthier way.

In the cab, I remember how Hannah was so upset about her looming milestone, the big, scary 3-0. The morning of the bombing she told me she always imagined herself as a young, twenty-something bride, with two adorable kids and a fabulous career in place by the start of her thirties. She said it in a way that implied failure to live up to some preordained life timeline. And I told her to stop being an idiot.

Oh God. That was the last thing I said to Hannah: *"Don't be such an idiot."* The call dropped as she stepped on the elevator and neither of us bothered to call back. Which didn't strike me as unusual at the time. We planned to see each other at the restaurant that evening.

I pay the cab and briefly consider waiting outside, but it's too windy. I climb the steep steps up to the law school's main entrance. Once through the heavy revolving doors, I loiter by the main desk, stepping aside to let others check in. Diana shows up on time, looking unduly radiant for such a somber occasion. She wears her black cashmere coat cinched around her narrow waist with a multicolored scarf peeking out at her breast. She's done her hair in hot rollers and the effect has more birthday va-va-voom than memorial gravitas. She must register my skepticism.

"It's supposed to be a life celebration!" she says, watery eyed, as her impossible heels clatter against the stone floor.

We hug. From the corner of my eye, I catch the agents looking Diana up and down with unmasked approval.

Although nothing untoward has happened in over a week, the agents stick with me everywhere I go. Even to the doors of public restrooms, if they happen to be out of view of the action. Smerth has apparently placated Acheson enough that I can continue to work on his case. There's been no further discussion of his offer to transfer me since I reported my husband's lack of interest.

Hours of document review have turned up nothing as interesting as the mysterious map. Henry registered zero excitement over it. He agreed it was gubernatorial and made me feel like a world class idiot for making a big deal out of it, even though it surfaced in two unrelated folders. Both agents were far more impressed with the substantial transfers from Clearwater Partners to the Lotus Group, and from Lotus to BXE.

Diana and I make our way to seats about twenty rows back in the auditorium where Hannah and I presented our moot court arguments as first year law students and where we sat through an interminable multistate bar review as newly minted graduates. The agents sit one row behind us, on the aisle.

I scan the space for familiar faces. I recognize a few classmates, slightly aged by life on K Street or Connecticut Avenue, in the crowd. We're fifteen minutes early. By the seven o'clock start time, the whole theater is packed, even the upstairs gallery. A Jesuit priest I vaguely remember from my second year professional responsibility class presides over the ceremony, which includes a recitation of highlights from the professional and academic lives of seven missing alumni and two current students. The program manages to strike a dignified yet detached tone, but I suppose that's normal whenever the officiant has no personal knowledge of the deceased. Still, I'm glad I decided to attend. The ninety minutes I spend in the auditorium, contemplating Hannah's life cut short, reinforce my resolve to get to the bottom of whether my firm was somehow complicit in her death.

This being Georgetown, a reception follows the memorial service. Party grade wine and beer flow freely in the student lounge that takes up much of the building's lower level. Diana and I accept glasses of Chardonnay from a cafeteria worker I recognize from my student days.

Diana raises her glass and says, "Well, happy birthday to Hannah." We toast our friend and fight back tears. Nobody else in the room seems upset. Most of the attendees haven't lost a best friend, and many appear more interested in networking than in remembering our fallen comrades. They'll leave here tonight feeling refreshed, unburdened, ready to "heal."

As if reading my mind, Diana says, "These people have no idea how much it hurts to have a friend murdered." Giant tears stream down her cheeks. She dabs at them with a cocktail napkin.

Evidently concerned that her watery eyes will ruin her face, Diana shoves her glass into my free hand, whips out her phone, positions it inches from her nose and takes a picture of herself. She studies her likeness, dabs at her perfectly made-up eyelids and sniffs, "Just checking that my eye shadow's even. I did my face in a hurry on the way out the door."

Across the room, one of the agents smirks at Diana's show of vanity. I thank God she's standing with her back to them. I exchange hollow platitudes about the horror of it all with some former classmates, with whom I was never close. Diana and I abandon our mostly full wine glasses and head for the doors.

We emerge onto New Jersey Avenue to discover a line of cabs idling in front of the building. I went to school here for three years and never once found a taxi within three blocks of the place. Diana and I decide to pop over to the other side of Capitol Hill to grab pizza and beer at Matchbox.

It's busy but not packed. I marvel at how everything can be so back to normal, yet not be. The popular eatery buzzes with the banter of the after work crowd, short blocks from the gaping crater at the Capitol South explosion site.

We put away a large fig and prosciutto pizza and two beers a piece in uncharacteristic quiet. Neither of us has the emotional steam to reminisce about Hannah, and it feels irreverent to chat about lighter topics. Two tables down, the agents nurse Diet Cokes and devour a pepperoni pie. I'm ready to crawl into bed by the time our check arrives. Nobody close to me has died since I lost my last grandmother seven years ago. I had forgotten how dealing with a death (or in this case, the prickling uncertainty of a presumed death) can sap your strength. I can't wait to get home, snuggle up to Damien and close my eyes. Diana looks spent, too. She suggests paying cash so we can leave the too-happy restaurant that much sooner.

We snag a cab discharging its passengers on 8th Street. The driver flies up Massachusetts Avenue, gunning the accelerator to make every light. The special agents stalk a couple of car lengths behind. As we turn onto T Street, Diana, who's been rifling through her bag, says, "Fuck. I don't have my keys." She roots around for another second before remembering she left them in her desk drawer.

I tell her to come get the spare set from our place. We pay the driver and spill out onto the sidewalk. As we fumble with our wallets, the special agents pull into a space three buildings down. I bet they had a car towed so they could park.

I feel sorry for my security detail. They must get bored. I'm not the most interesting person to watch. At least tonight, they got to eat decent pizza.

The lights are off in our living room but the blue glare of the TV shines out through the windows.

Diana looks at her watch: 11:54 p.m. "How sweet," she says in a syrupy voice. "Hubby waits up for you."

"I bet he just got home," I say, though I know he would wait up anyway. We're still gooey newlyweds and I'm not ashamed to admit we're excited to see each other, even if we've only been apart for a long work day. I hope we still act this way when we're old.

I reach for the lights and call to Damien, "Hi!"

"Hon, I think he's asleep," Diana whispers loudly.

He won't sleep long with the two of us banging around the apartment. I try to think where I left her keys. Probably in the kitchen junk drawer.

The weak overhead light illuminates only the hallway, but I can see Damien's silhouette in his favorite leather chair.

"Damien, we're home," I trill, in what I hope is a warm, wifely tone.

No response. "Damien, Diana's here. I need to turn on the lights and find her spare keys."

Still no response. He must be exhausted, and he's probably been drinking beers since the terminal at LaGuardia. I kick off my heels and turn on the living room lights, because he's going to have to wake up to move to bed anyway.

When the lights come on, Diana screams the scariest, most blood-curdling, bone-chilling scream I've ever heard. I lurch towards my husband, open mouthed, and crumple to the floor. Then I experience the unimaginable sensation of my whole world imploding.

Damien sits slumped in his favorite chair, feet spread on the floor in his usual manly Sports-Center-watching stance, with a half-eaten slice of pizza in his lap. Most of his gorgeous jaw, cheekbones and nose are missing, and what appears to be his drying blood and brains are splattered on the wall behind him. A handgun lies on the floor at his sneakered feet. We don't own a gun, is all I remember thinking, before my head spins and the whole world turns black.

8

When I come to, an army of unfamiliar faces blinks back at me. It takes me a second to register Diana at my shoulder. A pimple-faced EMT pushes her aside so that he can shine a flashlight in my eyes. Two DC cops, two detectives, two forensics experts and an ax-wielding guy from the fire department, whose role seems unclear, surround me. Someone holds up a white sheet to block my view of the living room. The EMT props me up against a rolled up blanket and tries to persuade me to drink some juice, but the thought makes me gag. I slump back down.

The senior detective starts to say something to me, then stops and addresses Diana. "Ma'am, we're going to need to speak with each of you separately."

"Excuse me?" Diana is indignant, green in the face and trembling with fear or rage or indignation, or perhaps some of each. "I have no intention of leaving her alone. She's obviously having a complete psychological meltdown. Understandably."

He takes a deep breath and scratches his jaw line with the backs of his fingers. "I understand your concern, ma'am. But we need to get everyone's independent version of events, to preserve the integrity of the investigation and catch the son of a bitch who did this."

Diana blinks back at him, looking dumbstruck.

Henry tears into the room. He's a bit winded, probably from bounding up the stairs. "FBI!" he yells and whips out his badge.

Everyone freezes. The junior detective, who is peppering me with questions I'm having trouble following, pushes himself up from his crouch on the floor. He puffs out his chest like an angry gorilla and strides over to Henry. "I think there's a mistake," he says. "This here is a plain, garden variety suspicious death. We've got it under control. But thanks for coming by."

Henry's already straight spine straightens further and he somehow manages to look down his nose at the detective, even though the latter is only an inch or two shorter. They lock eyes. Neither man blinks. When Henry finally speaks, his tone is beyond condescending. "Young man, there is no possible way for me to describe how little you know about this matter. We have reason to believe this death has implications far beyond a regular homicide."

"Oh really?" says the detective. "Here I was investigating a probable *suicide*."

His words, or the snide delivery of unthinkable news, or perhaps the ridiculous male posturing in the midst of the collapse of my life, blasts me out of my shocked stupor. I sit up straight and find my voice. "Damien did *not* commit suicide," I insist, loud and clear, before my voice crumbles. "He didn't. He wouldn't." My face drops into my hands and I sob deep, painful sobs from the bottom of my gut. Diana rushes to my side and wraps her arms around my shoulders, protectively.

I have no idea how long we crouch on the floor, me sobbing into Diana's chest, but eventually the detective shoves past Henry and squats next to me. "Nothing's certain at this early stage, ma'am, but you need to understand that we see no signs of a struggle or a forced entry."

"Damien would never kill himself," I repeat, as I struggle to process the detective's words. Would he? No. Never. Not a chance.

The forensics report on the handgun, which bore no serial number, comes back around five in the morning, midway through my three-hour "interview," which consisted of the cops asking nonsensical questions while I alternately cried and offered nearly incoherent answers. The police say that since the gun yielded no prints besides Damien's, they are ready to make a preliminary finding of suicide. I understand the words as the detective pronounces them, but I feel disoriented by them, as if I've been catapulted into some dark parallel universe where all rules of logic are suspended.

I can't believe this is happening. I have the sickening hunch that someone connected to the law firm killed Damien, but I have no idea how to find proof. And I feel too battered, too broken, to even begin figuring out how I'd go about trying.

Diana calls in sick, something she's never done before, even when felled by walking pneumonia last winter. She has me pumped so full of Xanax that I feel numb enough to face the apartment. Henry says we need to get it over with, and for some unfathomable reason, he insists I cannot delegate this task to anyone.

It's freezing rain outside, the worst kind of weather, which feels appropriate. One bleak blessing: the cops' suspicion of suicide keeps the press away. And the cold rain keeps would-be gawkers moving along.

The cops have roped off our place with yellow crime scene tape. Even though the coroner removed Damien while we were at the police station, the horrific blood stains remain. The sedatives must be nearly coma-inducing, since the hysteria I expect doesn't materialize.

Henry and one of the detectives accompany Diana and me to the bedroom. She assembles a pile of clothing while the FBI men hover in the doorway. I can't decide what was more upsetting about my interview with the police: the fact that these playground bullies turned DC cops kept saying Damien killed himself, or that when they weren't jabbering about suicide, they were treating me like a murder suspect.

Henry didn't say much, but I suppose I should feel grateful for his moral support and his comforting, old-man-in-charge presence. I suspect the detectives donned their kid gloves with me in deference to him. They certainly checked our alibis – Georgetown and Matchbox – in a hurry.

Diana wordlessly stuffs clothes into an overnight bag. I'm saying I've got enough things when Diana asks. "Did you grab shoes?"

"No," I say miserably. I'm wearing last night's clothes with my sneakers, because they were by the door when we walked out. Diana must have wrestled them onto my feet.

I wonder how long it will take to process that he's gone. I know it, but I don't feel it, if that makes any sense. My whole body feels heavy and stuck, as if every one of my bones and muscles is water logged.

I stare at my shoe rack, which displays three long rows of footwear. My bleary eyes snap into focus and I scream so loudly that everyone, including Henry, jumps.

There, right between my sensible navy interview pumps and a pair of purple slides from last summer, are the ankle boots I left in

Acheson's office twelve nights ago. Everyone starts asking if I'm alright. Somebody takes my arm.

I shrug the hand away and shove the shoes into my already full bag. Diana wordlessly picks up a pair of simple black heels and carries them out for me.

On the stairs, Henry whispers, "What did you see?" He bends close to hear my response.

"The shoes in my closet, the ones I have in my bag right now, are the same ones I left in Acheson's office," I hiss into his ear.

His face betrays no emotion. "You're sure?"

"Positive. They've still got the sample sale stickers on the soles."

"Alright," he whispers, as we reach the foyer, open our umbrellas and step outdoors. "I'm glad I made you go in. I would never have noticed this overture towards you." Then in a normal voice, he asks, "You're staying next door, right?"

Diana answers for me. "Four doors down."

Henry whispers into the mouthpiece by his cufflink that it's time to move down the block. Not that the agents' presence makes me feel safer. Damien died on their watch. But then, the agents were following me and Diana around Capitol Hill last night. Maybe if we'd skipped dinner, if we'd come home earlier.

I must voice my thoughts, because Diana says, in a strained voice, "Maybe if we'd come home earlier, you and I would be dead, too." She tries to stop herself from shuddering and wraps her arm around my shoulders. "Come on. Let's get out of here."

9

The funeral and its aftermath pass in one massive haze. I fly Damien's body to Rhode Island and bury him there instead of sending him back to the west coast. Selfish, maybe, but I need my own people around me. His parents and sister fly in for two days and stay in their hotel rooms as much as possible. They seem willing to accept the ridiculous ruling of suicide, and I suppose they blame me, by default, for Damien's supposed unhappiness.

I can't summon the energy to defend myself against such unfair condemnation. I know Damien and I were happy. Beyond happy. I don't need to demonstrate that to anyone, perhaps because I blame myself for Damien's death, too. Even though I'm convinced he didn't die by his own hand.

The autopsy comes back with the conclusion "probable suicide." The police leave the case open, but turn their attention to fresher crimes. Henry and Max assure me that when the FBI's investigation wraps up, they'll have the necessary evidence to secure a conviction for Damien's murder.

I can't tell whether Henry and Max agree the suicide ruling is bullshit.

Maybe they want to placate me so I'll continue to cooperate against Acheson and Smerth.

They no longer have anything to worry about on that score. Sitting in the funeral director's office I realize that I've never experienced true hatred before. I don't care how long it takes. Acheson will pay for this, I promise myself silently, as I sign off on white lilies for the casket.

The morning of Damien's funeral, Hannah's apologetic mother emails me and Diana to tell us they plan to hold a memorial service for Hannah in two weeks. I cry for two hours and try to process the knowledge that I will, at the not-advanced age of thirty, bury my husband and one of my closest friends during the same miserable month. Then I put on a black dress and float through the service and burial as if it's all an out-of-body experience.

Diana notices my security detail sitting in the last pew of the packed church. She confronts me the next morning. We perch opposite each other on the twin beds in my old room, under the shelves that still bear the full Nancy Drew series and my old tennis trophies, and I tell her everything. For the first time in our twenty-five plus years of friendship, I render Diana speechless.

After the funeral, I spend several days at home, hiding in bed, trying and failing to regroup. The firm sends an enormous floral arrangement with a card encouraging me to take as much time as I need.

Smerth, however, calls four days later and suggests that I show up if I wish to continue working for him. He proposes we revisit the question of a transfer upon my return.

I consult a therapist recommended by Diana's mom. She listens and nods solemnly for the fifty-minute hour and wraps up the session by encouraging me to keep busy. Reluctantly heeding her advice, I fly home, return to work, and list the apartment for sale. The realtor predicts it will go for the asking price in one weekend. She swears a gruesome death will not deter buyers bent on real estate in desirable Dupont Circle. I move into Diana's spare bedroom. My parents hire movers to pack my things. I swear I'll never set foot in my old place again.

Every time I'm alone with my thoughts, I shake with frustration. I'm a fool. Why on earth would I presume I'd return to Washington and find a smoking gun right under my nose in Interior Conference Room C? As if life ever unfolds like a primetime police drama.

Still, awake in my new, unfamiliar bed at night, I visualize the cops hauling Acheson away for capital murder, my tearful testimony moving a faceless jury to despair, and a judge sentencing the soulless bastard to die.

Never mind that I don't believe in the death penalty. Or that DC has no capital punishment. My revenge fantasies stoke my rage. I'm not a vicious and bloodthirsty person. I only believe in vengeance under specific circumstances. My specific circumstances.

On the way into the office for the first time since the murder, I cross Q Street and call Max, for no other reason than to vent my frustration that the FBI has yet to produce a suspect. I stand in the middle of Dupont Circle and shriek into my phone like an escapee from a lunatic asylum. Even the drug addicted homeless drifters pause from whiling their lives away on the brown winter grass to gawk at me.

I have no idea why Max doesn't hang up. Finally I run out of steam, fall silent, feel sick. I don't believe him when he tells me Damien's murder investigation is his top priority. My tirade, which already feels remote, like a dream that dissipates in the morning, has exhausted my meager reservoir of energy. I apologize for my hysterical outburst and hang up, feeling sheepish and unhinged in a previously unknown and wholly frightening way. I detour down 18th Street and enter my building's lobby through the back so I don't have to see the construction and clean up on Connecticut Avenue.

The elevators open and expel Smerth and Acheson. I jerk backwards so violently that I fall on my butt on the marble tile. Tears spurred equally by fury and shame stream forth without warning. Smerth extends a hand to help me to my feet. Acheson says he's sorry for my loss. I feel my eyes bulge like they might pop from my face when he steps closer and adds, "Good for you, for getting right back to work. I see Randolph's managed to rub off on you."

Acheson punches his lawyer playfully in the arm. I can't be sure, because I'm so stunned that he's speaking to me, but I think I catch Smerth wince. My whole body starts to twitch with revulsion. I turn on my heels and make a mad dash to the security desk's new miniscule post-bombing trash can, fling myself over it, and heave up coffee and stomach juices for what feels like an eternity.

Smerth appears at my side and holds my hair back, taking care to keep his wingtips safe from the line of fire. He offers me a mint and suggests I take one more day "to get my head back into the game."

At home, I spend nine hours curled on the bed in my suit. I lie in the fetal position and stare at the cheerful yellow walls of Diana's second bedroom, wishing I'd never met Henry Redwell and Max von Buren, and that my life could magically return to the way it was. Or alternatively, that the night could last forever. I could lie here, doing nothing, feeling nothing. I wouldn't have to face another dawn. Diana comes in around dinner time and forces me to eat a few bites of soup, drink some water and take a sleeping pill.

Something strange and wonderful happens before sunrise.

Hannah is found alive and, if not well, then certainly in fair to good condition.

Three weeks after the bombings.

Diana barges into my room, half dressed, happy tears streaming down her face. She shouts the unbelievable news and urges me out of bed so that I may view the 6 a.m. newscast for myself.

Last night, construction workers in Arlington found a thin, filthy but coherent Hannah and a barely conscious, wheelchair bound senior citizen named Bertha Sue Fitts in an elevator car at the Pentagon City metro station. The elevator car had been buried behind a wall of rubble that somehow wasn't excavated in the immediate aftermath of the bombing. The first responders had concluded that nobody could survive past the initial three to four day search and rescue period.

The television shows medics loading two stretchers into ambulances but neither patient is visible. The anchor reads a statement from one of the medics who quoted the younger woman, a Ms. Hannah Smith, as saying, "Good Lord! I'm fixing for the longest bath of my life!" before passing out from exhaustion.

Diana and I grin at each other. "It's her alright," she says. "It has to be her." She smiles from ear to ear. The good kind of tears start to flow down my cheeks. It's been ten days since I last smiled and the muscles in my face feel out of use.

A young, perky reporter tells us the elevator car ended up on its side during the blast, not far from a metro carriage in which twenty-seven people perished, but walled off by a mountain of concrete rubble. The medics transported the two women to the nearest emergency room, but Ms. Smith was transferred overnight to George Washington University Medical Center, at the request of her parents. The anchor inserts an inane comment about how she herself suffers from claustrophobia.

"Get in the shower!" Diana shrieks. "We're going see her and you are not going to smell worse than she does." I look down at myself. I slept in yesterday's suit, minus the jacket and my bra, which I must have removed sometime overnight. I do as I'm told.

Diana hands me a coffee in a travel cup when I emerge from the bathroom fifteen minutes later. We dash to the end of the block and hail a cab on 18th Street.

Over the cabby's cranking go-go music, Diana catches me up on what she learned while I washed: Hannah's train stalled in the Pentagon City station. The driver advised his passengers there would be a ten minute delay, due to a problem with a switch. Hannah looked out from the train to the platform and saw the wheelchair lady struggling with the elevator doors. They kept closing before she could get herself, her wheelchair and her luggage inside. "She had one of those old lady carts," Diana says. "She was trying to drag it behind the wheelchair. The poor thing is like, 86 years old. Anyway, Hannah offered to help her when nobody else could be bothered."

The bomb exploded after the elevator doors shut behind the two women, but before they reached the street. They were found twenty-five yards from the elevator shaft, but neither sustained injuries beyond cuts and bruises.

Fortunately for both women, Ms. Fitts was making her way home from the grocery store, where she had procured, among other things, two huge cases of Ensure, or some similar nutrition shake marketed towards the elderly and infirm. The elevator's alarm system failed them, but its fire blanket (which only about one in five metro elevators evidently carry) didn't.

Astoundingly, there was even more serendipity to Hannah's good fortune. Ms. Fitts hadn't even ridden the Metro. She finished her shopping at the Harris Teeter in Pentagon City and descended into the station when she remembered she had a hair appointment in the mall. So when Hannah's train pulled in, there she was, trying to get back up the elevator to make her hairdo on time.

Everyone else on Hannah's train died.

Diana stops talking and searches her phone for the latest. I spend the rest of the taxi trip contemplating whether the Chinese are right. I learned in a college seminar on faith that many Chinese believe some people come into the world lucky. Others, not so much. It has a lot to do with the zodiac. Hannah must be one of the charmed souls whose good fortune leads her to do good acts which in turn beget more good fortune. Or maybe that's the Hindu explanation for the luckiest among us.

A lump swells in my throat as I consider Damien. Maybe he was born under an inauspicious sign. Why else would he have to pay for *my* naiveté with his life?

A chill surges up my spine as the taxi stops under the medical center's portico. My breath catches in my throat. I've never given much thought to ghosts, and whether they exist or not. But I can't describe the cold, tingling sensation between my shoulder blades except to say it's as if something ethereal has brushed past me.

With a warning.

Hannah is lucky.

You, not so much.

Diana flings a twenty at the driver, tells him to keep it.

We race into the hospital to see our extraordinarily fortunate best friend.

On the way out an hour later, I call Max and demand a security detail for Diana. To my surprise, he agrees immediately. My whole body heaves a sigh of relief that she won't be in peril because she opened her home to me.

MARCH

10

It's after ten on an ordinary Monday night. I'm hiding in bed trying to read the *Chicken Soup for the Soul* book my therapist recommended. Not that the day of week makes any difference. I have no motivation to venture out anymore. Hannah's rescue buoyed my spirits temporarily, but while her life returns to normal, mine continues to crumble. Every once in a while I indulge an ugly thought I'd never admit to anyone, because I love Hannah. Truly, I do. But if I had to lose someone, why did Hannah get to live while Damien had to die? I know the events are unrelated, and I hate myself to the core whenever such a vile thought forms in my head. But I can't help myself.

I feel stuck in my own head, a prisoner of inertia and gloom. Which isn't always as bad as it sounds. My apathy provides a salve, compared to the intense pain, rage and despair I felt when the earliest stages of grief stung like a fresh stab wound. Every morning I haul myself to the office, accomplish enough to stay employed, return home and do nothing until it's time to go into work again. My hopes of finding anything useful to the FBI fade with each passing day I come up empty. I feel useless and bitter and unable to snap out of it.

My therapist urges patience.

As the days pass, nothing changes but the weather, which fluctuates madly between frigid and unseasonably balmy. I survive. But I'm not living.

I wander out to the living room to see Diana, who's back from a late workout – something else I haven't bothered with in recent memory. What's the point? My clothes hang loosely. I have no appetite. I can't manage to cook, or even order in. So why would I beat myself up at the gym?

I swallow prescription antidepressants every morning, right before I brush my teeth. They do nothing. My doctor assures me they will, in four to six more weeks. Max calls to say he needs to pick me up for a meeting tomorrow.

"Are you feeling any better?" he asks in a cautious tone.

"About the same. I'll see you in the morning."

Diana flips through her mail and scratches Buster's ears. "Who was on the phone?" she asks.

"The FBI. I'll have an early morning."

"Are they getting closer to arresting Acheson?"

"No, and if they don't make some progress soon, they're going to be without my services."

"You're quitting?" Diana asks, eyebrows raised. "Like actually telling them you're out? I didn't realize bailing was allowed."

"I don't know," I whine. "I don't know anything anymore. I've had a headache for longer than I can remember. I can't sleep, but I can't focus because I'm so exhausted. So I accomplish nothing. Which sucks." Diana nods sympathetically but she's run out of encouraging things to say. I rub my temples in a vain attempt to soothe my migraine. "Why can't they arrest that bastard already?"

She doesn't answer me. We've hashed this out countless times. We both believe the boots alone should be sufficient to render Acheson a "person of interest," if not an outright suspect. I think Henry has shelved Damien's murder investigation because the FBI has bigger fish to fry. But if I start making noise, they can arrest me for interfering with an investigation.

My alarm jolts me from my slumber at six-thirty. Buster the cat, who hasn't budged from his post on the pillow next to me all night, launches his furry form toward the ceiling as if shot from a cannon.

Max arrives forty minutes later. He looks like he's slept in his suit and skipped his morning shave. He's bearing a cup of Starbucks for me, the sight of which almost provokes tears. I need to get a grip, I tell myself as I bite the inside of my lower lip and will the waterworks to retreat.

"Skim milk and no sugar, right?" he says, by way of greeting.

I say yes, thank you, even though I use whole milk for my coffee, and these days I might actually benefit from the extra calories.

We pile into his black government SUV and two agents in a sedan pull up behind us.

"Where are we going?" I blurt ungraciously. The unbalanced feeling I've tried to suppress since the FBI first knocked on my door creeps back. It takes an enormous act of willpower to focus on drinking my coffee instead of fidgeting like a child.

He ignores my question and asks whether I've been sleeping.

"Surprisingly, yes," I admit. "Though I always feel wiped." There must be something wrong with me. Every night at bedtime, without Damien, I feel so alone. I'm convinced I'll suffer relentless insomnia. But I'm out when my head hits the pillow. It's pretty amazing since I've never, in my adult life, been what you'd call a "good sleeper."

"I understand it's pretty common," he says. "Depressed people often sleep soundly but wake up tired."

"I see," I say, though I'm not sure I do. I play with the lid of my coffee and change the subject. "What's new with you?"

"We've made tremendous progress on the case. I got in from Bermuda an hour ago. Your boss unwittingly told us where to look for more evidence."

"How so?"

"Through that microphone you planted on his desk, of course. He sent us right to a storage facility, full of documents, that enabled us to close in on Katya."

"Katya?"

"We believe Katya is a code name for a prominent terrorist leader, one whose group was waiting for funds siphoned from a casino owned by Korov. It seems they're expecting a wire transfer from Korov's Swiss account to some Western Union office in the middle of nowhere, in southwestern Russia. Henry claims to have a source who can pinpoint its timing."

He pauses to see if I'm following. I am, mostly. Max adds, "We plan to intercept the wire. The money is an installment for the attack on K4."

"Wait a minute," I say. "Smerth actually talked about this 'Katya' on the phone?"

"No. He talked about file storage in the basement of a restaurant in Hamilton, Bermuda, on the phone. With Acheson."

Max pulls into a metered space by the row of upscale shops in Cleveland Park. He leads me through the nondescript side entrance of a small specialty grocer and we climb dusty wooden stairs to a landing with two doors. There's no heat. The cold, damp air smells stale.

Max raps his knuckles on one of the doors so gingerly that I wonder whether the occupants can possibly hear him. But I hear the security chain being undone and the door swings open. Henry admits us into an apartment worthy of the rundown stairwell. It's a small place, made smaller by ridiculously low ceilings. As if that's not bad enough, filthy blinds are drawn shut over the windows. The lime green linoleum floors, circa 1972, if I had to guess, curl upwards at each seam. The apartment lacks any furniture except a ratty orange-red couch, a plastic-topped card table and a few metal folding chairs. One of these is occupied by a slight, jumpy looking man with a dark complexion and a dingy brown wool hat that's completely incongruous with his white dress shirt and blue tie.

Henry has his sleeves rolled up and he wears two handguns strapped to his body with the kind of vest sometimes seen on cop shows.

"Where are we?"

"FBI safe house. This unit is completely wire-proof. We can speak freely here."

"You can't speak freely at FBI headquarters?" Surely they have better security at the nerve center of the FBI than they do in an abandoned flat above a grocery shop.

"Just trust us on this one," Henry says, more curtly than usual. He looks tired, and his glasses magnify the darks circles under his eyes.

Satisfied that he won't have to conduct any further Q&A, Henry clears his throat and says, "Max and Lena, meet Casper—obviously not his real name."

The man in the chair doesn't bother to rise or extend a hand, but instead reaches into his tattered shirt pocket for a cigarette, which he raises to his lips and lights with a match from a book on the table in front of him. I bet he's smoked for a long time, based on how the cigarette hangs from his mouth as he lights it.

Casper inhales deeply, holds his breath for a second and releases a plume of smoke that lingers right above his head. It has no place else to go in this airtight hovel.

Henry motions for me and Max to pull up chairs around the table. He rolls out a map of the Caucasus, with both the existing and proposed pipelines clearly marked. It's a detailed rendition, peppered with countless tiny villages.

"Here's what you need to know," he says. "Casper led a band of Chechen freedom fighters in the Russian–Chechen war, during which Russian soldiers kidnapped his wife. A local CIA operative secured her release in exchange for Casper's services. Specifically, the CIA wanted him to provide information about the movement of money and arms from the Russian opposition—by that I mean Korov—into Chechen fighters' hands."

"Wait a minute," says Max. "Since when does the CIA share informants with us?"

"Since I called in an old favor," says Henry. "We don't need to get more specific. What you need to know is that Casper has recorded conversations between Korov and the rebel leader, in which they finalized the logistics of a deal exchanging arms and money for a spectacular, crippling attack on K4. More importantly, Casper was present when Acheson and Aziz pledged to finance the building of the replacement pipeline, but he never saw any documents memorializing the transaction."

I decide to interrupt. "I understand why Korov wants K4 destroyed: he stands to benefit by building the replacement. But why is its destruction so important to anyone else?"

Casper, who's working on his second cigarette, and who had been studying his fingernails while Henry spoke, looks up and interjects, in heavily accented but unbroken English, "Sometimes there are subtleties to these arrangements. Perhaps Acheson and Aziz are getting something else from Mr. Korov."

Casper takes a huge drag on his cigarette, and before he can exhale, Henry says, "That's why you're here, Lena. We need to find out what Acheson and Aziz, and possibly Vice President Prescott, could gain in exchange for their help in destroying the pipeline."

And here I was thinking, naively, that I would get some answers to my own questions this morning.

"Well," I say, looking from Henry to Max to this Casper character, who is picking at the unruly cuticles around his left thumb, "They all invested heavily in Clearwater Partners, which owns the

Burtonhall Corporation, which wins no-bid contracts in sketchy corners of the world all the time."

They're all listening to me with rapt attention. Could it be they didn't see something as obvious as the Burtonhall connection? But nobody looks surprised by my theory.

As if to confirm that this is some type of early morning test of my wits, Henry says, "Exactly right. Now we need you to go back into R&S and find proof that it's a done deal."

Casper looks up from his assault on his fingers and reaches under his jacket. My heart catapults up my throat. Max's hand flies to his gun. My brain processes what my gut sensed two seconds ago – he's going to shoot us.

"Take it easy," Casper says to Max, without looking his way. He produces a book, which he slides across the table to Henry. "Go always with your God as I go always with Allah, most gracious, most merciful." Casper stands up, raises his right hand as if offering a benediction, and leaves the room without another word. The door shuts softly.

"What was that about?" Max says.

Henry shoots a sharp look my way, and tells him to escort me back to my office. We leave the deputy director seated at the shoddy table, poring over Casper's pocket Bible.

Max and I pile back into his vehicle. "There was no need for Henry to have us meet this Russian character," he says, as he blasts the heat and maneuvers the car into traffic.

"Chechen," I correct him. I don't mean to sound obnoxious. It just comes out. "And isn't that war over?"

"It is, but all the Chechens got in the end was *de facto* independence and a bunch of corrupt warlords, some of whom would like to establish Chechnya as a wholly independent Islamist republic. Obviously that would be undesirable from both the Russian and American points of view. Others among them would prefer to bring about Russian regime change. And God knows where Henry's new friend stands." Max pauses to make sure I'm following. "But, to get back to *my* original point, Henry knows that the fewer people who lay eyes on a high value informant, the better. Something doesn't add up. I can't figure it out and it's going to drive me nuts until I do." He grips the steering wheel too tightly, as if wringing out his aggression on it.

I sit quietly for about a block and try to process this information. Henry must have his reasons. He's more experienced than Max and maybe plain smarter as well. I congratulate myself on having the good sense not to verbalize this. Since I seem destined to spend time with Max, why piss him off?

Connecticut Avenue is a sea of brake lights, all heading downtown. It's nine o'clock, the height of rush hour. Walking would be faster, but a cold rain has set in. I watch the water pelt a colorful banner promoting the Friends of the National Zoo.

I stare up at the images of smiling cartoon monkeys and pandas and say, "I bet Henry wanted us to see Casper because he doesn't trust the guy. Maybe the meeting was a bit of insurance."

Max shakes his head, but doesn't say I'm wrong. We stop and go in silence over the Taft Bridge. When we cross the intersection at Kalorama, he says, "The going with God bit creeped me out. It came out of nowhere. I'm not accustomed to doing business with religious yahoos."

"I thought he was reaching for a gun. Relief surged through every vein in my body when I saw all he had was a book. Besides, Henry seemed more curious than anything."

"Fair enough." Max plucks his Starbucks cup from the holder in the center console, takes a large sip of coffee and complains it's gone cold. We stop and go another block in silence.

"Alright," I say finally. "Since we both think there was something off about this morning's *rendez-vous*, do you still want me to focus on finding documents linking Burtonhall and Jack Prescott to the new pipeline?"

Max exhales loudly. He's visibly trying to keep his frustration in check. "Do you honestly believe they'd be stupid enough to leave something that major lying around the law firm?"

"No. Especially with Acheson under such microscopic scrutiny. And why would he want to bring his best friend, and likely next president, down with him?"

"Exactly," says Max. "And then there's Smerth. I don't know how he ties in. I mean, other than possibly profiting from Acheson's original scheme to bribe some senators."

"But if Smerth's not involved in anything more sinister than that, wouldn't Acheson and the rest of them stop funneling money through the company in Bermuda?"

"I'd assume so, unless..."

"Unless what?"

"Unless the rest of the gang has set up Smerth as their fall guy."

I hadn't thought of that possibility. "So," I say, "You *don't* want me to spend today looking for a no-bid contract for Burtonhall to build the new pipeline?" I feel desperate for a project, some structured diversion with a tangible goal.

"You do what Henry says. He's the deputy director. We don't get to ignore him just because I think he's on the wrong track."

"Okay," I say, though I suspect Max will conduct some extracurricular research of his own.

"His methods probably made sense at that other agency."

"What other agency?"

"Henry worked for years in the CIA's arms-smuggling unit. He was undercover for ages, in some kind of joint operation with Britain's MI6. That's why he has that strange ex-pat accent. Don't tell me you haven't noticed."

"I thought it was a private school affectation or something. Why did he quit the CIA?" I ask as Max pulls up in front of R&S.

"Blown cover. He's been driving a desk at the FBI ever since, but he misses the field. He loves all this cloak and dagger stuff. I can't blame him, but I wish he'd take an interest in someone else's case. I'm not used to having my boss breathe down my neck."

I slip through the revolving doors into the dry heat of the building's lobby. A few dozen people in suits have stopped to gape at the giant screen in the elevator bank.

A massive bomb exploded twenty minutes ago, in a hotel in Abu Dhabi where Jack Prescott was staying for a series of meetings with Arab leaders. The vice president escaped unharmed, but at least six hundred souls, all presumed lost, were assembled in the conference center where the blast originated. Two of Aziz's half brothers are among the dead.

The grim-faced hotel manager looks up at the smoldering shell of a glass and steel tower and says he expects the death toll to rise. He was fortunate to be outside at the marina, escorting Mr. Prescott to a last-minute yachting excursion, when the explosion rocked the ground under his feet. He says that even from a distance of five hundred meters, the smell of burning metal and flesh permeated his pores and lodged in his mouth. His eyes water, whether from sadness or chemical fumes I cannot say.

CNN's breathless anchor describes the decimated skyscraper as a "seven star ultra luxury property" owned mostly by Clearwater Partners, which bought out Prince Abdul bin Aziz's personal stake in the tower thirteen months ago for $843 million.

My BlackBerry goes nuts. Smerth. I push past my colleagues and dive into the elevator.

Violence never touched my life before, and now it's everywhere. Six hundred people dead. This morning they were alive and minding their own business. Each one leaves someone—a spouse, a parent, a child—as bereft as I am over Damien. I shake my head as if the back and forth motion will clear my mind. Smerth won't want to discuss the senseless, brutal loss of life.

Not when Clearwater is out almost a billion dollars. I jog through the beige hallways of R&S to my boss's office.

11

"Acheson might actually be screwed," Charlie says, as I hurry into Interior Conference Room C the next morning. Two empty *venti* Starbucks cups sit discarded on the table to his left. I should have been in before eight, but I was still awake at four and couldn't bring myself to set the alarm. I assume Charlie arrived early, in order to make as much headway as possible on the Acheson matter before he and Smerth depart for London next week.

That was the upshot of yesterday's meeting after the hotel bombing: A wild-haired, red-faced Smerth announced that he and Charlie will fly to London on Monday to meet with Clearwater Partners' insurers. The insurers will argue that they shouldn't have to pay out hundreds of millions because the attack wasn't garden variety terrorism, but rather a targeted assassination attempt which generated collateral damage. Regrettable, of course, but not covered by the letter of the policy. As insurance suits go, it would be an interesting case, and a great line item on my resume.

I am to stay here and mind the fort.

Charlie snaps my attention back to the task at hand. "It's been clear for a while that Acheson paid various Senators and Congressmen *millions* in bribes – much of it disguised as campaign contributions. If you ask me, Acheson is the single most arrogant fuck ever to work K Street. And that's saying a lot. I'm just amazed he spelled out so many *quid pro quos* on email. He didn't bother to delete anything. But for technology, he would probably get away with all of it. And you and I would be adding a huge acquittal to our CV's. But it's looking ugly."

"Smerth is going to stroke out if we can't find some facts he likes. He's already popping blood pressure pills like they're tictacs." He's been doing so since the appeals court ruled last night that the firm had to recover and fork over Acheson's deleted emails. The three-judge panel held that as a lobbyist, rather than a practicing lawyer, Acheson could not hide his communications behind attorney-client privilege.

"Yeah, Smerth basically ripped Acheson a new one this morning. He couldn't believe Acheson didn't have the brains to keep anything so incriminating off the firm email system, where anyone could retrieve it." Charlie shakes his head in disbelief at the mind-boggling stupidity of our client.

"Do you think Acheson will go to prison?" I wonder if Charlie detects hope in my voice. Most of Rutledge & Smerth's white collar clients never see the inside of a cell.

"Smerth says the odds are fifty-fifty."

"He said that? Seriously?"

"Oh, right. You missed his 8 a.m. briefing, so you wouldn't have heard the other big news." Charlie gets up and checks that nobody's loitering within earshot.

"What other big news?" I ask his back. I'm starting to feel whiplashed. Why is Charlie so edgy? He's sweating even though the thermostat is set to a frosty 65 degrees. I have a sweater on over my blouse and I'm chilly.

Satisfied that the coast is clear, he explains, "Aziz and Smerth had some massive falling out late last night. Evidently this firm no longer represents Aziz, effective yesterday. Something to do with how to handle the aftermath of the attack in Abu Dhabi. So we won't have to go through those after all." He motions towards the mountain of files pertaining to the Aziz matter.

Charlie looks relieved that we'll be spared this tedious task. I try to mirror his expression, but I'm panicking.

Charlie tells me that the files will be out of our hair before lunchtime, per Mr. Aziz's orders. "Since our guy is pretty much screwed and the Aziz thing is off my plate, I've been digging around a little, to see if there's anything to my hunch about election tampering," he says.

"So since our remaining client is fucked anyhow, you're proactively looking for evidence of some *additional* federal offense he may have committed?"

"I know, it's kind of bad."

"Well, you agree that the map is gubernatorial, right?"

"Duh, but Acheson obviously cares about something in the notations."

Charlie's right, of course, but we can discuss the map later. Right now I need him to leave so I can glance through the Aziz files before they're carted away forever.

I'm concocting ruses to distract Charlie – beg him to go for coffee or page him to another floor – when someone knocks on the door. Two burly men in work boots, accompanied by Janet, who hovers like a bad waitress, brush past us to load the files onto carts for transport down the block.

Charlie closes the door behind them. "What I was trying to say before was, the box with the map is gone."

I roll my eyes at him. "Of course it's not. That was an Acheson file. They took Aziz files. There's no way Janet was letting them take so much as a sticky note beyond what's absolutely necessary to turn over."

"Not Aziz's new lawyers. Someone came in here, overnight I presume, and took that file. So gubernatorial or not, it's important to somebody."

"Are you sure?"

"Positive. I looked for it first thing this morning, before you came in." He says this last part almost snidely.

I glare at him, and although Charlie isn't the most perceptive person when it comes to reading other people's feelings, he receives the message and starts apologizing.

"I mean, of course you're justified in taking some extra time. You've been through, are going through, something hideous."

I cut him off. "Thanks, but since we're both stuck here, let's get back to the salt mines." I don't want to discuss the missing evidence with Charlie until I've had a chance to talk with Henry and Max.

The afternoon drags on forever. At six, Charlie excuses himself, saying he has plans.

Plans? He never has plans. I can't help myself. "Hot date?" I ask, hopeful for some trivial diversion that has nothing to do with the nightmare that is my personal life.

"I have to meet my accountant," Charlie says, without looking up from his shoes. "See you in the morning. I'll be here early."

As I wish him good night, I try not to read anything into his remark about being here early. Bereaved or not, as the junior person, I should try to arrive first once in a while.

It's late, after nine, and I'm getting bleary-eyed hunched over one of Acheson's telephone logs when I hear the door open behind me. A heavily accented male voice says, "Good evening, Lena."

I reel around in my chair to see Volodya Korov, closing the door behind him with one hand, and raising the other to his lips in the universal be quiet gesture.

"What are you doing here?" I hiss, as I try to suppress the panic rising in my core. My mind's eye races back to my last late night run-in at the firm.

"I thought I might catch you alone," he says.

Korov towers over most mortals. He has strong, masculine features but his face bears deep scars from what was probably a vicious case of adolescent acne, and his smile is marred by a glinting gold tooth in the space where his right canine should be. He looks older than his thirty-eight years, weathered and even world-weary.

"May I sit?" he asks, and I suddenly realize who he sounds like. Boris. From Boris and Natasha, the diabolic caricatured duo in the old *Rocky and Bullwinkle* cartoons. I stifle an inappropriate giggle and motion to the empty chairs across the table from me. He picks the closest one and sits. He reeks of cigarettes. No wonder his teeth are falling out.

I close the folder in front of me and rest my shaky hands on the table, trying my best to appear composed. There's no reason for him to be here.

"I believe we can help each other," he says finally.

I feel my eyebrows rise about an inch on my forehead. "How so?"

"I know who killed your husband," he says matter-of-factly, as if he's saying, "I've decided what I'd like for lunch."

My jaw drops open. I will myself to close it. "Who?"

"Patience," he says, condescendingly. "But I want them to suffer for it every bit as much as you do." He sits back in his chair.

What am I supposed to say? The familiar thirst for revenge pulses through me. I've grown to welcome my vengeful moods. They provide a respite from debilitating grief.

My mind races as I try to decide how to respond. After what feels like a long silence, I blurt, "Why do you care about Damien?"

"I don't give a fuck about Damien. But the men who killed him stole an astronomical sum of money from me. I can't get them on my own. I thought you might be persuaded to assist me."

His answer hits me like a slap in the face. How can he say that about Damien and then expect me to help him? I fight back the familiar welling of tears by biting the inside of my lower lip. I clamp down so hard with my teeth that I taste a tiny trickle of blood on my tongue. Sick as this sounds, it helps me focus.

Unbelievable. First the FBI wants my help, and now him. I don't understand. I'm a nobody. Third year lawyers like me exist in droves in this town. Korov is one of the wealthiest men in Russia, one of the oligarchs whose dealings and escapades get reported in newspapers around the globe. I can't imagine there's anything he'd want to accomplish that he couldn't do without my assistance. I stall for time. "Why should I trust you?"

"Because you lack a better offer." His self-satisfied smile says, *checkmate*.

His gold tooth glimmers. I try not to stare. I wonder why someone so rich doesn't get a regular crown and silently congratulate myself for not asking out loud. I look down at my hands to avoid his intense gaze and attempt to process what he's suggesting. The little voice in my head screeches that I should tell him thanks, but no thanks, and beat a hasty retreat downstairs to the relative safety of the crowded street. We could pretend this *tête-à-tête* never happened. My life is complicated enough without the addition of a creepy oil baron.

I must take too long to reply because Korov clears his throat and interrupts my private dialogue. "I assume you're missing this map?"

He holds up the map that went missing, the one Charlie hopes to link to his election rigging scenario. I feel my face register surprise.

"That's what I thought," he says, leaning forward again. "But I imagine it would be much more interesting with these pages attached."

He passes a two-page list across the table. I regard it with suspicion, as if touching it would burn my hands, or worse. "Well, have a look for Christ's sake. You've been puzzling over something so simple for *ever so long*."

I pick up the papers. It's a state by state list, of all governors and U.S. Senators, broken down by party. I skim the two pages and glance back at the map, which he's courteously positioned in front of me. "So the map is gubernatorial, and the numbers refer to how many Republican senators each state has." Henry was mostly right, and would have seen the whole picture if he'd given the map more than a passing glance.

Korov nods his approval from across the table. "Exactly. You've been losing sleep trying to deduce completely public information. Acheson should have let you keep it in the first place. Fool."

The room spins. Can this be? Did Damien die because Acheson caught me holding a map I could have printed off the Internet?

"There must be something more," I say, without stopping to consider that it could be sub-ideal to hash this out with Acheson's crony.

"What a bright young lady you are. Of course there's more. Your clients want to change these numbers."

"Yeah, well that was part of Acheson's job. He got Republicans elected," I snap. I'm emotionally fried and Korov's patronizing tone strikes some nerve I didn't know I had.

"Ah, yes, but sometimes ambitious people lack patience. They look for other ways to change the things which displease them."

"I'm listening."

"It's so obvious. You'll kick yourself," he taunts.

"Are you going to tell me or not?"

"Acheson and his associates plan to assassinate several Democratic senators." He lets his voice trail off.

Even though my mind feels full of cobwebs, it takes me less than a millisecond to catch on. "From states with Republican governors, so the governors will appoint Republicans to serve out the terms."

"Smart girl," Korov says. "You get a gold star."

"There's one flaw with your theory."

"What's that?" His expression suggests that he's already familiar with any and all problems with his reasoning, but he's decided to indulge me.

"I don't believe for a second that Randolph Smerth would get even tangentially involved with a plot to assassinate anybody."

"Nobody said Smerth was involved in anything."

"You said Acheson and his associates."

"Smerth only thinks he's Acheson's associate. He's merely Acheson's lawyer. You lawyers always forget your station in life," he says, shaking his head as if this is an enormous pity.

I ignore the lawyer crack. "Can you prove it?"

"Otherwise I wouldn't be here soliciting your assistance."

The little voice in my head has sounded every possible alarm bell, but I ignore the flight command my brain is desperately transmitting to my body.

"Jed Carmichael of South Dakota, Maria Perez of Florida, Kurt Lundquist of Minnesota and Barry Stein of Pennsylvania will all travel to Moscow next week as members of a bi-partisan Senate delegation. In exchange for certain assurances relating to my oil empire from both Clearwater as a whole, and from Acheson and Jack Prescott individually, I will allow Clearwater's private special forces to take down their plane as soon as it enters Russian airspace."

He stops for breath. I don't bother trying to hide my shock. "Clearwater has a private army? Private special forces? The arsenal to take down a jet?"

Korov brushes aside my inquiry with a wave. "Of course they have a private army. Clearwater owns BXE. Your government contracts hundreds of millions of dollars of military dirty work to them year after year. They are very efficient at killing people."

He's not wrong about the feds outsourcing dirty work, but can Korov be right about how BXE intends to use its substantial resources? Like anyone who follows the news, I know they win all the big military security contracts because they're the largest player. Pre-indictment, they kept Acheson on retainer to help maintain their favorite child status.

BXE was founded by a first cousin of Vice President Prescott, a family black sheep named Royce, whose only prior life accomplishment was flunking out of West Point. When Clearwater acquired BXE three or four years ago, the board handed Royce Prescott a gold parachute and shoved him out the door. I remember reading that he used part of the severance to start some hyper masculine weekend warrior camp for wannabe fighters in a swampy corner of southeast Tennessee.

Under Royce's tenure, BXE's employees made frequent headlines for thuggish behavior such as gunning down foreign civilians. His people developed a reputation as salty at best, brutish at worst. They caused their fair share of embarrassments for the U.S. government and they kept our diplomats busy backpedaling and explaining their actions in the most volatile corners of the globe.

They've made fewer headlines since Royce's departure and this is the first time I've heard anyone suggest that BXE's upper management—meaning Clearwater—would scheme to bite the government hand that feeds it. I imagine using a private army to assassinate federal officials could constitute treason.

Korov shifts forward in his chair and continues his narrative. "I was going to help them make the assassination of four American senators by American hands in Russian territory look like the work of separatist terrorists. Choreographed well, the public would buy it. They'll blame anyone who looks remotely Muslim for anything these days." Korov studies his fingernails as if bored by having to explain this. "It would be terribly embarrassing for the Russian president for such a tragedy to occur on his watch, but that for me would be, how do you Americans say it? *Frosting*."

My mind races. I can practically feel my neurons struggling to push aside the cobwebs spun by hours of tedious work and too many mood boosting pills. A treasonous private army. Framed Islamists. Casper. Max says it doesn't add up. Offshore blocker corporations. *Yesterday's fatal explosion in Abu Dhabi.* I hear Henry's initial speculation echo in my head. *"A war started, financed and prosecuted by a corporation."* What if Clearwater launched a massive attack on itself in order to position its key players beyond suspicion? And to stoke resentment between the Saudi and Russian governments and the Islamists?

Korov keeps talking. "But as I alluded earlier, the deal has gone awry. I no longer have any interest in helping Acheson or Prescott do anything."

"If this is about oil, don't you want Clearwater Partners to invest in your pipeline?"

"I see you've done your homework, Lena." A chill shoots down my spine when he pronounces my name. "But I have a plan for alternate funding."

"Alternate funding?"

"The Russian government."

"Wouldn't they like to throw you in prison? Confiscate your assets?" I'm surprised I manage to spit out such a direct challenge.

"And they say Americans don't follow world news. I'm not talking about the *present* regime. I want to use Clearwater's money to remove President Perayev. I think I have an excellent chance of succeeding him. In which case I will have enough on my plate without worrying about a private army, commanded by people I no longer trust, running amok in my backyard. Not that any of those details concern you."

I swallow hard. My mouth has gone totally dry. "So it sounds like you have everything figured out. Why do you need me? And what can this possibly have to do with Damien?" I play with my wedding ring as I ask the last part. I haven't taken it off, or even switched it to my other hand as some of my friends have suggested. It's too soon. I feel naked without it.

Korov rocks back in his chair and hoists his feet onto the table, as if he's just now settling in for a long interview. He's wearing expensive Italian loafers, which for some reason strikes me as odd. I guess my stereotypical Russian thug would sport steel toed combat boots. He clears his throat. "BXE plans to bid in a private auction of former Soviet nukes and weapons grade uranium. Such an event is possible because of various introductions I made for Acheson several years ago. I now regret my role as facilitator."

My eyebrows rocket up my forehead and my mouth drops open.

Korov says, "I want you to purge your firm's files of evidence of my involvement. And once you've done so, please feel free to set your FBI friends on the trail. The world has changed seismically since I started doing business with Acheson fifteen years ago. I no longer trust Clearwater, which means I can't allow BXE to win the auction."

I blink at him, unsure what to say. I can't believe he has his feet on my desk and he's chatting about loose nuclear warheads in a normal conversational voice. Is he full of nonsense? Or could this auction be somehow connected to the arms and money Casper alluded to? Of course, the whole story about BXE could be horse shit.

"Who's running this auction?" I can't hide the fear in my voice. It's as if discussing the proposed sale of loose nukes makes the event itself more real.

"People I no longer trust." Korov's cobalt blue eyes flicker almost playfully. "The same people who launched the pretend assassination attempt against Prescott in Abu Dhabi."

"Pretend?" I swallow hard. So my gut was right.

"What better way to remove suspicion from oneself than to play the victim?" Korov studies the signet ring on his right hand while I process. He clears his throat. "Call me old fashioned, but I find my former associates' willingness to kill *innocent* women and children distasteful. Let's leave it at that."

I feel my head tilt to the left in something between awe and bewilderment.

"But you shouldn't worry your pretty head about my motives. All you need to know is that BXE should not be allowed to win the upcoming arms auction."

I sit up straighter in an attempt to appear more confident than I feel. "Wouldn't it be better for BXE to buy the weapons than some unknown foreign extremist group? At least they're an American company, with shareholders to consider, instead of a band of religious fanatics."

Korov stares at me as if I'm an idiot. "The end result will be roughly the same, regardless of who wins the auction. BXE will turn around and sell much of its cache to various bidders who left the original auction disappointed."

"Why?"

Korov rolls his eyes as if he's running low on patience. "They're war profiteers. BXE needs global strife to stay relevant, which means sometimes they need to spend money to make money. They'll buy the weapons, sell them to both sides to stoke some endless conflict, and then reap the profits in the form of a taxpayer-financed windfall."

I stall again. "You've been a client of R&S for over a decade. The firm will have literally tens of thousands of pages of documents, all of which are backed up electronically. Even if I wanted to help you, I can't access files from more than three years back. The firm ships them to a vault inside some no-name mountain in West Virginia."

Korov adjusts one of his gold cufflinks. "So start with the recent files, which remain on site. Now please, stop stalling. Are you interested or not?"

"What about Damien?" I feel way off balance. It might be time to listen to the voice in my head and hightail it out of here.

"You help me with my hassles. I'll give you incontrovertible, video evidence to solve your husband's murder." He crosses his arms over his chest and leans back, waiting for me to respond. He almost tips his chair too far backward, but saves himself from falling by anchoring his loafer-encased feet to the table more securely.

I feel bile rise up my throat. *Video evidence?* "You *taped* a murder?" I ask, afraid of his answer.

"Standard operating procedure," he says, in a dead on impersonation of Henry. He enunciates those three words without the slightest hint of his accent. He looks me in the eye and asks, in his normal Russian-accented English, "I'm not scaring you, am I? You didn't think you were the only one around here listening to other people's conversations, did you?"

"You're sickening me," I blurt, again without thinking. I really need to stop doing that. "What if I don't want to help you? What if I say no deal? Why shouldn't I turn you in to the FBI?" As I pepper him with questions, I wonder how long it would take me to reach the phone and summon help.

"If you say no deal, we part ways and forget this conversation happened." I'm about to interject that I could live with that, when he adds, "If you turn me over to the FBI, or any other authorities, I will kill you."

He lets his words sink in for a few seconds before hoisting his feet off the table and collecting his briefcase. "You've had a long day. Why don't you tell those boys downstairs you're ready to go home to T Street? You can give me your answer tomorrow. My chief operating officer will be in touch regarding the logistics." Korov produces a business card from his wallet and passes it across the table to me: *Mikhail Borofsky*, it reads, *Managing Director and Chief Operating Officer, VK/Victory Group Ltd.* While I study the card like it holds the secret to life, he gets up, nods in my direction as if acknowledging an acquaintance in a crowd, and disappears into the hallway.

I doubt I exhale before I'm in the car with my agents, cruising up Connecticut Avenue.

12

I arrive home at ten-fifteen and almost collapse with relief because Hannah is camped on the sofa watching TV. Diana recruited her to baby sit me so she could spend a night at her new boyfriend's place. I understand I'm lousy company these days, but I dread solitude and am grateful beyond words that my friends are so supportive.

Hannah has her feet propped on the coffee table next to an almost empty bottle of Chardonnay. She's trying to steer Chinese food to her mouth from the carton while Buster twists and turns on her lap. He rubs his head against her hand as she maneuvers the chopsticks, which causes her to miss her mouth and slop noodles and sauce on the sofa.

"Just in time," she says. "I feel guilty opening a second bottle alone."

I kick off my shoes and drop my bag in the hallway. I take a deep breath, exhale slowly and attempt to collect myself. I'm sure I look spooked. Or at least twitchy. "Thanks again for coming over."

"Any time."

I step into the kitchen to search the fridge for another bottle of white wine. I've been desperate for a drink since I sank into the relative sanctuary of the agents' car. I should have told them about Korov, but I was too scared.

I peer out the window behind the kitchen sink, over Diana's immaculately arranged flower pots. All quiet out on T Street. I take a long sip of the wine, hoping it'll slow my heart rate, and join Hannah on the couch. "Still, it's nice of you to come. It's not like you have nothing to do with the wedding coming up."

Hannah shrugs. "Please stop talking nonsense and eat something. Your clothes are starting to hang off you."

"Says Miss Size Zero." She's right, though. I settle under a yellow blanket crocheted by Diana's mom sometime during our youth.

Buster abandons his perch on Hannah's lap and comes over to investigate whether my carton contains anything more enticing than hers.

Hannah digs the remote out from between two sofa cushions and kills the newscast she was watching. "Big surprise: Some new group called the Caucasus Intifada tried to kill Prescott," she says, presumably catching me up in case I've been stuck in a work-induced news outage. "I guess if you're a startup radical, taking out the vice president is one way to get your name on the map."

I nod dumbly and help myself to a child size portion of veggie lo mein. Buster kneads my leg through the blanket. Hannah's brow furrows as if she's trying to figure something out. I wish she'd turn the TV back on and tune in to some lighter fare. I'm too freaked to speculate on world events. Never mind the royal mess that is my life.

"Diana told me everything," Hannah says finally.

Wine almost shoots out my nose. "What?"

"About your new 'job' with the feds, the 24/7 security detail, your boots appearing at the apartment the night Damien died. Why didn't you tell me?"

"Because it's a felony, for starters," I say, in a sarcastic tone that I regret as soon as the words cross my lips. I soften my voice and add, "And because it's dangerous for you to know."

"You told Diana!"

"Only because she pieced most of it together on her own. I thought reality would be less strange than whatever her legendary imagination could concoct. When did she tell you?"

"Today, when she swung by to give me the keys. I knew something was on her mind. Normally she'd messenger them over. She's worried that you're more depressed, not that you aren't entitled. But seriously. You don't even eat unless one of us brings you food and the pills don't seem to help you at all."

Hannah looks flustered, as if she's stuck her foot in her mouth and has no idea how to extract it. I have that effect on people lately. Nobody knows how to deal with a young widow. I'm outside the natural order and therefore make people uncomfortable. "It's okay." There's nothing else for me to say.

"Lena, she's afraid for you. Maybe a little for herself, too, but mostly for you."

"So now she's endangered you as well."

"I suppose, but I'm glad I know. I can't imagine you having to go through this alone."

I finish my wine and pour us each another generous glass before re-arranging myself under my blanket. Hannah watches me expectantly.

Against my better judgment I say, "Since you're in the loop, things got more intense today."

"What happened?"

I motion for her to lean in closer and whisper the details of my encounter with Korov. By the time I finish, I'm fighting the urge to cry again. Hannah looks like she's had a drink tossed in her face.

"What would you do in my shoes? Would you tell the FBI?"

"I have no idea. I'd be paralyzed by panic," she says. "But since you've already broken whatever attorney-client privilege Mr. Korov could have claimed by telling me, maybe you should tell the FBI. They're supposedly the good guys, right?"

"Yes, but—"

"But what?" she asks, suddenly snippier.

"They don't seem motivated to solve Damien's murder. Korov says he has proof." Even as I say the words I know I sound unhinged. Who in her right mind would trust Korov? He amassed his power and fortune through brute ruthlessness. That much is common knowledge.

"Wait. Now you and Volodya Korov, notorious Russian gangster, oligarch and international macho man, are on a first name basis?"

Instead of answering the question, I set down my glass and bury my face in my hands.

The next morning I feel like I haven't slept at all, though I imagine my sleeping pills bought me at least an hour or two of uneasy rest. When I look in the mirror, a bleary-eyed woman who looks older than I expect stares back. I give my tired reflection a pep talk. *Today I will find something important. Something that will put away Acheson for good.*

The day drags. Charlie and I hunch over documents in Interior Conference Room C. My task feels inconsequential, indeed ridiculous, after my interview with Korov. Maybe Smerth's right: the FBI are a bunch of bumbling idiots. Seriously. Who cares about Burtonhall building some silly overseas oil line when its sister corporation could be plotting to undermine the entire U.S. government?

And more importantly, will there ever come a day that I close my eyes and see anything other than Damien, slaughtered in our living room?

At three in the afternoon, our managing partner, Evelyn Peabody, announces via email that an explosion caused by a gas leak has occurred in a coal mine in West Virginia. Rutledge & Smerth's offsite storage facility is a total loss. The CEO of the data storage company called her personally to share the news. Evelyn expresses shock that the files were so proximate to a mining operation. An email to clients is in the works. She calls a meeting of the senior partners for six p.m. to discuss the firm's losses and inevitable insurance claim. I feel my face turn green.

"I feel like I could faint," I tell Charlie. He offers to fetch me a Diet Coke.

When he returns with the soda, he says, apologetically, "I'd say go home, but I imagine you can't spare the billable hours."

Sometime after seven, when I emerge into the welcome warmth of a shockingly mild evening, I'm surprised to see Max waiting outside across Connecticut, by the curb where I used to hail my late night cabs home. Though I'm loathe to admit it, the sight of him lifts my spirits.

I should rat out Korov right now.

His overture towards me and the mine blast must be more than a convenient coincidence.

No. I should worry about my own neck. Fourteen miners died today. That "gas leak" was no accident.

But maybe Korov's allegation that a tape of Damien's murder exists would spur the FBI back onto the murderer's trail. They'd have a chance to save those senators, along with who knows how many staff and flight crew. I should be brave, take a chance and tell all.

I pull the car door shut and snap at myself to dismiss this foolish fantasy. Korov would never confide plans that weren't already in motion. The explosion in West Virginia underscores that point.

Acid rises in my throat. That sadistic bastard is waiting for me to answer a moral dilemma that shouldn't exist outside of those hokey after dinner discussion games they sell in novelty shops. If I try to save a planeload of innocent people, Korov will kill me. Or at the minimum, he'll make it so I can never go home, or see my friends and family again. I'd need to disappear, reinvent myself from scratch. *Become a farmer in the witness protection program in bumblefuck*, I hear Damien's voice ring in my head as I fasten my seat belt.

My head pounds with the worst stress headache of my life. The pain is so intense it blurs my vision. I scrunch my eyes shut and try to force myself to focus.

Max makes small talk as we head north on Connecticut Avenue, apparently oblivious to my physical distress. I'm agreeing with some remark about rain in the forecast when it hits me.

Henry would never utter a word he didn't intend to share. But Max might. He's been bristling more and more under his boss's authority.

In my heart and gut, I don't want to help Korov. I don't want any more of any of this.

Unless I can help put away the murderer. I can't explain it. Maybe my obsession borders on insanity, but I have a visceral, primeval drive to know what really happened that hideous night.

"Max?" I say. "There's no nice way to say this, so here goes. Have you guys done *anything* to solve Damien's murder?"

His eyes narrow.

"I think I've more than kept my end of the bargain. Every day I go into R&S, sift through boxes and pass along clients' secrets, even though I could get fired or worse. Henry tells me to be patient, but I'm sick of waiting. Especially since I'm convinced Smerth has purged the files." My voice cracks.

"We think we'll solve the case once we collar Acheson and the others on this criminal finance ring. You know they killed Damien to scare you off. They couldn't get you, so they took him out instead. Don't hate me for saying this, but you're actually safer with him gone."

"What the hell do you mean by that?"

"If you turn up dead, the cops reopen their file on Damien. It would be too coincidental, you know?"

I fight to keep my voice level. "So you're saying no one will bother with Damien's murder unless I get killed, too? You're actually saying that? Out loud? To my face?"

Max lets out a put upon sigh. "Henry and I would love to catch those bastards, but it's not the right time, you know?"

"No. I don't know." I'm yelling now. "All I know is that you spend all your time chasing some non-existent money trail while the murder case goes freezing cold. Any idiot knows that the more time passes, the less likely a crime will be solved."

"The DC police are on it."

"The DC police have buried the file in some sub-basement in South East!" I feel tears starting to flow. "But *you* know they're wrong. If Damien had killed himself, which he didn't, he wouldn't have wiped down the doorknob."

Max softens. "Of course he didn't kill himself. Please trust me. We *are* doing everything we can."

"Bullshit. My whole life is stalled in a nightmare holding pattern. Henry keeps saying he needs more evidence. But it's so damn obvious. I left my boots in Acheson's office. Someone returned them after the murder. Therefore, Acheson was in our apartment. Or at the minimum, someone he hired was. That's still murder one."

I try to glare through my tears. Max offers me a box of tissues from the console between our seats. "Henry won't allow us to blow your cover."

"My *cover* was blown that very first night, when Acheson *and* the nanny saw me."

"Not them. Henry doesn't want any attention from the press."

"Maybe *I* should go to the press. The big tabloid shows would love my story. Who knows? Some media attention could produce an arrest." I'm making an empty threat. Henry would have me locked up, key thrown away, before I could spit out half my tale.

Max must realize I'm not serious, because he says, "It'll work out. Give us a little more time. I know it sucks." We're at a stop sign. He turns and looks me in the eye. "It really, really sucks." He reaches over the console, as if to pat my arm or leg, but stops himself.

At least he's finally being honest. I blow my nose loudly.

Max drives on. I seethe and stare out the window until we stop in front of the apartment. Diana won't be home until later. She's got some function on the Hill. I dig out my key and take a deep breath, screwing up my courage to face the next few hours.

"Do you want me to come in?" Max asks.

I'm preparing to protest, to say it's not necessary, but I hear myself say, "Would you?" Relief floods over me. Max may not be my favorite person, but he'll spare me two or three hours of nervous pacing in the living room, jumping at every little noise. Normally I might kill the time on the phone, but tonight I don't have the energy. Everyone expects me to want to talk about my grief and I can't do it all the time. Which makes me feel like an inadequate widow.

"Sure. I don't have plans." Max locks the double parked car and follows me up the short walkway.

His presence in the apartment makes me jumpy. I ask him to hang up his coat, make himself at home and perhaps find something to read, before my brain seizes control of my mouth and stops the flow of inane niceties. I manage to silence myself and evaluate the contents of the fridge. "Heineken?" I ask. Diana doesn't believe in light beer, although she practically lives on Diet Coke. This quirk used to bug me, but these days the extra calories don't matter.

"Thanks," he says.

I open two bottles. We settle on the retro red bar stools around the kitchen island. I reach across the granite for an economy size bottle of Advil. I pop three with my first sip of beer.

Max takes a swig. "It doesn't add up."

"What doesn't?"

"Any of this mess. The investigation in Bermuda has turned up information on dozens of companies and non-profits, which Acheson and Aziz seem to use as pass-throughs, but the trail goes cold. Every time. And while we're investigating a plot to attack a Clearwater asset, another one blows to pieces? And almost takes out Prescott? Who has more ties to Clearwater than anyone else in public life?" The pitch of his voice increases with each unanswered question. He rubs his forehead as if in pain. "Then we have Henry's new pal Casper. To save my life, I can't fathom why he would work with us."

"Money?"

"Guys like Casper consider themselves freedom fighters. They're notoriously difficult to buy off."

"Maybe political asylum?"

After another swig of Heineken, Max says, "If he wanted asylum, there are easier countries than the U.S. I think the Swedes will take almost anybody. And maybe the Dutch or French."

"Henry doesn't hear the same alarm bells?"

"Too many years with that other agency. Henry believes the enemy of my enemy is my friend."

"You don't?"

"Not always. A lot of times the enemy of my enemy turns out to be another enemy. Still, old spooks will make a deal with anyone to get information. That Casper character gives me a bad vibe. I don't relish the thought of racing overseas on his intelligence."

"So don't."

"It's not up to me."

Max sucks down more of his beer. He only has a sip or two left in the bottle. I ask if he wants another.

"Sure. Why not? And let's talk about something else, if that's okay. Something other than K4 or the Lotus Group."

I get up and retrieve another Heineken from the refrigerator.

"So, uh, why do you hate lawyers so much?" I try to strike a casual tone, but my segue into more trivial territory sounds contrived.

"Why would you think I hate lawyers?" Max flashes his toothpaste commercial smile.

"Just a hunch. You've said a few snide things about my job."

"I can't hate lawyers, because I don't do self-loathing."

"Were you a prosecutor?" That would be a natural leap to the FBI.

"For a few years, right out of school, in Boston."

"Harvard?"

"MIT."

"They don't have a law school." I wince at my snippy tone.

"Sorry. MIT undergrad. Engineering. After two years with a software company I decided to become a lawyer. I worked during the day, went to school at night and had no life, only to discover that my new career in patent law bored me sick."

"Unsurprising."

"I decided I wanted to be a 'real lawyer.' I was an assistant DA for five years. One day, I answered an ad for the FBI."

"So am I wrong to say I detect some resentment towards your former profession?"

"Not the profession. Just firms like R&S. When I came out of law school, none of those firms would give me the time of day, much less an interview, unless I wanted to work in patents. But whatever." He shrugs. "That's ancient history. I'm glad things worked out the way they did. I like my job. It keeps me thinking. Like right now, I have this hunch that our buddy Casper is bad news."

So much for changing the subject.

"Well, it's your job to pursue hunches, right?" I am suddenly frantic to keep our conversation away from all things Russian. Of course I feel guilty about my deal with Korov. But for the moment at least, he could be my best option. I want to sleep on everything for one more night.

Desperate to re-direct Max's focus, I ask the first inconsequential question that comes to mind. "Did you like law school?"

Max stops his beer in mid-air between the counter top and his mouth and considers my question. "I did."

"I hated it from the get-go."

"Really? Huh. You seem the type."

"That's me. The law school by default type. I fainted in biology 101 when we dissected a fetal pig. That pretty much ruled out medicine. I also can't draw, carry a tune or get my head around calculus. Law school seemed like a no brainer. I studied hard, made good grades and got my job at R&S. Which was exactly what everyone expected from me. I guess that's part of being 'the type.' Doing what's safe instead of what's interesting. See where that got me."

Max heaves a deep sigh. "Lena." He looks me straight in the eye. "You need to find a way to move on."

Some wiring in my brain short circuits. I fly off my stool, get right in Max's face and screech. "How dare you tell me what I need to do? I don't need to do a God damned thing! You have *no idea* what my life's been like since you and your self-absorbed boss showed up on my doorstep."

Max opens his mouth as if to speak, then clamps it shut.

"No. Wait. I'm the idiot. I actually believed I could help, just by leafing through some files. I thought I'd be doing *my civic duty*. Like jury service. You *must* have known how dangerous these people are, what they're capable of. And you didn't give a fuck."

"That's not fair."

"You know what's not fair? It's not fair that you sugar-coated the assignment when you first approached me. It's not fair that I'm a fucking widow before my thirty-first birthday. It's not fair that Damien got robbed of his life! He wasn't ready to die. Not even close."

"You're right. None of that is fair," Max says, in a quiet, calm voice.

I'm too incensed to listen. "You know what?" I shriek. "Just get out." When Max doesn't move I scream again. "Get out!"

I'm sure the neighbors can hear me. Who cares?

Max sets down his nearly full beer, grabs his coat and leaves the apartment without another word, or even the briefest parting glance in my direction. I sink to the floor. My limbs shake and my whole body convulses with sobs surging from the deepest part of my gut.

When Diana's key turns in the lock half an hour later I don't bother to peel myself off the kitchen tile. She rushes to kneel by my side. "Oh God. What happened?"

I recount my evening with Max. She nudges me onto my feet, reinstalls me on one of the bar stools, dabs my eyes with a tissue and gets herself a beer. I tell her I'll take one, too.

She pauses, as if considering whether feeding a distraught person additional alcohol is a good idea, but then shrugs and opens another Heineken. "I hope you didn't let him snoop around or plant any bugs or anything," she says, in a half-joking tone as she passes me the bottle. She perches on the seat next to mine and goes to work unbuckling the ankle straps on her impossibly high heels.

I lower my voice and confess that I stupidly left Max unsupervised for a couple of minutes when I went to the bathroom. I didn't think of asking him to step out into the hallway while I peed. Now, thanks to my small bladder, the government is probably snooping on Diana, too.

"Why did you invite him here in the first place?" Her eyebrows arch accusingly.

"Because I'm still scared to come home to an empty apartment. My nerves are shot. Each day feels a little easier, until I have to spend time alone, and then I become a basket case." I'm not even trying to suppress the undertone of desperation in my voice. "I was glad to have a little company at first, even if it was just Max. But then he made some remark about understanding what I'm going through and I got so angry. Unhinged, even. But Diana, can we please talk about something else? Anything else? I'm desperate to sleep tonight. My whole body aches from exhaustion. Can we please talk about something light?"

Diana gushes about the many wonders of her new boyfriend, celebrated pollster Tobey Weissman, until we finish our beers. I pop an Ambien. Hopefully the little pink pill, working in conjunction with four beers on an empty stomach, will be enough to knock me out until morning.

I spend the next several hours tossing in my bed, kicking the sheets on and off my person, and stewing over the many wrongs, real and imagined, that have been perpetrated against me by Max and Henry. At some point the sleeping pill must kick in. I awake refreshed for the first time in months, with an unfamiliar but wholly welcome sense of clarity about what I need to do in order to get my life back.

13

My sense of clarity lasts about twenty minutes. When I emerge from the shower wrapped in my well worn green bathrobe with my wet hair in a towel, Diana has switched on the morning shows. She clicks through them obsessively each morning, anxious to confirm that no network has anything her boss doesn't already know.

Prince Abdul bin Aziz, Saudi Ambassador to the United States and former client of R&S, toured the mine that exploded yesterday. His delegation, which included several muckety-mucks from the Saudi energy ministry, had been invited to inspect a new, state-of-the-art natural gas extraction site in the vicinity, with a view towards buying hundreds of millions of dollars of the extraction equipment from Clearwater for use back home. Several members of his group expressed interest in seeing a coal mine.

Or so the news reports claim. They were running almost an hour late when Aziz insisted they abbreviate their tour in order to return to the city for a reception with the Secretary of State.

The mine blew to pieces less than five minutes after the Saudi motorcade exited its parking lot.

Now Korov is on the news, swearing that his "sources in the Russian intelligence community" tell him that the mine was blown up by a sleeper cell operative hired by the Iranians to assassinate the Saudi ambassador. He reminds viewers that Russian President Perayev's government sells lots of weapons to the Iranian regime.

"Holy Mother of God," I say, over my untouched coffee.

"Indeed." Diana twists her hair into a bun and fastens it with several pins without diverting her gaze from the television. "The Saudi ambassador almost gets killed on U.S. soil and your Russian gangster friend says the ayatollahs did it." She seizes the remote from underneath Buster's front paws and flips through the other news channels.

I take my coffee back to my room, turn on the radio for white noise and call Henry on my secure phone.

If Deputy Director Henry Redwell is peeved that I sat on my conversation with Korov for over twenty-four hours, he seems disinclined to harp on his displeasure. In fact, he doesn't sound at all shocked by my account of the encounter. Not even when I tell him that those four senators are set to fly into a lethal trap.

After listening to my recounting, Henry conferences Max into the call. I explain everything again. Max protests that I could've mentioned this last night, instead of making chit chat about law school, but Henry tells him to cool it. "She's under a great deal of stress, von Buren."

"You think I don't know that? I was against bringing her in from the get go."

Henry cuts Max off. "Your objections are duly noted. But I decide. And I want Lena to pretend to play along with Korov."

"What?" yells Max.

"Really?" I ask. The muscles in my back and neck clench futilely against the beginning of a new stress headache.

"Yes. Think about it, von Buren. It's so simple, it's like a gift. She'll copy his files for us before she destroys them."

"I will?" I know this isn't much different from what I'm already doing by passing Acheson's secrets to the FBI. But Acheson wasn't supposed to know. I suspect Korov might make it his business to find out.

"Relax, my dear. We'll double your security. We'll add a detail inside the firm. We'll cover your floor and the conference room floor. The files are at your fingertips, and they could be valuable. Think about it."

"Right, Henry. Except yesterday if she got caught, Smerth would have fired her. Or shipped her out of harm's way. Now it'll be out of his hands. That Russian will dispose of her, if he even begins to suspect she's a liability."

I try and fail to swallow the enormous hard lump in my throat.

"Don't kid yourself, Maxwell. Lena was in as much danger before. Perhaps more. Korov wants her alive as long as she's useful. Acheson's another animal. He'd wring her neck with his bare hands right now, given the chance. He doesn't give a damn what Smerth thinks."

"Stop it! Both of you. You are not helping." I feel as if all the air has been sucked from the room. I hear our front door close, Diana leaving for work, off to face an ordinary day. I'd kill to have my old boring life back.

"Let's see what's in those files and go from there, shall we?" Henry says.

"What about their plan to kill those senators? Do you think Korov told me the truth?"

"Possibly," Max says.

"And do you believe what he said on the news, about Iranian extremists trying to kill Aziz?" I ask.

"I believe it's time for you to get to the office." The line clicks and they're gone.

I settle into the secure anonymity of the government's sedan and check my BlackBerry. One new email from Charlie. "Acheson has DISAPPEARED. Smerth is acting like he's dead, but I bet he skipped town to sip mai-tais on a yacht somewhere tropical. All work on the matter is suspended until further notice. Maybe you should consider a mental health day or two. You look worn out. You wouldn't miss anything billable, only the most exciting thing to happen in the history of the firm. DOUBLE DELETE THIS. – C. W."

Wow. I didn't see that coming.

The sedan catches up to a sea of brake lights. I glance at my watch, a delicate bracelet studded with tiny diamonds, last year's Christmas gift from Damien. 8:42. I write Charlie back: "I'm on my way in. Let's grab coffee."

Charlie sits on a sunny bench in MacPherson Square and tries to process the avalanche of information I've unleashed on him. By the time I finish, he looks as petrified as a patient facing surgery without anesthesia. He takes a deep breath, forces himself to exhale slowly, removes his glasses and rubs the bridge of his nose with his thumb and index finger.

"Holy shit," he says finally, as he fumbles with Mikhail Borofsky's card. I offered it to him a couple of minutes ago, as a sort of visual aid in support of my unbelievable story.

"I'm sorry. I shouldn't have told you." What the hell am I thinking? I've endangered Charlie for no good reason. Other than that I'm in over my head and he's in a position to help.

"No. I'm glad you did." He passes the card back to me, looks around, glances over both shoulders, and lowers his voice to a barely audible whisper. "How much would you bet that Acheson is out there somewhere, wining and dining prospective bidders in the salons of Arabia and Asia, doing whatever he can to drive up the price and create a favorable secondary market for BXE?"

Instead of answering, I pepper Charlie with all my pent up questions. "Do you think the FBI could be right about Acheson and Smerth? You don't find it ludicrous to suggest that a couple of white collar guys we know would slaughter hundreds—or even thousands—of innocent people for nothing but financial gain? And slap the taxpayers with the bill for the weapons while they're at it?" Because that's exactly what BXE plans to do: use U.S. government funds to buy illicit arms, then keep the profits when they flip their haul, possibly to some unfriendly entity.

Charlie takes a long, helpless glance up to his right, as if seeking heavenly guidance. "I've been defending white collar criminals long enough to know you can never underestimate the blinding power of greed."

I frown.

His eyebrows creep up. "Do you think I'm wrong?"

I gaze down at my shoes, plow the gravel with my toe. "I don't know what to think anymore." I force myself to look Charlie in the eye. His expression struggles between fear and excitement. "So will you help me?"

Before he can answer, my phone rings in my coat pocket. Henry. "I'm sorry. I need to take this." I leave the bench and walk across a patch of grass to stand behind a tree. My heels sink into the turf. "Hello?"

"He has a *vault* in his office. Can you believe our luck?"

"Excuse me?"

"We heard him access it through the device you planted. Meet Max at the coffee cart on Connecticut and K in fifteen minutes." Henry disconnects before I can ask for clarification. When I turn to walk back to Charlie, I notice a tall, exceedingly muscular jogger slow down and stare at me through mirrored shades. A tattoo of an eagle with enormous talons peeks out from under the collar of his Nike shirt. His hair is buzzed in military style. I glare at him and he smirks at me before veering towards I Street and picking up his pace. He's the first man I've noticed checking me out since I lost Damien, and I'm surprised, with everything else going on, that I feel oddly violated. The rude jogger disappears from my line of sight when I cut behind the square's namesake's equestrian statue.

Charlie springs off the bench as I approach. "Let's get started. Shall we?"

Max stands me up.

I wait a full half hour, and finally buy myself an unnecessary cup of coffee when the cart's proprietor, a heavy set woman with bushy eyebrows and an unfortunate chin, growls at me for loitering in front of her business. My security detail hangs out by the side entrance to the nearest building, where they chat about the Redskins and pretend to chain smoke. I call Max for the fifth or sixth time. Both his lines roll to voice mail. I leave an annoyed message and start walking back to the office. The agents follow close behind.

I ride the elevator to the 7th floor, home of Interior Conference Room C, where I duck into the ladies room. It's nicer than the bathrooms upstairs, featuring silk orchids, upholstered chairs and soft classical music, all for the benefit of visiting clients. The restroom and its adjacent lounge are empty. I race into the nearest stall, suddenly desperate since I've sucked down seven cups of coffee this morning.

I emerge from the stall, thinking I'll make more progress with Charlie's help, and that I should call Henry before I do anything else. Alert him that Max was a no-show.

In the mirror over the sinks, I see a towering figure in a black mask fly out of the center stall. He grabs me before I have time to turn and run. A hand clamps over my mouth and stops my scream. I try to sink my teeth into his gloved fingers. No success. I aim my fingernails at his eyes, but can't reach. For the first time in my life, I feel the kind of primordial panic that could make a person lose control of all bodily functions. I kick and struggle and stomp on my attacker's boots in a vain attempt to shake free of this unknown man who is apparently brazen enough to assault me at work in the middle of the day. Surely someone will hear our struggle. I realize with a sinking heart that the agent Henry promised for this floor is probably "working" in the mailroom around the corner from Interior Conference Room C.

A needle plunges into my neck. The muscles spasm in protest. My stomach lurches with nausea. My vision blurs, my heart races and my legs feel separate from the rest of my body. Everything goes black.

14

I wake with a pounding headache, my eyes glommed together with dry mascara, my stomach lurching. Why am I sea sick? Wait. Where am I? I lift my head and yowl in pain. My neck throbs like I've been stabbed.

Then I remember the bathroom. The man in the mirror. My pulse quickens. I have to get away from him.

Blue lights flash.

For a split second I wonder how the cops drove right into the law firm to save me.

It's only when unfamiliar sirens wail somewhere nearby that I grasp the fact that I'm no longer in the 7th floor ladies' room.

I'm lying face down in the back seat of a black sedan, one indistinguishable from those favored by the FBI, but for the overwhelming stench of stale tobacco. My head feels stuffed with cotton. My mouth is as dry as if I'd slept with one of those suction devices dentists use in there, and my limbs feel like they're chained down with weights, too heavy to move. My winter coat is draped over me.

Through the privacy glass, a stocky driver in a black cap keeps his eyes trained on the road. The back of his square head looks unfamiliar. I brace my neck with one hand, hoist myself to a sitting position and gape out the tinted window. I must be dreaming. This can't be real.

We're hurtling down a highway I don't recognize. One populated by foreign looking cars.

"Good morning, and welcome to Moscow," a male voice with a posh British accent says, at close range.

I whip my aching neck around.

A handsome man in a pinstriped suit sits as far from me as possible on the seat, palming an iPhone. He has a shock of brown hair that was due for a trim a week ago. His curls flop down his forehead towards features that are almost too pretty, but not quite. I'd guess he's in his thirties. I don't know him from the FBI. He looks nonplussed by the presence of a kidnapped woman in his car.

"Mikhail Borofsky," he says, in a tone that implies I should have been expecting him. He starts to offer me his right hand, but thinks better of it and rests it back in his lap. "Sorry about the unorthodox circumstances. I'm sure you understand. We need to respect the schedule." He looks at me with haunting gray-green eyes, the kind of eyes that stand out in a photograph whether the rest of the picture is any good or not.

"Excuse me?" I hear myself croak in a raspy morning voice. "Who are you? Where are we going? And why the hell would you expect me to understand?" I tell myself I must be asleep. I pinch my cheeks, dig in my nails so hard it hurts. "Wait. Did you say *Moscow*?"

This must be a bizarre dream, brought on by a cocktail of sleep deprivation, stress and liberally ingested anti-anxiety meds.

The pain I inflict on my face does nothing to snap me out of my supposed somnolent haze.

"Mikhail Borofsky," the man repeats, though this time it sounds more like a question. "Mr. Korov's right hand man. I have instructions to escort you to your hotel, and to apologize for any unpleasantness yesterday. Please be assured your safety is my top concern."

"*Unpleasantness*? Yesterday? You're the one who attacked me in the restroom?" My brain flounders for clarity and finds none. I can't say I've ever had an out of body experience, but this feels as disorienting as I imagine floating outside oneself would be.

"I had no idea you suffered an attack. I'm sorry to hear that. Airport toilets are dangerous places. You need to take care." Mikhail studies me as if weighing whether he should say more. I shake my head in a vain attempt to clear my confusion.

"Wait. You work for Mr. Korov? You don't sound Russian." I'm not sure why the specifics of my captor's nationality matter. Maybe because I can't wrap my head around my current predicament. My overwhelmed brain is seizing on foolish details.

"My father was in the foreign service. We spent most of my adolescence in Britain. I went to Eton," Mikhail says, as if I'm a stranger he's chatting up at a cocktail party.

I feel my heart thump harder and my eyes narrow. I glance at the door. I could hurl myself out. Escape. I wonder whether the child locks are armed.

No. Even if I could get the door open, I would never survive the jump. We're flying down the middle lane of a freeway. Cars cruising at inhuman speed blow past us on both sides. I glance around the car for any sign of my purse or more importantly, my phone. No luck. I can picture my bag perched on the brownish-red granite of the seventh floor ladies' room, my phone in its outside pocket. Fuck.

I turn back to face this Mikhail. "Where are you taking me?" I ask, as levelly as possible. My throat constricts and my face starts to crumple. I bite down on my lower lip until the shaky feeling starts to subside. Crying won't help. This Mikhail character must know I'm scared, and it obviously doesn't faze him. "Why am I here?" I enunciate each word carefully.

"For Korov, of course." He shoots me a pitying look, as if suddenly concerned that he's saddled with an idiot. "You're booked at the Hotel Belgrade, in the heart of our main tourist district."

I feel catapulted into the twilight zone. I'm kidnapped. But this guy, whoever he is, is acting like I'm his *guest*. Is this how people land with Stockholm Syndrome? The bad guys make nice until they stir some affinity in their victims? *Stop it, Lena. You've read too many crime novels.*

"You do realize I was assaulted, drugged and brought here against my will?"

Mikhail looks at me like I've tossed a drink in his face. "The flight attendant who wheeled you out told me that she saw you take some pills with your third or fourth glass of Bordeaux."

"What? What Bordeaux?" And what does he mean, wheeled me out? I don't recall a wheelchair. But why would I remember a wheelchair when I can't remember anything else? I snap at myself to focus.

Mikhail smiles what looks like a reassuring smile. A dimple flashes across his left cheek. My breath catches in my throat. Damien had a dimple just like that when he smiled. Mikhail and Damien look nothing alike, but seeing Mikhail smile is like seeing a ghost.

"All I know is what the stewardess told me. I'm sorry." My antenna shoot up. Is this all rehearsed? He assumes a more formal tone. "Perhaps you suffered a particularly vivid nightmare. That happens with sleep aids on occasion. I do hope you feel better soon. For now, I'm to escort you to the Belgrade, so you can rest and freshen up. I'll pick you up a bit later so you can start work on your article."

"My article?" My head spins again. What article? What the hell is he talking about? If Mikhail detects the panic in my voice, he doesn't let on. "Can I go home?"

His brow wrinkles. "Sure, but wouldn't that be a waste of your time? Don't you need to do some research here first?"

I ignore his ludicrous line of inquiry. "So, just to be clear: I'm free to leave?"

"Of course. Why ever would you think not?" I blink at him in confusion before he adds, "But you'd risk offending Korov."

We ride several miles in silence. I struggle to process. We pass a sign indicating the city limits. The chauffeur steers us off the freeway. A sea of brake lights appears in front of us as we merge into stop and go urban traffic. After maybe fifteen minutes of incremental progress, Mikhail looks up from his BlackBerry and points out a 1950's style skyscraper directly in front of us. "One of Stalin's Seven Sisters. He built them when the Americans were building skyscrapers. Stalin wanted eight of them, but ran out of cash for the last one."

The structure was obviously designed to intimidate. The effect is magnified, whether intentionally or not, by the fact that none of the other buildings come anywhere close to striking distance of its size. Also, nobody's bothered to remove the hammer and sickle motif from the façade.

The driver makes a U turn in the middle of a busy four-lane street and barrels onto the sidewalk, before screeching to a halt beside an unremarkable glass and concrete tower. I follow Mikhail through the revolving doors into a white marble lobby, which could be anywhere in the west, but for the cigarette smoke that hangs in the air like a curtain. Mikhail says something in Russian to the pretty but unsmiling girl at reception, and hands over a U.S. passport.

The clerk turns to me, "Claudia Lane?"

"Excuse me?"

She waves the photo page of the passport under my nose. It's my passport photo, but the name reads Claudia Marie Lane, and Korov's minions have subtracted two years from my age. The marble floor shifts under my feet. Why do I need a fake I.D.? My brain snaps at me to forget the minutiae. I should concentrate on learning why I'm here in the first place. And why I'm following Korov's supposed lieutenant around like some eager puppy dog. I contemplate making a run for the street, but I have no money and no phone. Besides, this Mikhail looks plenty fit enough to run me down without breaking a sweat. I nod and sign Claudia Lane's name to the form the clerk passes over the counter.

While she processes the paperwork, I survey the lobby, as if it might offer some clue to Korov's plans for me. There's a bar to the right, and a small terrace with a few empty tables abutting the parking lot. Three late-middle-aged men in inexpensive suits hunch over highball glasses. A bleach blonde woman, with enormous breasts spilling out of a turquoise top, hovers around them. She wears garish blue eye makeup and several pounds of costume jewelry.

The clerk shuffles a stack of papers into a manila envelope along with Claudia Lane's passport. Mikhail explains, "They register all foreign guests with the police. It saves you from going to the station, which would take hours. You'll get your passport back after five tonight, alright?"

I watch, feeling more confused by the second, as the girl hands Mikhail two card keys.

"Let's go," he says.

My breath catches in the back of my mouth. He better not think he's bunking with me. Or taking any liberties whatsoever. He struts towards the elevators, towing a small black wheeled bag I hadn't focused on previously.

"You're coming up?" I ask, alarmed about my short term safety. Just because someone is good looking and articulate doesn't disqualify him as a rapist or axe murderer. Though if Mikhail wanted to attack me, he probably wouldn't take the time to check me into a hotel first. Especially one with obvious security cameras installed all over the place. As soon as he leaves me alone, I'll call the U.S. Embassy for help. *Good plan*, I tell myself silently. *Except if I don't play* by Korov's rules, he'll never give me the tape. Screw the tape. This is too weird and probably very dangerous.

But I want that tape. More than I've ever wanted anything. Maybe I'll wait a teeny while longer. See what happens next. The embassy isn't going anywhere.

The elevator car abruptly halts at the eighth floor, though Mikhail pressed twelve. The doors open to reveal an empty landing, with dingy carpeting and ripped vinyl chairs with dirty foam spilling out. A huge, unoccupied round desk sits between the elevator and the hall of rooms. One bare light bulb hangs above the whole scene, suspended by a thick black cord.

"I don't want to stay here," I hiss at Mikhail, as the doors close. The elevator resumes its ascent.

"But I heard you were the adventurous type," Mikhail says with a smile. His lone dimple flashes across his cheek. I don't know why I find that so haunting. My brain kicks in and tells me to get a grip, because aside from his lone dimple and his height, Mikhail couldn't resemble Damien less. Damien had that athletic, laid-back California guy look going on, and Mikhail seems more lithe, more urbane, more *European*, if that's a way to describe someone.

The doors open on the twelfth floor and it's like the elevator whisked us to a different hotel altogether. We step out into a gleaming foyer adorned with fresh flowers and French doors.

"All Moscow hotels have two classes these days, business and tourist," Mikhail explains, as he swipes the key to get us past the French doors. "And trust me, I don't care how intrepid you are, you don't want to stay in the tourist class rooms."

"Are they as bad as the lobby on eight?" I'll feel safer if I can keep the conversation moving. Make him like me. Make him see me as an individual. Someone worthy of basic consideration and respect. Not an anonymous victim.

"Worse." The dimple flashes across his cheek again. "Think bugs. Bugs with lots and lots of legs. Red Army blankets circa 1952. Toilets you need a wrench to flush. Enough about that. Here we are."

But for the creepy shadow cast by Stalin's Sister across the street, the room is indistinguishable from one you'd find in a Holiday Inn back home. Serviceable but nothing special. Mikhail hoists the bag onto the luggage rack and steps towards the door. His feet don't make a sound as he moves. "Mr. Korov will see you tonight. Get some sleep, okay?"

What? Minutes ago, I was afraid he'd attempt to encamp in my room, but now I feel panic brewing at the thought of a whole day here alone, pacing the carpet, waiting for whatever they have in store like some kind of hapless damsel.

My heart rate accelerates so rapidly I feel dizzy. "I'm fine!" I protest. "We can go now." I sound like a kid asking for permission.

"Korov sets the schedule." Mikhail backs out the door. "And for your own sake, take a shower."

I blush bright crimson as he disappears into the hallway. Do I really stink? It's certainly possible, seeing as I have no idea exactly what day it is, and I'm still in the suit I wore to work yesterday. Or was it the day before? I slump on the edge of the bed and hold my head in my hands. What is wrong with me? Too many things to count, I think as I rub my temples. First of all, I was a fool. I thought I could help the FBI. Then, because I obviously learned *nothing* from the awful events that followed, I lost whatever was left of my mind and made a crazy deal with a modern-day desperado. Who apparently had me kidnapped for reasons that remain utterly unclear. And this Mikhail. Is he friend or foe? Both?

I sniff gingerly at my shirt and concede it's possible that I could use a washing up. God knows when I'll get another opportunity. But I'm humiliated to have a handsome stranger suggest it. I unzip the black suitcase.

There's my handbag, the one I thought I'd never see again, resting right on top.

I ransack its contents, but whoever stowed it in the suitcase confiscated my phone. My wallet is intact, minus my emergency twenty and my bank card. I should cancel it. Not that Korov needs my paltry balance. And if one of his henchmen uses the card, maybe it will help the FBI find me. Better not to alert the bank yet.

I dump the rest of the contents on the bed: keys, lipstick, hairbrush, all undisturbed. My fingers dig underneath a small tear in the lining.

Apparently some things do get past Korov. The bugs, nestled in their gum wrapper, are still exactly where I stashed them. I nudge them back under the lining and re-load the bag with my sundries before turning to the suitcase. I wonder what their range is. If I affix one to my body before leaving this room, will the FBI be able to hear me?

A plastic bag packed with sample size high end toiletries sits on top of some neatly folded shirts, skirts and extravagant underwear. My gut churns. Why would Mikhail, or Korov, or whoever packed this bag, include expensive lingerie?

My mouth goes dry. What are they going to make me do in exchange for the tape?

If the tape even exists.

It has to exist. I need it to exist.

I guzzle a bottle of Evian labeled complimentary before climbing into the shower. As the hot water pours down my aching neck onto my shoulders, I reassure myself that things happen for a reason. I'm meant to be here because I'll have the tape in my hands soon. Why would Korov drag things out? I just need to get through today. I can hold on for a few short hours.

I emerge ten minutes later, wrapped in a threadbare hotel robe that smells reassuringly of bleach, and feeling surprisingly sleepy. I suppose it can't hurt to close my eyes for ten minutes. I double check the chain on the door and drag both the standard issue hotel chairs to block it. My makeshift barricade won't stop a determined intruder, but it might serve as a primitive warning system, if I do manage to fall asleep. My eyelids ache to close. The bed is soft. The sheets feel starchy and clean. I feel myself drifting off, almost floating amidst a jumble of musings over Damien, the FBI, Korov and the Acheson case. My last cognizant thought as I fight the urge to sleep is of Max and Henry. Are they looking for me?

The phone rings.

15

I don't hear the phone at first, but rather sense it on some semi-conscious level. By the seventh or eighth ring, I jolt upright and lunge for the receiver, knocking over the bedside lamp in the process. It crashes to the floor but doesn't shatter. "Hello?" I'm shocked at how raspy I sound, way worse than my usual morning voice. Wait. Is it morning?

"Hello? Mikhail Borofsky speaking. Did I wake you?"

"No. Yeah. I guess you did. But it's okay, I should get up. Get onto local time and all." I sound stoned. "Sleeping during the day is supposedly horrible for jetlag. It's better to get into the sunshine, take a walk, stretch your legs. My mother swears by those melatonin tablets, but they don't work for me..." *Jeez, Lena, stop babbling! He doesn't need a recitation on jetlag.*

Mikhail stifles a laugh. "If a walk is what's required, can you be ready in twenty minutes?"

Twenty minutes? He must be joking. I feel drunk. Susceptible to a massive room spinning problem. Unable to function.

"Absolutely," I say.

"See you shortly."

I disentangle myself from the sheets and stumble to the bathroom, where the hoteliers have positioned the room's sole clock. Local time: 4:40 p.m. I slept all day. I pull my hair back into a knot that I hope looks presentable. I douse my face with cold water and decide there's no time for full makeup. Mascara and lipstick will have to do.

It feels strange, slipping into new underwear provided by whoever packed my suitcase. It probably cost as much as some of my suits. Wait. The tags are still attached: La Perla. Definitely pricier than any of my suits. I select a light tan skirt and one of the less revealing tops, a deep blue V neck sweater, and snakeskin Manolo

Blahnik boots. I press one of the FBI's bugs, which means I have only two left, onto my skin under my neck line. I send up a quiet prayer that Max and Henry will be able to hear me.

Someone raps on the door. I look in the mirror, check for lipstick in my teeth, and note that the fancy bra gives my unremarkable chest so much lift that a sliver of black peeks out above my neckline. Too late to change now. Anyway, nobody here knows me.

The heels feel higher than they look. I lurch forward and prevent myself from face planting onto the carpet by grabbing for the bureau. I teeter across the carpeting to peer through the peephole. Mikhail stands immediately outside, carrying a camera bag and holding a room key in one hand, poised to admit himself. I glance down at my clothes. I look like I'm going on a date. This whole situation feels wrong. Mikhail works for Korov. Korov claims to have the tape. I should ask Mikhail for it. Cut the crap. Get what I need and get home.

I undo the deadbolt and open the door.

"Ready?" he asks. "You must be famished." He's wearing freshly pressed pants, an untucked striped dress shirt and Ferragamo loafers, and holding a black cashmere top coat. His hair is done to make it look like he stepped out of the shower and ran his hands through it, but I bet he achieved the effect with fifteen minutes of effort and a large blob of styling gel. Mikhail's metrosexual. I congratulate myself for not saying this aloud.

Instead I say benignly, "Sure. Let me grab a coat." He watches with thinly veiled amusement as I tiptoe back to the suitcase. My eyes settle on the empty Evian bottle. Could they have spiked the water—the only available beverage, since the tap is labeled nonpotable – to knock me out? I can't possibly feel this groggy from one lousy sleeping pill ingested yesterday. But why would they care if I slept all day? I tell myself to stop indulging paranoia. I was exhausted, physically and emotionally. So I took a good nap. End of story. Now I can regroup.

No, Lena. Stop thinking like a drug-addled crazy person. Someone, possibly Mikhail, assaulted me, painfully I might add, and dragged me halfway around the world. Yet I can muster neither appropriate outrage nor terror. Just a touch of anxiety, and that can't be because I have nothing to lose. Isn't self-preservation supposed to kick in when the body is under threat? Even in depressed people?

They must have medicated me.

From this moment forward, I will only accept food and drink when I see others partaking.

The hotel corridor seems longer now than on the way in, because I have to focus on walking without turning my ankle and ending up in a Russian ER. We ride the elevator with three British businessmen. Outside the sun sits large and low in the sky. To avoid six lanes of speeding cars, we cut through an underground passage that reeks of urine. Old men and women squat behind card tables, selling cigarettes, vodka and lottery tickets. At least one of the peddlers catches me shuddering at the stench and shoots me a disdainful stare.

"The Arbat," Mikhail announces as we emerge onto the sidewalk. He takes out his camera and shoots a few photos while he narrates. "Moscow's major pedestrian thoroughfare. It's always been a market street, and as you can see, many western businesses have opened here." He points to a Hard Rock Café. "If you keep walking in this direction, you'll arrive at the Kremlin."

"And which way should I walk to arrive at Korov's doorstep?"

"You don't drop in on Korov. You wait for a summons."

The Arbat bustles with people trying to earn a few rubles. Countless artists exhibiting various degrees of talent peddle their work in the middle of the road. Vendors at stands sell everything from fur hats to second hand cookware to pictures with children stuffed into elaborate national costumes. Under normal circumstances, I'd be fascinated, but I'm too busy wondering whether our sightseeing expedition has anything to do with catching the murderer.

The spiky heels keep catching between the cobblestones. Mikhail steers us onto a cross street and hails a cab. I should keep track of our route, but the street signs are useless, all in Cyrillic. We pass a farmers' market. Tired, dirty people, wearing sweat stained clothes hawk potatoes and apples, bread and fish. We turn a corner and exit the cab in front of an electric blue awning. Mikhail places his hand lightly against the small of my back and a little jolt shoots up my spine as he steers me through the doors. The restaurant is busy, considering the early hour. "Tourists," Mikhail says. "Locals eat much later, but we may as well dine with your audience."

I want to say we both know I'm not a writer, but I stop myself. Some sixth sense says I should figure out Mikhail's real deal before launching into mine. Also several patrons are speaking English. It doesn't seem like the right time to bring up the cold blooded shooting of my husband, or the fact I was Shanghai-ed from my office halfway around the world. I still feel woozy and drugged. And suddenly really angry. At everyone and everything, and at myself. I feel a flush of blood race to my head and understand for the first time how rational adults can snap. Destroy things in a blind rage. I want nothing more than to smash all the plates and glasses to bits. To punch and kick Mikhail, whether he deserves it or not. To run outside and scream.

A tinny voice from the farthest recesses of my conscience begs me to hold it together. To find out why they dragged me here. Whether I can still hope to gain anything from my ordeal. I take a deep breath, exhale slowly and resolve to try.

A grey haired maitre d' with a bushy mustache leads us to a corner table, next to a window framed by heavy red velvet drapes that clash violently with the awning outside. A young waiter with a dirty blond crew cut appears, toting a liter of San Pellegrino. Mikhail takes it from him and breaks the seal himself. "You can't be too careful," he says, as he fills our glasses. "And you definitely don't want to risk the water here. My sister caught an amoeba fifteen years ago. It was dreadful. Her stomach's never been the same."

I've brushed my teeth with it twice and now he tells me. I foolishly figured I'd be alright as long as I didn't swallow it.

I think I pick out the word *borscht* from Mikhail's exchange with our dour, gap toothed waiter. Sure enough, two bowls of dark red soup arrive promptly, along with two beers. I will nurse my drink. I want to remain fully alert. And I need to eat before I pass out.

The borscht is too rich. It's like drinking warm heavy cream. I make a valiant attempt, but can't finish half the bowl. Instead I scarf all the black bread from the table. It looks rich and grainy but tastes like salty sawdust. The waiter sniffs his disapproval and takes away the empty bread basket, only to return it refilled.

"*Spaseeba*." I toss out one of few words I recall from an ill-advised college course in Russian.

"You know some Russian?" Mikhail asks, with seemingly genuine interest.

"No. Basically *Spaseeba* and *Dasveedanya*."

"Thank you and good bye. It's a start." He smiles and his lone dimple flashes. "I can teach you a few words, if you like. Say 'Ztrasveetiyeh.'"

"*Shtrazveetiyeah*," I repeat. "That's hello, right?"

"Yes it is. Not bad. Now say '*ya shpiohn*.'"

"*Ya shpiohn*," I repeat gamely. *Be human, Lena. Be likable.*

"Very good," he laughs. "Now never say that again."

"Why not? Is it the f-word or something?"

"No, it's nothing like that. '*Ya shpiohn*' means 'I am a spy.'"

"You're not funny."

The waiter clears the soup course and brings out a platter of meats, most of which resemble sausages, along with a casserole dish of some type of potato and onion concoction and a whole broiled trout. The fish is dry but palatable, not unlike the casserole. I screw up my courage and try the sausages. They taste like hair and grease shoved into a crackly tube I'd rather not contemplate. I try to swish discreetly with beer.

"Russian cuisine is an acquired taste that some Russians never acquire. My mother always had French chefs when we lived abroad."

"No, it's fine," I lie. "I enjoy trying new foods." By which I mean I'm not the kind of person who seeks out McDonald's while abroad. Not that I want to sample anything you'd have to dare someone to eat.

Mikhail looks over his shoulder, then leans in closer. "Tonight I have some management issues to attend to, at Mr. Korov's newest casino."

"You manage a casino for a living?" I ask, still utterly dumbfounded as to why Korov hauled me here. Or why he hired this man, who is clearly not a photographer, to squire me around Moscow.

"Among other things. I'm the CFO for many of his ventures. I'm responsible for financial oversight of the Victory chain of casinos, the VKOS oil company and the Titan Import-Export Company. You're familiar with them of course." He stares me straight in the eye.

I nod and mutter, "Of course," because he's waiting for acknowledgment.

"In addition to my financial oversight role, I generally make it my business to ensure that Mr. Korov's life goes as smoothly as possible."

"That sounds like a challenging job." I sip my water and curse myself for having no plan for the eventuality that Korov might fail to fork over the tape. An eventuality that, with the benefit of hindsight, looks more than likely.

"Challenging is a fair description." Mikhail leans back in his chair and gives the waiter the universal hand gesture for check, please. The bill appears, on a tray with two black coffees.

We collect our coats, emerge from the restaurant and walk two long blocks before turning onto a main drag. Mikhail stops in front of a massive strip-mallish building that's lit up like Las Vegas. I hope this is it, because the magnificent Manolo boots are brutal. Every step is agony.

"This is the Moscow Circus, the latest addition to the Victory Casino Group's empire," Mikhail says. "I had nothing to do with the exterior design." Multi-colored lights, all flashing at different times, race along the roof, like a massive holiday display on speed. A lit up outline of an onion-domed cathedral shares space with a lit up windmill and several lit up can-can dancers.

Moulin-Rouge-meets-Kremlin. Wow.

Uniformed doormen hold the doors for us. Mikhail greets each of them with a handshake. A scantily clad hostess in impossible stilettos and bright red lipstick rushes over to relieve us of our coats. The décor in the foyer rivals the showiest lobbies of Vegas in terms of gaudiness. Despite a loud ventilation system, smoke hangs in the air, as it seems to do everywhere in Moscow. Mikhail kisses the hostess, whose nametag identifies her in Russian and English as Natasha, on the cheek. She coos something into his ear.

Mikhail responds by introducing me. He says something in Russian. Natasha smiles and nods in my direction. He explains that he told her I'm an American writer, I'm doing a profile on Moscow's newest casino and its owner, and that Natasha says it sounds very exciting.

We leave Natasha at her post and step through another set of doors manned by uniformed staff, onto a floor dotted with table games. The noisy, flashy slot machines that form a gauntlet into every casino in the States are conspicuously absent. Patrons, on the other hand, are abundant. Some tables are already two or three deep with eager customers.

Clear booze, presumably vodka, flows freely. Waitresses wearing even less than Natasha ferry glasses to patrons from bars at either end of the vast space. I follow Mikhail as he snakes through the crowd, occasionally pausing to shake some hand or other. We go up a flight of stairs, through a mezzanine packed with the slots absent from downstairs, and round a corner into a private area where four men sit playing poker. The room is designed so that its occupants can see the casino floor, but people on the floor can't see them. Three of the men are dressed in the immaculate white robes favored by members of the Arab elite. The other wears a western suit and has his back to us.

Mikhail turns to me as we approach the group. "Let's play a hand. It'll give you a real sense of the atmosphere."

I don't feel like gambling, and even if I did, I don't have one lousy ruble to my name. I don't get to voice these immediate concerns because my legs buckle and my breath catches at the sight of Volodya Korov striding into the room. He walks right to me.

"Miss Lane," he says, with a smile. His gold bracelets glitter as he extends a hand in welcome. "I'm pleased you could make it. Welcome."

"Thanks," I mumble, in the general direction of my feet. Mikhail and Korov shake hands and exchange a few words in Russian.

Am I supposed to know Korov? None of this was scripted for me. I feel like I'm floundering. Korov alerts a waitress. He says something to her and she scurries away. He turns back to us and says, "You must join us for a hand."

"I'm afraid this particular game is too rich for me." I shuffle from left foot to right, grimace inwardly at my lame attempt to diffuse one of the richest men on the planet, and wish fervently that I'd run out of Interior Conference Room C the other night and never looked back.

"Nonsense," Mikhail insists with a smile. He takes my arm and ushers me towards the table. None of the players acknowledge us. How odd.

Mikhail says, "We'll play a hand together. Perhaps you'll bring me luck." He nods the dealer's way and a stack of purple chips appears.

"How much is that?" I whisper.

"One hundred thousand."

"Rubles?" I ask, though I don't know the exchange rate.

"U.S. dollars."

I swallow hard. At least it's not my money. Mikhail pulls out a chair for me. One of the men in Arab dress studies me over his scotch. I don't know him, though he looks oddly familiar, but for his overbite and unflattering goatee. His retro G-man style glasses slip down the bridge of his nose. One of his companions adjusts them for him without being asked. Mikhail pulls up a chair next to mine, and slides in closer than appropriate for a guide-slash-photographer. He leans to my ear and whispers, "Your friend across the table is Prince Muhammed al Sultan bin Aziz al Saud. His father, the king, is scheming to bypass Abdul and put his son on the throne."

Muhammed is Abdul's nephew. Of course. Now that he says it, the family resemblance is obvious. The prince not only looks like his uncle, he also shares Abdul's easy arrogance. Although Muhammed's facial hair obscures his age at first glance, on closer examination, I can see he's not far beyond twenty.

"Can't the king do whatever he wants?" I whisper to Mikhail.

"Your government prefers Abdul." He accepts our drinks from the waitress with a fleeting smile and places an overflowing glass in front of me. If I drink even half of it, I'll be a puddle on the floor within the half hour. But assuming I can dispose of the vodka by other means, perhaps Muhammed's presence is a gift. He might know who really tried to kill Abdul in the mine. And Prescott in the Abu Dhabi hotel. I've been here over twelve hours, and no one's even mentioned Damien. Maybe it's time I end my accidental foray over to the dark side, or whatever this twilight zone I've hurtled into is.

The man in the suit finally looks up from his cards and our eyes lock. His widen slightly. He recognizes me at the exact moment I recognize him. His body language and clothes could not be more different; he's coifed and clean-shaven, but his slight build and haunting, almost black eyes give him away. I'm staring Casper in the face. I will my jaw to remain shut.

Strange bedfellows, indeed. Isn't Casper supposed to be helping Max intercept a wire meant to fund an attack in the middle of nowhere?

Maybe the wire is a ruse, a trap for Max. I should warn him. If he's even available to be warned. My heart sinks as I remember his failure to show at our meeting. How could that have happened only yesterday? But if I tip off Max, these guys might kill me. And what brings Aziz's nephew here?

Casper recovers quickly from the surprise of seeing me, someone he believes to be *bona fide* FBI employee, in the high stakes room of Korov's shiny new casino. He takes a gulp of his vodka and studies his cards without emotion.

Mikhail leans over to show me the underwhelming hand we've been dealt. I furrow my brow to make it look like I'm focusing all my faculties on the game. Korov sits to my left, and launches into conversation with Muhammed. It takes me a second to register that they're speaking French. I can't even make out the gist, though I studied it for four years in high school.

Mikhail, Casper and one of the Arabs trade in cards and toss more chips into the middle of the table. The Arab who traded for a new card folds, as does Korov. Muhammed wins the hand. The man next to him gets up and rakes in the winnings. Korov buys the players another round. I wonder whose money Mikhail is gambling with, because he appears unfazed by the lightning fast loss of a small fortune. Muhammed stares across the table at my breasts. His lackey does the same. I feel my face redden.

I need to get away somewhere and think.

I excuse myself to go to the ladies' room. I forget that I'm wearing four-inch heels until I almost capsize.

The ladies' room features the pinkest granite countertops I've ever seen in my life, and whimsical Murano glass light fixtures. It's deserted except for a wrinkled, uniformed woman, who's wielding a mop. She's positioned herself between the sinks and the doors, with a generous array of towels and perfumes. The room smells like stale Chanel Number Five.

I lock myself in a stall and reach for my purse before realizing they must have surveillance cameras in here. As I silently congratulate myself for possessing such superior spying instincts, I look up at the ceiling and discover that, sure enough, one of the bulbs on a glass chandelier is aimed directly at me.

Still holding my bag, I sit on the toilet, which not only features one of those automatic seat covers, but also turns out to be heated. I rifle around in my purse, so that the security crew, if they're watching, will assume I'm searching for some female product. My hand rests on one of the remaining bugs. I push it into my hand and then produce a tampon, which I hold up to display to the presumed secret camera before unwrapping and flushing it. I emerge from the stall and head for the sinks, thankful that these bugs are water resistant enough to be placed in a potted plant, but wondering whether they're actually waterproof.

I rinse my hands extra quickly to avoid soaking the bug. The attendant frowns with disapproval as she extends a pink towel towards me. Her frown deepens as I dash out without placing any coins in her dish, because I still don't have a single ruble to my name.

The players, engrossed in their new hand, ignore my return to the table. I'm unlikely to get a better opportunity.

I pull out my chair with one hand as I plant the bug under the rim of the table, painfully close to Korov, with the other. I slide into my seat, cross my legs and lean over slightly so I can pretend to study Mikhail's cards.

Suddenly the hum of conversation stops. I look up from Mikhail's hand. Korov is staring right at me. The prospect of certain annihilation washes over my body like a tidal wave. I can't breathe.

16

Everyone turns to watch Korov, who clears his throat and asks, "You don't like vodka, Miss Lane?"

I can't believe my ears. He didn't see me plant the listening device. I'm not about to die, here and now.

"No, err, yes," I manage to stammer. "I'm, uh, usually not a drinker, but when in Rome, or Moscow." I wince at my lie as I reach for the glass and take the tiniest sip before proclaiming, "Excellent. Fantastic vodka. Top notch. Truly."

Korov rolls his eyes and says something to the players in French. They look at me and laugh. I feel my face burn crimson.

Mikhail trades in two cards and shifts position so his hand rests on my thigh. My muscles tense and I fight the urge to run (because I wouldn't get anywhere in these cursed boots) or to throw my unwanted drink in his face (because Korov might not react graciously to a scene). For a second I forget my panic over the bug and wonder if Mikhail seems the type to assault a woman.

I close my eyes and will Max and Henry to burst through the doors and rescue me, but of course they fail to materialize.

The players make their bets, pushing piles of chips into the pot. Mikhail leans in so close that his lips brush my ear and whispers, "For your own protection. It seems the prince fancies you. Unless you wish to become his consort for the evening, I suggest you play along. Korov told him you're all mine."

Alright. Maybe Mikhail isn't a rapist.

He leans back in his chair. His hand swoops up and around my shoulders in the classic male protective gesture. I will myself not to inch away and wonder how much more of this charade I'm meant to endure before Korov will see fit to discuss Damien.

Mikhail loses the hand to Muhammed, whose sidekick springs from his seat like a jack-in-the-box to sweep up the spoils of his boss's victory.

"I'm out," Mikhail says, in English. "Korov doesn't pay me enough to keep up with assembled company. If you'll excuse us, I'm going to escort Miss Lane back to her hotel."

My whole body sighs with relief when I hear we're leaving. Maybe Korov will have the tape sent to my room. Or not. He has yet to drop the slightest hint as to why he brought me to Russia. Transporting me 6,000 miles away from his files doesn't seem like the best way to help me fulfill my end of our deal. I can't possibly find the documents he wants from here.

Curiosity aside, I can't get out of here fast enough. I've been waiting, for what feels like an eternity, for Korov to reach down and pull the bug off the side of the table. It seems inconceivable he hasn't noticed. Why did I have to be so rash? I wonder if I can fish the bug out as we make our exit.

Some primal self-preservation instinct kicks in and prevents me from trying such a foolish move. I feel cold sweat start to form on my neck and at my temples. I send up a silent prayer that nobody notices, and quietly berate myself for never asking about the device's range.

Korov wishes us a good night. Only Casper eyes me with suspicion as I stand up to accept my coat from the hostess. I can't begin to guess what he'll say to Henry.

Mikhail steers me through a side door camouflaged in the wall. We walk down a short, unadorned corridor. "Administrative offices," he says. His hand releases my arm and grazes my back. We go down an escalator and step through the building's rear exit into a parking area. The lot is walled in with brick, like a fortress, with a lethal-looking coil of razor wire along the top. I count seven Bentleys in the first row alone. Two thuggish men the size of linebackers guard the only gate with assault rifles slung over their shoulders. Mikhail produces a key from his pocket. When he presses the button, the lights on a platinum-colored Porsche beep to life. He holds the door while I arrange myself in the passenger seat, which is upholstered in leather so soft it could be used to make clothing.

"Nice car," I say.

"It is, isn't it?" He closes the door for me, walks around the back and slides in behind the wheel. "It was a gift. Unfortunately, I've only put a couple of thousand kilometers on it."

The oversized guards step aside to let us pass. Mikhail fits a hands free device over his left ear and says he needs to check his messages. I stare out the window. On both sides of the street, the flashing lights of countless casinos illuminate the night. Bejeweled women in impossibly high heels and even higher hair prance down the sidewalk. We stop at a traffic light and Mikhail removes his ear piece.

"I can't figure out what Moscow smells like," I say. "Isn't that odd? It actually *smells* different from any other city I've visited."

"That's easy." Mikhail puts the car in gear and peels off with the traffic. "Moscow smells like money. It's like the Wild West. People get obscenely rich or they lose their shirts. If they manage to get rich, they either end up on top of the world or in an early grave."

"Interesting. Maybe I should mention that," I say, suddenly remembering I'm supposed to be a writer.

The skin at the bridge of Mikhail's nose wrinkles in puzzlement. We stop at an intersection and turn left.

Red Square is way larger than it looks on television. St. Basil's Cathedral presides over the far end in all its fantastical multicolored glory. The red brick walls of the Kremlin dominate the entire right side of the square. Spotlights reflect off the gold onion domes behind them.

"Let's take a stroll," Mikhail says. He parks the Porsche on the cobblestone sidewalk and produces a few bills for an imposing man who's appeared out of nowhere, presumably to watch the car.

We navigate through a large Japanese tour group and pass about a dozen uniformed police officers, whose green hats feature freakishly vertical brims. One of the cops looks us up and down before lighting a cigarette. He drops the used match onto the ground and takes a drag, eyes still trained on us. I pull my coat more tightly around myself. Mikhail starts lecturing like a tour guide. We walk down the square, towards the St. Basil's side, and stop between Lenin's austere tomb and the flashy shopping mall directly opposite.

"In Soviet times, that was the G.U.M. department store," Mikhail explains. He sounds relaxed but his eyes never pause from scanning our surroundings. "The queues were legendary back in the bad old days."

I try my best to feign interest, but between freaking out about the bug in the casino, berating myself for trusting Korov, and puzzling over Mikhail's intentions with regards to me, my brain feels overloaded. I hope the FBI can hear whatever Korov and his guests are discussing.

Henry and Max must know I was abducted, which means they must be looking for me. At least I hope so. Suddenly my gut pinches. A world-altering realization hits: I might be on my own. Mikhail tells me that Ivan the Terrible moved the czar's residence to the Kremlin in 1547, and he added various towers and improvements to the six churches.

From what I've read and garnered from the movies, intelligence agencies leave people behind, if not all the time, then not infrequently. Why would the FBI be different? I stop mid-stride and start to hyperventilate.

Mikhail reels towards me and yanks me to his chest. I freeze, unsure how to react. My heart leaps, not in a good way, and sticks in my throat.

He jams something hard and metallic in my gut right under my rib cage. I know it's a gun before I have time to turn my eyes down. I could pee myself with fright, but I somehow manage to hold it together.

My mind seizes with the effort of trying to remember what you're supposed to do when mugged at gunpoint in public. Scream? Fight? Make a scene? Offer up your valuables? Comply with whatever the man with the gun asks?

This is no mugging.

"Who are you working for?" Mikhail demands in a whisper.

"Korov, of course." I hiss back, but my voice shakes. My eyes dart around. Nobody's paying any attention to us.

"Besides Korov," he says, indulgently.

"Rutledge & Smerth. They're a big law firm in Washington."

Mikhail stares right into my eyes. I can tell he's not buying a single word. I feel my fingers start to tremble, then my hands, then my whole body. The barrel of his gun nudges under my ribs.

"Do not patronize me. I'm the only friend you have here. You think you're pretty sly, don't you? The way you planted that bug right under Korov's nose, that took real grit."

Oh shit. I'm about to die. My knees feel unsteady. He leans in closer. His breath warms my face when he whispers, "If you tell me, this will be far less painful."

Any resolve I might have ever possessed fades in under a millisecond. "The FBI." Some secret agent I am. I fold before hearing the "or else" part.

"Really?"

I can tell by his shocked expression that he expected some other explanation. Perhaps I should elaborate. "I'm not an agent. I'm a lowly informant who got in over her head. Didn't Korov tell you?"

"He claimed you were the daughter of an important associate of the Titan Import-Export Company, and he wanted to let you write his profile for some American magazine. Which sounded fishy, but not beyond belief." He slides the gun off my person and conceals it under his coat.

"So why all the fancy security, and um, with all due respect, if you're so busy and important, why are you stuck babysitting an aspiring author?"

"Female relatives of his close associates are major kidnapping targets who occasionally end up dead."

My head spins again. "Oh. Did anyone else see me plant the bug?"

"If they had, you wouldn't be here in one piece, asking me that."

"So why didn't you blow the whistle on me?" A familiar feeling of doom brews again, deep in my gut. "And why the Moscow-by-night tour?"

He considers my question for a long, uncomfortable moment. "Because I thought you might be one of our people."

"Whose people?" Dread creeps over me.

He takes a deep breath. "I'm with the FSB."

"FSB?"

"We're the domestic crime wing of what was the KGB. I've been undercover in Korov's organization for five years." He watches for a second as I digest his revelation and adds, "Technically we're on the same team."

"I guess we are." I'm not so sure. He could be lying to me, to keep me calm. It seems unprofessional to divulge his covert status to a stranger. Of course he could have some reason for telling the truth, or some variation thereof.

Mikhail takes my arm and starts to steer me back towards the car. "One thing worries me." He stops in his tracks and fixes his gaze back on my face.

"What's that?" Since about a million and one things are causing me extreme anxiety right now, we might as well start with his lone worry.

"You said Korov knows you're working with the FBI?"

"Yes, definitely."

"Why didn't he tell me?"

"Does he tell you everything?"

"Usually. Which makes me think you might not be safe at the Belgrade. Damn it."

He reaches into his pocket and switches off his iPhone. "Do you have one of these, or a cell phone?"

"No. Whoever brought me here relieved me of my Black-Berry."

"Interesting. You definitely shouldn't go back to the hotel before we find out why you're here. Which means you're stuck with me for a while." He holds the door of the Porsche open for me.

I balk. "Why should I follow you into the night? We only met this morning. You've got more questions than answers, and you've given me no proof that you are who you claim to be."

"If I were you, I'd try to keep my aggravation in check. Do you know how much trouble I'd be in, if anyone knew I let you get away with planting that device? He'd have me shot."

"I'm not *aggravated*. I'm fucking terrified. And if you could get yourself killed, why didn't you expose me in the casino?"

"I told you. I suspected you were one of our people. My story hasn't changed. Has yours?"

My eyes narrow. "How many American lawyers does the Russian government employ?"

"You'd be surprised," Mikhail says, dismissively. "Now that I know you're not working with us, I'd like to know what the boss has planned for you."

"What do you *think* he has planned for me?" I feel all the remaining color rush from my face. Why did I ever believe Korov would help me? Have grief and lack of sleep finally rendered me clinically incompetent?

Mikhail refuses to elaborate. He eases me into the car.

"Where are you taking me?" I demand, surprised at my boldness. He's armed. Nobody knows where I am. What if I'm going willingly into a trap? If only Henry and Max could see me now. I'm holding it together rather well, all things considered. Maybe that means I've completely lost it.

"Safe house," Mikhail hisses back. We fly down the road along the river.

Visions of the dingy apartment where I first met Casper fly through my head. That was an FBI safe house. I expect the Russian version to be even more depressing. I snap at myself to stop thinking like an imbecile. I have bigger worries than tonight's accommodations. Such as staying alive until morning.

Without diverting his eyes from the road, Mikhail says, "Why don't you tell me what Korov wants from you?"

"He claims to have something I need." I'm too nervous to care if I sound cagey. Better to say too little than too much. I can always elaborate, but I can't un-say something. "He promised to deliver that item to me if I helped him dispose of certain documents stored in the law firm where I work. Before I could even find the files for him, someone attacked me in a bathroom and brought me here." I rub my neck and glance at my reflection in the window. An angry purple bruise bulges under the skin where my assailant stabbed me.

Mikhail downshifts as we approach an intersection. He nods as if what I'm saying makes perfect sense.

"Well? What do you think?" I say, anger brewing that he's reacting to my story so calmly.

He says nothing and turns onto a smaller road. We snake through a series of winding, interconnecting streets and alleys. I try to keep track of the turns, but all the old buildings look the same. I feel my pulse accelerate. If I wasn't so scared, I'd burst into tears.

Finally Mikhail drives us through a nondescript gate into another walled parking lot. We leave the car and step inside through a back entrance.

The lobby is a showplace of decadence in decay. Well worn red carpets blanket the stairs. Ornate but tarnished chandeliers illuminate every hole and loose thread. The banisters look hand carved, but the wood, stripped by decades of hands holding the railings, could benefit from a fresh coat of varnish.

"This place must have been stunning in its heyday," I say, because the worst thing for nervousness is silence.

"It's a typical pre-rev building. They're rehabilitating them all over Moscow. Once they finish, I'll own some very desirable real estate."

"So the 'safe house' is your apartment?"

"Yeah. I thought if I told you we were going to my place, you'd be liable to make a scene."

"You thought right." I silently ask God to let the bug work from this distance, and spur the FBI into action.

We go up two flights of stairs and he uses two more keys to get into a small but tastefully furnished studio. "Home sweet home," he says, as he shuts the door, deadbolts it twice, and punches in a code to arm a security system.

The blinds are drawn, which makes the apartment seem cramped. There's a small kitchen in an alcove at the far end, a full bath immediately to the left of the doorway, and we're standing in the combination living and bedroom. A huge wooden computer desk takes up most of the space opposite the bed and overflowing bookshelves line the walls.

Mikhail turns on his laptop. While the computer thinks, he motions to a chair and says, "Let's get to work."

Although I have no idea what he means for us to work on, I eagerly sink into the desk chair and peel off the detestable boots. Mikhail pulls up a wooden chair from his kitchen table, turns it so the back faces the desk, and straddles it with his arms resting over the back. He types something and the laptop's speakers crackle to life.

"Our friends in the casino, in real time," he explains, with a touch of pride in his voice. "Don't worry. They can't hear us."

"You tapped into my bug that easily?"

"I'm not that good. I planted my own bug a long time ago. *Ya shpion*, remember?" He smiles. The dimple again.

The dealer asks the players to place their bets and chips click against each other. "English. Lucky break for you."

"Why English?"

"Muhammed doesn't speak Russian. Korov doesn't speak Arabic, and his French is intermediate at best," Mikhail explains, as if this should be self-evident.

We both fall silent and stare at the speakers, as if our concentration improves the sound quality. We hear the noises of the game, people trading in cards and raising bets.

A door slams and the murmur stops. I have no trouble identifying the next voice. Korov comes through in English, loud and clear, and he sounds furious.

"I thought I made myself understood!" he booms. "I said make it look like an accident, if possible a *car* accident, and you *idiots* went and blew him up with an old-fashioned ignition bomb! Now the Goddamn police, FBI and probably Interpol and the fucking CIA are all over this, not to mention every hack of an investigative reporter in the Mid-Atlantic region *and* it's going to be the top story on all the morning shows because you were *stupid* enough to do it at night."

A male voice answers calmly, "Don't question my methods. You wanted it done before news of the plea deal reached the press and I wasn't going to allow another day to go by with the potential for a leak. Let the FBI come. They won't find a thing. The blast incinerated everything within a twenty meter radius."

Mikhail turns to me, incredulous, and says, "They killed Acheson. The timing's not what I expected, but if he was going to make a plea bargain, maybe they saw no alternative."

"No. That can't be right. I worked on his case for months and nobody ever breathed a word about any plea deal."

In fact, at least in the presence of his associates, Smerth never mentioned the possibility of his client's guilt. While it's well known throughout the firm that if convicted on all counts, Acheson could face up to thirty-five years, we all expected Smerth to work his magic and make the whole matter disappear. After several years of billable legal wrangling, of course.

The same voice says, "Don't lose sleep over the FBI. Their point man is in the air as we speak, flying straight towards our special welcome." Someone grunts his approval and the original voice adds, "I frankly find it insulting that the Americans think we're unsophisticated enough to wire one lump sum, and through *Switzerland*, at that."

A chorus of snickers erupts.

"Are you confident their agent took the bait?" Korov demands.

"One hundred per cent. We intercepted a call between Agent von Buren and his Russian legal attaché three hours ago. They were both traveling to the Western Union office we specified, along with a swarm of FSB agents."

A wave of blinding panic washes over me at the mention of Max's name. I wonder if he has any idea he's flying into an ambush, and whether this swarm of FSB will be enough to thwart his adversaries.

And with my BlackBerry long gone, I have no straightforward way to warn Max. Would the FBI office believe my story if I called them with a warning? Would Mikhail let me do that?

Korov asks the man who described the trap to step outside. We hear chairs being pushed out. A door opens and closes. The game resumes, but the players switch to Arabic.

"I'll have to have this part translated," Mikhail says, shaking his head. He looks up at me, registers my distress and asks, "Do you know this agent they plan to dispose of?"

"Max von Buren recruited me to help the FBI."

"Well, I hope your friend Max has good instincts. He's going to need them."

I glare at Mikhail. I wonder what else he knows.

Mikhail, as if reading my mind, says, "I have no idea what's in store for him, but it's going to be unpleasant and professionally executed. On that you can wager your life." He adds, more quietly, "I'm sorry."

I'm about to protest that we have to warn Max, when we hear the door open through the speakers. The conversation abruptly reverts to English.

Korov speaks again. "Don't think that if you eliminate one lousy FBI agent, all will be forgiven for today's hack job. Your people couldn't do better than a car bomb in an office garage?"

I flinch at the word "eliminate." Mikhail glances in my direction, but avoids looking me in the eye.

The male voice from before says, "We first planned to pump carbon monoxide into his residence at night while the family slept, but you couldn't get close enough with the motion detectors and the ridiculous Bethesda Neighborhood Watch prowling the neighborhood at all hours. Look at the bright side. Less collateral damage this way. No women or children harmed."

"Still, it's not your best effort, and it better not come back to bite us, as they say in America." Korov snarls and clears his throat before announcing, "Gentlemen, let's adjourn upstairs."

Grunts of agreement come from all around. We hear the sounds of the players raking in their chips, downing their drinks and pushing away from the table.

"What's Bethesda Neighborhood Watch?" Mikhail asks.

"Sort of a citizens' vigilance program. Neighbors take turns keeping an eye on things around the neighborhood," I explain distractedly. This doesn't add up. Charlie's email said Acheson *disappeared*. There's no way that Charlie would fail to mention a car bomb in the building.

"Wait a second!" I almost squeal. "Did they say *Bethesda* Neighborhood Watch?"

"I think so, but I can replay the tape." Mikhail reaches for the keyboard.

"No need. They're not talking about killing Acheson."

"Sure they are."

"No. They're not. Acheson doesn't live in Bethesda. He lives in McLean. It's a different suburb in a different state. Korov spends too much time in Washington to confuse the towns."

"Then who are they talking about? Who else would they worry about in connection with a plea deal?"

"Smerth," I say, talking over the last part of Mikhail's question. "Randolph Smerth, Acheson's lawyer—and my boss—lives in Bethesda. With his wife and sons – the women and children that man referred to. Smerth would have known the intimate details of any plea bargain, because he would have negotiated it in direct talks with the U.S. Attorney. But you can bet your life savings that he would never leak without his client's blessing."

Mikhail rubs his temples, wrinkles his brow, shakes his head.

"There's another thing. Acheson disappeared hours before the car bomb. One of my colleagues told me in an email." My stomach churns uneasily while Mikhail digests this latest morsel of intelligence. As much as I detested working for Smerth, I hate that he suffered such a brutal end. And from a self-preservation standpoint, Korov's willingness to murder both Smerth and Max doesn't bode well. I struggle against a fresh surge of panic.

Mikhail, on the other hand, is thinking so hard that you can practically see the smoke streaming from his ears. "Smerth?" he asks. "Wasn't Randolph Smerth a partner in one of the pass-through entities in Bermuda that Acheson set up? The Lotus Group? I've written checks to them as the CFO of the Titan Import-Export Company."

Right. Mikhail doesn't snoop. He's actually infiltrated the organization and participated in its illegal activities. Maybe that's how the Russians do things. Not that I would put it past Henry for a second.

"Yes, but what do you mean, *one* of the pass-throughs?"

"Clearwater Partners maintains at least a dozen shell companies in the Caribbean. Whenever money moves from any part of Clearwater's empire to one of Korov's companies for an off-the-books deal, the funds come through one or more of the shell corps. That way Korov and other investors avoid paying taxes. You probably know that Acheson also established a private bank on Nauru. Also for tax evasion purposes."

"Where?" I ask. How can Max and Henry have missed this?

"A little island nation in the middle of the Pacific Ocean. You can establish a 'bank' there, anonymously and without the hassle of an in-person visit, in about an hour. There's virtually no paper trail."

That's why the FBI couldn't piece it together. You'd have to get inside and high up in Clearwater to know – a feat Henry's admitted they can't pull off.

Mikhail explains, "Nauru is a well known tax haven, especially in criminal circles."

"Wow. And this is legal?"

"That depends on how you look at it. Your country's law enforcement, or mine for that matter, can't interfere with bank transactions completed wholly outside their borders. So once the money moves through a series of bank accounts and shell companies, the crooks can spend their laundered cash anywhere. And the shell corporations always meet the letter of the law in their host countries.

They often appoint nominal officers and directors nobody has heard of, to keep their key players' names off the paperwork."

"You mean like Randolph Smerth's former nanny."

"Exactly. It seems she's Abdul's lady friend these days."

That answers a few lingering questions about the night Acheson caught me in his old office. "I knew she was a source for the FBI, when she worked in Smerth's house. But wait. What if the alleged plea deal involved someone other than Acheson? Maybe Smerth was about to make a deal *for himself* because he saw the feds closing in. What if he planned to blow the whistle on Acheson's plan to assassinate all those senators, in exchange for immunity for his role in the Lotus Group?"

My fundamental views on Smerth have evolved since Henry first suggested he had a hand in the DC bombing. Maybe my boss could be capable of terrorism and murder. Even if the prosecutors couldn't prove his link to the violence, his use of the Lotus Group to repatriate untaxed income could land him in a federal prison camp for decades.

Mikhail ignores my question and navigates to the BBC website. Sure enough, Smerth is the top news item: "BREAKING NEWS: Prominent Washington Lawyer Killed by Car Bomb." The single paragraph explains that police have no leads, and that Randolph Smerth was representing embattled lobbyist William Acheson, whose wife reported him missing earlier today.

Mikhail rockets off his perch on the chair. He paces the studio almost frantically. "Who told you about the plot to kill those senators?"

"Korov."

"You didn't find it strange that Korov would get involved with murdering American lawmakers?"

"Not really. If they die, the Republican governors of their states would appoint their replacements. Presumably those appointees would cast the deciding votes in favor of whatever Clearwater Partners wants from the Congress, which would be good for Korov, since his oil company and Clearwater have joint ventures all over the globe."

"I'm pretty sure they've nixed that plot," Mikhail says.

"Why would you say that? The Democrats are all about investigating the Burtonhall Group and Clearwater for bribery and a host of other offenses. Which means Clearwater and its subs lose billions in contracts while those investigations drag on. If the Senate changes hands, the Republicans would presumably suspend the investigation. Which is exactly what Acheson, or whatever new K Street player Clearwater hires to replace him, will want."

"Korov didn't tell you the whole truth."

"Well, he did say he'd prefer to kill the Russian president instead. Not that I understand why he'd share that ambition with me. I guess I shrugged it off as self indulgent macho posturing. Kind of like, *look what I can get away with saying*. He also told me he fell out with Acheson and Aziz. Abdul bin Aziz. Not Muhammed." I stop when I realize I've interrupted.

"What I was trying to say, is that Korov wants to kill the American president at the same time." Mikhail stops pacing and re-straddles the desk chair. He pauses, presumably so I can process the information overload.

It takes me two seconds to decide I don't believe him. "If they kill the president of the United States, then Jack Prescott becomes the new president." I think out loud, slowly and deliberately. "But if Acheson and Korov had a major falling out, then why on earth would Korov want to do something as risky as take a shot at the leader of the free world, only to install Acheson's closest friend in his place? And why wouldn't Prescott bide his time until the next election? He's young enough, articulate, and likely to win."

Mikhail shakes his head. "I may not have ever set foot in the States, but I follow your politics. Prescott would love to avoid an election. The American public was willing to overlook his lack of financial candor when he was picked for the number two slot. If he wants to run for the top spot, he'll be forced to release a decade's worth of financial statements and unedited tax returns – something I'm sure he's keen to avoid."

Before I can ask what details Mikhail might know about Prescott's offshore dealings, his phone rings.

"*Da?*" He gestures at me to keep quiet. As if I need that directive. He listens for a moment and then says in English, presumably for my benefit, "She's right here."

Conversation ensues in Russian. When they hang up Mikhail says, "Korov wants to see you."

"Now?" I am incredulous. And nervous. And scared.

"Afraid so." Mikhail shuts down the laptop and waits as I wrestle my throbbing feet back into the boots.

I decide to stall. "One of the men at the card game is an FBI informant."

"Oh yeah? Which one?"

"Casper."

"How do you know?" He squints at me as if that helps him judge my truthfulness.

"I saw him meet with FBI agents."

I have Mikhail's undivided attention. "Do you think he recognized you?"

"Absolutely. We did that mutual double take people do, when they can't place someone."

"Volodya would be very interested to know he has a mole in his organization." Mikhail rubs the stubble on his chin. "I'm curious about one thing. Would you know if Casper said anything to the FBI about going with God?"

Of course I remember Casper saying exactly those words to Henry when he gave him a Bible that rainy morning in Cleveland Park. My hand flies to the bug on my chest. If Henry can hear us, I doubt he'd want his conversations with an informant shared with Mikhail. I've probably said too much already.

So I say, "I don't remember."

17

We step out into the raw night air. I don't know whether to feel anxious about the timing of Korov's summons, or excited that whatever happens next could bring me a step closer to getting my hands on the tape. "Does he normally do business in the middle of the night?" I ask Mikhail.

"He never stops. He's one of those people who has a thought at three in the morning and needs to share it with someone. Usually me."

"I'm scared." It feels cathartic to admit out loud. I grasp Mikhail's arm, too overwhelmed by the past two days to care if I'm out of line. He makes no motion to liberate himself from my grip. He reaches his other hand over to pat mine and picks up the pace. My feet throb, but I soldier forward. To a casual observer, we would look like an ordinary couple out for a midnight stroll.

Mikhail navigates through a gloomy maze of back alleys. I don't think I could find my way back to the main tourist district if my life depended on it. Every now and then a street lamp flickers. They're spaced too far from each other to properly light the way. The effect is eerie, mostly dark with intervals of bright light. Anything or anyone could be lurking on the sidewalk, completely sheltered by the shadows.

He stops abruptly in front of a doorway along an especially poorly lit stretch. "Here we are."

"Volodya Korov lives *here*?" It can't be true. We're on a trash-strewn, dank back street. There's no way one of the richest men on the planet calls this tenement home.

"It's a *pied à terre*." Mikhail disentangles his arm from my grasp and produces a key from his pants pocket. It turns loudly in the lock. In the distance, strains of American hip hop blare. Traffic hums on some nearby thoroughfare.

The door opens to a marble lobby.

"Doesn't someone like Korov attract attention coming to this neighborhood?"

"He likes the amenities."

I blink at him, confused.

"The house is connected to one of his casinos by an underground passageway," Mikhail explains, as if this is the most normal arrangement in the world.

We ride an antique elevator—the kind with a cage door—to a fifth floor sitting room.

Mikhail smiles and says, "You didn't expect an apartment, did you? He's restored the whole house."

It's not that. I'm worried I'll say something stupid when we come face to face with Korov. Blow my chance of getting what I so desperately want.

I focus on breathing without panting or hyperventilating, and on mimicking Mikhail's relaxed demeanor. An aging tuxedoed butler, who looks ready to present *Masterpiece Theatre*, greets us in Russian. We follow him down a short hallway and cut through a beautiful old library, lined from floor to ceiling with leather-bound volumes. The butler swings open a door camouflaged in the library's paneling and steps aside so we can enter the next room. Korov rises to greet us.

As does a haggard and unshaven Acheson.

My breath catches in the back of my throat.

"Welcome," Korov says. "Please, make yourselves at home."

Every fiber of my being itches to shriek at Korov, to demand an explanation for Acheson's presence. Korov promised to solve Damien's murder. Is he sadistic enough to do so by orchestrating a face to face confrontation with my prime suspect?

Mikhail must sense my anger brewing over, because he shoots me a glance that could turn a weaker woman to stone.

Korov clears his throat. "Mikhail, this is William Acheson, my most zealous American advocate. He's secured hundreds of millions of dollars in contracts that have benefited my various companies, all courtesy of the U.S. government, and all nicely dressed up as foreign aid." He nods towards Mikhail. "Mikhail Borofsky, one of my most trusted employees."

Acheson shakes Mikhail's hand without even a sidelong glance my way. Korov stands over their handshake in the manner of a peace broker bringing two adversaries together, then turns to me and says, "And you two are already acquainted."

I nod uncertainly. My mind's eye fixates on those stupid boots that resurfaced in my apartment when Damien was shot. Acheson has to be guilty. No other scenario makes sense. I also have a strong, though utterly unsubstantiated, suspicion that Acheson had a hand in killing Smerth today.

Acheson looks me in the eye. "Good evening, Lena."

I can't bring myself to speak to him. I turn away and gaze at my feet.

"Lena?" Mikhail says.

Acheson shrugs, as if the question is too basic to dignify. Korov says to Mikhail, "Miss Lane's name isn't Claudia, it's Lena. But let's not get bogged down in such tedious matters." He rings a bell. The butler appears and pours snifters of brandy all around.

Mikhail leans in close to my ear and says, mockingly, "Lena *Lane?*"

"Lena Mancuso," I correct him, and turn to thank the butler, who evidently merits no introduction, for a generous pour of the sweet smelling liqueur. I glance around furtively to make sure everyone else is drinking from the same bottle. They are. At least I can be fairly certain Korov's not planning to poison me. I remind myself to be rational. If Korov wanted to kill me, he wouldn't bother to fly me out to Moscow and entertain me first.

Mikhail and I arrange ourselves in the side by side arm chairs Korov indicates. Mikhail sits back and crosses his left ankle over his right knee. He looks very much at home. I try my best to mirror his ease, but fail miserably. My hands shake so much I have trouble holding my glass.

Our host studies me from his enormous leather chair for an uncomfortable moment, during which I force myself to refrain from fidgeting. I take a sip of the brandy, which goes down surprisingly smoothly, considering the panic gurgling up from the deepest part of my gut.

"I'm impressed by your patience," Korov says finally.

I have no idea what to say. I search Mikhail's face for a hint. Nothing. Acheson swirls his brandy in what looks like a concentrated effort at boredom, but I can see he's keenly interested in the exchange.

Since I say nothing during the pregnant pause, Korov continues. "Your husband was killed on orders from Abdul bin Aziz, and over the objections of myself and Mr. Acheson."

I let my glass slip through my fingers. Mikhail swoops in and catches it before it hits the Persian rug.

I can't believe Aziz would contract for a murder without at least the implied consent of his usual partners in crime. And if they did object, they obviously didn't do so very loudly, because their alleged protest changed nothing. Disgust creeps in to replace the abject terror I've felt since we arrived in this house.

"But why?" I manage to stammer.

"I'm afraid you neglected to stipulate explanation of motive when we made our bargain," Korov says. "I will provide you with a video of the crime, as I promised, *if* you hold up your end of our little arrangement."

He reaches into his suit pocket, and for a terrifying, disgustingly exhilarating moment I think he's going to produce the tape. He pulls out a cigar, which he puts in his mouth unlit. All eyes fall on me.

"I already started on your files, and was making decent progress before I was, um, diverted. Why did you bring me here?" My mouth is so dry that I take a large sip of the brandy to wet it. It doesn't help, and leaves a cloying flavor hanging at the top of my throat.

"I want you to be abducted by extremists."

"Excuse me?"

"From time to time, agents of Russia's break away republics, or Islamists, if you will, take a western hostage. Usually they seize a journalist or a relief worker, but occasionally an intrepid tourist wanders too far from the beaten path."

"Well, I'm none of those things." I'm surprised how defiant I sound.

Acheson, who had seemed content to let Korov do the talking, speaks. "I suspect the FBI will expend significant resources to look for you, if only to try to prevent a leak of your activities as a Patriot

Act informant. They use so many ordinary citizens as insider informants that your outing could draw unwelcome scrutiny to other corporate surveillance operations the FBI would prefer to keep clandestine."

Korov makes a expansive gesture with his hands in apparent agreement with Acheson's analysis. "Your disappearance will also serve to silence any rumors percolating among your law enforcement that Mr. Acheson may have kidnapped you himself."

My pulse skyrockets and alarm bells shriek in my head. They killed Damien in cold blood. They blew up Smerth, their supposed friend and advisor, in the heart of downtown DC.

Nobody is going to care about insignificant me.

As if reading my thoughts, Korov says, "You're young and pretty enough to spark an American cable news frenzy, especially if we plant the story with the right media outlets."

Which could be a mixed blessing. I don't want to become the star of some Russian police rescue effort. They botch those operations all the time, often with lethal consequences for the hapless hostages.

I feel the color leave my face. Korov says, in a saccharin voice, "There, there, don't fret, Miss Lena. Mikhail will be taken with you."

"I will?"

"Yes. It'll play in the Russian media as an American agent, posing as a writer, and her local guide, held by separatist fighters who desire to embarrass the government during the summit."

"But I'm not even an agent. Or a writer."

And I can't possibly be that valuable to the FBI. I glance at Mikhail. Maybe he'll tell them their plan is stupid. Maybe they'll listen. Korov appears to possess a certain affinity for him.

Mikhail says, "You can't have me kidnapped. Everyone who matters in Moscow knows I work for you."

I know it's ridiculous, but his matter-of-fact betrayal stings me. Acheson studies his loosened tie, waiting like the rest of us for Korov to respond to this challenge to his authority.

Korov looks as if his patience is dangerously close to running out. "Nobody's really being kidnapped, you half-wits," he booms. "We're going to make a little film and then everyone can go off and get a good night's sleep."

He rings the bell and the butler comes running. Korov explains that the butler will show Acheson to his quarters. Acheson's expression registers offense, but he doesn't argue. He leaves us with as much dignity as a man who's been iced out can summon.

Mikhail and I follow Korov back to the elevator. I'm trembling, but Mikhail seems cool and collected, as if all this is normal.

Korov presses a button that says " -2". It would have to be the basement. I steel myself for arrival in some damp dungeon and attempt to breathe deep breaths while we descend.

"Do you like my little hideaway, Miss Lena?" Korov asks, as if he's making polite small talk with the wife of a social acquaintance.

"Uh, yes, it's lovely," I manage to stutter.

"Many of my antiques belonged to Catherine the Great."

I nod dumbly. Mikhail comes to my rescue. "Mr. Korov is a major patron of the arts and he has a special passion for Russian antiques."

The elevator lurches to a halt before I can formulate an appropriate response. We're standing in a finished basement that could be in any suburban American home. There's a plasma television and a row of leather armchairs, as well as a pool table and a full bar. Framed sporting prints dominate the decor, but one wall features unadorned white paint. Korov clears his throat forcefully. He sounds like Buster clearing a hairball.

Casper and one of the Arab men from the casino emerge from behind a door at the opposite end of the room. The latter has abandoned his white robes in favor of jeans and a black turtleneck.

I start to gasp, catch myself and stifle the sound with a false hiccup. Mikhail shoots me a look that begs me to remain calm. Casper carries a newspaper and a video camera. He avoids making eye contact.

"Let's get this on the first try." Korov glances at his watch and settles onto a bar stool.

I can't decide if it's good or bad that Mikhail suddenly looks as lost as I feel. He's evidently decided not to advise Korov of Casper's FBI-snitch status, at least not tonight.

"Miss Lena, you will sit there." Korov gestures towards a spot on the floor, by the wall with no artwork.

"On the floor?" I blurt without thinking, as if my dignity makes a difference to anyone present.

"It's alright," Mikhail says. He takes my arm and steers me in the general direction his boss indicated.

Casper hands me tomorrow's *Herald-Tribune*. Today's actually, since it's after midnight. Smerth's murder is one of two stories above the fold. There's a big picture of a mangled, burnt out car in the R&S garage. My hands start to shake.

"I think you should hold it up and try to appear petrified," Korov directs.

That won't be hard.

Casper hands the camera to Mikhail.

Korov pours himself a glass of vodka. Casper and the Arab, as if on cue, don black ski masks, which make them look far more menacing. The Arab pulls a handgun from the back of his waistband and strides towards me. I feel the horrible, powerless sensation of having a firearm aimed at my skull at point blank range. There's definitely no need for me to *try* to look scared. I'm terrified. Korov tells Mikhail to start filming.

From the corner of my eye, I see the masked Casper walk into the frame. He produces a folded sheet of notebook paper from his pants pocket. He unfolds it deliberately and reads a brief statement in Russian. Then he motions for Mikhail to stop filming.

We all wait motionless while Mikhail shuts off the camera. As soon as the red recording light goes out, Casper and the still anonymous Arab remove their ski masks. I don't resume breathing until the latter holsters his gun. Mikhail takes the camera over to the bar so that Korov can review the footage. He says, in English, "Very nice. Perfect on the first try." He downs the not insubstantial remainder of his vodka.

Unsure what to do with myself, I continue to kneel on the floor, clutching the *Herald-Tribune* at chest level as if my life depends on it, until Mikhail offers me his hand and says, "You can get up now."

I clamber to my feet. He guides me to one of the empty barstools. Casper and his nameless companion retreat through the door from which they came with a little salute in their boss's general direction.

Once the door closes behind them, Mikhail gestures towards the camera, and asks Korov, "Where would you like it sent?"

"I'll take care of this one myself. Let me walk you out."

18

Korov thanks us for coming and wishes us a pleasant night, as if we'd stopped over for a nightcap. The door swings closed behind us. I'm about to say something about how surreal, scary and frustrating this whole experience was, when Mikhail's forefinger flies to my lips and he whispers, "Wait a block, alright?"

Once we pass the second cross street, Mikhail looks around, and seeing nobody, whispers, "What was *he* doing as a guest in Korov's house?"

"No idea. Like I told you, Korov said he and Acheson fell out."

"Was there any hint that wasn't for real?"

"None that I noticed," I whisper back, as I almost launch forward onto my face, my heel wrenched between the cobblestones. I manage to catch myself, but when I try to jerk my foot free, my boot breaks. I stumble forward. The heel sticks out of the sidewalk like it grew there. Mikhail stoops to the ground and bends the stuck piece of my ruined Manolo this way and that. Finally the heel breaks free. He stands up triumphantly and hands it over. I try to pick up my left foot to inspect the damage and almost keel over again because I can't balance on my remaining intact stiletto. I lean on Mikhail's arm and try again, only to discover what should have been obvious in the first place. There's no way to re-attach the heel. I limp home on uneven feet, attracting snickers from the two pedestrians we encounter along the way.

As we're shuffling along at the slower pace dictated by my lopsided heels, Mikhail says, "I didn't know your husband was murdered. I'm so sorry."

"Thank you."

"What happened? I mean, I understand if you don't want to tell me."

"No. It's fine," I say. Suddenly talking feels almost cathartic. I give him the whole story, starting with the gruesome scene that Diana and

I discovered when we returned from Hannah's premature memorial, to the nightmarish night with the police and the return of the boots I left in Acheson's office when he caught me snooping.

When I finish my story, his expression shows something resembling pain. "I'm so sorry," he says again.

"It's okay." Of course it isn't, but what else can I say?

We're quiet for a few paces. Maybe we're both contemplating my loss. At least I am. When we come to the next cross street he says, "I'm impressed."

"Excuse me?"

"I'm impressed with how cool you were tonight. If you'd told me earlier what you shared now, I would have expected you to have a full blown meltdown upon seeing the man."

"What can I say? I must have nerves of steel." Though I never thought I did. Maybe humans *can* adapt to almost anything.

"Do you suppose Korov's telling me the truth?" I ask.

"About what?"

"About Aziz being the culprit. He claims to have evidence."

"Bluffing is one of his many talents."

As soon as we walk in the door to Mikhail's studio, I peel off both the intact Manolo and its damaged mate. If my feet could cheer, they would.

Mikhail logs onto the computer. "Why does Korov want to stage my kidnapping?" I ask over his shoulder.

He rotates to face me. "I don't know for certain. I suspect it's part of a larger strategy to make the administration to look inept, on the eve of the American state visit."

"So why don't they really kidnap someone?"

"I'm afraid I don't have an answer for you." He turns his attention back to the computer screen.

"Mikhail?"

"Yes?"

"Do you think they're going to do something awful to me? I mean, when they don't need me anymore, for whatever it is they need me for?" Even as the question comes out, I hate myself for asking it.

Mikhail looks right at me and says, "No. I promise I won't let that happen."

For some reason, whether it's that his demeanor inspires confidence, or that I'm so overwhelmed that I'll latch onto any lifeline someone tosses my way, I believe him.

He stares at me for a moment too long and shakes his head. "Your hair," he mutters. "We've got to change it." He goes into the bathroom, roots around in the cabinets and emerges with a box that features a woman who bears a strong resemblance to the hooker lurking by the elevators at the Hotel Belgrade.

I shake my head no as he foists the box on me. I've invested thousands of dollars over the years, having Washington's toniest salons paint just the right highlights into my brunette locks. There's no way I am going to let a Russian spy turn my hair into a peroxide nightmare.

"It says to leave it in for half an hour, then rinse and shampoo," he reads off the box. "You have to do this. Your eyebrows, too. Otherwise you'll be too easy to recognize once your photo hits the newsstands."

"Maybe I don't care anymore."

"I'm afraid it doesn't matter what you think. Korov will be furious if your abduction gets exposed as a hoax, and then you'll never get what you came for."

I shuffle into the bathroom. My eyes water from the stench of bleach as I apply the lotion to my hair. I decide that after all that's happened, a hair disaster doesn't matter. I'm angry at myself when tears start to roll down my face while I wait for the timer. I was such a pathetic fool to think I could take charge of the murder investigation by dealing with Korov. And if Mikhail is really a KGB agent or whatever, why can't he deliver me to the U.S. authorities? Aren't we at least sort of allies these days?

I slap at my face. *Don't be a moron, Lena. He's not going to ruin his career for your sorry self.*

I shampoo under the handheld shower with no water pressure and study my handiwork in the mirror. I look horrible. My hair has turned brittle and yellow and my dark eyebrows underline the blatant fact that it's a botched home job. I brush the solution on my brows and my eyes water at the chemical smell. When I wash it away, my carefully waxed brown arches have disappeared into my forehead. But for my brown eyes, I'd look almost albino.

I'm brushing my teeth when Mikhail raps on the door. "What?" I splutter, ungraciously.

He cracks the door and passes me a pair of scissors. I don't have the energy to object. I hold up a fistful of hair and chop it to chin length. Mikhail watches in the mirror as I inflict the same cut on the other side. "Do you want help with the back?" he asks.

I pass him the scissors and stare emotionlessly into the streaky mirror as the remainder of my tresses drop to the floor. He grabs a comb off the vanity and does a passable job of evening out my new bob. It's kicky, tapering forward from the back, and might even look cute if my hair weren't lemon yellow.

"Do you need something to sleep in?"

"No, uh, yes, that'd be great," I say, tearing my eyes from my unfamiliar reflection. He steps out. I close the door and brush my teeth with my finger.

He knocks, opens the door a crack, and hands me a clean blue Oxford shirt, which I accept without turning to face him. Of course I have nothing in the way of sleepwear. It's not like I planned on spending the night in the apartment of a man I just met.

I emerge from the bathroom, wearing Mikhail's shirt, which smells faintly like some expensive cologne I can't name. I walk over to the desk, where he's shutting down his laptop.

"It's not so bad," he says, too quickly,

"It's terrible!"

"You're right. I was being kind."

"And I'm trying to have some perspective," I say, as I gingerly finger a strand that's fallen on my face. It feels like straw. I'm screwing up my courage to ask what happens next, when he says we need to try to catch a few hours of sleep.

"You take the bed," he says. "I'm fine on the sofa."

"Absolutely not. I can't possibly put you out of your own bed. I mean, after all you've done for me today. You basically saved my life by keeping your mouth shut in the casino and I didn't even say thank you." A chill shoots up my spine as I hear the words come out. I'm beginning to wonder when my luck, if you can even call it that, will change.

"I don't think the statute of limitations on that has run out yet," he says, almost playfully.

"Well then, thank you. Korov would have killed me."

"Yes, he would have."

I wince.

"I'm still not letting you sleep on the sofa," I say. "I'll be fine there. I'm smaller than you."

"Nonsense," Mikhail says. "You're my guest and the subject is closed. Now try to get some sleep. It's going to be a stressful day." He folds his arms across his chest and blocks my path to the couch.

I cross the room and throw back the covers to climb into the bed, which also smells faintly of the same mystery cologne. I pull the sheet over me as he busies himself with retrieving a pillow and blanket from the closet. "Mikhail?"

"Yes?"

"You've worked undercover a long time, right?"

"For long enough, I suppose."

"Are you always terrified?" I feel ashamed, but I'm scared beyond the capacity for rational thought, and I want validation that my reaction is normal.

"Maybe not terrified, but always a little on edge," he concedes as he comes to stand over me. "You're going to be okay," he murmurs.

I look up at him and his expression *does* look reassuring. I fight back tears, successfully for once, probably because I'm too shocked by what he does next. Mikhail looks at me for a moment and plants a gentle kiss on my mouth. His lips only graze mine for a second and then he stands back up. "Goodnight, Lena."

I say goodnight back, and then I do something completely out of my normal character. I reach up and grab Mikhail by the opening of his shirt collar, pull him down towards me and kiss him. For real.

He freezes at first and his eyes fly wide open in shock, but that reaction only lasts a split second and then he kisses me back. His lips feel soft and full and taste a little salty. His tongue grazes the inside of my upper lip. I pull back. We pause, take stock of each other before he leans forward to kiss me again.

Mikhail climbs onto the bed next to me, not under the covers, but just on the edge of the mattress. I pull him towards me and lose myself in the feeling of his hands running up and down my sides. At some point his hand finds its way up my shirt (his shirt, really) and grazes my breasts. A quiet, almost sad moan escapes my lips. I feel his mouth on my neck and my ears. I moan again as he deftly unbuttons the blue oxford shirt that already smelled like him. Somewhere in the recesses of my brain, a little voice tells me this is wrong, but I silence it and enjoy the moment.

Somehow he ends up under the sheets on top of me. I pull his shirt over his head without bothering to undo the buttons. He hovers over me. He has a lithe, chiseled torso, with long, lean muscles reminiscent of an elite swimmer. His stubble scratches my face but I don't care. I close my eyes and breathe in his scent. And then he's inside me.

I am having sex with someone other than Damien. The little voice inside my head springs to action and shrieks, "SLUT!" My eyes fly open.

But then I see his eyes staring into mine, and for some reason I feel that everything is alright.

Afterwards we lie together for a long time, without saying anything. I close my eyes and order myself to go to sleep. At some point, Mikhail disentangles himself to get a glass of water. I watch him get up and cross the room, completely at ease in his own skin. He comes back with a glass for me, and says, "Now you really need to get an hour or two of rest." He kisses me on the mouth and climbs into bed next to me.

I must manage to doze, because the next thing I notice is that I'm in the bed alone. Mikhail's in the chair by the window, poring through some papers by the weak early light. I watch him through half-closed eyes for a while. He's somehow more self-possessed, more together, than any of the other men I know. He even scratches his chin with panache.

I close my eyes and contemplate what I've done. I am not cheating in the strict sense of the word, since Damien is *dead*. But while part of me is enjoying the afterglow, another part of me feels disloyal, embarrassed, guilty and maybe even a little dirty. I prop myself up on my right elbow and pull the sheet to cover my chest.

"Good morning," Mikhail says from his seat by the window. He's wearing blue plaid drawstring pajama pants, but hasn't bothered with a shirt. The ancient looking radiator throws off a surprising amount of heat.

"Good morning," I say, tentatively. "What time is it?" I don't wait for an answer, because as I form the words, my tired eyes focus on a picture on the nightstand.

It's a framed photograph of a bride so beautiful she could be in a magazine. She has sparkling eyes and impossibly high cheek bones, and long, elegant, mind-bogglingly thin arms. She's wearing a fluffy, multi-layered veil that most people would say is over the top, but on her it's gorgeous.

"You're *married*?" I shriek, and something in my gut tells me I want to kill him. Fortunately, my brain kicks in and stops me from following that base instinct. Mikhail, being a KGB spook or whatever he calls himself, could probably dispatch me with his bare hands.

19

"I was married," Mikhail says quietly. His tone could not sound more opposite mine. "Nadia died almost a year ago. Ovarian cancer."

Now I feel like a heel. "I'm so sorry."

Mikhail puts down the papers he was reading and stares out the window. "She was probably already sick on our wedding day."

I study the photo of a glowing, radiant, young woman. She couldn't possibly be dying.

"By the time she got the diagnosis, it was too late. They gave her six months, but she was dead before she made it to five."

"How awful."

"She didn't go to the doctor until the pain in her abdomen got so bad it affected her work. And by then it had to be awful, because she always powered through pain."

"What did she do?"

"She was a ballerina. At the Mariinsky Theatre. She was young, but her star was rising fast." Mikhail continues staring out the window.

A ballerina. They must have made a stunning couple. "She was a beautiful woman," I say, because I feel I should say something.

"Yes, she was, in more ways than one. She's the reason I'm so torn about my job."

"What do you mean?" Now I'm sitting up in bed all the way. This is too serious a conversation to have lying down.

"When Korov found out Nadia was sick, he used all his connections to try to help her. He got her in to see experts in London, Boston and Geneva. Nadia, thanks to his intervention, had the best possible shot at beating the cancer. He got her access to new drugs an ordinary Russian would have never received. Unfortunately, none of them helped. The doctors caught it too late."

I nod slowly, but have no idea what I should say.

"So, while as an agent of the government, my job is to ensure that Korov gets put away for a long time, and stripped of his empire, it's not so black and white for me. I know he's done a number of disgusting things, and been involved in God knows how many shady deals, but I've learned to admire his good side. The man's loyal to his key people and he thinks I'm one of them. And my job is to get close and betray him."

He takes a breath. "To make it all worse, over the five years I've been with the FSB, I've lost a lot of faith in our government. Maybe Russia needs a guy like Korov at the helm." He runs his hands through his tousled hair and scrunches his eyes shut as he rubs his temples.

A thud at the door shatters our contemplative silence. I jump.

"The paper." Mikhail gets up to retrieve it. "You need to see this."

He hands me this morning's *Moscow Daily*. Most of the front page, above the fold, is dominated by my picture. I knew it would be there but it still takes my breath away. I look more terrified than I expected. The photo shows the gun pressed to my right temple, but Casper and the other man have been cropped from the frame.

I stare at my image for a second, before letting the *Moscow Daily* drop to the floor.

"Are you okay?" Mikhail asks. He picks up the paper and studies my photo more closely. "It's not a bad shot, actually."

"Easy for you to say."

"Sorry. But seriously, it's a good thing we changed your hair last night. You could never venture out today otherwise. People would recognize you for certain."

"Can you read me what it says, instead of babbling about my looks?" I swipe the newspaper from his hands.

Mikhail says nothing during the brief moment it takes me to realize that the paper, of course, is in Russian. Instead of grabbing it back, he translates the article over my shoulder. It's not very long. Even so, I don't think he goes word by word, but rather gives me the gist.

"It says they believe a small group of Chechen rebels seized an American tourist *en route* from the airport into Moscow. It says the hostage's driver is believed to have escaped. Police are searching for him. The terrorists claim to represent the Caucasus Intifada, the same group that claimed responsibilty for the hotel bombing that targeted Vice President Prescott. They want the Americans to cough up a ransom of $100 million. They want the United States to recognize Chechnya as an independent state. They also demand that the U.S. government reopen its investigation of the January attacks on Washington, D.C."

"That will never happen." The whole world tilts under my feet, as if I'm suffering my own personal earthquake.

"Agreed. So it's a good thing this is only a staged kidnapping. It really doesn't matter what this says." His eyes scan the rest of the article.

"Read me the rest."

"The Caucasus Intifada says, that if its demands aren't met within seventy-two hours, they will behead the hostage," he recites apologetically. "But obviously that's impossible."

My left hand shoots up to shield my throat. I frown at Mikhail.

"Oh, come on, you're going to be something of a celebrity. Every Russian cop within a thousand miles will be looking for you. Our president would love to free the hostage, so he can have her, or you, home safe and sound before the American president arrives tomorrow."

I can't say anything. I feel as stunned as if I'd been smacked in the side of the head.

"We need to get moving." He goes to the closet and roots around the back shelves before emerging with a pair of jeans, a button down shirt and some socks. "Try those," he says.

I reluctantly do as I'm told, but I know there's no way I'm going to get a professional ballerina's pants over my hips. I'm shocked when they zip right up. I really need to start eating again. Mikhail flings a pair of brown and pink Puma trainers at me. "My wife's only practical footwear." Only half a size too small.

Mikhail gets on the phone. While he converses in Russian, he digs a pair of over-sized Bulgari sunglasses and a black ball cap out of a drawer. "Wear these," he mouths.

After he hangs up, he stands in the bathroom doorway and brings me up to speed. "The FSB is on it, as I knew they would be. But listen to this: They think the hostage's driver was also an American, a male FBI agent named Maxwell von Buren, who escaped. The

FSB thinks he was the intended target, but the terrorists grabbed the woman instead. They received a conflicting report, by way of an anonymous tip, which I would bet anything came from Korov's organization, claiming the hostage takers got the driver, too, and that his photo will be released later. They must have him, or they wouldn't have promised proof."

The world starts to spin faster. "What are you saying? Who has Max? There was no driver. The whole thing was rigged. You were there. Max had nothing to do with it." I can't form an entire coherent thought.

Max has been taken by real terrorists while I'm kidnapped by pretend ones? How can that be?

Mikhail, who appears oblivious to my confusion, has eased me out of the way so that he can brush his teeth and run a razor over his stubble. His calm infuriates me. I take a deep breath so I can explain myself without shrieking, but he beats me to the punch, "Don't you find it an interesting coincidence that some previously unknown band of operatives has taken a keen interest in abducting the same agent that Korov's concerned with?"

I don't get what he's driving at, so I say nothing.

"Damn it. I should have seen this coming, but *no*, I have to eat right out of his Goddamned hand. I'm such an *ass*. I believed him when he said he knew as little as I did, but of course his people, whoever they are, did this. " He switches to Russian and presumably continues to berate himself for reasons vague to me at best.

He lets out an almost anguished growl of frustration and punches the wall by the mirror. The plaster cracks. I scramble backwards out of Mikhail's path, hold my breath, pray he regroups fast.

When no further assaults on the building appear forthcoming, I ask, cautiously, "So what now?"

A hunk of broken plaster drops to the floor and shatters.

Mikhail scans the room with frantic eyes as if he might hit something else. Instead he pauses, collects himself and explains, "Casper and his associates, the men from last night who supposedly abducted you, might actually have grabbed this FBI agent. It's also possible that Korov is using new people, but hasn't seen fit to share that development with me. Which would beg the question, why?"

He slips past me into the living-slash-sleeping area and produces a clean shirt from his closet.

"Did you know before I said anything, that Casper is an FBI informant?"

He stops buttoning his shirt and turns the question over in his mind before answering. "Yes and no."

"What?"

"Yes, he's a known FBI informant, but I wouldn't vouch for the quality of his information."

"What do you mean by that?"

"I mean, sometimes he's right on. Other times he deliberately passes along bad intelligence, because some third party pays him to do so. Casper's a mercenary. He's for sale to the highest bidder. Lately, that's been Korov."

"I thought the Chechen separatists considered themselves freedom fighters and freedom fighters can't be bought." I hear myself parroting Max.

"Most of them can't. But Casper's been corrupted by power and money and the promise of influence. I've watched him devolve from idealism to pragmatism over the years. He sees a brighter future for his people under a friendlier Russian regime and not necessarily through the birth of an independent new state. I can't say he's wrong. An independent Chechnya would be tiny, devastated by years of war and landlocked by its sworn enemy."

"Okay. But if real terrorists kidnapped Max and are threatening to kill him if their demands aren't met, I honestly don't care whether they ever get their stupid Godforsaken country or not." I also don't care that I sound like a stereotypical ugly American. Mikhail's too serene in the face of this latest catastrophe and it's starting to piss me off.

"If your agent friend is indeed kidnapped, I suspect Korov's plans for him might be more violent than his plans for you. Anyway, are you ready to go?"

"That depends where you want to go."

"Well, I told Korov that we'll lie low until he gives me new marching orders." He's nonchalantly throwing a few things into a brown leather day pack: his camera, a notebook, a bottle of water. Banal stuff.

He can't be serious. I look at Mikhail with disgust and contemplate throttling him.

He must get the message because he adds, hastily, "But I have other ideas. We're going to find out what Korov's people have been up to, and if we get a little lucky, that'll lead us to your FBI handler."

It takes me a second to register what he means by handler, but I suppose the spy terminology isn't wrong. "Good. But how do you propose to do that without Korov catching on?"

"The FSB isn't the amateurish organization portrayed in so many Hollywood films. I'm certain I'm not the only government mole in Korov's empire. For security reasons, we're never aware of each others' identities." He pauses, as if considering whether to tell me more, slings the backpack over his shoulder and decides to keep talking.

"We have ways to reach out to one another in emergencies. I've sent a message asking for a meeting. We need to go to the appointed place."

"We?"

"I can't leave you unsupervised."

"I'm at least glad Max's predicament rates as an emergency."

"On its own it wouldn't," Mikhail says. *Bastard.* "But I thought I was on top of things and obviously I'm not."

"What if Korov finds out you're doing your own investigation?"

"He has no reason to suspect that. He has no idea I'm FSB or I'd be dead. I'm a loyal employee, remember?"

I can't think of a snappy retort, so I say nothing and watch with apprehension as he produces a black handgun from the nightstand and slides it into the waistband of his jeans at the small of his back, so his shirt conceals it.

"Just a normal precaution. Don't look scared. I'm sure your FBI friends have their Glocks with them at all times."

My mouth feels dry. I have a terrible premonition that I'll have to watch him shoot someone before the day is over.

His plan sounds dubious and vague at best. Maybe everything he's said to me is total bullshit. I'm worried sick about my family, who will wake up in a few hours to see me halfway around the world, held at gunpoint by terrorists. And I'm a little scared for Max. Maybe more than a little. But I don't know what I can do to help him, besides follow at Mikhail's heels as he steps out into the hallway and bounds down the stairs, two at a time, somehow almost silently.

Out on the street the sunlight blinds me until I remember the designer shades perched on my head. We walk three blocks to the subway and pass through the turnstiles into a tiled hallway with signs pointing in every possible direction. We ride down the longest escalator I've ever seen in my life. Its steps are made of wooden slats that look a hundred years old. Intricate wrought iron chandeliers with electric candles illuminate our descent. It's crowded, mostly with locals. I glance at my watch. Almost eight o'clock. The tourists are still snoozing in their hotel beds.

I attract more than a few sideways glances while we stand on the platform, but none of the commuters registers anything close to obvious shock or recognition. Maybe I just look foreign. Mikhail launches back into tour guide mode. "When the Soviets closed and looted Moscow's churches, they took much of the marble and artwork to decorate our world famous subway stations."

His narrative does the trick. Passersby lose interest in us and go back to their morning papers, all of which display me on the front page. I fight a fresh wave of nausea. The train arrives and we shuffle on board. It's cleaner and nicer than I would have expected, but crowded with commuters. Mikhail ushers me into one of the few open seats along the wall and he stands in front of me, holding the overhead bar as the train lurches forward and picks up speed. I see him studying someone else's newspaper.

Since his attention is momentarily elsewhere, I allow myself a couple of seconds to contemplate what we did last night. I guiltily admire his chiseled frame, impressive even underneath clothing, and tell myself that it had to happen sometime, and it might as well have been him. Even though I don't know him, really. They say stressful events bond people, but I hadn't expected to enjoy the first time with someone new quite so much. I wouldn't mind doing it again, I decide, as my eyes wander down below his belt. The sex was like a luxurious half hour suspension of the nightmare that is my life.

The man whose paper Mikhail had been reading prepares to disembark. I notice too late and Mikhail catches me staring at the bulge in his pants. I blush bright red. To his credit, Mikhail remarks only that we're getting off at the next stop. We push past an array of grouchy passengers and charge up an escalator that seems even longer than the last one.

I'm practically winded when we reach the top and emerge into sunny late winter morning. Vendors already crowd the sidewalk. Those selling beer appear to be doing the briskest business.

"We need to cross the street." Mikhail grabs my hand, sending an electric charge up my arm. He leads me through the traffic, his body between me and the relentless wave of Ladas, to the other side of the six-lane road, where we take a flight of stairs down to a small park by the Kremlin wall.

The park boasts a large café, populated mostly by locals. Mikhail steers us through the maze of tables and chairs to a spiral staircase and gestures that we're going up. I follow him upstairs to the first landing, to a door that says something in Russian. Underneath the neatly painted text, a hastily scrawled sign in English reads, "Only Employees."

Mikhail checks behind us to make sure we're alone, produces a key from his jeans pocket and thrusts it into the lock. I hear the click and he grabs my arm, pulls me inside and closes the door behind us. We're in a windowless room, illuminated by greenish fluorescent lights and littered with cardboard boxes and other debris.

When I see the man waiting for us all the air rushes from my lungs.

Casper and Mikhail stand and regard each other, mirror images of unmasked surprise. Each man has his right hand on his gun and his left hand raised halfway between greeting and warning.

Everything stands so still that I can hear them breathe. I look slowly from one to the other, wondering if this is it – has my luck, if you can call it that, finally run out?

Casper breaks the silence. "I should have known," he says in perfectly serviceable English, apparently for my benefit. The thick accent I heard back in Washington has vanished.

I feel my eyes bulge in disbelief and my breath catch halfway up my throat. Casper's voice is the one we heard last night, defending the use of a car bomb to kill Smerth. Mikhail must have known then that Casper killed my boss.

"I won't even pretend to have guessed," Mikhail says, eyes still locked on Casper's. Then he switches to Russian.

They have a measured exchange of some kind of pass phrases. At least that's what I presume they're doing based on my knowledge of spy protocol, which of course comes mainly from Hollywood.

After four rounds of back and forth, the men seem satisfied. By which I mean they lower their guns.

Mikhail asks in English, "But why would you, a proud Chechen and Muslim, *ever* work for the FSB? I can see how a relationship with Korov could benefit your people and your cause, but the regime? I don't get it."

Neither did Max, from what I recall of that strange morning in the hovel in Cleveland Park, where Casper and I first laid eyes on each other.

"Every man has his price," Casper says. "I'm well past the point of shame about that. It's money, pure and simple, but I'm not so interested in discussing our mutual career choices as I am in knowing why you called this emergency meeting."

Mikhail considers for a second, takes a deep breath and says, "Korov knows he's infiltrated. I'm not sure which of us he's onto, but this morning he flatly denied any connection to the missing FBI man in the papers."

"It's the girl," Casper says, as if I'm not standing ten feet from him. "Korov should have let Acheson's man in Washington kill her. But no. He can't do the ladies. So I had to swoop in and fix everything. And for what? I bet Korov saw her plant that listening device on the poker table. In one evening she compromised years of our work."

So much for thinking I was all slick. Casper glowers at me.

"No way. She'd be dead by now," Mikhail says.

"We tried. It seems she was not in her room, despite the lateness of the hour." Casper's eyebrows rise slightly.

I feel my blood go cold. Mikhail was right to keep me from returning to the Belgrade.

"Who's we?" he asks levelly.

"Acheson wants her dead and he's willing to pay. He finds Korov's kidnapping charade unnecessary, affected and stupid. His words, not mine. You know Acheson doesn't share Korov's squeamishness for killing the ladies."

Vomit rises in my throat and I feel like both my bladder and my legs could give out.

Maybe I've been right all along about Acheson being the killer.

But if Korov was about to implicate Aziz, and Acheson and Aziz fell out, then why wouldn't Acheson let Aziz take the heat for Damien's death?

If Mikhail can't smell that this is all profoundly wrong, we are screwed. Maybe Casper came here to kill us both. Or just me. He's here to finish last night's job and Mikhail marched me straight into the trap.

Frantically, I try to stall.

"I'm beginning to think someone really doesn't like me. I mean, first my office gets rocked by a terrorist attack and then my husband gets shot, and now I hear that someone came looking for me at my hotel last night." Both men regard me as if I've cracked. *Just keep talking, Lena, until you find a way out.* "And as of this morning, I've made the international headlines and not in a good way."

I shoot Mikhail a glance that's meant to communicate every doomsday scenario racing through my mind, but it probably comes across as a wild-eyed glare.

Casper grabs for his gun.

A sharp crack shatters the silence. Mikhail's shot hits its mark and Casper's gun flies out of his hand. Mikhail lunges for Casper, who's ignoring his injured right hand and diving for the gun, which Mikhail manages to kick across the floor in my general direction.

"Pick it up!" he shouts.

I scramble for the weapon. Mikhail kicks Casper in the chest with astounding force. Ribs crack.

Casper howls in protest but regains his footing and takes a swing at Mikhail with the closed fist of his left hand. Somehow Mikhail manages to duck the punch. Before Casper can regroup and swing again Mikhail raises his gun in the air and brings the barrel crashing down on the back of the other man's head. Casper drops into a heap on the floor.

"For God's sake, don't point that thing at the floor. Point it at him!" Mikhail lowers his own weapon and starts poring through the contents of Casper's pockets. He tears open the unconscious man's shirt.

"Is he d-d-d-dead?" I stammer, unsure of whether I want him to be or not. The gun is far heavier than it looks and I need both hands to hold it steady. My fingers start to cramp because they're shaking, but I'm trying so hard to keep them still.

"I don't think so, but his head will hurt for a while," Mikhail replies as he pulls apart Casper's undershirt. "Fuck," is all he manages to spit out. I peer over Mikhail's shoulder and see what even I can tell is a wire.

"Fuck," Mikhail repeats. Then, with eerie calm and a steady hand, he rips the wire from Casper's body, places the barrel of his gun between the slumped man's eyes and squeezes the trigger. I wrench my eyes closed and bite my tongue to keep from screaming.

When I peek out of one eye, most of Casper's face is gone, reduced to a bloody mess on the grimy tile. I start to gag. Mikhail, looking nonplussed, reaches under the dead man's waistband and produces a little black box. I presume it has something to do with the wire. He empties Casper's pockets and takes a phone and a small, thick book.

"Holy Quran?"

"It's a Bible, oddly enough." He shoves the book in his bag along with the spy paraphernalia. He yanks down the dead man's pants.

Casper has the biggest knife I've ever seen in my life sheathed and strapped to his leg.

They'll decapitate the hostage.

I stumble backward, delirious with panic, blind to the fact that the would-be knife wielder can't hurt me anymore.

"We're out of here," Mikhail says.

His cool tone snaps me back to reality. Everyone downstairs must have heard the shots. Mikhail can't possibly expect us to walk out the way we came in. He takes Casper's gun from me and places it in his waistband. He switches the lights off and we're plunged into darkness until he opens the door a crack and sticks his head into the corridor. "All clear. Let's go."

I freeze.

"Don't worry," he says, as if reading my thoughts. "Soundproofed room." I follow Mikhail down the stairs, trying to look as cool and natural as possible. It was self defense, I tell myself.

We hurry out of the café, up a stairway by a fountain that's getting crowded with people taking pictures and children launching toy boats. I jog to keep up with Mikhail as he bounds up the steps, two at a time. We shove past a French tour group and finally reach the sidewalk. Mikhail's arm slices the air. A taxi swerves towards us from the far lane, cutting off two other cars and setting off a symphony of horns. Before the vehicle comes to a full stop, Mikhail yanks the door open. He shoves me inside, slides in beside me and directs the driver in Russian.

"How did you know he was ready to kill you?" he hisses.

"Lucky intuition, I guess. And his remark about me not being in my hotel room made my blood run cold. How did you know I had a hunch?"

"Your eyes. They had blind panic in them," Mikhail whispers. "But hunches like that will serve you well."

"I'm not so sure. I'm not accustomed to my hunches getting people killed." Tears start to well once again.

"If it makes you feel better, I would've preferred to keep him alive and interrogate him. Then I saw the wire and did what I had to do. Besides, he was working too many sides. I had to do away with him before he screwed me over. It's better that he's out of the way."

I nod, and a lone tear trickles down my cheek. I brush it away. I am not going to have a meltdown. At least not right now. "I saw my husband murdered. I mean, my friend Diana and I found him, but I've never seen anyone actually die before."

I don't know whether it's the recollection of that horrible night in DC, or the hideous experience of having witnessed a killing, but I feel myself start to unravel.

Whoever was listening to Casper's wire now knows I am spying on Korov. Did I just sign my own death warrant? Or maybe it was Henry's wire and I just witnessed—indeed provoked—the murder of an American agent.

Then again the wire could have been Clearwater's. Or Acheson's. Or Korov's. The possibilities hurt my head. Which I guess is Mikhail's point.

Mikhail gazes at me. "I know it's been an awful twenty-four hours. You're holding up great." I feel unreceptive to his pep talk, possibly because he's not the first agent to tell me I'm hanging in there. Not that my supposed grit has gotten me anywhere good. I shrug and look through the grimy window at the city whizzing by.

"Where are we going?" I ask. I run my fingers under my eyes once more, to head off any lingering tears, waiting to take advantage of the next, inevitable emotional speed bump in the road.

"Railway station. My cover's totally blown, as is yours, I'm afraid. That room was soundproof to the outside but his wire was working."

So that's it. We're hunted prey.

And I've burned my bridge with Korov, which means I'm no closer to proving who killed Damien.

"What about Max?" I protest.

"I'm working on it, but I've made one massive tactical error today and lived to tell about it. I can't afford another." He looks racked with guilt.

I hesitate a moment, then tentatively place my hand on top of his. I half expect him to pull away.

He doesn't. He takes my hand and holds it for the rest of the fifteen minute trip.

20

We pull into a parking area crowded with vendors, travelers and loiterers of every type and description. Fruit sellers hawk their wares next to booths offering pirated movies, many of which haven't even opened in theaters yet. As we disembark into the chaos, a scraggly girl with French braids and a backpack almost her size rumples up a subway map in frustration. She tearfully announces to her equally overburdened boyfriend, and any other English speaker within a fifty-foot radius, that they are taking a taxi. They waylay our abandoned cab.

Mikhail grabs my hand and we weave through the throng into a gigantic departure hall. I follow for a few steps and stop.

Now I'm supposed to join an outed KGB agent as he barrels out of Moscow to points unknown? On the other hand, the number of scary individuals who would prefer me deceased is mounting at an alarming rate. Maybe sticking with a highly trained professional would be smart, given the dearth of more attractive options. My mind's eye focuses on the threat of decapitation. Just because Casper didn't finish the job doesn't mean Acheson can't hire someone else to try.

I gaze longingly at an ordinary Russian cop enjoying a cigarette not thirty feet away. He looks non-threatening. He's no more than a kid. Maybe I should turn myself in to him. He could help me get to the American embassy.

Or maybe Korov owns plenty of cops. Stop being a dummy, Lena.

Better to follow the devil I know.

Mikhail whisks us down two flights of urine stained stairs to the lockers, a dark cavern deserted except for one filthy, nearly comatose man who's slumped against the wall, using what little energy he has to probe his arm with a needle.

I've watched a man die, shot, point blank, a few feet away from me. I'm going to have to tell the FBI that while kidnapped and bundled off to Russia, I attempted to freelance and imperiled their efforts along with my own safety. In my temporarily insane state, I slept with a complete stranger. My mind settles on this last fact, perhaps because it's the easiest to digest.

While we were together last night, all my problems were momentarily suspended. But now I feel like I've betrayed my dead husband by hopping into bed with Mikhail because I felt fragile. Which is ridiculous. I should put the whole episode out of my mind. It was a blip. A moment of frailty brought on by severe emotional strain. Nothing more.

A small key from Mikhail's front pocket opens an eye-level locker in the farthest corner of the hall. I watch him empty a packet of papers—money or passports, I imagine—as well as a gun and an ammunition clip into his backpack.

"Next stop: your embassy." He closes the empty locker and leaves its key in the lock.

We hurry back upstairs, stepping over a man passed out on the concrete at the top landing. He's hugging an empty vodka bottle like a child would hold a teddy bear and sleeping the unconscious slumber of the totally inebriated.

Mikhail grabs my hand and steers me to the station's depressing little bar, the only permanent enterprise in sight. My eyes bulge in disbelief. He's stopping for a cocktail? Mikhail waves the barman to a row of empty seats at the far left. The half dozen customers at the other end all look half in the bag.

I think I catch the barman's eyes flicker at Mikhail with recognition, but by the time I process what this could mean, he's resumed his blank expression. He's young, probably in his early twenties, average looking in every way. He and Mikhail go through a laborious exchange of clipped phrases that sounds too complicated for ordering the two shots of vodka the barman pours. Mikhail passes him some money, which he drops into a drawer under the bar. When he pops back up, he passes Mikhail an envelope along with his change. In one motion, Mikhail settles onto a bar stool, shoves the envelope down his pants and says we need to move along.

We leave without touching the drinks, and exit the station through a side entrance. We hurry past a couple of farmers attempting to sell old onions and potatoes to commuters passing through. Across from their stands, a woman with a wart on her nose peddles scratch tickets from behind a rickety card table. A janitor shuffles along with his crude broom made from sticks, pushing dirt and debris from one spot on the platform to another.

A long queue of cabs waits along the curb. Mikhail approaches a forty-something man with cloudy eyes, a mustache and an olive-green Lada that's seen better days. They have a brief conversation in hushed Russian. The stranger's face lights up with delight and an envelope brimming with cash changes hands.

The man holds it close between himself and Mikhail as he counts, so that none of his nosy neighbors can see what's transpiring. He feels the bills one at a time between his thumb and forefinger and counts them twice. Satisfied, he folds the envelope and tucks the money into his pocket. He hands Mikhail a single key, which he removes from an overloaded keychain, and walks away. He's trying to look casual, but there's a slight spring in his step.

"You just bought this piece of crap?" I can't help the incredulity in my voice. The conveyance Mikhail has procured for fifteen hundred dollars, if I counted right, looks as if the wheels will fall off at any moment.

"I did. Now get in, before anyone takes an interest in us. If that man lets it slip that we have this kind of cash, the entire neighborhood will swarm us in a matter of seconds."

From the passenger seat of the Lada, I see a muscle bound blond man in fatigues watching us from only a few feet away. He sports combat boots, a crew cut and mirrored aviators. An enormous tattoo of an eagle graces his neck. Its outstretched talons graze his Adam's apple. He's the kind of guy I might cross the street to avoid if walking alone after dark. And I can't shake the feeling that he looks awfully familiar. He watches me studying him through the car window. He turns and walks into the station.

21

The Lada produces an impotent clatter when Mikhail turns the key. He tries again. The engine splutters in protest before rattling to life. Whatever the state of its motor, the heat works all too well. Hot air blasts my face and no amount of fiddling with the rudimentary controls tempers its assault. Mikhail wriggles out of his coat and tosses it into the back seat. I do the same.

"What did the bartender give you?"

His eyes don't leave the road. "Something I need. It couldn't wait." Right. Why would he share with me? I hear a noise that's half sigh and half growl of frustration escape my lips.

Mikhail grinds his teeth, tightens his grip on the wheel and navigates around the biggest potholes I've ever seen onto the ramp for an elevated highway. "I'd like to deliver you to your embassy, not the airport. I don't like the idea of leaving you unaccompanied, and not even Korov is brazen enough to take a shot at you on diplomatic soil. Any objections?" He maneuvers the Lada between an endless series of car swallowing craters.

"Yes, If we're going to the embassy, why are you leaving the city?"

"Traffic. It's much faster to jump on the ring roads than to snake across town."

Fair enough. Part of me can't wait to get back on U.S. soil. For the first time in my life, I understand how a person could be thankful enough to be home that they'd kiss the ground. But if we go to the embassy, I'll never get that tape. I wonder if there would still be a chance. We merge onto a larger, divided highway and the pace of traffic picks up.

"Whoever killed Damien is going to get away with it, aren't they? Korov's never going to give me that tape. Right? Am I right?" I sound shrill, and more than a little unhinged.

Mikhail gets no chance to answer. We hear a sharp crack, like the sound of a large vehicle backfiring. One of our rear tires blows out. Seconds later another tire explodes. Mikhail screams at me to get my head down. I dive face first into the foot well with my hands protecting my skull as much as possible.

A bullet takes out the Lada's back window. Glass flies and I hear myself shriek again as the bullet rockets out the windshield.

Glass rains onto us. Mikhail slams on the brakes. I think he screams, but it might be me again.

The Lada careens into a cement barrier, spins twice and comes to a halt facing oncoming traffic. I slam against the dashboard at least twice before landing in a heap. When the motion stops, I move one arm slowly, then the other, followed by each leg. I feel my face for signs of injury and realize I'm bruised but alright. When I turn my head up a narrow sliver of glass tumbles from my hair and spears the well worn vinyl seat.

A white and blue police van appears out of nowhere, pulls up immediately behind us and blocks the far right lane. Traffic cruises by as if the drivers saw nothing. At home people slow to a crawl and rubberneck at car crashes, even without the added excitement of a shooting. Here they apparently speed up and mind their own business. At least the police presumably saw the whole incident. That means someone will be hunting whoever is trying to kill us. Things could be worse, I try to persuade myself. Things could always be worse.

Five or six men in camouflage clothes and black ski masks pour out of the police van. My heart sinks. These are not good Samaritans. I doubt they're even tangentially connected to any branch of law enforcement. I choke rising vomit back down my throat. Mikhail yells something in Russian. The men say nothing.

These thugs, who presumably shot us off the highway mere seconds ago, surround the mortally wounded Lada. Mikhail has his hands up by the time he's yanked from behind the wheel. Four men train their sizable guns on him. The Lada's passenger door flies open. Someone grabs me by the upper arm and pulls me out.

"You come with me," the man says. He tightens his grip on my bicep. He reeks of sweat. My teeth chatter as every muscle shakes with fear.

I summon the nerve to look up at my captor. An eagle tattoo peeks out from under his mask. I hate myself for not voicing my concerns earlier. But what was I supposed to say? A creepy guy looked at me and walked back inside the station?

Yes, Lena, that's precisely what you should have said. Especially since he looks like the jogger who leered at you when you were in MacPherson Square with Charlie.

We are so screwed. The fingers of my free hand touch the lump in my throat.

Mikhail protests vigorously and in multiple languages. One of the men smacks him in the side of the head with the butt of his rifle. He starts to drop but catches himself. I wonder if they will shoot us right here on the side of a public highway in the middle of the day. My heart feels like it's about to give out. The barrel of a gun jabs between my shoulder blades.

"Let's walk, darling," Eagle Tattoo Man says, in what sounds an awful lot like a Texas twang.

I manage to stumble forward. Out of the corner of my eye, I see one of our captors begin the process of confiscating Mikhail's weapons. Eagle Tattoo Man hurries me towards the back of the van. My mind might be playing tricks on me, but I think I see Mikhail bolt away from the group and run towards oncoming traffic. Horns blare, tires screech and gunfire rattles. Male voices yell. I see none of it.

Eagle Tattoo Man shoves me into the back seat of the van and slides the door shut. The engine rumbles to life.

22

"Who are you?" I demand, my voice equal parts terror and disdain.

The driver jerks the van into traffic with the police lights flashing. He sits alone in the front seat, with a thick glass barrier behind him, and all I can see is the closely shaven back of his head. I wonder if he plans to circle back to collect either his comrades or Mikhail. My captor and I are in the back row of the van, with an empty bench seat in front of us.

"CIA," he says.

Bullshit, I think, as I acknowledge his response with a slow nod.

"Where are you taking me?"

"I'm afraid that's classified." He pronounces it class-ih-faad. The driver navigates into the left lane and accelerates. Eagle Tattoo Man places his gun in his lap and removes his mask with one hand. Not an auspicious sign. He clearly isn't concerned about my ability to identify him at some vague later date.

The eagle on his neck and jaw clutches a confederate flag in its foreshortened talons, along with a banner which reads: "Freedom ain't free!" The "ain't" moves up and down with his Adam's apple and creates the illusion that the middle of the cartoonish banner is waving.

Cold sweat beads along my middle back and down my chest, between my breasts. "I thought CIA men couldn't wear tattoos." I know I sound less than diplomatic, but this brute is probably going to kill me. For some difficult to explain reason, I'd like to know my future murderer's identity.

"What would you know about it?" He strokes the barrel of his gun almost affectionately, like someone might pet a much-loved kitten.

The driver pumps the brakes. We're approaching what must be a merge point with another major road. Traffic is markedly heavier, but still moving. If I had to guess, I'd say we're going about thirty or forty miles per hour. It's hard to tell for sure. The driver raps on the barrier with his knuckles. Eagle Tattoo Man switches on an earpiece and tells him to drive on.

My captor has ice blue eyes. The whites are bloodshot. Fuck it. "You want to know what I know about it? I know enough to say that CIA operatives don't abduct their fellow American citizens at gunpoint."

"Don't they?" he asks, with a grin far too lascivious for my liking. I try to suppress the shudder climbing my spine, a futile effort that results in my shoulders twitching neurotically. He removes his earpiece and looks me up and down. I follow his gaze to the floor and feel my face go white. For an awful second, the rush of blood makes me think I'm about to faint.

Inches away from my feet, stowed neatly under the seat in front of us, are several yards of rope and three cinder blocks. He follows my gaze to the suspicious provisions and shoots me a sadistic grin. Not only does he plan to kill me, but he might derive considerable pleasure from doing so. My breathing has turned so shallow and short I'm afraid I may hyperventilate. Get a grip, I order myself. If you panic, you're dead for sure.

"Alright. I'll play your game," I hear myself say. "Why would the CIA want to do away with little, insignificant me?"

"Because we eliminate anyone who stumbles *close* to interfering with our business," he says, as if this is obvious. "And your mucking around pisses my bosses off."

"Which bosses?"

He shrugs and glances out the window at the traffic.

"So why didn't you shoot me back there?" I ask.

"C'mon, aren't you supposed to be a smart little bitch, what with all your hoity toity Yankee education and all? Do you need to ask?" He pauses to study my face for hints of comprehension. "You're a mighty pretty girl. Mighty, mighty pretty. I'm gonna enjoy what I didn't have time for the other day. It's so much better if you're awake, all nice and scared and full of fight." He wags his tongue at me. I feel my eyes bulge at him, appalled. His hand lands in my lap. I recoil towards the far edge of the bench seat but his fingers grasp my thigh with the finesse of a steel vice. The tips of his fingers fondle the inside of my leg. I feel like I'm trapped underwater and out of air.

Because I can't breathe, I throw up.

The minimal contents of my stomach spew all over myself and his hand, which he jerks away as if he'd inadvertently submerged it in acid. The gun crashes from his lap to the floor. For a split second neither of us moves or exhales. The weapon comes to rest quietly, its bullets presumably secure in their chambers.

"Jesus Christ!" he barks, as soon as he looks sure the firearm won't discharge and blow off a chunk of his leg. "You vile, stinking bitch." He rolls down his window and gulps at the highway air. Then, without warning, he lunges at me and rips my shirt off. I swat at his arms ineffectually, but he's too fast and too strong. He balls the shirt up and flings it out the window. I cross my arms over my chest as defensively as possible.

He lights a cigarette and inhales deeply. "That oughta fix the worst of the stench, dontcha think?" He pronounces "think" as "thank." He ashes on the floor of the van. Up front, the driver appears oblivious to the disturbance. I glance out and notice a sign with a symbol for some kind of campground or wilderness recreation area. I wonder how big a park it is, and whether it's the kind of place criminals would use to dispose of bodies.

The exit is ten kilometers away. Which means we'll be there in no time, since we've reached a well maintained, likely newer, stretch of highway. There's a neatly mown grass median, and far fewer ruts and potholes pock the asphalt.

Eagle Tattoo Man tosses his cigarette onto the highway and reaches for another.

"Could I please have one?" I ask.

"You smoke?"

"It might help get rid of the vomit taste in my mouth."

"Fair 'nuff." I hold the cigarette in my trembling fingers while he lights it for me. He lights his own and swishes the match to extinguish it. I take a deep drag and cough. He laughs at me.

Now or never. I take another, much smaller puff. As I breathe out the smoke, I lurch towards Eagle Tattoo Man and ram the smoldering cigarette into his right eye. He yowls in pain. I fling myself over the back of the seat. He grabs for me but his hand only swats at my waist. The back door of the van has an emergency hatch. If it's locked I'll be dead in the next three seconds.

Without thinking, I fling up the latch. It gives.

Eagle Tattoo Man fumbles over the seat after me, still mashing one hand into his wounded eye.

The brain is a bizarre organ. Instead of contemplating the slim chance that I will survive the next minute, I wonder whether I blinded my tormentor as I push the rear door open and lunge out of the moving vehicle.

23

I try my best to tuck and roll as my unprotected shoulder crashes onto the gravelly shoulder of the road. Brakes screech. Tires squeal. Metal crashes. Someone screams.

I pick my face out of the breakdown lane in time to see Eagle Tattoo Man's body crushed by one of those monstrous, clattering eighteen wheelers that transport cars.

I push the ground away and roll my bruised body down a short, steep embankment. It seems like a good idea to put as much distance as possible between me and the speeding cars, which are cutting left and right to get around the accident scene as quickly as possible. When I glance up at the roadside, I see a few vehicles pulled over. My heart sinks.

I force myself to look again. A busload of orthodox nuns scoot down the embankment towards me. Their black robes flap in the breeze as they advance. They resemble a flock of super-sized ravens.

A matron with a tight brown perm peeking from under her head covering reaches me first and squats at my shoulder. She fires a series of questions at me in Russian. I blink back and finally find the presence of mind to ask if she speaks English. She shakes her head no as a dozen of her holy sisters encircle us. Someone helps me sit up. My hips ache as if they've been slugged with a sledgehammer. My pants are torn. I'm bleeding from both knees, both elbows and my right shoulder. My left ankle throbs, but I don't think I've broken any bones. One of the sisters starts reciting something I recognize by its cadence as the Lord's Prayer.

One of the younger nuns yells a word resembling "ambulance." She hikes her robes to knee level and rushes back up the embankment, presumably to summon help from their driver. I sit on the ground, dazed, and study the shreds of filthy fabric framing my bloodied kneecaps. Tears of relief well in my eyes as I process that this busload of nuns probably does not desire to rape, torture or kill me. And whoever Eagle Tattoo Man's friends are, they might think twice before massacring a busload of nuns.

I wipe my eyes with the backs of my grubby hands and notice that I've got more than a little gravel ground into the bloody scrapes on both palms. It will hurt to clean them out. This stark and clinical observation snaps me back to reality. A young nun, who doesn't look much past twenty, extends a hand to help me up. "Do you speak English?" she asks haltingly, her blue eyes round with disbelief.

"Yes." Her companions watch as I take a deep breath, clasp her wrist and hoist myself to my feet. It hurts to move, but it's not impossible.

"Did you see where the van went?" I ask, suddenly frantic to know. Because upon further consideration, I doubt Eagle Tattoo Man's associate would think twice about circling back and mowing down every last nun with a machine gun, in order to secure the privilege of tearing me limb from limb.

"No," the young nun says. "A man fall out. A big truck runned him over. I'm sorry."

"Don't be." I sob with relief that his death wasn't a mirage. One of the older nuns steps forward and drapes an arm over my shoulders. She smells of moth balls and her habit is scratchy but I lean into her and shake and cry until I hear ambulance sirens shrieking, way off in the distance. I realize that the nuns, in their rush to help me, have registered zero concern about Eagle Tattoo Man. Perhaps they saw the whole thing and understand that nobody could survive that kind of crush. Though you'd think at least one of them would be curious enough to go poke at his corpse or say whatever prayers they recite for the dead.

Horns blare much closer by. Up the hill brakes squeal and gravel flies. My body tenses. If I have to run, I have nowhere to go but across the median and into highway traffic.

Uphill, car doors fly open and slam shut. My stomach crunches under a fresh wave of fear.

"Lena!" Mikhail barrels down the embankment, yelling "FSB!" in English, as if that means anything to the nuns.

Mikhail pushes through the flock of holy sisters. He holds me at an arm's length by the shoulders. "I think I look worse than you do," he says finally. His head sports a nasty gash that looks like it could resume bleeding with the slightest wrong move. He probably needs stitches. As he looks me up and down, I realize that I'm still shirtless. The young nun with some English skills must make the same observation, because she dashes up the embankment to the bus and returns bearing a men's white dress shirt. She must have taken it off the driver's back.

I stammer thank you. I put on the shirt and roll up the sleeves so they aren't flapping over my hands. I turn back to Mikhail. "How?" is all I can manage to ask.

"Let's say these particular weekend warriors won't bother us again. I also commandeered us a much nicer ride." He gestures uphill at a black Mercedes sedan in the break down lane. His eyes study every face in the small crowd. Finally he makes some kind of announcement in Russian. I get nothing but "FSB." The nuns listen attentively and file back to their bus as soon as Mikhail stops talking. A few mutter quiet prayers as they pass me. The one whose shoulder I cried into crosses me and herself and tells me in barely recognizable English to "Go always with God." She presses a Russian Bible into my hands and makes the sign of the cross over me before joining her sisters up the hill.

Their bus rattles to life, emits a blast of diesel exhaust and clatters away.

Ambulance sirens wail, closer now. More horns blare. They can't be far away.

I wonder if I need tests for internal bleeding. Or if I should have my hips x-rayed, just in case. My various aches are growing more pronounced by the minute, probably because the surge of adrenalin that propelled me out of the van is wearing off.

Mikhail says abruptly, "Let's move."

"You don't want to wait for the ambulance?"

"You look healthy enough to skip the hospital." He hurries me back to car. I sink into the black leather seat. Mikhail sprints around to the other side. When the engine starts with a purr, he smiles and says, "You didn't think I'd let those animals drive away with you, did you?"

"I honestly didn't know what to think. All I knew was that I had to get away from that man." I shudder again and wonder if his menacing face will be seared in my brain forever.

Mikhail puts the car in drive but creeps along in the break down lane instead of joining traffic. He stops abruptly, flips on the hazard lights, jumps out and runs toward the front of the car. He hoists Eagle Tattoo Man's lifeless form by the armpits, drags it to the back by way of the passenger side, and heaves it into the trunk, which he slams shut.

We're on our way again.

As far as I can tell, nobody but the nuns slowed to process the scene. I can understand folks being busy, or minding their own business, but this is ridiculous. I say something to this effect.

"Unfortunately, we live with so much gang violence that bystanders have learned it's best to keep their heads down," Mikhail says, as he shifts lanes.

"Who is he?" I motion towards the trunk.

"His friends were all BXE employees. You know, Vice President Prescott's cousin's firm. Might as well be called Thugs-R-Us. Mikhail makes a disgusted face. "Our friend in the trunk was probably called in to finish the job when Casper failed."

"You mean an American security contractor just tried to kill us?"

"You've got it. Let's move before they call in their reserves."

24

The Mercedes accelerates and Mikhail steers into the left lane.
"Where are we going?" I'm annoyed I need to ask.
"I owe you an apology," he says.
Great. A non-answer.
"I should have taken you to the embassy before running my errand at the station and finishing my job. After the thing with Casper. I didn't handle my blown cover as well as I should have. I panicked. I'm sorry."
I ignore his apology. "What job do you mean? I thought a blown cover meant game over in your line of work."
"I shouldn't say any more. The less you know, the better."
"You're saying this to me *now*? Seriously?"
Mikhail responds with stony quiet.
We veer onto an exit ramp. Mikhail slams on the brakes to slow to the pace of city traffic. We pass endless rows of depressing concrete apartment blocks. The buildings sit so close together that it's hard to tell where one ends and another begins. Many have dirt yards, littered with household trash, broken toys and construction debris.
A few hundred meters later, we turn a corner onto an immaculate, tree lined residential street. I deduce from the flags on each façade that we've arrived on Moscow's version of Embassy Row. The U.S. Embassy is an enormous stone building, surrounded by heavily armed guards in bulletproof vests who patrol in the shadow of its iron fence. There are cameras everywhere.
At first I think my eyes are playing tricks on me.
Henry waits, pacing at the gate like an anxious watch dog. He must assume Mikhail's merely a hired driver, because he orders the guard to wave us through, without asking any questions. Mikhail parks among a fleet of a dozen Mercedes sedans, all bearing diplomatic plates.

His eyes boggle when he sees Henry Redwell. "Cheshire," he says under his breath, with a mix of reverence and surprise. "You must be really important to someone."

"Cheshire?"

"Henry Redwell."

"Why do you look more like a recent veteran of an armed conflict than like a high level attaché?" Henry demands of Mikhail before turning to me. He's beaming. "My dear, I am thrilled to see you. We thought you were dead. Were you mistreated? You look like you've run through the ringer."

"All these people who want me dead are awfully tenacious." I feel my face start to crumble. "Why didn't you come for me? Didn't you hear me through the bug?"

"We had no contact, no knowledge of your whereabouts," Henry says. "I was afraid Acheson had done away with you. I'm delighted to see that's not the case." He turns to Mikhail. "Who exactly are you?"

Mikhail shows his FSB credentials and sarcastically thanks Henry for being so grateful for the rescue of an American civilian. I resist the urge to interject that I pretty much rescued myself.

Henry marches us up the cobblestone walkway, past several scrupulously maintained flowerbeds, to the entrance.

As the doorman admits us, Henry whispers, "Don't forget, the place is wired by us, you and God knows who else." He turns to Mikhail. "Young man, you have a choice. If you wish to accompany us, I must insist you submit to a biometric scan. Which should pose no problem, if you are who you say you are." Henry looks the Russian up and down. "Afterwards, you're welcome to avail yourself of the house medic's services."

"Of course," Mikhail says, as if being offered a coffee.

I'm surprised he'd agree, but what do I know about international spy relations? Maybe this is normal protocol.

A pretty receptionist with a bun and funky pink-framed eyeglasses greets us from behind an enormous mahogany desk with ball and claw feet. On Henry's instructions, she summons an escort for Mikhail. She does a double take when she notices that we're both in rough shape. She stares longer than would be polite at our cut up faces and torn clothes, but refrains from commenting. Instead she emerges from behind the desk and ushers us down a hallway lined with portraits of men in suits to a lavishly appointed sitting room occupied by a diminutive woman. Her face is obscured by a colorful Missoni scarf.

Henry closes the door behind us as soon as the receptionist leaves. "Lena, meet Katya."

The woman straightens in her chair and lets her scarf fall.

I know her. She's the waif of a woman who saw me at R&S the night I broke into Acheson's office. She looks exhausted and something about her body language, the way she's looking into space to avoid eye contact, conveys fear.

Smerth's *nanny* is Katya? The terrorist Katya, who Casper claimed was in charge of blowing up K4? It seems impossible. I know some terrorist groups use women these days, but the female operatives you see on TV normally fit a mold – brooding, hardened, determined. They have a score to settle and nothing to lose. This Katya looks like a garden variety scared rabbit. Albeit a well-dressed one.

"Katya is a key informant." Henry winks at me conspiratorially. I have no idea if he's serious or not.

I'm about to blurt that Mikhail said Katya and Aziz are an item. But something about Henry's overall demeanor stops me from sharing. I want to know what he's cooked up, and if it's a trap for this Katya person, perhaps I shouldn't be yelling, "Hey! Terrorist Lady! Look! A trap!"

Henry motions for us to sit around the ornately carved round table. "The Smerths hired Katya, who's a Bulgarian national, to look after their youngest son." He looks me in the eye and cocks his head as if to ask whether any of this sounds familiar.

"So she got caught overstaying her visa, and that's why she cooperated when you started asking questions about the blocker company in Bermuda," I recite.

"Exactly," says Henry. "Except she failed to convey all the relevant facts. For starters, she never mentioned that Aziz caught her red-handed in Smerth's home study, reading Lotus bank records to us over the phone while her charge napped in his nursery."

Katya looks like she could die of shame.

"What was Aziz doing at the Smerth residence when the nanny was home alone?" I ask.

"Our bug heard him explain he was in the neighborhood. He wanted to drop off an invitation to some charity ball," Henry says. "But, somewhat curiously, he'd admitted himself through the back door."

Katya nods emphatically.

"That's ridiculous. Aziz doesn't run his own errands. And even if he did, nobody saw him?" I ask.

"He drives a brand new Mercedes. He blends right in, and if he were questioned about breaking and entering, he has diplomatic immunity," Henry says. He clears what sounds like a bullfrog from his throat. "Getting back to the crux of the matter, Aziz told Katya that this could be 'their little secret,' on the condition that she leave the Smerths' household to come work for him. Katya, in a panic, agreed on the spot. Smerth didn't object. He saw it as a win-win. The embarrassing illegal domestic would be off his hands, but he wouldn't need to remove her name from any corporate documents. Aziz was cunning enough not to mention that he caught the nanny snooping. Smerth, for his part, simply assumed that Aziz thought Katya would make an attractive addition to his household entourage."

I finish the analysis. "And Smerth was too arrogant to consider that his nanny might take an interest in the affairs of his offshore entity, even if she was nominally on the board."

Henry nods. "Aziz kept at least a portion of his bargain. He provided Katya with a new identity and a diplomatic passport from the Dominican Republic."

"Why?" I don't see what diplomats from the Dominican Republic have to do with this whole mess. I'm tired, feeling defeated, and increasingly anxious about why Henry is telling me any of this. But still curious.

"So I could run his errands unchallenged and come and go from the United States," Katya says. "Mostly I accompanied Mr. Aziz wherever he went. The diplomatic passport from the Caribbean was believable. Lots of rich Arabs procure them for their servants. They only cost about a hundred thousand dollars."

I feel a rush of sympathy for Katya. She's been sucked into a dangerous mess, way over her head. She's been a pawn. Not unlike myself. I doubt Mikhail's right about Katya being Aziz's girlfriend. Henry would never rely on her to pass along good information, if he suspected her of harboring even a passing affection for her employer.

I ask if I can have a private word with Henry.

"No need," he says. "Our plans have evolved within the past twenty-four hours."

"What do you mean *our* plans?" I feel spent from all of this fruitless dashing from point to point with only vaguely defined objectives, like "stopping explosions," "following the money," and worst of all, "running for my life."

None of which has brought me a single step closer to learning the truth about Damien's death. *I need to stay in Russia, get one last chance to confront Korov about the tape.*

Henry interrupts my train of thought. "When Aziz learned that Katya was working with us, he exploited a golden opportunity. He had her pretend that the INS was still hounding her, so that she could relay all kinds of information that was good enough to send us scrambling in a certain direction, but which ultimately dead ended."

"Like all the files in Bermuda. They looked promising and led nowhere," I say.

"Precisely," says Henry. "But now it turns out Aziz wants to help us stop his former associates from pulling off the assassination. Since Acheson and Prescott became cozy with his nephew Muhammed, Aziz believes the status quo is preferable to a Prescott presidency, which might move quickly to help Muhammed consolidate power in Saudi Arabia."

Compliance with the assassination plot must be the "other assistance" Aziz was threatening to withdraw if Prescott allowed Muhammed into the Clearwater Partners inner circle.

Clearwater's internal politics aren't high on my list of concerns. I hear myself shriek, "I'm not working on anything with that cold-blooded monster! He killed my husband. Acheson didn't want him to, but he did it anyway, to scare me away from helping you. And now you want to make a deal with him?"

Henry softens his tone, but only slightly, and asks, "How can you be certain about that?"

"Korov," I mumble miserably. "He said he had a tape."
"Ah. And have you seen this tape?"
"No."
"That's what I thought. Now, I understand you're upset, and perhaps justifiably so, but you need to understand two things. First, in this business, we deal with a lot of people we'd prefer to have nothing to do with. Second, a significant percentage of those people lie. A lot. And convincingly. We do the best we can, try to verify information if possible, and go with the lesser evil whenever we can. And right now, thirty-plus years of experience are telling me to listen to Abdul al Sultan bin Aziz. He does not want his former partners killing the president."

Henry pauses and I presume the lecture is over, but then he adds, "And I will not tolerate you interfering with the FBI's objectives any longer. Am I making myself clear?"

"Yes, but—"

"But what?" Henry's eyes narrow.

"If you believe everything Aziz says about the plot against the president, then wouldn't you punt to the Secret Service?"

Henry's face turns crimson. He growls, "I have it on reliable authority that the Secret Service has been infiltrated. I believe that more than one agent on the Commander in Chief's traveling detail is taking orders from Prescott. There won't be a gunman in the crowd tomorrow. It'll be something more sophisticated."

"Why are you telling me this?"

"The night before Smerth was murdered, we heard him over the wiretap you planted. He was talking to the U.S. Attorney. Smerth sounded panicky. He wanted to sing, turn in Acheson and the others and make a deal for himself. He said he had reason to believe that they had hatched a plot, with the cooperation of some men inside the Secret Service, to kill the president. The prosecutor pushed throughout the phone call for more details or a face-to-face meeting. Smerth said he would think about it overnight. Then he hung up."

"And Smerth was dead within twenty-four hours of placing that phone call," I say.

"Exactly."

"Isn't it odd that he made it from his office telephone? He'd know the firm records every conversation. Why would Q. Randolph

Smerth, one of the best lawyers in the country, make a recording of a self-incriminating call?"

"Maybe he knew he was in mortal danger and he wanted to leave a record," Henry says. "He's trying to cross back over to the good side and he's scared for his life. He'd know that his phone records would be searched in the wake of a homicide."

There's a knock at the door. Henry's hand moves to his hip. Mikhail brushes past his military police minder and joins us.

"Just me," Mikhail says, shaking his head. "You damn Yankees. So trigger happy." Then his eyes land on Katya and his expression changes to register shock. Katya leaps to her feet. Her open mouthed expression mirrors his.

"You two know each other?" Henry says, incredulously, then barks at the MP to close the door. I watch from the corner of my eye as his fingers reach under his clothes for his Glock.

Mikhail notices, too. Without taking his eyes off Henry's gun, he says, "You could say that. We were classmates at the former KGB academy."

"I went undercover immediately after graduation," Katya explains, in markedly better English than she deployed previously. "I made a point of losing track of my classmates."

We gape at her in disbelief. I steal a questioning glance in Henry's direction, but it's obvious from his flummoxed expression that the deputy director feels as thrown as I do. He sits back down and motions for everyone else to do the same.

My head starts aching dully and I rub my temples without taking my eyes off Katya, who's morphed from cowering to commanding in the blink of an eye. Mikhail slides into the chair next to me and pulls in closer than necessary.

Henry bellows at no one in particular, "Our key informant was working for the Russians?" He looks at Katya. "Would you mind telling me why your government was so interested in Acheson that they planted a spy in his *lawyer's* home?"

"First we tried to get into Acheson's house. He has three young children and it made more sense, but Acheson's wife wouldn't take a Russian au pair. She only hired French girls. The Smerths were our back up strategy. It was a pleasant surprise that he kept files at home." Katya shrugs. She's wearing a don't-blame-me-I-just-work-here look.

Mikhail's hand surreptitiously reaches down to graze my leg and I feel a tiny electric charge that makes me blush. Henry's gray eyebrows go up, but he says nothing.

"You didn't answer the question," Henry says irritably.

"It should be obvious, but since it's not, I'll enlighten you," Katya snaps back. "The Russian government was interested in Acheson because of his ties to Korov, whom the regime views as a major threat."

"Or perhaps your government wanted to help Acheson take out K4. So you could have a new one built on your terms. Your president would let Korov do the legwork, and then arrest him on trumped-up tax charges or some such nonsense, before deprivatizing the project."

Katya glowers at Henry, but Mikhail nods and says, "That sounds right on the money."

"Oh really?" Katya adds and then barks something indecipherable yet clearly accusatory at him in Russian. Mikhail shrugs in response.

Henry loosens his tie and unbuttons his top collar button.

I turn to Mikhail. "So, when you worked as CFO of Titan and you processed paperwork from the Lotus Group, bearing Katya's name, you didn't have any clue that she was a Russian agent?"

"None. And by the way, thanks for exposing *my* undercover role. That's truly helpful."

"I knew you were there all along," Katya says, in as patronizing a tone as I've ever heard from anybody. She could give Q. Randolph Smerth a run for his money.

"You didn't recognize the name?" Henry asks Mikhail.

"It's not her name, as I recall." Mikhail glances Katya's way, but then turns to Henry. "I knew the Lotus Group's directors were all domestic employees of Acheson, Smerth and Jack Prescott."

Which explains why the name of the third owner was so carefully blacked out on all the Lotus Group's files. Relief washes over me and I blurt excitedly, "So that's it!"

All three of them stare at me as if little green aliens are shooting from my ears.

"Don't you think that if we call *The New York Times*, or CNN, or whoever you want, and tell them the Vice President of the United

States owns a secret offshore company, together with a disgraced, indicted, and on the lam lobbyist, that this whole mess will be over? The American public will be outraged." My words run into each other because I'm in such a hurry to spit them out.

"I'm afraid it's not so simple," says Henry. "Although your sense of moral indignation is frankly refreshing."

He's talking to me but he's looking at Katya with what appears to be a mix of disappointment, disgust and flat-out admiration.

"Why isn't it that simple?" I protest. "Vice President Prescott has committed a crime. The press will have a field day. They'll investigate the assassination plot. It'll blow open the biggest political scandal since Watergate. Bigger even."

"Because," says Henry, "we have the word of the two Russian spies and a gut feeling. There's no trail linking Prescott to any offshore entity. Nor do we have a scrap of concrete evidence that he's invested with Clearwater Partners—or anyone else—since taking office, because it's all in blind trusts." He glowers at Mikhail. "In America, we don't ruin people on hunches alone."

"Sure you don't," Mikhail says.

"Can I ask a stupid question?" I say. "Why doesn't the FBI have anyone inside Clearwater or one of its subs?"

"It's an impenetrable fortress," says Henry. He removes his eyeglasses, the old guy hipster ones that make him look like Harrison Ford. He wipes them on his shirt.

"Nothing is completely impenetrable. It depends on who's doing the penetrating," Katya says, with a sardonic smile.

The phone on the table rings. Henry readjusts his glasses on his face and frowns at Katya as he answers. "Redwell here," he barks in lieu of any greeting. He listens before insisting, "I need the ambassador in here, on the double."

On the double? Who says that?

Henry clears his throat again. "Change of plans, people. Our mobile command post has been compromised. Our legat's been shot along with several men. I've summoned the ambassador so we can finalize Plan B in a secure area."

Mikhail frowns at the mention of the murdered legat. I wonder whether the guy was someone he knew. And whether Max von Buren is among the casualties.

25

Whoever called Henry must hold sway over the ambassador's schedule because within minutes, we hear footsteps in the hall. The door swings open to admit a well fed fifty-ish man and Abdul bin Aziz.

My stomach lurches. When I stand my legs buckle as if both knees could give out at the same time. The corners of Abdul's mouth turn up slightly in recognition, or perhaps in satisfaction that his mere presence inspires dread. Mikhail extends an arm to steady me. I shove him away, too embarrassed to cower behind him in front of Henry.

Henry looks at the other man, who's presumably our ambassador to Russia and says, "We need to talk in the tank."

"All of you?"

"Except our new Russian guest, obviously."

"Fine," says the ambassador. He turns to Mikhail. "Please make yourself comfortable. There's a full bar to the left, a washroom down the hall and the entire house has wireless access, of course."

Mikhail nods politely, but makes no move to avail himself of the amenities.

The ambassador directs us into an old elevator. We ride in silence down to the basement. The ambassador ushers us down two more flights of stairs to a concrete room. In the middle, suspended by what look like ordinary cinder blocks, is a gigantic metal vault. It resembles a safe out of a cartoon, something the Roadrunner would drop on top of Wile E. Coyote.

"What is this place?" I ask.

"That's the tank," says the ambassador, with a hint of pride.

"It's the only completely secure place in Moscow," Henry says. "The downside is the air supply is limited."

Maybe Mikhail is lucky to be upstairs. I'm not leaping for joy at the prospect of being sealed in an airtight canister with Aziz.

Henry asks the ambassador, "How much air will we have?"

The ambassador consults his watch, as if it might produce the requested information. "About ten minutes," he says confidently.

What does he mean, *about*? If we're going to risk asphyxiation, I'd prefer a more precise answer. Aziz looks mildly concerned as well. He's rubbing his sweaty palms on his otherwise immaculate white robes.

"Alright," Henry says. "Let's go."

The ambassador swings the heavy metal door shut. The walls look about a foot thick, with some sort of rubber sealant framing the doorway. He locks us inside with a series of nerve-rattling clicks. My eyes settle on two meters on the wall. One's a Celsius thermometer and the other presumably measures oxygen supply. The mercury sits high in both tubes. Despite their reassuring presence, I catch myself breathing in rhythmic gasps, like a first-time scuba diver.

The tank is little more than a hundred square feet. The only breaks in the grey metal are glaring fluorescent lights, which feel too bright for such a small space. The air is stale, like on an airplane several hours into a long haul flight.

Only Katya seems at ease. "First time in here?" she asks.

Henry, the obvious addressee, nods. "In this one, yes. I've been in our tank in Tehran, but that was years ago."

It must have been, since we haven't had an embassy there in decades.

"We don't have much time." Henry says. "The president arrives overnight, and tomorrow he has a full schedule of meetings with President Perayev, followed by a reception at the Kremlin and another at the Ritz. The next afternoon, the Bolshoi Ballet will present a special performance. Then, at eight o'clock, the president will arrive at the Presidential Palace for the state dinner. He flies out the next morning."

"If he's still alive by then," says Katya.

Henry says, "I think they'll wait for the Ballet. It won't be the Ritz. The hotel has brought in enough extra security to launch an invasion of a small country."

"Casper didn't share your confidence in the hotelier's measures," Katya says, in a tone implying that however imminent events play out, it doesn't make a great deal of difference to her.

"Why would you trust Casper?" I ask, before I can stop myself.

Aziz turns towards me, sighs as if bored, and demands of Henry, "Why is she here, Redwell?"

"Because *I* want her here."

"She's a foolish girl, and for some unimaginable reason, you're all pretending she's an agent," Aziz says. I'm surprised he chooses to express any opinion about me. If he's the primary culprit in Damien's murder, you'd think he'd want to minimize our interactions. Maybe I should want to lunge at him, rip his throat out with my fingernails or grab Henry's Glock and shoot him in the face. But I'd honestly be happy to get away from him and never see him again.

"Whore," he mutters under his breath.

Henry swings at Abdul without warning. His jab hits squarely in the jaw. Abdul's glasses fall to the floor, revealing incensed eyes. I brace for a fight in this cramped cube. There's no place to get out of the way.

Aziz looks stunned but doesn't swing back. I suppose, given his royal status, he's never been hit in his life. He's running his tongue around the inside of his mouth, inspecting the damage. His fingers clench into fists, but then unclench. I look up at Henry gratefully.

He says, "Now don't get all teary-eyed, my dear. I'm not so much protecting your honor as preserving our oxygen supply."

I nod. The temperature's rising and I'm starting to sweat.

"My dear," Henry's tone is softer. "You're down here because we need your help in neutralizing Mikhail."

I'm not sure I follow. 'Neutralize' sounds like something you'd do in a high school chemistry lab or worse, in a Mafia movie. I don't like the sound of it.

"He's on our side," I protest.

"No," says Katya, who's made the transition from glowy to sweaty like the rest of us. "Mikhail works for Korov."

"Korov planted him inside the FSB," Henry explains. "It's ingenious, really. Korov hand selected him and oversaw his training. From a distance, of course. He's a patient man. He let Mikhail cut his teeth on a few legitimate FSB matters before pulling some strings at the agency to get him assigned inside his own organization."

"That's not possible. He's the one who told me about the presidential assassination plot. Why would he tell me, if he's in on it?"

Three pairs of eyes stare back at me blankly. Maybe I've rattled their resolve. I decide to press my case a little further. "And if you really wanted Mikhail out of the picture, why didn't you shoot him already?"

"Because we want to watch him a little longer before we dispose of him."

I cringe, though I'm slightly relieved that the prospect of killing someone remains distasteful, even to a veteran like Henry. His mouth is contorted as if he's bitten down on something bitter.

My eyes blaze with anger. "You mean you want to use him for information. Then kill him. How do you know your information is correct? You haven't exactly been batting a thousand."

"Mikhail's regional director was arrested recently and he confessed," Katya says.

"You expect me to believe information extracted in a Russian interrogation?"

Nobody answers me. Nor does anyone inquire as to what crime Mikhail's boss supposedly confessed to. "Everyone who reads a newspaper from time to time knows you use torture to get your suspects to say whatever you want to hear."

Katya looks as if I've slapped her across the face. I hold my breath, which, under the circumstances, seems like an act of community service. The oxygen meter has fallen by at least a third.

Henry suddenly looks eager to change the subject. Aziz, who'd been dabbing at his bloodied mouth with a handkerchief, seizes the moment and announces, "It's time to discuss the specifics of my deal. That is if all of you can stop bickering about that insignificant boy from St. Petersburg."

"Fair enough," says Henry.

Aziz removes his sunglasses. "If you expect me to hand over Prescott's head on a silver platter—which I'm prepared to do, mind you—I will require a significant reward. Jack Prescott and I share a long and fruitful history. His betrayal won't come cheaply." He delivers the last statement like a dare.

Henry glances at the air meter, which is sinking, and the thermometer, which is rising proportionately. "What is it you want? Because I know it's not money."

"I want assurances."

"What kind of assurances?" asks Henry, feigning patience, when I can plainly see he's fighting the urge to lose his cool.

"One: The president, in consideration of my small role in helping you save his life, will support my succession to the Saudi throne upon the death of my ailing older brother Fahd. Fahd likes to pretend he can leave his son Muhammed in charge without the blessing of the United States, but that's not entirely true. We Saudis only do what we like when the Americans are indifferent."

Katya gestures at Aziz to get to the point. Her sleek hair has begun to go frizzy and her white blouse, which no longer looks crisp and pressed, is clinging to her chest and arms. She fans herself futilely with her hands.

"Item two is equally important: I require lifetime immunity from all criminal prosecution in the United States and its territories, whether I continue as ambassador or become head of state, or not."

I cut him off. "No way."

Henry takes my arm and tells me that he will handle this. He says to Aziz, "You know I can't do that for you, until you tell me what you're prepared to do in return."

"I'll give you evidence that Prescott is providing money and arms to terrorists, on a scale that makes Iran-Contra look like a game of Risk. I'll expose his plot with my brother to choreograph a war against a supposed Saudi 'insurgency,' one armed and led by BXE employees, and pinned on the Iranian mullahs. Such a conflict would suck the U.S. military into yet another inevitably unpopular Middle Eastern quagmire, drive up oil prices and enrich Prescott personally. Imagine: U.S. taxpayers digging into their pockets to fund a war manufactured by a Fortune 10 company. It's bloody brilliant. But as I'm no longer involved, I can't very well let it happen."

For a moment I forget how hot, anxious and uncomfortable I feel. Time stands still even as the clock on the wall ticks off the seconds. Henry and Max were right all along. Clients of my law firm actually plan to start an international conflict and get rich off it. Not in an incidental way, either. They're providing the weapons and the opposing army. And then igniting the uprising.

"As an added bonus, I'll let you know how Clearwater Partners infiltrated the Secret Service. In short, I'll make the deal you wanted to offer Acheson before he disappeared, only better."

My stomach sinks. The FBI would be crazy to turn Aziz down, especially as their investigation is going nowhere, despite a tremendous expenditure of time and resources.

"Not good enough," Henry says, to my surprise. "I need physical proof."

"There's no paper trail for the Secret Service compromise. The money was wired through a series of offshore accounts, into a set of numbered Swiss accounts, opened by one of the Secret Servicemen's wives. As for the arms financing, that money left Bermuda within minutes of entering, mostly through a set of anonymous accounts in Cyprus. Profits traveled into Prescott's coffers by the same route, in reverse. He has a secret fortune sitting in the Lotus Group."

"There must be a record of the first wires into Bermuda. Their banking isn't completely secret," Henry presses.

"No."

"Then, how?"

"In my hand luggage," Aziz answers with a satisfied smirk.

"Of course." Henry's shaking his head as if embarrassed he didn't see it. "Diplomatic bags," he mutters.

Aziz, visibly satisfied with himself, stands even taller and presses his position. "So, *Mr.* Redwell, if you're prepared to meet my conditions, I will hand you Jack Prescott and anyone else you want from Clearwater Partners *and* I'll help you identify the rogue Secret Service agents."

"And if you don't deliver your end of the bargain?" Henry asks.

The fact that Aziz seems moments away from lifetime prosecutorial immunity turns my stomach. I need air. Mercifully, a warning bell chimes. Two minutes of oxygen left.

Aziz looks Henry straight in the eye. "Then we have no deal, of course. I'm a reasonable business man."

I can't believe this is happening. "Wait. You don't need him to lead you to Acheson. Acheson is right here in Moscow."

"I have a team scouring the Caribbean for him."

"Well, have them call off the hunt. I saw him with my own eyes, having a drink in Korov's living room less than twenty-four hours ago. He could still be a guest in that house."

"Or he could be anywhere in the world by now. Twenty-four hours is a long time. My sources believe he's fled to a private island hideaway in the Caribbean," Aziz says. "And they are professionals. Rarely mistaken." He shoots me a nasty glare with this last remark.

Henry nods and glances at the meters. "We only have a minute left. We need to address the problem of the Russian."

"I can make him disappear," Katya offers.

"Not yet," says Henry. "But I don't want him hampering our efforts, either." He reaches into his pants pocket and produces a tiny plastic vial of clear liquid. "Lena, you need to slip this into his drink, the first chance you get."

"What is that?" I hate this plan. Katya looks disgusted, too, but I suspect for different reasons. She sees no need for childish games when a simple bullet to the brain would solve the problem.

"GHB," says Henry.

"You want me to slip him the date rape drug?"

"Precisely. This dose should be enough to produce a coma, but you have to make sure he drinks all of it."

Henry presses the vial into my sweaty palm and forcibly wraps my fingers around it as the tank's lights flash red and the bell clangs. A knock at the door echoes through the tank. The entrance swings open and a flood of room temperature air, that feels as refreshing as the freezer aisle in an August heat wave, rushes in.

"Time's up, Mr. Redwell," says the ambassador. I slip the vial into my front pocket and wipe my sweaty, scraped up hands on my pants, because I don't think handing the drugs back to Henry with a polite but firm refusal is an option.

"Thank you, sir," Henry replies. He wipes his brow for the hundredth time with his wet handkerchief.

I hang back and let the ambassador, Katya and Aziz shuffle into the elevator first. I grab Henry's arm and whisper, barely audibly, "Why me?"

"Because he'd never trust me with his drink," Henry says.

26

Upstairs Henry and the ambassador confer behind closed doors. I seize the opportunity to dash into the restroom. My hands, elbows and knees are scraped raw, but my face sports only a few minor scratches. I pick several pieces of highway gravel out of a cut above my left eyebrow. I scrub with soap and water, not caring that I soak the entire counter in the process, and emerge, still disheveled but hopefully disinfected.

Katya catches me by the sleeve as I exit, pulls me close and whispers, "Go home. If you stay here you'll be dead soon." She releases her hold on me and brushes past as breezily as if she'd alerted me to lipstick in my teeth instead of peril for my life. When she re-joins us she stops the deputy director in his tracks with her smoky eyes and pouty red lips. She's transformed from withered to stunning in mere minutes. Her clothes even seem to have ironed themselves back into pristine condition.

Henry exhales appreciatively. He puts his hand on the small of her back and escorts her towards the main lobby. Mikhail seizes the opportunity to grab my arm and when I slow my pace he slides his hand down and presses a piece of paper, folded into a tight little package, into my left hand.

I glance around, afraid someone else noticed, but they're all charging ahead. Katya's shoes click loudly on the marble tiles as she hustles towards the exit with Henry. Aziz walks closest to us. He's busy re-examining his face for signs of swelling, gingerly, with the tips of his fingers. The outline of an ugly bruise has started to form and his cheek will turn a half-dozen shades of purple and yellow by tomorrow.

A big black limousine idles out front. Henry reaches for the door himself, without waiting for the driver.

"After you," Henry says to Mikhail.

"This is where we part ways," Mikhail announces.

"You sure about that?" Henry asks. "It seems to me that you've made some enemies out there." He motions vaguely towards the world outside the embassy.

"I'll take my chances, if it's all the same to you. I'm not accustomed to working with such a sizable entourage."

"And what if it's *not* all the same to us?" Katya asks.

"Then I'm still going my own way," Mikhail says, in a voice that cuts off further debate. He swings his backpack over his shoulder and walks towards the gate.

"Suit yourself, young man." Henry says.

"You might want to take a peek in the trunk of that Mercedes," he yells as he crosses back onto Russian soil.

Katya looks monumentally displeased. She opens her mouth to say something but stops herself. Instead, she purses her lips, which emphasizes her high cheekbones.

I bet she weighs under a hundred pounds soaking wet. I'm no Amazon, but I feel large and ungainly standing next to her. We've been outside less than sixty seconds and the wind has ripped my hair from its ponytail holder. Loose strands fall on my face and whip into my eyes. Henry herds us into the car, taps on the glass and tells the driver to get moving.

We pull out slowly over the cobblestone drive.

"Henry?" I ask as the driver stops to wait for the guards to clear him through the gates.

"Yes?"

"Why isn't Max here with you?"

"He's indisposed. Change of plans, as it were."

"Excuse me?"

"I'm sorry. I'm not at liberty to elaborate. But don't worry about it, alright? And don't get too settled in, my dear. I've changed your plans as well."

What the hell does he mean, *indisposed*? My brow furrows. Screw his plans. What if I don't feel inclined to do anything but fly home? Henry announces that I'm to get out of the car and follow Mikhail. My eyes bulge at him. I can't believe he's about to allow me out of his sight again. I feel my pocket. Next to the vial of GHB, Mikhail's note is tucked, unread.

"We're counting on you. Do you still have the vial?"

"Of course," I say, and pat my pocket for emphasis. The chauffeur tries to nose into a steady stream of oncoming traffic, without much success.

"Good," Henry says. He hands me an iPhone. "I notice you lost your old one."

Henry raps on the glass and instructs the driver, who's managed to break into the traffic, to pull over. Out the window, I see Mikhail's back moving steadily away, half a block ahead of us.

"Catch up to him and knock him out. Call us if you need anything. The numbers are in your phone."

"Okay."

"By the way, what's in the Mercedes?"

"Dead BXE guy, probably American."

Henry blinks at me, momentarily dumbfounded. Whatever answer he anticipated, I guess it wasn't a contractor's corpse. "Good luck," he says.

When I climb out, I'm only about thirty yards behind Mikhail. I can't tell if he sees us stop. As the limo disappears down a side street, I hurry to catch up to him.

I close the gap between us to about fifteen feet and call out his name. He stops dead in his tracks, turns and smiles. The single dimple that reminds me of Damien flashes briefly on his cheek, then vanishes even though he's still smiling. Maybe the resemblance I keep seeing is a mirage – Mikhail reminds me of Damien because that's what I want to see.

"You read the note and couldn't resist," he says, in a normal conversational voice as I fall in by his side. But for the dirt on my coat and the conspicuous holes in my pants, we could blend in this desirable neighborhood full of beautifully restored pre-revolutionary buildings.

"No. I haven't had a second alone yet," I answer truthfully, without thinking whether that's wise. What if Katya's telling the truth and he's not on our side? Whatever side that is. "What is it I couldn't resist?"

"If you didn't read my note, I need to assume Henry sent you out to persuade me to come back into his fold. Or does he expect you to kill me?" He asks, in the kind of mildly curious tone one might use to inquire about the specials in a restaurant.

I feel my face burn bright red. "No. I don't think he wants you dead." I'm stumbling over the words, improvising. "You intrigue him. He thinks if I follow you, you'll lead us to Korov. I think, and this is just my theory, that the FBI would love the opportunity to question Korov."

They have to be worried about the loose nukes.

As I say the words I know I sound preposterous. Even if the FBI believes Casper's tip about the imminent auction of arsenal, our elite law enforcement must have better countermeasures than *asking* Korov to halt the event.

"Korov wants me dead," Mikhail says emotionlessly. "So perhaps it's good to hear Henry doesn't share that ambition."

He walks us down a short flight of steps into one of those underground crosswalks. It's empty, except for two teenage boys with shaggy haircuts, strumming guitars with their cases lying open in front of them. Mikhail tosses them a few rubles and says, "Korov's making you an offer that I suspect you can't refuse."

I instinctively reach for the note in my pocket.

Mikhail smiles. The dimple dances across his face again. "That's all the note says. I'd never put the details in writing." He motions towards the dusty beam of daylight coming down the stairs at the other end of the tunnel. "Walk with me."

As we press forward, I take out the note and unfold it anyway. Sure enough, it reads, in simple block print: "Korov has extended an offer you may find impossible to refuse."

Mikhail clears his throat. "I assume you plan to remain focused on the reason you came to Russia."

"Of course. But with the way things have gone today, I'm thinking any offer to help me has been yanked off the table. Doesn't he want you dead? And me, too?"

"You'd think so, but right now he wants to orchestrate your rescue."

"Excuse me?" I stop in my tracks, but Mikhail keeps walking, so I have to jog a couple of paces to catch up.

"Don't you remember?" He lowers his voice, not that anyone's listening. "The little vignette you starred in?"

"Seriously?"

"The whole point of the staged kidnapping is that Korov wants to rescue you. He'll make the government look inept, swoop in, save the day and steal the headlines during an important summit."

Mikhail explains this like it's the most rational idea in the world, as if people allow ruthless desperados to choreograph their disappearances and recoveries every day. Who knows what my other options are, but I'm not feeling great about this one.

"How do you know it's not a trap?" I demand.

"You're going to have to trust me."

"I don't have to do anything of the sort."

He pulls back a bit. "What other choices do you have?"

My head pounds with alarm bells and stress and what feels like mental fatigue. "You just said Korov wants you dead. But you want *me* to skip off and do his bidding? When did you even talk to him?"

"I didn't. Korov has a man in your embassy. He passed me a note while you were in the tank."

I don't believe him. "The embassy is wired. I'm sure cameras catch every move. There's no way you read a secret missive without the cameras seeing."

"Indeed. The cameras watched me flip through several books in the sitting room. It helps to know where to find the secret missive. Any more questions?"

"When does he want to liberate me?"

"Soon, Within the next forty-eight hours."

I could hang on for two days. Get the tape from Korov. Help put Damien's murderer in prison forever. "Fine. But if forty-eight hours go by with no summons from him, I'm on the next plane home." I say this with more bravado than I feel.

"Suit yourself," Mikhail says, as if it makes no difference to him what I do. Which of course it probably doesn't.

The quality of the neighborhood starts to decline. We turn onto a quieter residential street, one featuring utilitarian apartment buildings and copious amounts of litter strewn in the gutters.

We stop in front of one of the towers. He glances over each shoulder before producing a key and admitting us to a grimy grey lobby, unadorned but for a row of metal mailboxes installed on the wall to our right.

"Where, exactly, is here?" This is precisely the kind of place you picture when someone says "Russian apartment building." Unwelcoming. Concrete stairs, littered with cigarette butts and a few crushed beer cans, lead up to a dark landing. A battered foam mattress rests under the stairwell. Beside it, someone has stowed a wash basin and a modest but neatly folded stack of clothes. "Someone lives under there?" I ask, knowing the answer.

"It's common to let someone, usually a pensioner bewildered by the new order, live under the stairs in exchange for building maintenance."

When I make a face he says, "It's better than the street, especially in the winter."

I nod.

"I have a studio here," Mikhail says. "I paid cash for it in the early nineties, when we Russians were first allowed to buy real estate, and before I signed on with the FSB." He's lowered his voice to a whisper. "As far as I know, nobody knows about it."

A chorus of alarm bells begins to chime inside my head. First of all, it seems unlikely that he'd be able to keep a secret residence. I'm not an expert on the FSB, but Korov seems to make it his business to know everything.

Secondly, I wonder where Mikhail got the money, even for a dump like this. If my math is right, he would've been a student back then.

I follow him upstairs. He takes them two at a time, noiselessly. I tell myself that if he wanted to harm me, he would have done so already.

We charge up four flights and stop in front of a grey door that features a steel knocker but no other adornments, except screw holes where a nameplate has been rather conspicuously removed. He fishes the envelope he collected from the bartender in Elista from his pants. A key and a card key. He uses the regular key to admit us. "You'll have to excuse the housekeeping. I haven't been here in a while."

Mikhail deadbolts the door before turning on the lights. Thick blinds block the sole window, which overlooks a tiny kitchenette in the far corner. An empty hat stand appears to be the lone frivolity, if you can call it that. The walls are bare. Spartan might be too generous a word to describe the furnishings. He has one of those futon couches that pulls out to a bed, a big metal computer desk and a couple of folding chairs. I glimpse ugly, hospital green tiles through a door on the left, which I presume leads to a bathroom.

Mikhail crosses the room and dives under the desk to plug something into the wall. An alarm screams.

"Good, it's working," he mumbles, as he silences the police-siren-like noise.

"What's working?"

"Heat detection sensors."

"So it's a burglar alarm?"

"Better. Standard burglar alarms are motion detectors. This was tens of thousands more expensive but it's also much harder to disable."

He says something else about the technology, but I fixate on the fact that his system was expensive. Where is he getting his cash? Would he dare steal from Korov?

An explanation seems unlikely.

I try a more neutral line of inquiry. "Can I ask what we're doing here?"

"Surveillance," comes the one-word reply from under the desk. When I ask him if he might elaborate, he tells me to hang on. Discouraged, I drop myself into one of the cheap folding chairs.

My phone rings and catches Mikhail off guard. He leaps up and smashes his head on the underside of the desk. The cracking sound of skull against metal makes me flinch. He barks something in Russian, I presume a curse, and then adds, in English, "Don't answer that!"

My finger is poised above the green talk button. "Why not?" I demand as the phone continues to sing insistently. I answer. Before the caller can spit out a word, Mikhail's extricated himself from under the desk. With one swift motion, he knocks the phone from my hands. It skips across the floor like a flat stone on water before hitting the baseboards at the far side of the room. His backhand sends me reeling off my chair. I stare up at him in shock. I can't tell if he meant to hit me or whether he got me by accident in his dive for the phone. Whatever the case, no apology seems forthcoming.

"What the hell do you think you're doing?" I yell.

"Keep your voice down," he growls, but his own voice begins a steep crescendo. "What do *I* think I'm doing? *I'm* trying to keep us alive, that's what *I* think I'm doing! You can't use a phone in here. It lets them pinpoint your location."

His eyes flash with rage. He's scaring me. I try to pick myself up off the floor, as gracefully as possible. Mikhail scoops up the phone and switches it off.

"I think you need to apologize."

He ignores my request and demands, "Didn't it occur to you that they use the phone to track you? So you should only use it when they know your location anyway? Because if it didn't, you're not nearly as smart as I thought."

Mikhail stares at the phone as if it's radioactive before double checking that it's switched off and putting it in his pants pocket. "Don't you think it's strange that they give you a new phone at the very same time they send you out to trail me?"

His voice has leveled off but his eyes are accusing. Even if he believes I want the tape from Korov, which I do, desperately, he has to assume that while I'm at it, I'll continue helping the FBI.

Of course he's right. Instead I say, "Not really. They want me to have a line of communication." Shouldn't he, an alleged elite agent, have been smart enough to *ask* me if the FBI issued me a new phone *before* he brought me here? Especially if he was so worried about its stupid GPS? Maybe he's cracking from stress. My face hurts, and as I rub my newest bruise, I decide that maybe I'll slip Mikhail the roofies after all.

Mikhail turns away from me and fires up his laptop. Maybe he knows he's crossed a line. At least I hope he does. I'm so angry at him and myself and the whole world really, that I can practically feel the heat rising from my head.

"That was probably the FBI, you know. Henry will come after me if I don't answer his calls." Even as the words come out, I hear the doubt in my voice.

Mikhail spins in the desk chair to face me. His expression is still angry, but the look in his eyes is almost pleading. "Cheshire, I mean Henry, is the least of my worries. You just don't get it. *You* may have had enough of moonlighting as an agent but *I* still have a job to do. It's up to me to get into the Bolshoi tomorrow *and* keep up the pretense of your kidnapping so Korov doesn't smell a rat. In case all that isn't enough, we're definitely being hunted, possibly by more than one highly lethal person. So I'm sorry if I have a short fuse and if I'm being a jerk. I certainly didn't mean to whack you like that, but I cannot have you getting us both killed."

It's not a gracious apology, but I bet it's as good as I'm going to get. If *we* really are being hunted by a professional hit man, or God forbid a series of professional hit *men*, it would seem foolish to storm out on Mikhail now. Still, part of me doesn't want him to feel completely forgiven, so I nod curtly instead of verbally accepting his apology.

I watch him work in silence for a moment before something so obvious occurs to me that I can't believe I didn't think of it earlier. "The FBI has no power to make arrests in Russia, do they?"

"No, of course not. They have no jurisdiction outside the U.S. Technically, they shouldn't even be armed over here, but we let that slide."

I'm not interested in whether Henry carried his Glock into Russia illegally. "Then the pipeline plot is a red herring." I'm surprised at the certainty in my tone.

Mikhail spins his chair away from the keyboard and faces me.

I continue, emboldened, "Remember the conversation in the casino? They seemed pretty sure that Max, the other agent I worked with, was heading to the Chechen frontier, all because of some bank wire. If Max can't arrest anyone or seize any assets why would he be so desperate to go south? It's not like he would be traveling with a television crew, who could expose the plot with cameras rolling."

"If the FBI has a tip about some high value individual connected to a pipeline sabotage plot, they'll take him out, regardless of the jurisdiction issues. They'd rather ask Russia for forgiveness than permission. Nobody cares about catching terrorists alive anymore. American prisons around the globe are full of alleged terrorists who won't talk. Your friend Max wasn't planning to intercept a bank transfer. He was planning to kill some high value target."

"Isn't that the CIA's job?"

"Job descriptions in your agencies and ours have gotten blurry."

Right.

Maybe Max was *en route* to an aborted assassination mission. That would explain his traveling alone. But then what about the dead legal attaché? I'm not sure what to think about anything any more. My brain feels fried from the overload of fear, excitement and frustration.

"You maybe right about the FBI and CIA. But there's something else. I'm fairly sure that Henry and Max got the information about the pipeline from Casper. And wasn't he a double agent?"

"At least, if not a triple agent," says Mikhail. "That's what I'm trying to figure out. I'd wager that his wire went to Korov, but I want to rule out the possibility it went to the FSB or the FBI." He holds up the apparatus ripped off Casper's dead chest this morning as if it's an exhibit in a trial.

"Henry couldn't be dead wrong about his sources," I protest. "He hasn't had such a successful career by accident."

"Old-fashioned spies like him solicit information from all kinds of unreliable people. And some of the stuff Casper passed along might well have been true. Double agents frequently supply a mix of good intelligence and bad, so their handlers keep asking for more. I don't know about the pipeline plot, but I do know that many of those half-empty Titan Import-Export Company containers went to rebels in and around Chechnya, fighters who would prefer Korov to the current regime. Something of interest to the U.S. government is going down."

Like an international auction of loose nuclear arsenal. I feel myself blanche. The world feels unsteady under my feet. But I manage not to voice my theory aloud. Either Mikhail already knows about the loose nukes from his work in Korov's empire, or the auction is horseshit invented to throw the FBI onto the wrong scent, or, at least as far as Mikhail is concerned, I'm not supposed to know about it. Better to wait and see where he steers the conversation.

"This kind of speculation gets us nowhere. First we need to know who's chasing us, and then we need to focus on evading them, at least long enough to head off the assassin tomorrow."

Mikhail turns his attention back to the laptop, obviously done with outlining our plans for the moment. The appearance of his homepage, a news site, drains the color from his face. "Fuck."

"What?"

He points to the screen. "The barman. One of ours. Dead, in what the police are calling a botched hold up." Mikhail takes two seconds to cross himself, something he didn't do for any of the other corpses he helped make today. He shakes his head as if to clear it, then plugs the transmitter from Casper's wire into one of the USB ports. The computer whirs under the exertion of communicating with the foreign device and then, within seconds, Mikhail has his answer.

"Definitely one of ours," he announces. "Dammit."

"Ours? Who exactly do you mean by ours?"

"Korov's. Which means he knows, beyond any reasonable doubt, that I'm a government mole, and also that you're in the loop. I'd much rather have the FSB on my tail than him."

I feel the color in my face go to ash. Mikhail's turning a bit green himself as he processes the confirmation of his worst suspicions. He swallows hard, in an unmasked attempt to regain his composure. His Adam's apple bobs up and down. "I need to know if you trust me."

Excuse me? I've once again ignored the unambiguous orders of the deputy director of the FBI, only to be advised that the man to whom I've figuratively hitched my wagon has become the quarry of one of the most ruthless men in Russia, if not on the planet. Not to mention the fact that my friends and family must have worked themselves into a frenzy over my disappearance. And Mikhail is asking if I trust him as if we're a couple of earnest teen stars in a feel-good summer flick?

"What the hell is that supposed to mean?"

"I need to know if you're with me. I think we can stop the plot tomorrow and expose the terror financing and maybe even some large scale arms smuggling. I also think I can help you solve your husband's murder, but I need to know whether you trust me. Because if you don't, it's going to radically alter my plans."

This does not seem like a good time to sit around second guessing my gut. I hear my voice answer, "Sure, I trust you."

"Good. I need to know where your FBI friends were going after they dropped you off, since you seem convinced K4 is a red herring."

Even if I did know the details of Henry's plans, I'm not sure I'd share everything. I can't even decide if I should divulge the tip about the infiltration of the Secret Service. Aziz could have made it up. Although it would explain why, with all these rumors swirling about a threat on the president's life, the Secret Service hasn't changed his itinerary, or come up with some excuse to cancel the summit altogether.

Instead I try a different tack. "Katya said something interesting about you."

"Oh, did she?" he asks. "By the way, her name's not Katya."

"Well, whoever she is, she seems to believe that Korov sponsored your education and career with the FSB. She claims he handpicked you and waited while you studied and cut your teeth on some legitimate cases." I look Mikhail in the eye as I recite all this and try to read his reaction.

"That's dead wrong." He makes a point of looking me straight in the eye. "You don't believe her, do you?"

The question hangs in the air a little too long and finally I shake my head and say, "But if you're a legitimate Russian agent, why aren't you and the FBI on the same side? It seems to me that both governments have an interest in keeping their leaders alive through the summit."

"Of course we should be on the same side, but the FBI thinks I've gone rogue, over to the criminal side or whatever you want to call it. I'm confident Katya is using all her wiles to support that notion."

"You're not far off. In my humble opinion, even Henry seems smitten with her. But why does she mistrust you so much?"

"She's the true rogue agent. She works for whoever pays the most."

I'm confused. Mikhail's acknowledged a certain degree of admiration for Korov before. But Mikhail has never, at least in my presence, described himself as anything close to a rogue agent. Sure, he's participated in shady dealings, but as far as I know, he hasn't turned on the FSB. My head swims. Could it really not have occurred to Henry that Katya's been working for some combination of Korov, Acheson and Aziz for years?

Nothing is turning out to be as it seems, and my face still hurts from where Mikhail hit me—accidentally or not—when he confiscated my phone. Not that the phone theft alone wouldn't be enough to make me furious. I tell myself that I'm co-operating out of an interest in self-preservation. It doesn't mean he's forgiven.

As if to add deeper insult to my injury, *his* cell phone interrupts my moment of reflection. He frowns at the caller ID and announces it's Korov, before answering in Russian. What I get from his tone is that Korov wants something and Mikhail is pushing back. Mikhail paces a tight circle as they negotiate. Once or twice he runs his fingers through his hair and rubs his scalp in an agitated manner. For lack of anything better to do, and because there's nothing worse than not understanding the conversation unfolding right in front of me, I study the holes in my pants. Maybe I could fix them, if I had a needle and thread. Or not. My mother always told me I'd regret opting out of home ec in the seventh grade.

Mikhail finally hangs up. He starts pacing around the flat, as if arguing with himself over what to do. I clear my throat and try to will him to bring me into the loop.

After a few more agonizing laps around the room, he says, "He is grievously disappointed by this morning's events."

"Isn't disappointed better than furious?"

"No. In Korov's case, disappointed means he is way past furious."

"Oh. So he called to tell you that?"

"Not exactly. He still wants to stage your 'liberation from terrorists' tomorrow. He says he'll deal with me later, but his offer to you still stands. He was very anxious to know whether you were with me."

"And did you tell him?"

"I said I was aware of your location, but left it at that."

"What about your phone?" I can't suppress the accusation in my tone.

"The best GPS scrambler money can buy. Please don't worry about that."

"Do you think he wants to kill you?"

"Not immediately. He knows I'm an agent but he believes, rightly, that I also know where all the bodies are buried." I cringe at the word bodies. He adds, "Figuratively speaking."

"Isn't that more reason to silence you sooner rather than later?" Leave no witnesses: the motive for countless murders.

"No. Since he couldn't secure my demise earlier, he assumes I've tipped off someone else about all the sordid things I've learned during my time inside his organization. He'd like to extract the details of any such tips to third parties before he dispatches me." Mikhail tries to explain this with a smile, but he's clearly shaken. The corners of his mouth twitch slightly, refusing the command to turn upwards. I force myself not to speculate on the ways Korov might go about extracting information from an unwilling subject.

"Does anyone else know the full extent of whatever it is you know?" I ask.

"No, and that's why I'm glad you're here."

I flinch, and try to reassure myself that it sounds like Korov prefers me alive. Maybe, if I play the poor bereaved little ingénue he wants, his rage towards Mikhail won't explode all over me.

While I'm ruminating over my options, none of which are tempting, Mikhail drops to his hands and knees and produces a Swiss Army knife from his pocket. He drives the blade between two floorboards. One of them pops up easily into his waiting hand. He sets it aside and pulls up a number of the adjacent boards, stacking them neatly in order to his left. Curiosity exiles my admittedly spotty self-preservation instinct to some remote corner of my brain. I crouch on the floor next to Mikhail, leaning so close that I notice his breath smells of coffee. He must have had some at the embassy, while I was sweating in the tank.

I have no idea what I expect to see as I peer into the exposed space under the floor. Perhaps a small safe, a pile of cash or maybe even a tunnel. I dismiss this last option as ridiculous, given our distance from the ground.

"What is all this?" I ask.

"Proof that a small group of very greedy, very evil men, working together, can engineer chaos all over the world."

27

Mikhail picks up one floorboard after another, revealing a crawl space filled with dozens of plastic storage bins, all carefully labeled in Russian. The hiding place under the floor is roughly waist-deep, a narrow, grave-like rectangle.

Mikhail jumps in once he's cleared enough room. "Come on down. I want to show you something," he says.

I climb down. "What is all this and how did it get here?"

"Copies of every transaction made by the Titan Import-Export Group and by Korov's Victory Casino Group, going back four years and eleven months." Mikhail starts pointing out boxes. "Wire transfers to anonymous offshore accounts. Emails to leaders of various upstart terror groups located in southwestern Russia. These guys are willing to create chaos on demand in exchange for infusions of cash. Communications with individuals outside Russia, whom I originally believed to be good, old-fashioned mercenaries, but who actually work for BXE. Not that there's much difference." Mikhail pivots one-hundred-eighty degrees and points to another stack. "These are Titan's shipping records, mostly Soviet-made weapons mislabeled as farm equipment, purchased by various Clearwater entities, and shipped to middlemen all over the world. The end user certificates are almost always BS. Behind that, we have millions in payments by Korov to Acheson. Money transfers, always in small sums, to the Lotus Group in Bermuda, and then back into the States in the form of bogus charitable contributions. Maps of the oil pipeline, marked up to show the most vulnerable stretches. It's all in here. There's enough for the Russian government to lock up Korov and throw away the key."

My jaw drops. Mikhail has Max's money trail, sorted, filed and annotated. We're standing amidst proof that the Bermuda transfers are merely the tip of a Titanic-sized iceberg. *And* circumstantial evidence that a pipeline plot exists. It's better than any smoking gun the FBI could have imagined.

"How?" is all I manage to spit out.

"The miracle of modern technology," Mikhail says proudly. "It was as simple as email, especially after my wife died. Before that I had to hack into files when I could. After Korov tried to help with her cancer, he must have decided I owed him. He promoted me and granted me access to computer files that only one or two other guys can see."

"Doesn't email leave a trail? Even if you double delete or whatever?"

"Not if you swap out hard drives from time to time." Mikhail looks impressed with himself. "It's ironic. Korov hates for his employees to print anything. He's paranoid we'll carry out his secrets in manila folders, but he thinks it's adequate to have his IT guy spot check email from time to time. Collecting data from him was almost too easy."

It's too good to be true. "You really emailed all this stuff to yourself? That's it?"

"Yeah, and I always printed everything to be doubly sure. You'll see my files end abruptly, a few months ago. I thought someone was following me and decided to lay low for a spell."

I say a silent prayer that Mikhail was never followed here, because if he was, I imagine the apartment would top the list of places Korov's thugs would search.

"There's more," he says. He knocks out a few more floorboards. He bends down to enter the combination to a smallish safe. The door swings open. He uses what I thought was a card key to generate a pass code to open an interior door. Mikhail reaches inside and produces a handgun, a stack of passports and something that vaguely resembles a key. It has a key handle, but instead of teeth and grooves, the handle is attached to a thin metal tube, peppered with a series of metal dots that look like Braille.

"What you really want to know is how I smuggled copies of everything into a safe deposit box at UBS's main branch in Zurich."

I hold the key like it's radioactive. It sort of is, if you consider that there are at least a handful of people who would kill to keep the information it protects locked away. Mikhail looks at me expectantly.

"Why are you giving this to me?"

"Because I want to sell it to the Americans and you're the logical broker."

I was afraid he would say something like that.

"Since you aren't going to play nice and ask how I got the files to Switzerland, I'll tell you. I scanned everything, saved it all on memory sticks and mailed them to Zurich, with instructions for the bankers to place them in my safe deposit box."

"They do that kind of thing?"

"Sure, if you have the key," he motions toward the one I'm holding, "and the code, which I'll pass along, if and when the time is right. This box has two keys and two codes. The other set lives in a safe deposit box of its own at the Credit Lyonnais branch across the street from UBS. And the sole key to that box is in a railway locker in Roma Termini Station, with the combination known only to me. Can't be too careful."

"I guess you can't. But wait. Isn't all this information the property of the Russian government?"

"Technically, yes." Mikhail frowns. "But as I've alluded earlier, I'm not sure I want to send Korov off to waste to his death in Siberia."

I feel like I'm going to faint. He must be nuts.

Instead of fainting, I decide to appeal to reason. "You can't be serious. You said yourself that you think Korov wants to torture you to death. How can you still have doubts about turning him in?"

Mikhail scratches the stubble on his chin. "A couple of reasons. First, it's my duty to head off the assassination plot against your president tomorrow." I notice he makes no mention of stopping someone from killing his president. "Secondly, and less altruistically, I think the Americans will pay a fortune for this information. If I hand it to the Russian regime, they won't share intelligence. And personally, I wouldn't mind sending Acheson and Aziz to prison instead of Korov. To my mind they represent the greater evil."

"How so?"

"Korov's done a lot of bad, but he's also done a lot of good."

I roll my eyes. He can't be serious. "Helping your wife was a compassionate act, but you can't possibly believe he's a decent person."

"No, really," Mikhail says earnestly. "Think about it. He's our largest employer, besides the government. He treats his rank and file workers better than anyone else in Russia. He's single-handedly restored dozens of architectural treasures. He's pledged funds to air condition the Hermitage, which will add years to the life expectancy of its masterpieces. He brought the finest conductor in the world back to Russia, to the Mariinsky."

Of course he has to bring up ballet. That's what it all boils down to, for him. I listen to his laundry list, unswayed. Korov's a thug. Mikhail's argument is like saying we should let a serial killer go free because he was always kind to his mother and his dog.

Mikhail reads my expression and exhales loudly. "Alright. Can we at least agree to disagree on Korov for the next twenty-four hours? You want to stop them from killing the president, don't you?"

I hesitate. What I really want to do is erase the past several months and go back to the way everything was before. I offer God a little wager. I promise, if I could rewind my life two months, that I'd never again complain about my petty, inconsequential problems.

"I suppose so." I hope I sound convincing. I've never liked the president. I've called him an ass more times than I can count, but he's fairly benign, when held next to the evil genius of Jack Prescott.

Mikhail tilts his head and scratches his incoming stubble. "You don't sound so sure."

"I'm sure," I say, mustering a modest increase of conviction. I play with the key in my hands. Mikhail doesn't appear to want it back, but he hasn't given any instructions about what I should do with it.

He picks up on my unverbalized question and says, "Guard it with your life." I don't think he means it figuratively, as most people do when they employ that phrase.

Mikhail swings himself out of the crawlspace and starts replacing the floorboards. I watch for a moment before jumping in to assist. Soon all that's left is a hole in the corner by an air vent.

"I need to go out, but you can't go anywhere like that. You attract way too much attention with the free peep show." He motions towards my pants. I look down. One of the tears caught on the floorboards when I climbed out of the crawlspace. The seam split all the way up to my seat.

He says, "I won't be gone long. I'll bring you something to wear. Now, I want to show you something."

He crouches down by the hole in the floor. I watch as he fits the last boards together. They have interlocking slats that make a swinging trap door. There's a small wooden handle on the underside of the second to last board. I'm already not liking this.

He clears his throat. "I strongly recommend that you climb down there. You can keep the hatch open, but if you hear anything at all in the hallway, I want you to close it. There's a rolled up foam mat, a case of bottled water, and a flashlight. You'll be alright for a short while."

Although I'm freaked out by the idea of hiding in the floor, it seems, in principle at least, less threatening than explaining my presence to any nosy neighbors. I have to admit that he has a point about me not going outdoors.

Reluctantly, I step down into the hole. I arrange myself on the uncovered foam mattress and wonder how long he'll really be gone. This could all be a trap. My stomach lurches. But if he wanted to bury me under his floor, wouldn't he remove all his files first? Mikhail stops in his tracks halfway to the door, spins around and unplugs the laptop and the recording device he pulled off Casper. He passes them down to me for safekeeping and then pecks me on the cheek. "Don't answer the door, alright?" He tries to sound flip but fails.

I fight the urge to ask how long he'll be gone. I know the answer: however long it takes to do whatever he's setting out to do. Since he hasn't shared that, I can't begin to guess.

Neither can I stop myself from asking, "What if you don't make it back?"

"I'll make it back." He reaches into his waistband and passes me the handgun he pulled from the safe. "There's no safety. If you need to use it, aim and pull the trigger. Watch out. It kicks hard."

I swallow the panic rising in my throat and take the gun. I set it down carefully, as if it's breakable. I stow the laptop on the floor by my feet. As I place the wire down next to the computer, I notice that some of Casper's chest hairs are still attached to the swatch of tape. Normally this would turn my stomach, but I'm too overloaded to care.

As soon as I hear the multiple locks click shut, I take a deep breath, count to three and close the hatch. I don't hear anything unusual, but I'm still struggling to maintain my composure, shut under the floor. If I'm going to panic, I'd rather do it now, than when and if it becomes necessary to hide.

The building sounds strangely different from here. I'm probably sharing space with rats. I hear the distinct noise of metal squeaking against metal and then the water pipes gasp, sputter and swoosh to life. A few minutes later, someone below me flushes. Water races through the pipes again.

I lay back on the mattress because there's no other comfortable way to arrange myself, and concentrate on breathing evenly. I count to six for each inhale and eight for each exhale. I tell myself it's coffin-like, but not really any tighter than the bunks on Diana's parents' sailboat, where we slept so many nights as kids. Of course, those weren't closed to the outside air. Thankfully the vent, which is about two and a half feet from my head, allows in a faint beam of light. I cross my fingers and hope Mikhail returns before dark.

After fifteen or twenty minutes, I've convinced myself I can handle this. My hand is poised to open the hatch when I hear the unmistakable thud, thud, thud of footsteps in the hallway. They stop abruptly and then there's a mighty crash. I have to clamp both hands over my mouth to avoid screaming. Thank God I didn't open the hatch. There's no way I could've closed it in time.

What sound like combat boots but are probably only men's shoes stomp into the apartment. I can make out two sets of steps, possibly three. More than one anyhow. I expect to hear Russian, but a familiar voice pierces the quiet.

"Empty!" Korov proclaims, in English. Even though he utters only one word, I'm positive it's him. He's standing right above me. The heat sensor alarm wails. My fingers reach for the gun. I wrap my hands gingerly around the handle, terrified that my trembling will set it off.

"How can that fucking nitwit snitch possibly think you don't know about this place? I mean, he cuts the fucking checks for all your goons every week," Acheson shouts over the alarm.

It's him. There's no question about that, either. His voice has regained its usual authoritative timbre. His repeated use of the f-word also gives him away. I freeze and hold my breath. What if they can hear me breathing? I tell myself to stop being ridiculous.

"He presumes I don't delve too deeply into his affairs," Korov replies. He sounds testy and his English is more accented than before. "But look closely. He assumes we know. His computer's gone."

A chill flies up my spine and back down again. My stomach crunches. *I knew it!* Of course Mikhail couldn't get away with a secret apartment. Of course Korov knew about it. He just needed a real reason to pry. Now that he knows Mikhail went to a meeting and shot Casper, and presumably found the wire, he's got more than enough reason to indulge his curiosity about what Mikhail does outside the office. There's a crashing noise and the alarm falls silent. They must have yanked all the wiring from the wall.

I hear both pairs of feet walking a circle around the tiny flat, to the window and back. Then I hear the sound of a gun being cocked. I never heard that noise before today, but I'll never fail to recognize it again.

More footsteps stomp overhead and then there's a muffled thunk I can't immediately identify. I realize they're taking out the ceiling, which makes me almost sigh with relief before I catch myself. When they strike out overhead, will they turn their attention under foot? I hear them remove panel after panel of foam tile. They work quickly and Korov grunts his disappointment. I hear no efforts to replace the panels. My heart catapults itself to the top of my throat. I try, and fail, to breathe.

"What about the fire escape?" suggests Acheson. I hear him strain to force the apartment's sole window open. It creaks and squeaks but then gives. A moment later he yells, "Nothing out here but a filthy courtyard." The window slams shut.

One set of feet stops directly above my hiding place. I hold my breath again. A rush of panic comes over me, but then, as fast as it came, it's gone, replaced by a sense of resignation. They're not out to kill me, I tell myself. They want to stage my rescue. Perhaps I should simply climb out and say hello. Fortunately, reason edges out this impulse.

Acheson speaks again from across the room. "Not only is the computer gone. He removed it recently. There's a dust mark here."

I cringe at Mikhail's carelessness. He's supposed to be a professional. Even I would wipe away a dust ring.

"Dammit," grunts Korov.

"But he left the printer. Do printers have a hard drive or a memory or whatever you call it?"

"I don't know. Let's take it, to be sure."

I hear some more shuffling and clatter, which I assume is the sound of Acheson getting on his hands and knees to disconnect Mikhail's printer from the wall outlet.

He crosses the room and asks, "So our work here is done?"

"Unfortunately, it would appear so."

I feel like screaming with joy, or at least relief, as I hear them walk towards the door, or presumably, the gaping hole in the wall where the door used to be.

I exhale to sounds of their footsteps moving away, and then Korov stops abruptly. "Wait a minute!"

"What?"

"Let's pull up that air vent. Can't be too careful, right?"

My heart feels like it stops for a second. I hear them walk right above me. I'm about to be annihilated by two angry, unscrupulous men. They'll dump my body in the river, or worse, and when they find my remains, the police will need to ask my parents for dental records to identify me. I can't believe this is it. I grasp the gun more tightly, wondering if I should jump up and shoot. I decide that would be foolish. There's two of them and one of me, plus they're bigger, stronger, undoubtedly carrying firearms and generally more experienced with violent encounters.

Acheson sets the printer down with a thud. A shadow falls over the beam of light from the vent, as the two men count to three and yank its eight inch by six inch grate out of the floor. It must come loose more easily than they expected, because I hear them reel backwards when it dislodges. Unfiltered light floods down towards me and millions of dust particles float above my head. As the men regain their footing, I ease myself onto my side and move away from the vent as much as possible. I manage to slide back about a foot, but stop because I don't want to knock into anything.

A hand belonging to Korov (Acheson would never wear such jewelry) plunges down through the hole. He feels around but reaches nothing but air and the wall. "Nothing," he barks over his shoulder at Acheson. "But why don't you have a look? Your eyes are better than mine."

28

From my hiding place, I can't see Acheson peer through the vent, but I swear I can feel his eyes glaring into the darkness, trying to make out something besides the dust. Finally, he too pronounces, "You're right: nothing." I hear them pick up the printer before they disappear into the hallway.

I struggle to make out the faint strains of their retreating conversation. Korov says something to the effect that Mikhail (I assume that's who he means by "that despicable turncoat") will be easier to find than his computer. Acheson launches into something lengthier, but I can't make out his words. The elevator cage slams shut and they're gone.

Of course, the fact that the neighbors were using the plumbing mere minutes before Korov and Acheson arrived means that someone must have heard them smash through the door. How strange that nobody bothered to investigate. Then again, maybe Mikhail picked this place because the residents mind their own business. Still, it's unsettling that a sound of such magnitude would go unnoticed.

My breathing slows to a less panicked rate. I can feel the dust sucking into my lungs with each breath. I must have been too freaked out to care before. Suddenly, my accommodations feel unbearably claustrophobic. I can't wait to get out of this hole. I feel the urge to run, I'm not even sure where to, but first I force myself to count to a thousand and evaluate my options.

A strange sense of calm comes over me as I focus on counting off the minutes I spend curled on the natty foam mattress under the floor. I resolve to take charge of my destiny, starting now. There will be no more blind following of agents, American, Russian or otherwise. I will put an end to all cowering in spider holes, such as this one, while waiting for the men to secure my safety. It seems, as

I reconsider the events of the past twenty-four hours, that my gut instincts might actually be better than Henry's, Max's or Mikhail's.

And I have nothing to follow besides my gut. I'm in Russia, my husband is dead, I'm unarmed and sucked into a semi-central role in a massive international incident in progress. I've had a grand total of two hours of training at the very most, and that was when I thought my espionage would be limited to snooping in Smerth's files. The whole thing has spiraled way out of hand.

Because I've let it.

That stops now. And this isn't like some lame January resolution that sticks for two weeks. This will be for real.

When I decide enough time has elapsed for Acheson and Korov to put some distance between us, I give the trapdoor a good shove and hoist myself out onto the apartment floor. The door frame splintered where they kicked it in and the fragments of Mikhail's three wholly inadequate locks remain right in their posts, like a trio of incompetent sentries.

Other than the printer, nothing appears to be missing, probably because there was nothing in plain view to take. I walk to the window, which they left partially open, and lean out over the fire escape. No signs of life, other than a beehive dangling overhead.

I'm about to step onto the fire escape to check if I can see the building's back entrance, when I hear the elevator cage bang open. Footsteps fall in the hallway.

I freeze, and curse myself for leaving the gun under the floor. Especially since I don't see any fireplace tools or baseball bats conveniently laying around.

The footsteps quicken to a run. Mikhail bursts through the open doorway and stops short, standing on his flattened front door. He's holding a couple of plain plastic shopping bags. He surveys the scene, although there's not much to see, other than the ceiling panels, in small stacks dotting the floor. He looks at me questioningly.

"Who do you think?" I snap, in response to the inquiry he can't manage to formulate. Mikhail blinks at me blankly, so I add, "He had Acheson with him. Whatever differences those two may have had, they've clearly decided to bury the hatchet."

"Did they see you?"

"Of course not. Do you think they would have left me here? I hid in that stinking hole, like you said. Lucky for me, they didn't think to pull up the floorboards. Or maybe they did but they didn't have the right tools and they're coming back." This last thought hadn't even occurred to me before, but it seems obvious. "They did, however, rip out your air vent and stick their hands about six inches from my hair. I have to say, I wasn't feeling so secure in your little hideaway."

He ignores my complaints and states the obvious, "They took the printer."

"Yes, they weren't sure whether it had a memory, so they took it, just in case," I explain grudgingly.

Mikhail lets out a nasally half laugh, half snort. Not an attractive sound. He seems to have no idea what to do. I find this maddening, but then I remind myself that I'm no longer relying on him for a plan. I'm about to inform him when he snaps out of his daze and says, "I brought you some presents." He holds out one of the two bags.

I snatch the bag from his outstretched hand and pull out a new pair of cargo pants that look roughly the right size, a white shirt that looks less borrowed from a one night stand than the bus driver's, and a heavy but flimsily constructed wrap around sweater in a dull shade of purple. I reach to the bottom of the bag and touch something small and metal.

"I bought you a prepaid phone. You're welcome to use it once we're on the move again."

I'm touched in spite of myself. He didn't have to do that. The new outfit is one thing. Neither one of us was comfortable with me attracting stares and these new clothes look plain enough to prevent any heads from turning as I walk by. But the phone is a totally different matter. For one thing, it's probably the closest thing I'll get to an apology for his earlier behavior. "Thanks," I manage to say.

He nods, smiles slightly and says, "I took the liberty of sending your FBI iPhone by DHL to a made up address in Los Angeles. The FBI will have lots of fun tracking your fake trip home. But we need to get the hell out of here. You're probably right. They'll be back with a crow bar."

"How are we going to get out of here with all the files?"

"Unfortunately, we're not. That's why they're backed up in Switzerland. It's not ideal, but it's the best I can manage. Why don't you change and I'll grab the laptop and whatever else I can carry in my backpack." His voice has regained its usual confidence, but he keeps glancing nervously over his shoulder. He's obviously not thrilled about picking up the floor to retrieve his things, in full view of the corridor.

I wonder whether Mikhail managed to get to Switzerland and back without anyone noticing. Even if he mailed the memory sticks to a banker, wouldn't he have had to make one trip in person to set up the accounts? And he said his other key is hidden in Rome. Maybe Korov sent him on business and didn't bother to follow too closely. But if Mikhail couldn't keep this apartment a secret, then it's unlikely he wasn't shadowed while abroad, even if allegedly traveling on Korov's business.

In the bathroom, I pull on the new clothes, which fit fine. He guessed well. Then I take a deep breath and say a silent prayer that the trick Diana once showed me works. As nonchalantly as I can, I touch the tip of my index finger to the glass and study the reflection. There's a little gap between my nail and its mirror image.

According to Diana, that means I'm looking at a legitimate mirror. She showed me once that the ones in the Victoria's Secret on R&S's block are two-way. When she held her nail up to the glass in the dressing room, there was no gap. She declared that was conclusive evidence that we were being watched by "fat, donut-eating, drug-addled perverts" (her words, not mine). I remember being disgusted, and frankly traumatized, that afternoon. Now, compared to everything that's happened, I can't believe I got worked up about something so trivial as a possible voyeur in a lingerie store.

I take my hand away and test once more, to be sure. I still see a little space there. It's small comfort, because my heart's racing like it's going to sprint right out of my chest. I reach into the pocket of my dirty, ripped jeans and consider the contents of Henry's vial. I don't want to kill Mikhail. Nor do I want to render him comatose, so Henry can ship him off to some CIA hellhole for "enhanced interrogation." Because I'm pretty sure that's what the deputy director has in mind, given the high stakes of the investigation and how little headway they've made on their own.

I hold the vial over the sink and debate flushing its contents. Despite Mikhail's perverse affection for Korov, I believe he wants to help the FBI bring down Acheson, Aziz and Prescott. At the end of the day, I think Mikhail would accept Korov's arrest as collateral damage. He's smart enough to see it's the only way.

Maybe I won't use the roofies on Mikhail, but they're too valuable a weapon to chuck. I stow them in the front pocket of my new pants.

When I emerge, I feel inexplicably more confident. Mikhail's ready to go, his bag, which looks heavier than before, slung over his shoulder.

He sticks his head through the open doorway and looks both ways before calling, "All clear."

The back stairwell spits us out into the empty courtyard.

"How do we know that no one's watching us from behind a tree, or from the roof?" I whisper. We could have rifles aimed at our heads as we speak.

"You watch too many movies," Mikhail says. He's trying to sound encouraging but his brow furrows with worry. I stop myself from saying that movies are at least loosely based on reality. He adds, "Korov will presume I'm smart enough to leave and not return, if he thinks I've taken the computer. Why would I risk coming back here?"

He's trying his best to sound positive, but I'm still uneasy. "Your safe houses haven't struck me as particularly safe. We'd be better off hiding in a crowd somewhere."

"I was thinking the same thing."

I can't tell if he was, or whether this is silly, male face-saving foolishness. Either way, it makes sense. In a city of fifteen million people, I bet we're harder to find if we keep moving instead of hunkering down in one of Mikhail's flats.

We slink across the courtyard and out a back gate into a narrow residential street, lined with tenements on both sides. People have discarded significant quantities of household trash in the gutters. I breathe through my mouth to avoid inhaling the stench of decomposing chicken bones, banana peels and cardboard yoghurt cartons.

We round a corner onto a wider street where the residents must be richer, since there's much less of a trash problem. Two blocks up, I see a sign for the underground.

We disappear down the infinite escalator. The station is busy, considering it's not rush hour. I let myself relax a little as we merge into the crowd. The more people around me, the better.

A half hour later we emerge into the hazy sunshine across the street from an enormous marketplace, with people selling everything from dried fruits to fur hats. We skirt the chaos and stop in front of a colorful awning that declares in English and Russian, *Yalki Palki!*

"We need to eat," he says. "The tables here turn over quickly. You can make your phone calls in the bathroom because it's one at a time. No chance of being overheard."

We pass through the doors and a bored hostess in a red and blue national costume get-up waves indifferently at the few empty tables in the cavernous dining room. It's a kitschy place, with wood beam ceilings and colorful folk art dotting the walls. Mikhail grabs a table in the back, between the bathroom and the emergency exit. Under normal circumstances it would be the least desirable seat in the house.

I sink into the wooden chair. I haven't eaten in almost twenty-four hours. The adrenalin racing through my veins must have suppressed my appetite. We scarf our food, a motley array of bread, cheese, some sort of egg salad and various pickled vegetables. I excuse myself when I see a woman emerge from the restroom.

I latch the door behind me and take out the phone. Before I hear the ring tone, a tri-lingual, computerized voice tells me I have six minutes. My finger hovers over the keypad. I desperately want to call my mother, but I should take care of business first.

Diana answers immediately.

"It's me."

"Are you alright?" she shrieks. "Where the hell are you? We're beside ourselves here!"

"I'm fine. I'm still in Moscow. Who's we?"

"Who do you think? Your parents. Hannah and John. Your picture is all over the news. Your mom is frantic. Your congressman is calling on the president to put pressure on the Russians."

"Please tell mom I'm alright. I'm free now."

"Are you hurt?"

"Di, I'm fine. I called you instead of my parents because I thought you could keep it together and I don't have much time."

"Wait. Are you sure? Is someone forcing you to say these things?"

"I only have a few minutes on this phone. I need you to overnight my passport to the American Express office, here in Moscow. I think I'm really close to getting the thing Korov promised me. Then I want to come home, but I'm penniless. I don't even have five bucks to use an internet cafe. I hate to ask you this, but could you please book me on a bunch of flights? I don't know which one I can make, but if you book me on a few tomorrow and some more the day after—"

She cuts me off. "Consider it done. But how will you know which ones I booked?"

"Book me on British Airways to New York. There's bound to be several flights a day through London."

As I give these instructions, I wonder whether New York is any safer than DC. Maybe it won't matter by then. As soon as I get to London, I plan on handing the safe deposit key to the nearest available policeman. Maybe Acheson, Aziz and Korov will all be under arrest before I board my connecting flight.

"I think it would be better if you went to the embassy. Let them help you. Or find a cop and ask him to take you there."

"I can't. Just please, *please* book the flights."

"I will." She sounds awfully apprehensive. "Please be careful."

I heave a sigh of relief. "Thank you." As we're about to hang up, she says, "Wait a second! You need a visa for Russia, don't you? They won't let you leave the airport without one, because that would mean you entered illegally."

My stomach crunches again. I hadn't thought of this wrinkle. "I'll have to try to talk my way through. I can't hide for more than a day or two."

I don't know where I should cool my heels. I wish I could camp in the Amex office until my passport arrives, but they probably have rules about that kind of thing. The embassy might take me. Though they might hold me there indefinitely, if they didn't believe my rather incredible account of my "abduction."

When we say our good-byes, the computerized voice says I have three minutes left. Damn it. Someone knocks on the door. "Just a minute!" I call in English before realizing the knocker probably speaks Russian.

I dial the number for my voice mail and find my mailbox full. I force myself to delete messages from Diana and Hannah and every member of my extended family without listening to more than a few words. They're all the same. "We're worried/concerned/desperate to hear from you." A testy missive from Henry expresses outrage that I've failed to check in and asks "whether our friend is sleepy."

The person waiting outside knocks again. Charlie tells my voicemail he got into the vault under Smerth's desk. He found several pages of documentation that Clearwater Partners paid bribes totaling in the tens of millions to ensure that Congress grants Burtonhall Construction Corporation a no-bid contract to build the proposed oil pipeline connecting Russia to Turkey, should the Russian government approve the project. He doesn't think this makes sense. He says Clearwater must have received something more for its money. He finds it unfathomable that so many elected officials would risk the potential embarrassment, just for a construction project in another country. Even if the project would benefit an American firm.

Charlie starts listing the members of Congress and the sums they accepted when the voice mail system cuts him off.

The next message, left a minute later, is Charlie again. He wonders whether he should go to the media. He's afraid of being disbarred for violation of confidences, but thinks the "overwhelming public interest in the truth" might outweigh his concerns for his law license. He wants to know what I think. I think he should forget about the vault, keep his head down and hope nobody notices his snooping.

I'm about to call him back, but the voice tells me I have no more minutes, and the person outside has escalated to banging on the door instead of knocking politely. I emerge from the bathroom, wearing what I hope is an apologetic expression. A robust woman who's holding a visibly uncomfortable young boy by the hand shoves past me with a sniff and slams the door.

Mikhail pays the bill and we hurry out of the Yalki Palki.

I quietly plan my dash to American Express and out of the country as we step outside into the drizzly evening. I haven't decided whether to return Henry's call. I suppose I don't see the upside. He won't be happy to hear that Mikhail remains conscious.

As if he's reading my mind, Mikhail says, "We need to procure a passport for you. No hotel in Moscow will allow you into their rooms without one. And we need a hotel so I can get online in private."

"What about the hookers?" Not that I want to compare myself to them, but I assume they march past the guards without I.D.

Mikhail laughs, "You'd never pass for a Moscow call girl, even with your new hair."

"That's not what I meant!"

"I know. Those girls get upstairs by tipping out the clerks. The staff would charge an extortionary price to hide an undocumented foreigner. It's cheaper and safer to procure a passport."

We stop at the entrance of a photo shop with a big red sign advertising one-hour service. Only "one hour" has been crossed out and replaced with "same day."

Mikhail greets the clerk in a familiar way. He ushers us behind a heavy purple curtain, into a back room with a camera set up facing a stepstool which is pushed against a plain white background. The clerk snaps my picture and scans the photo into his computer. He fiddles with the image then turns to us. "Name?"

"Claudia Lane," I answer, without thinking. Might as well stick to the alias I know.

Mikhail overrules me. "Korov will check hotels for Claudia Lane. Use Anne Lewis."

Minutes later we emerge from the shop equipped with a perfect New Zealand passport, complete with a properly stamped Russian entry visa, for Anne Lewis of Christchurch, age 29. I figured there was no harm in making myself one year younger. When I suggested that maybe I should be Canadian or American because of my accent, Mikhail assured me that most Russians can't tell one English speaker from another.

The passport's presence in my purse restores a little spring to my step. I no longer have to sneak over to AmEx, because this passport is better than my real one.

But crap. Now I need Diana to rebook my plane tickets in my new name. I whip out the phone and text her.

Diana sends a text in return: All cards maxed out by airfare. Will see what I can do. Hang in there.

Of course she already booked the flights. I text back: PLEASE TRY.

We ride the subway a few stops and disembark into yet another station opulently decorated with marble and artwork from some looted church. We navigate through a maze of underground corridors before popping up across the street from one of those creepy Seven Sisters skyscrapers.

"Now what?" I liked my chances of blending better on the subway. The sidewalks here aren't exactly packed.

"We're checking into the Hotel Ukraina."

We make a mad dash across eight lanes of moving traffic, because the underground passageway is closed for renovations. The lobby is almost identical to the one at the Belgrade, only larger.

Mikhail goes through the elaborate check-in process in heavily accented English I haven't heard him use previously. The passport he hands over with my new one is issued by Poland. The clerk keeps the passports and hands Mikhail a card key. We ride the elevator up to a glassed in foyer that's utterly indistinguishable from the landing on my floor at the Belgrade. Once we're in the room, he hangs the Do Not Disturb sign and pulls out his laptop.

I survey our new quarters. There's only one major difference between this room and my last one. The room at the Belgrade contained one double bed, but this room has two. Tricky. Did he get two beds because he's a gentleman and assumes I will want my own? Or worse, maybe he doesn't want to sleep with me again? Or maybe he presumes I don't want to sleep with him, which I'm not sure I do, because clearly I'm obsessing about these beds. Maybe this was the only room available. I doubt we're staying long enough to use the beds anyway.

Mikhail snaps me out of my momentary neurosis. "Aren't you interested?"

"In what?"

He smiles and the dimple flashes. He looks relaxed for a hunted man. "Let's see if my microphones have picked up anything while I've been, what do you Yanks say? Away from my desk."

The screen divides into a dozen small squares, each with an idle audio band.

"You don't think they swept for bugs after they heard you shoot Casper?"

"Probably. That's why most of these show no activity. But I'd be surprised if they got them all."

No sooner has he said this than one of the little boxes on the screen crackles to life. We hear a stream of obscenities that leave me with no doubt as to the speaker's identity. Acheson.

"Where are they?" I whisper.

"Relax. They can't hear us. They're in Korov's main drawing room. You remember. We had brandy there. He has so much wiring in that room. I'm not surprised the bug survived his countermeasures."

Something slams, maybe a phone. Mikhail starts typing while we listen. One by one, he enlarges the boxes on the screen and checks their settings before shrinking them back. I watch over his shoulder and decide he's checking to see if any of his microphones recorded anything earlier. Only one did. He plays the sound back, without turning off the live feed, which has gone quiet except for the distinct sounds of pacing. I can picture Acheson wearing a track in Korov's Persian carpet with his overpriced wingtips.

The prerecorded sound turns up nothing but twenty minutes of vacuuming and other cleaning noises. Mikhail minimizes that window and we strain to hear the live feed from the drawing room.

Five or ten minutes later we hear Korov rush in, with his butler in hot pursuit. The butler serves drinks and leaves the room.

"Not a good day," Korov says, after the door closes behind his servant. "We've lost our point man for tomorrow *and* I learned that one of my favorite men is a traitor. Yet we have no way of knowing what, if anything, he's handed over to the government. Nor can we seem to locate him. Abdul Aziz has disappeared. God knows where to. And the day's not even over." Korov's palpable agitation increases as he spits out each consecutive complaint.

Acheson must be losing his mind, because he decides to add an item to Korov's list. "And the key financials have gone missing from the vault in Randolph's office. Maybe we should have kept the poor chump alive. At least he kept track of our files."

"He kept such good track that he practically had a slide show ready for the Attorney General. He had compiled and printed an indexed guide to every illegal act we've committed over the past ten years."

So Max and Henry were partially correct. There was a paper trail inside R&S, but I never would have found it by snooping where they directed me to snoop.

"Do you think Aziz has it all?" Acheson asks.

"No," Korov says. "I've considered that possibility, but it's unlikely. He and Smerth stopped speaking after he switched lawyers."

"Don't be so sure. Randolph was meticulous. I'm sure the bastard backed up everything and hid it somewhere in Bermuda. Aziz could've gotten the duplicates from the vault in Hamilton. God knows he spent enough time down there. I told you it was a shitty idea to invite Muhammed into Clearwater Partners." Acheson's voice crescendos. I can almost see the hairs on his neck stand on end.

"Muhammed's money's as green as anyone else's, and his pockets are deeper than everyone's."

Korov's right. The new Crown Prince is filthy rich, even by Saudi standards.

"Right, but because we got greedy, we put Abdul off the idea of a Prescott presidency," Acheson argues. "I've known Abdul bin Aziz for half my fucking life. If he has to choose between his investment in Clearwater and the throne, he will choose the throne. And if he has to choose between his millions and preventing his brother's son from sitting on that throne, the spiteful prick's going to spend every dime to make sure Muhammed never becomes king."

Korov grunts something indecipherable in reply.

Acheson adds, "You know as well as I do that Aziz never needed the money he made with Clearwater Partners. He used all his profits from the firm to funnel money to all sorts of fundamentalist nut jobs, while masquerading as a normal businessman. His westernized veneer and Oxbridge English gave him the perfect cover."

He takes a breath but he's not finished, "And because you couldn't fucking wait, you took out Smerth without considering that he was a smart fuck. He knew he was in danger. Before we killed him, we should have found out what he knew, beyond the bribes and the fake charities. Maybe we should have even paid him to go along with everything."

"You've never hesitated about killing anyone before. So please, try not to be disingenuous." Korov sounds almost put upon.

I swallow hard. Acheson could have killed me that night in his office. He could have strangled me with his bare hands. I bet he only held back for logistical reasons; it's problematic to cover up an unplanned murder.

"What the hell is that supposed to mean?" Acheson demands.

"That it was such a Goddamn foolproof plan you had before, to use the Secret Service to plant bombs in a bunch of laptops and frame those milquetoast Muslim post grads as mass murderers."

I feel the air rush from my lungs. Even tempered through the static laced sound feed, this bombshell hits me like a rib cracking blow.

"Excuse me. That almost worked. And now we know for sure that BXE owns an entire branch of the Secret Service. So I'd argue that operation was a resounding success," Acheson says.

I glance at Mikhail. His face gives away nothing. I wonder whether he had any advance inkling about the Washington attacks, if he could have prevented them.

Maybe I don't want to hear the answer to that. And what does Acheson mean by "almost worked?"

Korov again. "No, it didn't *almost work*. You set off the chaos of the train attacks without the tandem effect of a leadership vacuum. You should have waited until one of our men had a clean shot at the president and *then* blown up the subway. That's the problem with you Americans. You all want instant gratification and when it doesn't work out, you run crying to your lawyers."

Despite everything else, I wince at Korov's description of my countrymen. He can't possibly believe Acheson is a typical specimen.

"Taking out POTUS in favor of Jack Prescott was always part of the plan. Killing my old friend Randolph Smerth was not."

"POTUS?" I ask Mikhail.

"Insider lingo for President of the United States."

Right. I knew I'd heard the term somewhere before.

"It's not like you can return to the States, so please spare me this nonsense about your lawyer," Korov says.

"You can bet your shriveled Russian nuts I'm going home as soon as POTUS is dead. Prescott will pardon me."

"Or he'll decide you're not worth the political capital. The presidency corrupts people. They step into that Oval Office and sometimes they forget their old friends."

A buzzer sounds. Korov announces that he's taking a call in another room. Mikhail frantically clicks around the computer screen to see if he can pick up conversations from elsewhere in the house. No such luck.

Korov marches out to the escalating timbre of Acheson's voice. "What the hell am I supposed to do about my family? It's not like the girls can grow up on the run. And Helen has no idea about any of this, besides the bribes to Congress. What the fuck am I supposed to tell my wife? Sorry, honey, I made us a fortune selling arms and construction contracts with Clearwater but the fucking government's going to confiscate every last penny. And by the way, I'm fucking going to prison for the rest of my fucking life. Is that what I'm supposed to say?"

"That, my friend, is your concern." Korov closes the door behind him, leaving Acheson alone with his panic attack.

"Why is Korov keeping Acheson alive?" I ask Mikhail. "His life as an influence peddler is over."

Mikhail shrugs. "Jack Prescott must want him alive for some reason. Maybe he'll install him as CEO of Clearwater." He replays the last few seconds of the conversation and smiles. "That's exactly what I thought he said."

"What?" I demand. I could hear them loud and clear. I wonder what Mikhail missed.

"Acheson referred to arms money. I have the paper trail that shows Korov is running weapons in Titan containers, but a recorded reference is like extra insurance."

"Just because Acheson said arms money doesn't mean they're smuggling weapons in *Titan* shipments." It's like we're playing a board game and Mikhail has skipped a number of squares to get to the finish line. Of course he knows more Titan back story. I remind myself he worked there until a few hours ago.

And that knowing something isn't the same thing as having proof.

We hear Korov storm back into the room. "Tomorrow's a go. If we pull this off, I'll be the most powerful man in Russia. And perhaps I'll give you asylum, old friend." His tone is icy, menacing. I can't tell whether he's toying with Acheson on purpose or if it just sounds that way.

I can, however, practically hear Acheson gritting his teeth. "Don't you think that's a big *if*? How do you know Aziz isn't singing as we speak?"

"Don't be so melodramatic," Korov sniffs. "You're wrong about Aziz. He has too much invested to squeal. He'll keep the cash and let his nephew have the Kingdom. And once he calms down, he'll see that he got the better end of the deal. Arab Spring could yet come to Saudi. Off with their heads and all that. Were you in his shoes, wouldn't you rather have the cash?"

"I think you're wrong," says Acheson. "I think Aziz is a hothead. He's mad as hell and he's so fucking rich that he's incapable of imagining his life any other way. Which means he's undeterred by financial risk. But most importantly, he wants to rule Saudi Arabia. He's spent his entire adult life on the world stage, being groomed as their next great statesman."

"Your point?" Korov needles.

"He's also fucking brilliant. I bet Aziz plans to bid against BXE this week. Think about it. Two Saudis, each wants to be king, each commands a personal nuclear arsenal."

Mikhail says, "Aziz must have cold feet about the auction. Maybe he's concerned his nephew is too young. He's liable to start a nuclear war with Israel, just to look tough. Maybe the man has some scruples, at least where it comes to defending his homeland. Why else would he be running around Moscow with the FBI?" He looks at me, as if expecting me to enlighten him.

Korov's voice prevents me from speculating. "Why would Aziz want the Kingdom anyhow? Their unemployment's worse than ours. And the heat. Whether or not spring comes to Saudi, their neighborhood's going downhill. Who wants to be the only monarch left on the block?" I can't believe Korov's levity. Then I realize it's his way of closing the subject. "We have to stop spinning our wheels. We can wait a day and re-take Aziz's temperature, but we need to find Mikhail and the girl tonight."

My mouth goes dry. I wonder about our chances of evading them. A knock reverberates through the speakers. Some renegade part of my mind tricks me into thinking somebody's knocking on our hotel room door and I jump.

There's a quick exchange in Russian.

Mikhail explains, "That's Kolya, Korov's head of security. He says he's brought in a superior bug sweeping system."

"So no more listening in?"

"Afraid not."

We listen to the sounds of Korov's men scouring the room. We hear a beep and some yelling in Russian before the audio feed falls silent.

Mikhail leans back in his chair, which is made of flimsy wood and upholstered in green plaid. He runs his fingers through his hair and rubs his scalp. "At least we've confirmed they're looking for us."

That's no comfort whatsoever. "We already knew that. I think it's time for you to make your deal with the FBI and for me to go home. The tape of this conversation alone would be enough to nail them and the stuff stashed at your place—or in Switzerland—would be gravy."

I don't understand why he still looks so damn torn. This should not be a difficult decision. I try appealing to reason. "If you join forces with the FBI, you'll have the best chance of heading off the plot."

Mikhail looks unconvinced, and perhaps even mildly paralyzed by indecision. I curse myself for disregarding Henry's orders. If I'd followed directions, I could be on my way home. Russia isn't hiding answers to my questions. Nor has my adventure, or rather misadventure, done anything to ease my sense of loss and frustration. If there are answers for me anywhere, they're probably back in Washington. This insane chapter of my quest for justice should end here.

Mikhail says nothing. But at least he's thinking about it. I watch his face for clues for what feels like an eternity, but in reality is probably no more than a minute. Finally he says, "You had no idea what you were getting into, did you?"

I shake my head no.

"You really thought Korov would help you?"

I nod, feeling sheepish. Since this whole thing started, I've been played by the FBI, by Korov and quite possibly by Mikhail, too. I've been a pawn, who occasionally contributes something useful to the larger game.

Mikhail says, "He still might, you know. If he can pin your husband's murder on Aziz, he might want to do that, even though he's mad as hell at me. Because if Aziz is indeed the murderer, that conveniently makes him a less credible witness against Korov and Acheson, if and when their dealings come to light."

"If Korov wants to help me, he can send me the video. Not that I believe he has it. Or that one even exists." *And if he's going to send me anything at this point, it's likely to be an assassin, delivered right to my front door.*

Mikhail produces his mobile phone from his pocket. "Here," he says, holding it out to me. "Call your agents. Tell them you're ready to come in from the cold."

It feels like such a funereal moment. Mikhail looks defeated and I try to diffuse the tension by laughing at his silly spy talk. He rewards my effort with a sad smile. A sharp pain, probably a pang of misguided regret, jabs my chest, but resolve takes over. I'm not following him blindly anymore. And my instincts are screaming at me to get the hell out of Russia.

I take the phone. " Do you want me to tell them about the key?"

"I can't stop you."

"It's worthless without the code."

"Indeed it is."

"So are you ready to make a deal?"

Mikhail furrows his brow, chews his lower lip, and decides to punt. "Get Henry Redwell on the phone and see if he wants to talk to me."

I dial with shaky hands and listen to the beep of the foreign ring tone.

Max answers. "Where are you? Are you alright? I'm so glad to hear your voice."

And I'm stunned to hear his. "Detour," I say, hoping I don't have to explain. "I'm hanging in there. Where have you been?"

He ignores my question. "Henry's here with me. He says he's glad to hear from you, but he hopes you have something good to show for your detour."

Mikhail gets up out of his chair and walks to the window. He pulls the beige curtain back to peek outside at the rainy Moscow night. "As a matter of fact, I have a few interesting things to share with you. First, Charlie called to tell me he found the files documenting Burtonhall's no bid contract to build a replacement pipeline. They were in Smerth's office the whole time."

"Yeah, we know," says Max. "And I think you're going to want to sit down for this."

"I'm sitting," I lie. He can't possibly have discovered anything more shocking than the cache under Mikhail's floorboards, or the recording of the conversation Mikhail and I overheard. Acheson and the Secret Service were behind the Washington attacks. We may not have staved off the pipeline blast, but we've solved the biggest criminal investigation in recent American history.

"Lena, we know about the Burtonhall files because we've been listening to Charlie's cell phone. I also know your pal Diana's trying to book you a flight home, but we can speak about that later."

"So you have the files?" I ask excitedly.

"No. We have no idea where they are and I'm sorry to be the one to tell you this. Charlie Winthrop was found dead in his office, shortly after he left you that message. We think he was poisoned."

"No," I start to say, but my head spins and everything goes dark. I feel the phone slide out of my fingers.

When I come to, Mikhail's leaning over my face, holding the phone. "Yeah, she's conscious. You gave her a shock. No, she wasn't sitting down."

I push myself off the floor and lunge for the phone. Mikhail sidesteps out of reach. "Is Redwell there? Let me talk to him."

I take his desire to speak to Henry as a positive sign and stop grabbing at the phone. Instead I take a seat on the edge of the bed and put my head down. I still feel dizzy and I don't want to pass out again. Those bastards killed off poor, harmless Charlie. Charlie who was concerned about the ethics of sharing his treasure trove of new evidence. I wonder who actually poisoned him, since the usual suspects have converged on this side of the pond.

Mikhail graciously puts his phone on speaker. Henry's voice comes through. "Redwell here."

"Your lady agent wants to come in."

"I see. And why can't she tell me that herself?" Henry sounds blasé, almost bored.

"Because depending on your level of interest, I'm prepared to send her back to you with a key to a safety deposit box in Switzerland and the pass code that goes with it."

"I'm listening," says Henry. He switches his end of the conversation to speaker, so Max can hear. I wonder if Aziz and Katya are still with them. Somehow I doubt it. Mikhail must not care any more, since he doesn't ask.

"I think you'll find the memory sticks in this safety deposit box very interesting. They were compiled over five years in Korov's organization and contain enough information to throw the book at all the major Clearwater players. I have records of money laundering, terror financing, you name it. And as a special bonus, I'll provide you with a recording of Acheson, admitting his role in the DC metro attacks."

The other end of the line has gone silent. They must assume Mikhail is bluffing. But why would he bother to initiate contact if he wasn't serious about a deal?

I pick my head up out of my lap and realize they've put us on mute. Mikhail raises his eyebrows at me. I shrug. I have no idea what they could be saying.

We hear a click and Henry's voice comes back on. "I suppose you want something in return."

"I do. You're going to need a pen."

"Of course I have a pen, my boy."

Does Henry need to be so patronizing? At first I found his funny way of talking endearing. But it's actually just obnoxious.

"I want ten million dollars."

Max lets out a guffaw. "Is that all? We don't carry that kind of cash."

Mikhail doesn't miss a beat. "Ten million dollars is nothing to the U.S. government. They waste that much on disposable coffee cups every week at the Pentagon."

"I'm not so sure about that," says Max.

Mikhail says, "And I read recently that the First Lady flew her labradoodle to some pet psychic in LA. On Air Force One."

Max curses under his breath, but Henry cuts him off. "Assuming we could procure ten million dollars for you, I'm guessing you don't want suitcases of cash?"

"No. I want it wired from the U.S. Treasury – make sure it's the U.S. Treasury– into my account at UBS in Zurich. Half up front. Half when Lena delivers the key and the code."

"And if we're not happy with the quality of the information?" Max says.

"You will be more than happy." Mikhail pauses. Silence on the other end. "Are you ready for the wiring instructions?"

Mikhail recites a twenty-two digit account number and an eleven digit routing number from memory. "Call me when I can confirm the first transfer. Then we'll arrange for you to be reunited with your wayward lady agent."

He hangs up before they can object and turns to me. "Let's move."

I hoist myself off the edge of the bed. Mikhail takes a quick final scan of the room and hurries me out the door. In the lobby, he waves a hundred dollar bill at the initially recalcitrant clerk. She fetches our passports without further conversation.

I swear there's a spring in Mikhail's step as he pushes through the revolving doors. For a second, I despise him for it. But then I realize: Why shouldn't he be happy? If all goes according to his plan, he'll be a rich man by the end of the night. We disappear into the subway once again. Our train barrels into the station within seconds of our arrival on the platform.

I ask where we're going.

"Just one step ahead of everyone. We need another hotel."

29

Mikhail checks us into the Hotel Bucharest, an establishment resembling the Hotels Belgrade and Ukraina, even though there's a perfectly nice Intercontinental across the street. Mikhail notices me eyeing it and says, "Sorry. The Russian ones are safer."

He trades our passports for another card key, which he uses to admit us to another elevator, another glass encased lobby and another modern yet modest room. This one contains only one bed. Not that it matters. Based on our track record, we won't be spending the night.

Mikhail fires up his laptop and opens a series of detailed architectural drawings. I force myself to stop pacing and pull up a chair.

"What's all this?"

"The Bolshoi Theatre, the Ritz Carlton Hotel and the Kremlin Palace."

I squint at the screen. "Where did you get these?"

The drawings show painstaking details. Every tile, every pipe, every air shaft.

"I downloaded them about a month ago from Korov's database. I didn't know exactly what he had in mind when I took them, but they seemed too interesting to pass up. Getting into any of the Kremlin palaces without advance clearance, especially during a state visit, is a pretty thorny process. Which is why I suspect they'll try to take him out the day after tomorrow, at the special ballet performance in his honor. Which means I need to know all possible routes in and out. And I want to get inside before the rest of the audience."

What is wrong with him? Mikhail should be mentally spending his millions and plotting his escape, instead of pushing ahead with this suicide mission to help save the American president. This may sound awful, but it's not his job.

"How?"

"With press credentials. You're a writer and I'm your cameraman, remember?"

I laugh in his face. "Aren't you forgetting a key fact? The President of the United States will be there. I don't know what kind of lax security measures your presidential guards normally take, but I can assure you that the U.S. Secret Service will have an advance list of every person cleared into the event."

He shrugs as if this makes no difference. "So maybe we should dry run our disguises at the palace tomorrow. They finished a gut renovation last year, put in air conditioning, restored every piece of art in the place, and added state of the art security. I wouldn't mind a look." He grins.

"Haven't I made myself clear? I'm done with these insane spy games. I want to go home."

"And miss all the fun? We can't have that."

Alarms go off in my head again. He's planning to use me somehow. Otherwise he would insist on working alone.

"Trust me," he says.

That line may have worked before, but not this time.

Mikhail makes notes from his diagrams as I pace by the window and try to formulate my next move. The blinds are drawn so we can peer out, but others can't see inside. Across the street, the rain pelts a work site illuminated to make it look like midday. It resembles an enormous museum diorama against the darkness.

My prepaid phone chimes, announcing an incoming text. Diana came through, big time: "Booked U and Anne, all BA flights tmrw, next 2 days. Come home. T maxed out 2 cards 4 U. BE CAREFUL!!! Call me!!!! xoxoxo D."

It takes me a second to realize that T stands for Tobey. So he's still in the picture. I wonder how much she had to tell him to get her hands on his credit cards. *I have this friend who's in trouble. I can't tell you any details, but I need your MasterCard. And your Visa. And maybe your Amex, too.* If anyone can deliver such a speech successfully, it's Diana.

So now all I need to do is get Anne's passport from reception and dive into a cab to the embassy, where I will not leave Max and Henry's side until we're home. I'm racking my brain for a plausible excuse to step out when Mikhail says, "Hey, come look at this."

He's reading about Charlie's death. They published his picture from the R&S web site. He's wearing a blue suit and smiling too broadly for a business portrait. The story explains that Charles Ronald Winthrop, 34, an associate at the same DC firm where fabled litigator Quillan Randolph Smerth, 51, was murdered two days prior, was found dead in his Connecticut Avenue office. The coroner's preliminary report suspects poisoning by diarsenic pentoxide. I've never heard of it before, but it can't be healthy if its name contains the word arsenic.

While the police suspect foul play, they cannot speculate on a motive. The article says the victim had no known enemies and notes that Winthrop had received a "very positive" performance review immediately before his death, according to Managing Partner Evelyn Peabody. It goes on to report that Ms. Peabody was the last person to see the deceased alive. "We met this morning for his annual review. Charlie seemed pleased and eager to get back to work," she's quoted as saying. "It's obviously an incredibly difficult time at the firm, with Charlie's death coming so soon after that of our longtime partner, Randolph Smerth, and the unresolved disappearance of our associate, Lena Mancuso."

"Have you heard of that poison?" I ask Mikhail.

"It's an ingredient in a variety of pesticides. I'm not a poison expert, but I believe it would only take a miniscule dose to kill an adult."

"Right, but how would they get Charlie to eat pesticide? Wouldn't it taste bad?" Despite the evidence, I am in denial about Charlie's death. It's too much to process, and he was such an honest, hard-working, thoughtful person.

"The murderer probably slipped it into his coffee or some alcoholic drink, any beverage with a strong flavor of its own."

"It would've been his coffee. He wasn't one to drink on the job."

I think back to the day we went to lunch and pondered Acheson's electoral map over a couple of clandestine beers. Charlie would never drink before work and certainly not on the morning of his fifth-year review. The fifth year review is a huge deal, because that's when R&S associates find out whether they're on track for a chance at partnership.

"Was he a good friend of yours?"

"We were colleagues. He was a really good guy." I'd always considered Charlie too nerdy to count as a friend. Maybe he was one after all.

"Do you have any idea who did this?"

"No clue. As far as I know, all the suspects are over here, except Smerth, who's dead. Who else would feel threatened by Charlie's discovery of the Burtonhall deal?"

"The vice president?"

"Too far fetched. Prescott travels by motorcade and can't exactly sneak into law offices to poison people unnoticed. Could Casper have other operatives working in Washington?"

"Unlikely. He was an odd duck who worked alone. But it's worth checking out. It could also have been any number of Secret Service agents. Who knows how many they've corrupted?"

Instead of pondering Charlie's death, Mikhail spends the next couple of hours poring over his diagrams of the palace. When I tire of looking over his shoulder, I pace by the window and struggle to formulate an excuse to duck out and away from here. I doubt it's an option to say, "Well, so long," and head for the door.

I snap silently at myself to stop being stupid. Of course it's an option. Mikhail wants my company and questionable assistance, for whatever reason, but he's made no motions to force me to stay. I grudgingly admit to myself that I'm not leaving because walking further away from Korov—and his stupid tape, that might or might not even exist—feels like abject, inexcusable, shameful failure.

I've come so far. I've nearly been killed, more than once. My mind can't accept that it's probably been for nothing.

Another half hour passes before Mikhail picks up the hotel phone and orders room service. He doesn't bother to ask what I'd like. Overcooked burgers, greasy fries, a liter of water and a six-pack of Baltiskaya beer arrive in a respectable fifteen minutes.

We chew our food in silence. Mikhail looks far away, lost in his thoughts. Bags have appeared under his eyes and I notice a faint tremor in his fingers each time he lifts his water glass. He doesn't look at all like a man on the cusp of huge wealth.

I take a few sips of beer in a futile attempt to dull my nerves. I shred the label into shards and lay the pieces next to my plate. Once I've scraped the bottle down to the glue I ask, without looking up, "What's next on your agenda?"

"Press credentials, and hopefully a few hours of sleep."

I take another sip of beer. "What if I don't like your plan?"

He shrugs and pushes a French fry around a pool of ketchup, forming a track as if he's plowing a ketchup blizzard. It's all I can do to stop myself from snapping at him for playing with his food.

After another moment of no sound but my chewing, he says, "Look. I'm wiped out. I killed a man today, in case you forgot. I had to do it, but it's still weighing on me. So I'm sorry if I've got nothing to say."

While his little speech does nothing to ease my mind about the immediate future, I am relieved that shooting someone bothers him. It weighs against him being an utter psychopath.

After dinner, we fetch our passports from a clerk at a special window in the lobby. The Bucharest's system is more Soviet than the last two hotels. We have go to reception and get a rubberstamped ticket, then wait at the passport window while the same clerk sidles over there to hand us our documents. Mikhail stows both passports inside his shirt.

Back in the room, he suggests I jump in the shower. I hadn't thought of indulging in such a mundane ritual, but now that he says it, a shower sounds fantastic. The hot water surprises me by coming out hot. I stand under the spray long enough to fog up the entire bathroom and soak the floor and walls with condensation. When I emerge, wrapped in two large but threadbare towels, Mikhail's proudly displaying our press passes. It irks me that I didn't hear him run out to print them over the noise of the water. Nor did he warn me I'd be alone.

Mikhail says he wants a couple of hours of sleep. Has he lost his mind? He's running from one of the most powerful men in the world, who happens to be furious at him, and he's worried about catching a few z's. Worse, he doesn't shed the shirt with the passports in the pocket until after he disappears into the bathroom. I hear him latch the door. Damn. Maybe the steam cleared my mind, because a rush to the airport sounds appealing once more. Maybe there's no shame in going home empty-handed. It's not like I'm measurably worse off than when I started. At least in terms of solving the murder. My insides spin with indecision. I turn on the television and find CNN. They're wrapping up a report on Acheson's disappearance.

Mikhail emerges from the bathroom in boxer shorts, looking marginally more relaxed, with a towel slung over his shoulders.

"Do you really think it's safe to sleep here?" I ask.

"We won't stay all night, but I want to be here when the wire comes through. We can catch a power nap."

He sits on the edge of the bed and commandeers the clicker. He flips through the usual stuff: soccer games, *I Love Lucy* re-runs, an infomercial for a twelve-function kitchen wonder gadget, before stopping on the local news. They're covering a raging apartment fire. Mikhail's jaw drops.

"That's not—?"

"It is. Maria Petrovska Street. My building. Christ."

The reporter is interviewing an elderly woman who's wearing a dressing gown and clutching a cat. The black feline seems nonplussed by the surrounding chaos. Red fire engine lights flash against the night sky. Mikhail translates for me. Someone planted suicide vests throughout the building and detonated them remotely.

"Korov?" I ask.

"I think so, but the government will blame the Islamists. The alarms went off before anyone even smelled smoke. Everybody got out. This has Korov written all over it."

Firefighters douse the building, which looks like a total loss. Mikhail looks rattled, more so than after he shot Casper, or after our run in with the BXE men.

"That's why you backed everything up, right? You thought someone might discover and destroy your stash. It'll be okay." As I say this, I get out of bed and cross the room to grab my purse. I want the key within reach.

He nods, entranced by the images of his building burning to the pavement and his innocent neighbors watching all their worldly possessions go up in smoke. What was their crime? Living near Mikhail. The arbitrariness makes me ill.

The coverage shifts to a parliamentary debate on pension policy and he starts clicking again. It's after eleven when he kills the television and climbs into bed from the other side.

I pull the starchy covers up to my chin and will myself to fall asleep. When I peek out of the corner of my eye, I see he's doing the exact same thing. I can tell by his breathing he's wide awake. After twenty minutes of listening to each other breathe in the dark, he rolls over in one swift motion and curls up behind me.

We lie in silence for a spell. Mikhail nudges my hair out of the way and gently kisses the back of my neck. His hand cups my breast through my shirt, questioning. He pauses, waits for my answer. I take his hand in mine and guide it under my clothes so he's touching my skin. He rolls on top of me so his weight pushes me into the mattress, making me feel both caught and secure at the same time. When he moves inside me, the sex feels more reassuring than anything. *I'm not alone against all those evil men. We're in this together now.*

30

The phone jolts me awake at twenty after two in the morning. It takes a moment to remember where I am. Mikhail apparently doesn't suffer from any similar disorientation. He's out of bed, phone in hand, before it rings a second time. He says something is good.

He hangs up and places another call. While he waits for an answer, he grabs his jeans from over the chair and starts dressing. He looks like he could be in a fashion advertisement, standing there with slightly tousled hair and no shirt, jeans on but unzipped.

Finally someone answers. They converse in French. I don't catch much besides a series of numbers. I suspect he's confirming that five million dollars arrived in his account and he wants it moved elsewhere.

Mikhail reads another long series of numbers. The person on the other end puts him on hold. After a pause Mikhail says, "*Merci, Monsieur,*" and hangs up.

"What was all that?"

"I confirmed that five million dollars hit my account in Zurich. I divided the money into ten parts and wired it onward to other accounts."

"All Swiss?" I'm not sure why this should matter but I ask anyway.

"No. Swiss banking is private but not wholly anonymous. I've picked some more discreet places."

"Like where?"

"Like Liechtenstein, Palau, Cyprus and the Caymans. Among others."

He turns his attention to the laptop and logs into various banking sites to monitor his transfers. "Most of these are set up to forward deposits onward immediately." He looks at the screen, obviously satisfied that the international banking system is performing to his expectations.

I rub sleep from my eyes. "How long have you had these accounts ready to go?"

"I opened them when I acquired the safe deposit box in Zurich."

The money hits all ten accounts within an impressive fifteen minutes. Mikhail moves his funds three more times. I watch over his shoulder, fascinated. I had no idea it was so easy to bounce one's fortune all over the globe in the middle of the night.

Mikhail double checks several accounts before he seems satisfied. As he shuts down, he reaches for a beer and asks if I want one. Why not? I'm wide awake and feeling a tiny bit more secure now that Mikhail and the FBI have made their deal.

"3-3-0-2-8-7-4-4-9-1," he recites as he pops the tops off two bottles of Baltiskaya with the hotel's opener.

I don't register what he's saying until half the numbers are out of his mouth. He waits for me to repeat the code, which I somehow manage on the first try. I say it over and over to myself, determined to sear the numbers into my long term memory. Mikhail hands me a beer.

The first sip is still in my mouth when someone knocks on the door. I jump halfway out of my skin and almost choke on the lukewarm lager.

Mikhail grabs his gun from the nightstand. He holds a finger to his lips and motions for me to stand between the bureau and the window. I do as I'm told and stretch his shirt in a futile attempt to cover more of my legs. I mentally curse the FBI for sending me out after Mikhail without so much as a minute of self defense training. Our visitor knocks again.

The knocking turns to pounding. Mikhail walks to the door, looks out the peephole and heaves a sigh that sounds halfway between resigned and exasperated. He lowers his gun and admits Korov, who barges in, handgun trained on Mikhail's chest. Mikhail must have put down his own weapon to prevent the men from blowing each other away. Part of me thinks he should have shot Korov, though I doubt he could convince himself to do it. The same man who shot Casper point blank, without even flinching, has come to view this ruthless tycoon as a kind of dysfunctional father figure.

The door slams shut behind Korov. He's wearing an expensive suit and every one of his hairs is slicked into place with some type of styling product. Discussion ensues in Russian. Mikhail's ears redden as he repeats something over and over. In the end, he drops his gun to the floor and kicks it away. I flinch, afraid it will fire and send bullets ricocheting all over the room.

There's more conversation in Russian and Korov gestures in my general direction. His gold tooth glimmers. "I was explaining to Mikhail that you're coming with me."

I can't find my voice, but I feel my head shaking no.

"Yes," says Korov. "You'll be my *guest* tonight. Tomorrow you and I will have a little photo op. Then I'll present you with the item you came for and you'll be free to go."

I shudder. I doubt what he claims is what he has in mind. All the skin on my bare legs has gone to goose bumps. I shift from foot to foot and hold down the t-shirt as low as it will go, roughly mid-thigh.

Mikhail steps closer to me. "It'll be okay. We don't exactly have a choice," he says. I wonder what he's up to. Korov no doubt shares my curiosity. "Why don't you get dressed?"

He nods encouragingly and even musters a small smile as I gingerly step towards the armchair where I piled my clothes. It's on the side of the bed closer to the door and Korov.

Mikhail seizes the brief moment while Korov's eyes are on me. He rips his laptop from the wall and flings it at the window. I stop in my tracks, hold my breath and stare, knowing it will crash to the floor.

But it doesn't. Instead the shoddy construction of the Hotel Bucharest gives way, the window shatters into a thousand tiny pieces and the laptop soars out into the night and plummets fourteen floors to the street.

"Now we can go," Mikhail says.

Korov's eyes burn with anger, which I hope he won't take out on me. It's not that I don't care what happens to Mikhail, but my instinct for self-preservation has kicked in and shoved all my other emotions aside. Maybe if I cooperate they won't hurt me. I'll play nice until I can make a run for it.

Which isn't now. There are only two ways out of this room, the door Korov's blocking and the window exit used by the now deceased laptop. Neither looks tempting.

I pull on my pants.

Korov says, "Wouldn't you be more comfortable changing in the restroom? I want to speak to your friend in private."

I scurry past him like a panicked mouse and barricade myself in the bathroom. The floor's still wet and the lights buzz ominously for a second before flickering to life, but as I shut the latch behind me I wish I could hide in here forever. I hear heated but hushed Russian through the flimsy door. I wonder if Korov is threatening to kill Mikhail, probably in some highly unpleasant way.

I frantically search my purse for the safe deposit box key, which has sunk to the bottom. Thankfully, it's fairly small. I shove the key in my bra, not under the strap, but right above the underwire. It cuts into my skin but it's the only solution I can think of, other than attempting to swallow the thing, which I'm not prepared to do. I arrange my shirt as loosely as possible and study myself in the mirror, head on and from both sides. No strange protrusions.

With a deep breath, I undo the latch and step out of my safe room.

"Ready?" Korov asks, as if he's here to pick me up for a movie date.

I nod and try unsuccessfully to swallow the boulder sized lump in my throat.

Korov, hand on his gun, steps aside to let me and Mikhail into the hallway ahead of him. "Go left," he says.

We step into the deserted corridor. Mikhail pushes the stairwell door open and we're met by two of Korov's goons, one of whom immediately seizes my purse. The other shoves Mikhail against the wall and pats him down, more roughly than I'd think necessary. He produces our passports and passes them to Korov.

Korov instructs the toothless man holding my purse, "Hands off the lady."

The man looks uncomprehending. He doesn't speak English. These theatrics are for my benefit. Frankly, I don't see the point. The thug confiscates my prepaid phone but hands back my bag.

Korov gives the order to proceed down the stairs. I exhale as I realize I've been spared the pat down treatment. I almost smirk at the thought that our adversaries have underestimated me, but I catch myself. Any self congratulatory impulses are way premature.

We march down fourteen flights with no sound except for the noise of shoes stomping on cement. The stairs end at the hotel's service entrance. Korov's limousine waits. Mikhail tries to look cool and calm as he slides into the car but his normally resolute face betrays mounting anxiety. Nothing good is going to happen to him at the end of this car journey. As if to underscore my hunch, the thug who gets in next to him throws a black hood over Mikhail's face. I jump back in horror and smash into Korov's chest. He steadies me with his free hand like a boy scout might help a little old lady. The goon cuffs Mikhail's hands together.

Korov's free hand stays on my arm. "Don't worry. I treat my *guests* very well. Please get in the car."

We drive in silence for twenty minutes that feel like twenty hours. I struggle to commit the route to memory but the streets and buildings all look the same in the dark. We pull into a gated garage. The chauffeur kills the engine and a steel cage crashes shut behind us. Lights come on as we spill out. One of the thugs unlocks an entrance with some type of handprint identification device. We arrive in an elaborate foyer, not unlike the one in Korov's *pied à terre*. For all I know, we could be back at that same residence. It's not like he gave me the grand tour last time.

We walk down a hallway adorned with antique mirrors and huge urns of fresh flowers. Korov lets me walk on my own, but the sturdier of the thugs keeps an iron grip on Mikhail's cuffed hands. Mikhail stumbles forward blindly. Korov stops our sorry procession in front of a heavy wooden door.

The door might well be antique and hand carved in appearance, but it sports a thoroughly modern, high tech lock. Korov uses the handprint security system to open it. "Your quarters. I trust you'll be comfortable. I'll see you in the morning. Good night."

Before I have a chance to protest, or even form a question, the door slams shut and I hear nothing but the hum of the ventilation system. I wonder if they'll dump Mikhail in some kind of dungeon. Maybe he'll be able to escape, or at least talk his way out of his predicament, and rescue me.

Or maybe I shouldn't hold my breath. I remind myself that the only reason Mikhail got away from BXE's mercenaries was because they never managed to take him prisoner in the first place. But why on earth would Mikhail surrender to whatever fate Korov prescribes without any fight, moments after becoming economically self-sufficient? The U.S. government's millions would give him options he never contemplated before. He must have some reason for cooperating with Korov. I need to believe this is all choreographed, that it will turn out alright.

I walk over to my room's lone window, a thick glass shield designed to let in the most minimal amount of light. Perhaps Mikhail knew his days were numbered, and that's why he gave me the Swiss vault information. I try to put the thought out of my head but it keeps barging back in. If Mikhail hadn't confiscated my phone, the FBI could use its GPS to find me. Maybe I could convince them to storm the entire premises and rescue Mikhail, too. They've paid the first half of his ten million dollars, so wouldn't they want to keep him alive, at least until they have the files? Not that any of my silly speculation matters, because they have no way of finding me.

The opaque window is barricaded with wrought iron bars of the type used all over the world to deter burglars. They feel sturdy and appear recently installed. There's basic furniture and in the half bath, I find a couple of bottles of Evian on the vanity. Someone has left jeans, a short Burberry trench lined with the signature plaid, and a navy blue V-neck sweater folded neatly over the chair, tags still attached. A belt is coiled on the seat, next to a change of under things and a buttery soft pair of driving moccasins far too nice for springtime slush.

I sit down on the bed, but have trouble being still, so I get up and pace. I curse myself for getting into this predicament. I kick off my shoes and tread circles on the scratchy beige carpet. I doubt Korov truly intends to help me solve the murder. I'm almost positive I've been duped. But why? And does Mikhail know more than he's let on?

Will Korov have him killed before I can ask? I try to chase my gruesome thoughts away, but my imagination keeps going there.

Images of interrogation scenes from a dozen different spy movies float through my mind. I wonder what it will take for Mikhail to fork over the information they want. Not that they'd do anything with it. They might not even rush to Zurich to destroy the files. As far as they know, whatever evidence he has locked in a Swiss bank will rot there in perpetuity, so long as they remove Mikhail from the picture.

I get up again and press my ear to the door. I stay that way for a long time, straining to hear anything, picking up nothing but excruciating silence. After a while I give up. I curl up on the bed, clutching my purse. Hours later, I drift off on top of the covers. I have fitful dreams in which Mikhail succumbs to torture and tells Korov I can access the vault.

31

I wake to Korov's voice, relayed through a staticky intercom. "Good morning, Miss Lena. Please be ready to go in twenty minutes."

His footsteps retreat. I splash cold water on my face, use the toothbrush provided, and brush my new bob in the two way mirror. I wonder where they're taking me. Hopefully the reality won't be as awful as the possibilities I concocted at three in the morning. I get dressed in the new clothes and realize, with a fleeting moment of relief, that I look more like myself again.

A bell rings and Korov flings the door open. He looks ready to seize the day in a crisp white shirt and red tie under his expensive suit. A small pang grips my chest as I remember Damien getting dressed for a big interview once, tying and re-tying his red tie, and joking that serious players tie tight knots.

Korov shoves a large manila envelope at me and waits as I tear it open to reveal my recently procured Kiwi passport and an old fashioned VHS tape. My heart beats faster. I feel light headed, like I've had too much wine on an empty stomach. Korov watches me with unmasked satisfaction. His gold tooth gleams. "I am a man of my word. Let's get moving, please."

My feet feel stuck to the carpet but I manage to put one in front of the other and follow Korov to the garage.

"Where are we going?"

"To my press conference, of course. We'll pose for a snapshot or two and then you'll be on your way."

It sounds too simple. I scan the garage for an escape route, but of course the place is a fortress. Even if I make it past Korov and his driver, a man of considerable girth, I doubt the garage opens onto a major road. They'd tackle me well before I'd catch sight of a taxi or a sympathetic bystander. And I don't want to risk Korov re-possessing the tape. I take a deep breath and climb into the car, hoping to find Mikhail inside. No such luck.

I stow the VHS tape in my bag and set the bag on my lap. I try not to think about the particulars of its contents. I was so obsessed with *getting* the tape that I hadn't focused on the revolting prospect of actually *watching* it. An embarrassingly large part of me is glad a screening doesn't seem imminent.

"You'll need to say something," he says. "Keep it brief. Say you're relieved to be free and looking forward to going home."

That won't be a stretch.

We cruise a few more blocks in silence before he adds, "There will be sharpshooters in the crowd. It would be a pity if you fell as collateral damage during an attempt on my life."

"Excuse me?"

"Stay with the script, Miss Lena. No matter what they ask. You're happy to be headed back to the States."

"What about Mikhail?" I force the question out, because I can feel myself losing my nerve. "Did he go off your script? Pay with his life?"

Korov smiles, apparently considering his response. "So you've grown attached to him as well? I'm not surprised. He grew on me rather quickly, as I recall."

"You didn't answer my question." I don't care if I sound brash. For whatever reason, he's counting on me to play my part for the press. Maybe I can afford to push, just a little.

"Let's say that he and I reached an understanding last night and he's not here."

"Well, obviously he's not here," I snap, but then some of the wind leaves my sails. "Is he, is he—?"

"Is he what?"

"Is he dead?"

"I shouldn't answer that. In America, you'd say I'm taking the fifth, wouldn't you?" He relaxes a little further in his seat and spreads his arms. It's a confident posture. "That's what you call the refusal to answer a self incriminating question, isn't it?" He stares at me calmly, as if truly interested in clarifying this point of American criminal law.

My stomach churns. I can't wait to put this creep and his awful friends away for decades. I silently recite the bank code to myself. 33-02-87-44-91. Good. I can rattle it off as easily as my own social security number.

We pull into Red Square on the St. Basil's side, opposite from where Mikhail and I walked the other night. Could that have been only two days ago? It feels simultaneously like yesterday and a lifetime ago.

Five huge but well dressed bodyguards emerge from a black car that pulls up alongside us. The last guy holds the door for Korov and me. A slightly built man with a clipboard and headset scampers up to Korov and says something in Russian. Then he says to me, in heavily accented English, "This way, please, Miss."

The security men whisk us upstairs to the stage, where we're flanked by Russian and American flags. Korov waves and some members of the press pool actually applaud. He pushes me forward. I freeze. A surprising number of familiar faces stare up at me from the front row. I realize they're the White House correspondents who travel with the president, and they're here to see me.

Korov waits at the podium for the welcome to subside, before making a statement in both Russian and English.

"Ladies and gentlemen, I am pleased to announce that this morning, privately financed commandos acting on my orders raided a house in Moscow and freed Miss Lena Mancuso, an American tourist seized two days ago by Islamist terrorists. As you can see, the young lady is unharmed and looking forward to a reunion with her family. I have succeeded where President Perayev's government failed." Evidently he finds subtlety over-rated.

He switches to Russian. Camera flashes blind me. My overwrought mind for some reason seizes on the fact that Korov said *Islamists* rather than *Chechens*. He must have chosen that word for audiences outside the Motherland.

He nudges me to the podium and his bodyguard closes ranks behind me. I stand stock still, shell shocked and unable to speak, even though my mind is galloping at breakneck speed. A man I recognize as NBC's Washington correspondent asks me whether it feels good to be heading home.

Thank God. A softball question. All I can muster is, "Yes, it feels very good." A woman from one of the cable news channels inquires as to whether there's anything I'd like to say to Mr. Korov.

Well, since you ask, I have plenty of things I'd like to say. I'd like to scream that Korov is a complete nut job who plans to assassinate the leader of the free world, along with the incompetent President Perayev, so why don't they all forget about me and file stories about that? I'd like to tell them that he held me hostage last night, not some Muslim group. And on a tangentially related note, they might be fascinated to learn that BXE has its people running around Russia trying to kill American citizens. My eyes scan the crowd for Korov's snipers as I hear myself mumble lamely, "Only thank you."

A heavyset, red faced *New York Times* reporter wants to know whether I can share some details about the raid. I blink back at him vacuously. Korov, unable to prompt a tabloid worthy outpouring of gratitude from me, hands me off to his aide, who whisks me off the stage.

My muscles start to uncoil as I step out of the spotlight. I sneak a final glance down at the crowd and there's Max. He's weaving his way towards me from the back. Thank God. Someone familiar. Someone from home.

If Korov recognizes Max, he doesn't let on. He's too busy patronizing the press pool. "She's had a very difficult forty-eight hours. Please bear with her." He makes the most empathetic face I've ever seen in my life. Flashbulbs light up the overcast morning.

I lose Max in the crowd, despite my desperate efforts to keep my eyes on him. Up on the dais, Korov's still speaking in Russian. A number of reporters abandon him and push towards me, only to be rebuffed by his guards.

As if sensing I might inadvertently steal his show, Korov pulls one more trick from his French-cuffed sleeve. He announces in booming English, "Many of you covered the dreadful apartment fire that left fifty-four citizens of our great nation homeless last night. Yet you've heard no response from President Perayev's government. So I am announcing that my organization, the Victory Group, will pay each victim a lump sum of five million rubles before the end of business hours today. It's the least I can do in the face of such inaction by Mr. Perayev."

I try to calculate how much money that is. A few hundred thousand dollars, I think. A fortune for a working class Russian.

Two tall men sporting the signature sunglasses and earpieces of the United States Secret Service approach us, waving badges. Korov's rangy little assistant scampers at their heels like a terrier. "These American agents will be responsible for your transfer to the airport. Mr. Korov wishes you a safe journey home," he tells me.

He retreats, leaving me and the Secret Service agents to stare at each other over the noise of the press conference, which Korov has resuscitated with his announcement about the fire victims.

One of the agents starts to introduce himself when a hand comes to rest on my shoulder, and a familiar voice says, "No need, gentlemen. FBI. She's coming with me."

The Secret Service men look at each other, unsure. They inspect Max's badge and the more senior-looking one speaks into the microphone on his wrist, waits for a reply and tells Max, "She's all yours."

I can't decide whether I should apologize, or tell him I want to go home, or try to convince him to help me find out whether Mikhail's alive or dead. Korov led me to believe dead, but I don't want to wonder for the rest of my life. Instead of articulating any of this, I hear myself blurt, "Where's Henry?"

"I'm glad to see you, too." Max looks offended. Exhausted and offended. He's wearing a fresh suit, but he has enormous bags under both eyes. Not dark circles. Actual bags. A small animal could nest in them.

"That didn't come out right. I'm just happy to see a familiar face."

"Henry went looking for your Russian boyfriend. He's keen to make sure his investment pays off."

"Excuse me?"

"We knew you were scheduled to be here with Korov. So we split up."

Maybe Henry will save Mikhail from an unpleasant demise and the real bad guys will go to jail. Maybe Mikhail will get immunity from prosecution for his evidence against Korov. I'm smart enough to keep my premature excitement to myself. I whisper, instead, "What about heading off the assassination? Or the auction? Or the pipeline attack that started this whole chain of events?"

"I still have plenty of hours left in the day. When we made our arrangement with your Russian lover boy last night, securing the indictments became Henry's number one priority."

"Don't call him that. Mikhail might be dead. You shouldn't make fun. And since when does buying evidence trump protecting the president?"

"It doesn't, and in case you haven't noticed, when Henry's around I don't get the luxury of making decisions about what takes priority and what doesn't." He's not even trying to hide his annoyance with his boss. Maybe a transfer to Nowheresville is starting to sound tempting.

A gaggle of reporters approaches us.

Max shakes his head at them. "Enough about Bureau politics. Aren't you ready to get the hell out of here?"

Before I can answer, the Secret Service agents come back to tell us that the President of the United States would like a photo with me. I freeze, before finally managing to squeak, "No, thank you."

Judging by their confused expressions, this is not the response they expected. "Excuse me?" says the senior-looking agent. "I don't think I heard you correctly."

I feel my face turn red. Why does the basic concept of *think first, then speak* continue to elude me? Max comes to my rescue, "I'm sure you did. She said thanks, but no thanks. Certainly the Commander in Chief can understand. Ms. Mancuso is in a state of shock. Clinical shock. She doesn't feel able to face the cameras again. Maybe later, back in DC, if he would like to invite her to the White House—" His voice starts to lose some of its punch.

The Secret Service men ignore Max and ask me again, "Ma'am, are you sure?"

"Positive."

"Alright, then. He's not going to like this."

They retreat and we overhear the senior agent instructing the younger one to break the news to their boss.

As soon as they're out of earshot Max says, "I don't blame you."

"No?"

"Just because I work for the feds doesn't mean I like the president." He lowers his voice. "Between you and me, the man's a bumbling idiot." He pauses to see if I'm still with him. I am. Then he grins broadly and adds, "Besides, you look like death."

I take a pretend swing at him.

"Seriously." He lowers his voice to a whisper. "Even if you don't like the man *and* your hair looks like it belongs on a department store mannequin, turning down POTUS takes guts. I'm impressed." The corners of his mouth twitch up to hint at a smile.

"Thanks. But aren't you supposed to be saving the bumbling idiot's life right about now?"

"I am indeed. And Henry wants to debrief you personally. So I'm afraid any promises to whisk you home were premature."

"Can I at least call home?"

"Not yet. Sorry."

I swallow hard, nod and try to find a silver lining. Maybe by staying just a little longer, I'll be able to learn Mikhail's fate.

Max pushes through the crowd to a large black limousine. The driver starts the engine as we pile in. Max pours us two glasses of water from the bar.

"Henry was furious with you for not checking in after he sent you after the Russian. I've never seen him so steamed. He was trying to figure out what we could charge you with, so he could call the U.S. Attorney and make the case personally."

"Are you kidding me? He sent me out with no training and no ability to defend myself. He should be giving me a medal."

I decide there's no need to tell Max I didn't even try to incapacitate Mikhail.

"I said he *was* furious. Not anymore." Max takes a loud gulp of water. "Remember the bug you planted in the casino? We had a technical snag and couldn't bring it online until last night."

Then they didn't hear the conversation about Smerth's murder. Too bad. Hopefully Mikhail saved it on one of his flash drives.

Max chugs more water. Maybe he looks so haggard because he's dehydrated. Finally he says, "There was a card game. Acheson was there. Right after they called it a night, we heard him come back into the room, shut the door and place a phone call." He pauses dramatically.

We're driving in a big circle, along the river and back around the Kremlin. I make a rolling gesture with my hand that says get to the point.

"Acheson spoke to some unidentified person in English for five minutes. He told him to green light the site on the Georgian-Azerbaijani border crossing. He said that would give them the most bang for the buck because it would take hours, if not days, to hash out which government would deal with which aspects of the investigation. He said they wanted maximum chaos instead of maximum loss of life."

"How gracious of them."

Max refills his water. "Can you believe he was stupid enough to say the location of a pending terrorist attack on a cell phone?"

"It's not stupidity. It's arrogance. I'm glad you got some use out of the bug, but what good is the location if you don't know when the bombers will strike?"

"That's the best part. Acheson said they'd have the last payment wired into the account on Cyprus at 2 p.m., Moscow time. He said he wanted the blast to occur as soon as the wire was confirmed."

"So you found the bank and intercepted the wire?" Now it's my turn to be impressed. I've seen firsthand how easy it is to move money electronically. If they only got the tip last night, they've done some excellent detective work.

"No. The FBI would have no way of knowing where the money was coming from, or which of the thousands of small banks on Cyprus it was going to. So we tipped off Interpol, gave them the recording from your bug and had them send an international team into no man's land."

"What no man's land?"

Max gets the smug look that so many men get when they feel like an expert on something. "A three-hundred meter stretch of border zone between the two countries. If we'd done our homework more thoroughly, we'd have known the Azerbaijani side had a maintenance crew scheduled to conduct repairs this month in no man's land."

"So what do you do now?"

"Nothing. It's already done. A half-hour before your little press conference, the Interpol team, backed up with Azerbaijani police and border agents, stopped a maintenance crew of twelve on their way into the border zone. They were wearing the uniforms of Azerbaijani government workmen, but all twelve were carrying enough explosives to take down an airliner. And they weren't Chechens, either. They were all employees of BXE. Mostly former special ops guys who served in war zones, left the service and went home to massive financial difficulties. They're ideal mercenaries, really. Formally trained brutes desperate for cash and with no regard for non-American life."

I don't know what to say. It's too reprehensible. A corporation paying its people to perpetrate acts of war on foreign soil to line their shareholders' pockets. And the vice president's. Yet the public has no clue. "What happens to those BXE guys now?" I ask.

"I can't say for sure, but I imagine the CIA will whisk them off someplace where they can debrief out of sight of any human rights monitors. And I'm sure you won't find even a hint of the whole episode in the media. The White House will want this hushed up, forever if possible. Which might be possible, since the attack failed to launch." He shakes his head. "If Interpol hadn't caught up with them, the blast would have leveled villages a mile away in every direction and killed thousands of civilians."

"BXE and Clearwater have branched into murdering innocent villagers? Just to make money? For no other reason?"

"Come on. Are you really surprised?"

"Yeah, I am." Though maybe I shouldn't be.

Max shakes his head. "And we wouldn't have known to head it off, if it weren't for you having the *chutzpah* to plant a bug in Korov's casino. So that explains why Henry is ready to give you a medal."

"Wow." I stop myself from asking whether I'm back in Max's good graces, too.

He waits for me to say something besides wow but I've got nothing. I'm too stunned. All this time, I thought that we were waiting for some piece of incontrovertible evidence to fall into our laps, or some deductive burst of genius to strike, and it turns out that the huge break came by way of old fashioned eavesdropping. Albeit with a modern twist.

I can't wrap my head around the irony. They've solved the crime I was brought on to research, *but only because* they lost track of me and Korov smuggled me here.

Max looks perturbed by my silence. Maybe he thinks I'm finally about to crack from the stress. It wouldn't be the craziest thing if I did. I understand that people often power through traumatic situations, only to collapse after the action subsides.

"Won't they regroup and try again?" I ask. "Surely BXE has more men to throw at this problem. Or they could always make a deal with actual terrorists. Like the ones they planned to blame in the first place."

"BXE's brass will lay low for a while. Of course they could try to buy off some local freedom fighters, but they're harder to control and they would demand upfront payment. I want to catch Acheson before Clearwater has a chance to re-group."

"So what are we waiting for? Why are we wasting time driving in circles?"

"Because not even an emergency speeds up the glacial pace of bureaucracy. Why else?"

"What do you mean?"

"You're a lawyer. You know we can't arrest anyone on Russian soil. We have to wait for the FSB to do so. And they wanted to liaise with the legat, but of course there isn't one, because he was killed while traveling to Chechnya yesterday."

I nod sympathetically.

"And now the stupid deputy legat says he refuses to cause an embarrassing international incident during a presidential summit without rock solid evidence."

"What the heck does that mean?"

"It means he's a Republican appointee who doesn't want to arrest a Republican operative, even a disgraced one, during the visit of a Republican president."

"Right."

"So when Interpol handed him their report, which corroborates our evidence, he grudgingly sent the FSB out after Acheson twenty minutes ago. They have an arrest warrant, but we'll have to file for extradition. That's assuming they find him. He may well be off to the South Pacific by now, looking forward to years of frozen drinks under a beach umbrella."

I remember Charlie speculating that Acheson had escaped to the Caribbean. I shake my head, as if trying to clear my brain of all thoughts concerning poor Charlie.

Max lowers his voice. "So twenty minutes ago, the FSB put out their version of an all points bulletin for Acheson. They faxed his photo to every hotel, airport, bus and rail ticket desk in Russia. His mug is all over television, but it's the middle of the day. People aren't watching. If he's still here, he could try to buy his way out. We assume he has access to plenty of cash."

"Can't you turn off the tap? Flush him out by freezing his bank cards?"

"Only the American ones. We're sure he has ATM cards for various anonymous offshore accounts. Plus Acheson isn't the only man in Moscow withdrawing funds with an anonymous card. It's like the God damned wild west over here. So following the money is a crap shoot. But I need to find Acheson, or at the minimum find a way to communicate with him. Henry wants to offer him a deal in exchange for his testimony against the vice president. He thinks that's our best shot at heading off the entire plot against the president."

"What do you mean, the entire plot?" I ask.

"If we thwart one assassin but don't nab Prescott, he'll hire a new gunman. And past experience shows he'll use his old pal Acheson to broker the deal."

"Henry already promised Aziz immunity in exchange for his cooperation against his friends or rather, former friends." I'm still sore about that. It maybe irrational, but I'm inclined to believe Korov's assertion that Aziz arranged Damien's murder, if only because Mikhail said Korov wasn't interested in needless slaughter. Operative word being needless, which of course remains wide open for interpretation.

"We'd love to dangle a deal under Acheson's nose, even though Henry already offered a deal to Aziz. But we, and by "we" I mean law enforcement, can't *promise* a plea bargain without the prosecutor's blessing."

"Acheson would know that, even if Aziz doesn't," I say.

The driver, who's now on his third pass down this strip by the lazy Moscow River, halts abruptly by a crowded crosswalk. The door on Max's side swings open and Henry swoops in. He's wearing a fresh suit and looks more rested than either Max or me. The chauffeur drives on.

I sit in silence. To squelch the urge to fidget, I examine my fingernails, which have seen better days, while I wait for Henry to read me the riot act. Even if he's pleased with how things ended with the pipeline, he can't be happy that I let Mikhail slip away.

So I'm shocked when he booms, in a voice not unlike a circus ringmaster's, "Well done, my dear. I have to say we were skeptical. We thought you'd ditched us for that dashing young Russian, but you came through like a pro."

I don't know what I expected but it wasn't this. Even if Henry believes a desirable end justifies questionable means, I deliberately disregarded his orders more than once. I manage to spit out some acknowledgment of his praise.

"I'm very sorry about your friend," Henry adds, his voice more somber. "Terrible waste of a brilliant young talent."

His words hit me like a well delivered punch to the stomach. I feel like I can't breathe, like my lungs are clamped in a vise. Max notices my distress and offers a glass of water.

Henry looks taken aback by my reaction. "I'm sorry, my dear. I thought you'd heard. But you should know that the FBI has seized all the law firm's computers, phone records and reception log, and we're conducting a thorough forensic sweep of the building. We're not letting the D.C. cops bungle this investigation. Whoever put arsenic in that young man's coffee walked right into the firm to do it and probably on Acheson's orders. Charlie Winthrop placed a call to the FBI's regional office the night before he died. It was anonymous, but we traced it to his cell phone. He had unearthed some very incriminating documents."

My brain is swimming. I'm not really processing the details of Henry's discourse, but I'm certain he's talking about Charlie, not Mikhail. I feel relieved, like I can breathe again, but only for a second. A heavy shroud of guilt drapes itself over me. And reality kicks in.

I *am* truly sad about Charlie.

And furious about the unfairness of it all.

I restrain myself from asking Henry about Mikhail.

Max, who's shifted seats to ride backwards across from me in order to give his boss more room, sees my angst and asks the question for me. "What about our friendly FSB agent? You remember, the one we paid five million dollars? So far for nothing?"

"I'm afraid there's no sign of him. I accompanied the newly promoted legat and the FSB team to Korov's home. We spoke to a butler, who admitted us too readily. I knew we'd turn up nothing." Henry swallows hard and finishes his thought. "They may have already disposed of him. Which presents a bit of a problem, because he never communicated that he was ready to pass the information. So it looks like we flushed five million dollars down the tubes."

Henry's saying that Mikhail is dead. The news bowls me down like an avalanche. I only knew Mikhail for a couple of days, but I admired and despised him, all at the same time. We drive over the river.

Maybe my messy feelings for Mikhail mean I'm not doomed to be a numb shell forever. I stare out the window at the polluted water. Mikhail must have liked me too, at least a little. If he didn't, he could have exposed me to Korov and increased his chances of getting away with his own spying activities.

The car stops in a busy drop off zone set up by police by one of the Kremlin's many gates. Russian soldiers wielding machine guns patrol the area, looking tense but miserable, stifled by their wool uniforms in the relentless drizzle.

"Here we are." Henry's voice is all business. "Now, von Buren, as we've discussed *ad nauseum*, I'm going inside to meet with the head of the FSB while you meet with the new legat. I can't take anymore of that man today. Try to keep him out of our way. When the presidents make their entrance, the FSB men will give you the nod to take out the two agents Aziz fingered yesterday."

The surreal nature of the conversation snaps me back to attention. The deputy director of the FBI is authorizing one of his agents to assassinate two U.S. Secret Service men. In front of a witness. And Henry bases his unfathomable order on information garnered from a known criminal. This can't possibly be legal. I steal a glance at Max. He looks hesitant. Not mutinous, but not convinced either.

"Right." Max licks his lips. "Speaking of Aziz, where the hell did you leave him this morning?"

"With an FSB team supervised by Katya. They've confiscated all three of his passports. He's not going anywhere."

"Are you sure about that?"

Henry scowls before formulating his answer, which comes in a tirade.

"It's their Goddamned turf, von Buren. The Russians want to hold Aziz for questioning about his dealings with Korov. Katya, despite her Oscar-worthy performance as a timid suburban nanny, has turned out to be one tough agent. It's as good a situation as we can hope for. Now why don't you just try to keep your eye on the bloody ball?"

Max nods grudgingly. Maybe he's visualizing his career, circling the drain. Jersey City will look like a holiday. If he screws this up, Henry will dispatch him to someplace like North Dakota for the foreseeable future.

Henry bellows, "I'm glad we're clear. Now, figure out how to secure the young lady, and get your ass inside that palace." With that, Henry opens the door, unfurls an enormous golf umbrella and disappears through the security checkpoint, behind the impressive red brick walls of the Kremlin.

Something's not right. I can feel it. I've heard people talk about a sixth sense, though I never experienced it before the awful meeting with Casper. But it's back now, stronger. "Mikhail said that Katya, well that's not her name, it's Irina. He said that Katya is Aziz's girlfriend."

"She's pretending to be Aziz's girlfriend. Elite FSB agents are fiercely dedicated. It's amazing what they'll do for Mother Russia," Max says, his whole face tight.

Surely some agents will make extreme sacrifices for their missions, but a nagging voice in my head tells me that's not the case here. So I push a little harder. "No. If anything, she's pretending to be undercover for the FSB."

I start to explain further, but Max raises his hand and cuts me off. "Henry's checked her out twenty-eight different ways. He says Katya's legit." He notices I'm about to object again and adds, "Way more so than Casper. He was impossible to investigate. You maybe onto something or not, but it would be career suicide for me to go against Henry on this one."

"But you said Henry believes the end justifies the means."

"Only when the means don't involve overruling *his* judgment. And don't forget, whether Katya's legit or not, Aziz wants to scuttle the plan to kill POTUS for his own reasons. He doesn't want a Prescott presidency that's cozy with his nephew Muhammed. Never let a hunch cloud reasoned judgment in this job. If you do, you'll end up dead."

I glare at Max.

"Sorry. That was preachy." He tries to explain. "You know, I've never fired my gun on the job before and now he's ordered me to shoot two American agents, who may or may not be treasonous. It goes against my training *and* my conscience. Damn Henry. We wouldn't be in this predicament if he hadn't inserted himself into my case. Why can't I have a normal boss? One who's happy to drive a desk like everyone else?"

My glare softens a bit. Max's predicament sucks. "So don't do it," I suggest. "Walk away. Quit. Find another job. You could always fall back on the patent lawyer thing."

He shakes his head. "Not my style. So now I'm going in there. I have no idea how long I'll be, but I need you to stay out here with the driver. After yesterday's boondoggle Henry won't let you travel home without debriefing. I'm afraid you're stuck for a few hours longer. Try to catch a nap."

I glance through the barrier into the front seat. The chauffeur yawns, scratches his incoming beard, blows his nose loudly and reaches into his pants pocket for a bottle of pills. I watch as he tosses two back with a swig of coffee. Max pounds his fist on the barrier. "Hey! What is that?"

"Relax. It's Benadryl. I hated spring back home, and I come over here and they have as much freaking tree pollen as anywhere. The stuff's like the cockroach of the plant kingdom." The driver explains his complaint in that neutral west coast accent frequently heard on American television. I don't know why I assumed he was local. Of course the FBI would have American support staff in a major city like Russia. He shuts up when he notices Max has stopped listening. The privacy glass slides closed once more.

"Can I ask you something?" I need to know. "That morning in DC, when you were supposed to meet me at the coffee cart at Connecticut and K? Why didn't you come?"

A rush of color sweeps up Max's neck to his face. "It's embarrassing."

I give him a look that I hope conveys I don't give a fuck. I want to know.

"I was kidnapped. They grabbed me right before they must have taken you."

"What? How?"

"Carjacking."

"Oh my God. So you escaped?" I picture Max fighting off multiple armed assailants like some kind of real life James Bond.

Max fixes his steely eyes on mine and forces the corners of his mouth into a rueful smile. He looks down, rubs his scalp hard with the fingers of both hands. "Not exactly. Henry paid three million dollars to get me back."

"That was big of him."

"Not really. He was afraid I'd talk under pressure. The first thing he said to me when they dumped me at the agreed upon meeting point – some sparsely utilized overflow parking lot for a state forest in Brandywine, Maryland – was that he's issuing me a suicide pill before letting me out of his sight again."

I feel my eyes widen. "Was he serious?"

"I'm not at liberty to say."

Max reaches down to pat his ankle and for a sickening second I think he's about to offer me a cyanide capsule. I realize, with no small measure of relief, that he's double-checking his weapon is firmly in place. An icy chill rockets up my back. Max double checks he has his badge. Maybe he's stalling or perhaps this is some kind of luck ritual, like the ones certain baseball players perform before batting.

"Here goes." He reaches over to pat my arm. "Wish me luck."

Only after the car door shuts and he disappears through he same gates that swallowed Henry five minutes ago do I allow myself to bury my face in my hands and cry. And cry. And cry some more.

I wish I'd never let Max and Henry into my apartment. No, it all went wrong before that. I wish I'd never gone to work at Rutledge & Smerth. I could be like Hannah, slogging away at an equally prestigious but much less politically wired law firm. Then Damien would still be alive. We'd be living our lives, working, seeing friends, going on vacations and eventually starting a family, moving to a nice house and growing old together. I'd be blissfully unaware of the sinister ways of Acheson, Prescott and their cronies.

I certainly wouldn't be alone in the back of a car, halfway around the world from home, crying my eyes out over the life I've lost.

32

I don't know exactly how much time I waste on self pity. When I rub my eyes and look out the window, I see a steady stream of reporters filing through the checkpoint. The television personalities stand out, not only because of their familiar faces, but also because they're better dressed than the others. A number of the folks I presume to be print journalists wear decent suits, but there's also a large group of under dressed people Diana would call back-benchers. They're bloggers and writers who cram into the back of press briefings in order to write first-hand stories based on other reporters' questions.

Maybe I could pass for one of them. At least for long enough to find a reporter with some clout. Some big, trusted name who could relay the threat to the president and get taken seriously.

I dig in my purse and pull out the press pass Mikhail fashioned at the Hotel Bucharest. I hang it around my neck and fix my hair to the best of my ability. I have nothing to improve my appearance except lipstick, which I apply using the dark reflection of my face in the soundproof barrier glass. Even with these tune-ups, the scraggliest blogger in the press mob looks more presentable than I do. But only slightly.

I hold up one of the K cups from the bar's coffee machine and rap on the glass. "Want a refill?"

"Sure. Thanks." He passes me his mug. "Cream and sugar?"

"Just cream, please."

I dump the contents from Henry's vial into the coffee along with a generous dollop of cream. I brew myself another cup, pass the driver his mug, settle back in the seat and wait.

He's slumped, deep asleep, in under ten minutes.

I sling my bag over my shoulder and step out of the warm car into the unwelcoming afternoon. I close the door quietly and march towards the queue without looking back.

When I reach the end of the line, I realize I haven't the faintest idea which news agency I supposedly represent, because my counterfeit Kremlin press card is in Russian. I notice it has a bar code on the bottom. I hope Mikhail knew what he was doing.

I'm up before I have time to reconsider my plan. I put my card on the desk and mumble hello. The guard spends a moment comparing me to my photograph.

Oh God. He probably recognizes me. He knows I'm no journalist. As far as he's concerned, I'm a kidnapped tourist freed by President Perayev's arch rival, and I should be sitting on a plane to the States. He considers me and the photo for a third time. I start sweating. My mind goes blank. What if he looks up and says he knows I'm a fraud? He won't believe my story. I look too young and unimportant. I take a deep breath and arrange my face into what I hope is a competent, business-like expression. I remind myself that errant social climbers manage to slip into state dinners from time to time. Infiltrating the press pool has to be easier than crashing a twelve-course meal with the president.

If the guard thinks I look familiar, he can't place me, because he pulls the card through a scanner. It clicks and pauses. I hold my breath. The little light comes on, bright green. I exhale. He waves me through the checkpoint towards a metal detector. I remember the key in my bra. If it beeps, I'll have to fish it out and hope the guards believe I'm neurotic. It's only a key after all. Not a weapon.

I step through without incident while my bag rolls into the x-ray machine. The guards extract the VHS tape and send it through the scanner a second time before handing it back to me. I pray the machine doesn't fry film.

The inside of the Kremlin resembles a small, wealthy town. Cars displaying official plates park along the cobblestone streets lined with Medieval churches with gleaming onion domes and stately palaces. Manicured lawns surround most of the buildings. Security personnel herd me and various members of the international press corps towards an enormous yellow building with sparkling white trim. I know from reading over Mikhail's shoulder that this stately example of pre-Revolutionary architecture, with the tri-colored Russian flag flying proudly from the gilded flagpole on its green roof, is the Grand Kremlin Palace, the largest of the half dozen palaces housed within the Kremlin's walls.

We pass through an expansive foyer, adorned with oil paintings two stories tall. The guards rush us into a suite of rooms reserved for the press. All around me, legitimate journalists busy themselves with the abundant refreshments and laptop hook ups.

I'm inside.

It's frightening how easy that was, but as I survey the room, my heart sinks.

No sign of anyone recognizable. I ask a random reporter, whose badge reads *PolitiScope.com*, about the whereabouts of the White House press corps.

He laughs as if I've told a stupid joke. "With the important people, I imagine. Getting better access and eating better food. We're just the hangers on."

A Russian official appears and distributes an updated schedule of the day's proceedings. She announces that the joint press conference has been pushed a half hour. The reception will follow. As soon as the messenger retreats, the room erupts with grumbling about how the Russians never stick to their schedules, how it's always hurry up and wait, how they won't have time to file their stories and that they'd better get fed again soon.

The powers that be grant their last wish almost immediately. The room's huge doors swing open and a team of waiters marches in, bearing enormous trays of open faced sandwiches, little pancakes with caviar and sour cream, and all sorts of sweets. Most of the press descend like vultures.

Thanks to the ample buffet, nobody's paying me any attention. I walk towards the main exit. I should try to find the A-list press corps encampment. The worst they can do is kick me out.

Halfway down the hallway, I bump into an astonished Max. He grabs my arm, looks over both shoulders to make sure nobody's watching and marches me through a door marked, in Russian, French and English, *Ladies Powder Room*.

Max latches the door. "What the hell are you doing? Didn't I say to wait in the car?"

"I wanted to help. I thought—"

He cuts me off. "This is a dangerous operation. We could have a full-on Constitutional crisis if we fail. I don't have time to play bodyguard for you." He pauses, looks at me, hones in on the Kremlin press pass dangling from my neck and asks, "How the hell did you get in here anyway?"

I hold up my forged credentials. "It was easy."

"Where did you get that? Wait. I don't even want to know. You're going out to the car. And I'm going to get someone to make sure you stay there." He reaches for the microphone tucked under his cuff.

"No. I'm not."

"Is that so?"

"Yes. Well no. I suppose you could force me to leave. But you don't want to."

"Why the hell not?"

"I spent hours last night poring over maps of this building."

"I have a floor plan," Max snaps.

"Does your official floor plan show the HVAC renovations made this winter? Or which secret passageways they left in the walls and which they bricked up?" I'm on perilous footing. I'm not blessed with a photographic memory, and while I paid attention to Mikhail's hurried explanations of the drawings, I don't trust my ability to recall the details. At least not perfectly.

Max doesn't answer, but I can tell from his expression that he doubts he's seen the most recent drawings.

I press my case. "You said yourself you don't want to shoot anyone. Maybe you can get to them, before they pose an imminent threat."

"I'm listening." He leans back against the marble vanity. He's apparently slowed his campaign to get me out to the car.

"Mikhail says," I begin. Max frowns. I start again. "The FSB believes that the assassins plan to poison both presidents at the reception. It's quick, effective, clean and not nearly as suicidal for the perpetrators as firing gunshots from the crowd. You just need to get into the kitchen and catch them before they have a chance to act." I pause and wait for Max's reaction.

He rubs his eyebrows and lets out a muted growl of frustration. "How credible is this tip?"

"It's from the inner circle of Korov's organization. That's all I know."

Max buries his face in his hands and sighs, "I could pass your tip on to our legat. He'll relay our concerns through proper channels to the FSB and they'll make the arrests. Meanwhile, our people can evacuate the president." He looks up again. "The Bureau would come out of this looking good."

"Exactly."

"Wrong. Henry doesn't want the suspects arrested by the Russians. He wants them either eliminated or in U.S. custody. And we can't arrest anyone here."

"Fine. You can't arrest anyone. But you could abduct them and bring them back to the States. Or wherever you want them." I take a long breath to give Max time to bite. He's considering, but he's not there yet. "Abduction, even rendition, must be easier for you to swallow than assassination. Particularly since you seem to have doubts about their guilt." I arch my brows at him, daring him to shoot down this last argument.

Max's eyes narrow and he presses his lips together. He nods slightly, then frowns. "An unorthodox plan, but not without its merits. Especially since, if you're wrong about the food poisoning, I should still have time to get into place to carry out Henry's orders. There's only one minor snag."

"What's that?"

"There's one of me. And two of them. At the minimum. I can't let the legat in on a plan to modify Henry's orders. He'd have a meltdown. He'll think I'm an insubordinate wimp."

"That's why you can't send me back to the car."

Max weighs his options for what feels like a long time. He's probably picturing his career tanking here, today. Forget Jersey City or North Dakota. Right now he imagines a bleaker professional future, one that involves asking whether you want fries with that.

I hold my breath and look at the floor. Part of me wishes he'd escort me back to the limousine. He's shaking his head and muttering that it'll never work.

Then suddenly his head stops shaking side to side. He looks me in the eye, as if trying to measure my resolve. "It's so crazy it might work."

Inexplicably, I feel my face break out into the first real smile I can remember having in months. I take it as a sign that I've lost my mind.

Max consults his watch. "We need to move fast." He asks me to describe, in as much detail as possible, the drawings I saw last night. He's especially interested in the ground floor kitchen, which Mikhail spent a great deal of time studying.

The newly refurbished catering kitchen adjoins four huge pantries. Each one features an oversized dumbwaiter that goes up to a series of staging areas for the main reception hall. Last year's addition of central air conditioning necessitated the creation of a crawl space between the floors. The space above the kitchen is most easily accessible through the hatches for the dumbwaiters.

Another possible entry point would be through the enormous chimneys. If a particular oven isn't in use, a person could theoretically climb down the chimney. He would need basic climbing gear, wire cutters to dispatch the grates to keep out birds, and an astonishing amount of luck to avoid detection. According to Mikhail, a team of sharpshooters patrols the palace roof, and they'll have reinforcements during a major summit. The chimneys seem highly unlikely.

The kitchen also features a trash chute that empties into a dumpster in a locked and guarded basement. For anyone to get into the building that way, he'd need an accomplice in the bowels of the palace. Which is far from inconceivable, though it would add another moving piece to an already complicated plot.

I explain all this with a verbose disclaimer that I wouldn't swear to any details.

Max nods with approval when I pause for air.

"Now for the bad news," I say. "The catering kitchen is on the opposite side of the building. According to the drawings they've installed three-hundred-sixty degree ceiling cameras every hundred feet or so, throughout the palace's main thoroughfares."

Max frowns. "Can we get across without using the main hallway?"

"There's a servants' passage that's supposedly been out of use for decades. It runs parallel to the main hall. The doorway should be concealed in the wall about four-hundred feet from here, if I remember correctly. Alternatively, there's the crawlspace above the ceilings. When they renovated last fall, they dropped the ceiling height in all but the main ceremonial spaces to make room for central air."

"Fuck. How did we have such inferior drawings?"

I haven't a clue. In fact, I'm probably more surprised than Max is by the FBI's inability to procure the most detailed intelligence.

"I know why," Max says, in a tone that reminds me of a schizophrenic arguing with himself. "Fuck. Fuck. Fuck."

My brow furrows. I stare at Max, silently willing him to keep it together. "Why waste valuable time getting mad about the drawings?" I ask, as gently and neutrally as possible.

"Because the Secret Service made a big production of furnishing those plans. Fuck." He turns to me. "How sure are you about that crawlspace?"

His eyes follow my gaze upward. Ordinary tiles, painted to look original. Max jumps onto the vanity and removes one. It slides aside easily. He grins as he hops back down to the floor, his outrage seemingly forgotten.

"Any idea what the schedule for the press pool looks like?" he asks.

"Actually, yes." I hand him the schedule issued by the Russian press aide and feel like the most capable person in the world.

Max scans the sheet and frowns at his watch. "In about three minutes, they're supposed to have something called the undersecretary's briefing."

"The buzz in the room was that the Russians never run on schedule."

"We'll wait." He moves his ear closer to the door. I do the same. Precisely two minutes go by and we hear applause from down the hall. "I guess the reporter who said that was grousing for nothing."

"Who cares? That's our cue."

I suddenly feel sick. I imagine the color draining from my face, down into my neck and chest.

Max softens. "Are you sure you want to do this? I can take you back to the car and we'll never breathe a word of our restroom *tête-à-tête* to Henry."

"I'm sure," I say, with conviction I'm surprised to feel. I don't know where all this courage, or foolishness, comes from, but I make myself swallow my doubts. "Let's go."

Max climbs onto the vanity and extends a hand to me. "Let's avoid as many cameras as possible. We'll try to reach the passageway across the hall through the ceiling. You go first, with the flashlight."

"Why me?"

"Because I'm guessing I'll need to give you a leg up."

Max produces a pen-sized flashlight from his inside pocket and hands it to me. He laces his hands together and holds them at my knee level.

With the flashlight clamped between my teeth, I step my right foot into his interlaced hands and grab the edge of the ceiling with both of mine. He boosts me higher than I expected, and I pull myself into the crawlspace with no more effort than it would take to get out of the deep end of a swimming pool. I shuffle out of the way on my hands and knees and transfer the flashlight out of my mouth. I turn back to the opening in time to see Max's hands grip the edge of the hole. He pulls himself all the way up and slings one leg, then the other, into the crawlspace next to me in one controlled motion.

"Wow." I shine the flashlight his way.

He gets that self-satisfied look that suit-wearing men get on the rare occasions that a woman marvels at their physical prowess. "The obstacle course at Quantico. We're in pretty good shape for a bunch of geezers in suits."

"You're hardly a geezer."

"No time for flirtatious banter. Let's move."

I start to crawl forwards, stopping every few paces to readjust my grip on the flashlight and cursing the FBI. If they can't provide up-to-date drawings, couldn't they at least spring for head lamps? Max counts off our paces, trying to estimate the width of the hallway. If we remove a ceiling panel before we reach the passageway, the cameras will catch us for sure.

We'll be arrested by a kid with a Kalashnikov. We'll be tossed in the gulag, or the infamous Lubyanka Prison. Or worse. They'll summon Henry and he'll let the Russians shoot us.

Max taps my foot and whispers, "Time to peek." I hold my breath as he gently eases one of the tiles aside.

Darkness.

He takes the flashlight from me. He's counted right. We're above a narrow passageway. Max swings his legs down and dangles over the floor before dropping and landing on all fours with a sickening thud.

I dangle my legs through the hole and focus for the first time on the ceiling height. This could hurt. I lower myself gingerly until I have to let go. Max catches me, not gracefully, but capably enough so it doesn't hurt to hit the ground. We start walking. The ancient floorboards creak under each step. I cringe, certain of our imminent annihilation.

After about three hundred feet, we come to a door.

Max crouches down and peers through the keyhole. "Empty room," he announces.

We continue for what feels like a significant distance. The floorboards seem to grow creakier with each step. Finally, we arrive at a second door.

Max crouches again, checks the keyhole and positions his flashlight so he can glimpse through. "This is it." He tries the knob.

Locked.

I start to sweat. My stomach lurches in loops inside my abdomen.

Max whispers under his breath, "Nothing we can't handle. Don't flip out on me now, okay?"

I try to get a grip on my nerves as he whips out a credit card, with which he demonstrates the technique that got me into Acheson's office at R&S. Except Max gets the lock to turn on his first try. The door opens into a huge pantry, which is in the midst of a major renovation like everything else in Moscow. We hear American eighties music and the unmistakable sound of a bustling kitchen through the closed door.

"No good," Max decides. "We have to get closer to the action and we can't just waltz through that door."

"So what do you suggest?"

"There are four pantries that connect to the main ballroom by dumbwaiter, right?"

"No. The pantries connect by dumbwaiters to prep rooms adjacent to the reception room."

"Even better, because if you're right about the poisoning scheme, I'd bet any amount of money that they're planning to ride a dumbwaiter to the food supply. We just need to figure out which one."

"How?"

"Through the roof again."

He perches on a conveniently available stepstool and pops out one of the foam ceiling panels. He shines his flashlight into the abyss and grins. "No problem. Easiest part so far."

I wonder if this is false bravado. I've had enough of tight spaces and I'm still cursing myself for getting out of the car. But my adrenalin's kicking in, either galloping to my rescue or spurring me on a suicide mission, depending on how I choose to look at it.

I step onto the stool, but it's not big enough for two, so Max balances with one foot on a lower step as he gives me another leg up into the ceiling.

We crawl along on our hands and knees. Progress feels glacial.

Max removes one of the ceiling tiles. He doesn't pop it all the way out, but rather pulls it back a couple of inches, so he can evaluate the space below. It seems risky, but I see no viable alternative. Most busy people don't spend that much time contemplating the ceiling of their workspace anyhow. At least I hope they don't. My heart pounds so hard that I bet Max can hear it.

"Nope." He slides the panel back into place.

We inch forward. He tries more tiles as we progress. On the fourth or fifth try he whispers, "Jackpot," and motions for me to come closer.

We peer down through the narrow opening he's created into a well-lit pantry area that's clearly in use, but unoccupied at the moment. Strains of George Michael drift our way, urging us to wake him up before we go-go. My mind's eye darts back to elementary school. I remember my older cousins loving this music, and somehow that insignificant recollection makes my current circumstance feel more surreal. Max clears his throat quietly, but it's enough to snap me back to the here and now.

The pantry has a huge counter along one wall and an island in the middle. Bottles of champagne, nestled in buckets of ice, and rows of empty glasses arranged neatly on trays cover most of both surfaces. Cabinets large enough to qualify as closets line two walls. They're closed, except for the one nearest the doorway. Its floor length door has been left wide open, revealing what must be an outrageously expensive set of china. Opposite the kitchen door, the dumbwaiter waits, empty.

Max takes the flashlight, switches it off and pockets it. He double checks for signs of activity below. Seeing none, he eases the ceiling panel off to one side. It catches on part of its own framework and cracks in two. Max is left holding the smaller half as we watch the larger one cascade to the counter below. It misses the nearest row of champagne glasses by less than five inches. My stomach lurches again. Max wastes no time contemplating his near miss. He tosses the remaining piece of paneling aside and nudges me out of the way so he can swing his legs through the hole. He drops a good ten feet and lands like a cat, on all fours.

His landing makes a thump that explodes in my ears, but nobody bursts through the doors to check it out. Max gets back on his feet and in doing so knocks over a glass. Miraculously, it doesn't break. He doesn't bother to right it. Instead he reaches up both arms and whispers, "Come on down."

Is he crazy? Why do we want to trap ourselves? But I lack a sound counterproposal, so I swing my legs through the hole and force myself to push off the edge of the crawlspace.

We get down from the counter without causing further damage and huddle by the keyhole. Max looks first. "Damn. Only half the faces are visible from this angle. I need to see the other side."

He steps away and I sneak a peek. The kitchen is enormous, much bigger than I imagined from the drawings. A couple of dozen people, all in white chef uniforms, chop, dice, stir and mix ingredients. A white-haired man, clearly in charge, paces the perimeter of the room.

Max reaches into his back pocket and produces two folded photographs. "I want you to stay right here. Watch everyone who comes and goes and keep your eyes peeled for either of these two men."

The men in the photographs are white and in their thirties or early forties. Muscles bulge through their shirts. One has the squarest jaw I've ever seen on a human being. They look tall and rugged, too hardened to pass for kitchen help. Max must have it wrong.

But that's not my most pressing worry. Panic grips me again. "You mean you're leaving me here? Alone?"

"Only long enough to cross the room and take a look from the other side."

Neither of us knows how long that will take. It depends on whether the crawlspace is blocked, or if the ceiling panels move as easily as the ones we chanced to choose on this side, or of course, whether he's detected.

Max adds, "I don't want you confronting anyone. Just watch quietly. If anyone comes towards the door, hide."

"Where?"

"Back in the ceiling," he says, as if this ought to be obvious.

"I can't get back up there without help." This *should* be obvious. The ceilings are easily fourteen feet high, which makes the pantry appear larger than it is.

"Just hurry." I hiss. If he spends another moment dithering here, I'm going to lose my nerve and start begging to go back to the car.

Max clambers onto the counter. He looks up and realizes there's no way he can jump to reach the edge of the hole in the ceiling. It's too high and nobody's left a conveniently placed stepstool this time.

They have, however, left a number of wooden crates from the champagne, piled next to the dumbwaiter. We stack three of these on the island. Max hops on top of them and pulls himself back into the ceiling. I hear him moving around overhead and wonder if we were that loud before, or if the sound is amplified because the ceiling's open to the room.

As soon as his feet disappear, I move the crates back where we found them, resume my post by the keyhole and curse myself for not going straight to the airport when I had the chance. The eighties serenade continues with some song about a chameleon.

A sharp buzzing sound jolts me almost out of my skin. The dumbwaiter's sliding doors rattle shut. The indicator lights show it's heading up. I exhale. All that means is someone upstairs wants to send something down.

Which means someone will be sent to receive whatever they send. I frantically scan the room for a hiding place. Maybe I could summon super-human strength and pull myself into the ceiling. Unlikely. Although I've heard reports of individuals exhibiting exceptional athletic ability in crisis situations, I doubt I'm one of those people.

My only option is behind the open cabinet door. It's near the entrance to the kitchen. Maybe that's good. People tend not to look behind themselves when they enter a room. Damn Max for leaving me here.

I press against the wall. My chest tightens and I wonder whether I'm too young to have a heart attack.

I'm telling myself that healthy thirty-year-old women do not perish from cardiac arrest when a key turns in the lock. The person on the other side fumbles with it a few times, but finally the lock turns over and the door swings open. Someone enters, then closes and locks the door after themselves. That's odd.

I can't suppress the self-destructive urge. I have to look, even though I can't see anything from my hiding place without leaning out into the open. I inch my head to the edge of the door and lean out enough so one eye can peek. Whoever came into the room is wearing the white kitchen uniform, complete with the tall white hat. It looks like a woman from here and that's somewhat comforting. I'd rather be discovered by a woman than some angry, knife-wielding man. Not that this woman couldn't get angry. Or wield a knife, for that matter. I tell myself to breathe, to get a grip. She'll do whatever she needs to do and leave.

She starts rearranging the champagne glasses. Although my better judgment is screeching no inside my head, I lean out a little further. She turns towards the kitchen and I lurch my head back and press myself against the wall.

I hear her put the key in the lock. She's only a couple of feet away, but all I can see from my hiding place is a flash of white from the arm of her uniform.

The dumbwaiter buzzes again and its door clatters open. The kitchen worker turns and gasps. A male voice blurts something in Russian. I hear the new arrival jump to his feet.

I hear a metallic click and the woman announces, loud and clear, "Eff. Ess. Bay."

FSB. Aren't they on our side?

For a split second I contemplate showing myself and explaining the situation, but reason kicks in. Even if the woman is an FSB agent, I have no way of proving I'm with the FBI, nor do I have a plausible explanation for my presence in this kitchen. And who knows who the intruder might be.

The woman barks something at the intruder in Russian. He answers her angrily. I hear something fairly heavy drop to the floor. I have to look.

Some primordial self-preservation reflex kicks in to raise my hand to my mouth, to prevent me from screaming.

Mikhail, dressed head to toe in black, has dropped in by dumbwaiter. He's got his hands in the air and he's telling the lady chef something in hushed Russian. There's a handgun on the floor, a few feet away from him. That must have been what fell. I lean out an inch or two further so I can see her.

Both hands fly up to cover my mouth this time as I recognize the woman in white.

It's Katya. And she's got both hands on her own gun, which is aimed straight at Mikhail's head.

33

Mikhail says something in Russian, but Katya appears utterly disinterested in his version of events. She makes a downward motion with the gun, ordering him to his knees.

I can't watch. But I can't make myself look away, so I stare from my hiding place behind the door, almost afraid to breathe, as I scan my surroundings for anything that could serve as a weapon. Why isn't she guarding Aziz? And where the hell is Max? If this were the movies, he'd swoop in and save the day.

I tell myself to stop thinking idiotic thoughts.

Mikhail starts to lower himself slowly towards the floor. I bite down on my lip to keep from shrieking.

Before his knees reach the tiles, Mikhail dives for his gun.

He misses. The gun slips through his grasp and slides across the floor. Both my hands fly up to cover my mouth. Mikhail throws himself towards Katya's legs in a futile attempt to knock her off her feet. She dodges deftly and lands a well-placed kick on his jaw.

Her gun goes off with a quiet pop, almost like a fizzled firecracker.

In a split second several thoughts unspool in my mind's eye. I am going to die. It's going to hurt. A lot. Katya is about to execute Mikhail. Then she'll notice me and kill me without a second thought. I contemplate making a run for the kitchen, but Katya's blocking the door and even though my minutes are numbered, I can't summon the guts to run towards her gun.

Katya's bullet ricochets off one of the hanging pots into the china cabinet. It hits a piece of porcelain that crashes to the floor.

Without stopping to consider the consequences, I leap from my hiding place and grab the closest thing I can reach. Katya reels around, startled. I swing as hard as I can, and shatter a bottle of Perrier Jouet – the hundred dollar champagne that comes in those pretty painted bottles – on the side of her head.

She drops to the floor. I stand over her, holding the neck of the champagne bottle, stunned. For a moment I feel like I'm the one who's been hit in the head. I see stars and bursts of color, miniature fireworks going off inside my eyes.

"Thanks," Mikhail says, and snaps me back to reality. He retrieves his gun and Katya's, which has a long metal tube screwed onto the barrel, from the floor. "Very nicely done." When I continue to stand speechless, he adds, "You're a sight for sore eyes."

Even if I could formulate an adequate response, I'm not sure my mouth would comply. The sheer insanity of this situation has whipped up a storm of emotions. Part of me wants to throw myself into his arms, but mostly I am furious with him. He's the professional agent. He should have let me know he wasn't dead. Somehow.

He takes a step towards me but stops short. My eyes focus on Katya and without any warning, they start to well up.

Finally I manage to whisper, "Is she dead?"

I'm horrified by the thought.

I didn't mean to kill her. I only wanted to stop her from killing us.

I crouch next to Katya's motionless form. She looks like a sleeping princess from a children's story, with her utterly motionless, perfectly made up face.

"Don't touch her," Mikhail says. He steps over and presses a gloved hand to Katya's throat. "Not dead, just out cold. She has a strong pulse."

"How long will she be out?" On the few occasions I've fainted the blackouts never lasted long, but maybe getting walloped in the head produces a different result.

"Let's not stick around long enough to find out."

Sparked by relief that I am not a murderess, my brain shifts itself out of first gear and remembers I was beside myself over Mikhail's fate. And feeling guilty about it. And angry and bereaved, even. But I don't try to explain my emotional spin cycle. Instead I say, "Wait! I thought you were dead! Henry said—"

"You were misinformed." Mikhail smiles at me. The dimple that makes him look like a ghost flashes across his cheek.

"What? How? What happened last night?"

"Korov and I made a deal."

"What kind of deal?"

"Let's just say I'm working on fulfilling my end of it."

I nod. The left side of my brain tells me it's better not to know the details. The right side aches with curiosity.

Mikhail says, "I wasn't sure I would see you again, but here." He produces a skinny letter from inside his black shirt and hands it to me. It's addressed to Henry Redwell, care of the U.S. Embassy.

"Don't freak out now, okay? This is almost over." He glances at his watch. "It's closing in on penguin suit time up there. Go upstairs to the party and deliver this to Redwell. And please hurry."

I look at him like he's nuts. Does he expect me to waltz out through the kitchen? Because I'm sure that would go over with the palace staff like a lead blimp. I can picture it. "Excuse me, pardon me, don't mind me. I'm some random American woman who was hiding in your pantry during a presidential summit."

Instead of saying this, I ask, "How?"

"The express elevator, naturally." He points at the dumbwaiter. "It goes right to a small room adjacent to the reception. Henry's up there with all the important people."

Why does it have to be another dark, cramped space? I'm revising my opinions about espionage. It's not the least bit glamorous. It's dirty and sweaty and consists mostly of eavesdropping, scampering from point to point like a possessed rodent, and cowering in claustrophobic crevasses.

"How the heck do you know where Henry is? And how did you get in here?"

Mikhail sighs with annoyance. "I rode the dumbwaiter from the basement. I came in through the loading dock, rode up and checked out the scene upstairs. I was on my way back down to retrieve the rest of my gear. But the damn thing stopped and opened on this floor."

"What gear?"

"Nothing I need anymore." He keeps his eyes trained on Katya.

Too bad there's no rope or tape around. We could tie her up.

"In any case," Mikhail says, "I've revised my plan. Improved on it, really. But I need you to go find Redwell. Now."

He reaches into the dumbwaiter and retrieves a medium-sized black duffle bag that I hadn't noticed lying there. I wonder whether the ancient device will break under my weight. A ridiculous fear. It carried Mikhail.

I'm arranging myself inside the Victorian victual conveyor when Max's head pops through the hole in ceiling. "What the hell is going on down here?"

I jump back to my feet. "Don't worry. He's on our side." I'm not sure this is technically true, but at least I have a strong feeling, or maybe it's what you'd call an intuition, that he's on *my* side. At the minimum.

"FBI. Agent Max von Buren." Max sticks his badge out at arm's length for inspection. I wonder why he thinks a badge would impress anyone, since I've seen first hand how easily documents can be forged. Mikhail ignores the badge and looks to me for confirmation that Max is who he claims. I nod, slowly, afraid that if I make a sudden move, I could inadvertently unleash more violence.

Max drops to the counter with a thud. He looks from me to Mikhail and back again. His jaw is clenched. He looks angry and unsure of his next move.

Mikhail breaks the silence. "I've given Lena a letter for your boss. It explains the location of an incoming shipment from BXE to Burtonhall, handled by Titan. The papers say the containers left half empty, but I've gone over this a dozen times and the weights don't add up. If we're right about our arms-smuggling hunch, these containers should provide some answers."

"Why should I believe you?" asks Max. His eyes narrow and his fingers find his gun.

"You've paid me five million dollars, but I haven't delivered yet. Think of this as a bonus, a good will gesture."

Max looks partially swayed.

"He's telling the truth," I say. Not that I know for sure. I want to believe Mikhail's a good guy, although a strong circumstantial case could be constructed to the contrary. I want to believe the shipping containers exist and that they contain enough evidence to send Acheson and all his cronies away for a very long time. I'd like to believe that the FBI and FSB, working together, could shut down a massive arms smuggling operation and the evil corporation behind it.

But mostly I want to believe this nightmare will end soon.

"Take your hand off your gun," Mikhail says to Max. "See? Mine's holstered." He holds his hands up for emphasis. "Let Lena deliver the letter. She's safer upstairs. You and I have to go save your president."

That does it. Max nods faintly. It's a weak gesture, but his expression and posture change subtly. He's grudgingly on board.

He and Mikhail usher me back into the dumbwaiter with admonitions to hurry. As the door rattles shut, I see them making motions to empty one of the cabinets and stash Katya's inert form inside.

The dumbwaiter is dark, cramped and noisy. Clearly not subjected to renovation, recent or otherwise. As it clatters upwards, I clutch Mikhail's letter and wonder why God, or whatever supreme being calls the shots up there, saw fit to put Mikhail and Max together. They obviously mistrust each other, and why shouldn't they? There must be some other team on the planet, better equipped to save POTUS from his own security forces.

The ride is short. A buzzer announces my arrival, which is hardly necessary because the contraption slams to a halt. The hum of conversation carries through the walls.

I unfold myself out of the dumbwaiter, smooth Mikhail's letter between my hands and suck in a deep breath. I nudge the door open and find myself behind a row of overflowing buffet tables. The orchestra sits off to the left. Grand windows with even grander curtains line one long wall of the room, framing a panorama of the Moscow evening. Four impossibly ornate chandeliers hang from the ceiling. Protruding between them, I notice several security cameras.

There are about three men to every woman at this party, mingling in small groups. Most of them clutch wine glasses and nibble on passed hors d'oeuvres. Nobody has touched the display on the buffet table. As I scan the room for Henry, I realize the presidents haven't arrived yet.

The sea of tuxedos makes everyone look the same. Finally my eyes settle on Henry's familiar form. He stands halfway across the room, neither laughing nor sipping wine. He's engaged in what appears to be a serious conversation with two other middle-aged men.

It's now or never. I step through the door. At first nobody notices, although I don't exactly blend in my jeans.

I clutch the letter with two hands as if it's a winning lottery ticket and inch forward. A woman turns towards the buffet and her eyes fix on me. She points, presumably at my clothing. Her companions shake their heads in confusion and start looking around.

I panic. "Henry!" I yell. I break into a run. All frivolous worries about my attire vanish as I sprint towards the deputy director.

I don't get very far. Out of nowhere, two young Russian soldiers in dress uniforms tackle me to the ground and hold me down. They mash my cheek into the carpet and yank my hands behind my back. Everyone stops and stares. The musicians cut off Shostakovich mid-measure. Nobody speaks. I manage to crumple the letter in my fist. If they want it, they'll have to pry it forcibly from my fingers.

"Henry!" I shout a second time.

A crowd converges around me and Henry's familiar voice orders people to let him through. He comes to a halt at my head and barks at the guards, "Unhand her at once."

I strain my neck to look up at them. They're unsure.

Henry whips his badge out of his tuxedo pocket. "FBI. You've assaulted one of my agents. Release her this instant."

I don't know if they understand English, or whether his badge impresses them, or whether it's his tone, but the soldiers help me to my feet and even make motions to dust off my clothing. I shove the letter at Henry as the band abruptly strikes up a fanfare, probably the Russian version of Hail to the Chief. The entire crowd turns to applaud the two leaders, who have been turned back from the room by security personnel. Applause and music stop short. Hundreds of eyes pivot in my direction. A tidal wave of nervous murmurs starts at the far end of the room and washes towards us.

The Russian soldiers may have let me onto my feet, but they seem disinclined to release me. They each grip one of my arms despite Henry's protests. A grey-haired man in uniform, apparently their supervisor, marches towards us. A lively exchange in Russian ensues, during which the soldiers briefly release their grip on me to point at each other. I can't make out whether they're apportioning credit or blame.

Henry repeats his request that the security forces unhand his agent, but they ignore him. Someone sends for a translator. One appears almost immediately, accompanied by someone from the American president's entourage. From where I'm standing, I can see Secret Service men bunched around the man himself, visibly conflicted as to whether he should be allowed to enter the reception or whisked to some other part of the palace. The president bellows that he trusts Henry Redwell and he's going in.

Which shouldn't be all that surprising, considering the mountain of caviar, cheese and paté that awaits him on the buffet table. He's been called the most gluttonous Commander in Chief since that one they buried in a piano box, and I've always thought he looks one cruller away from heart failure.

I'm so lost in my own preposterous thoughts that the translator has to ask me twice for my handbag, which remains strapped across my chest. The guards release me so I can pull it over my head. The senior Russian army man snatches it.

He roots around. His fingernails are filthy, which seems like a breakdown of military discipline, considering he's decked out in dress uniform. He makes a show of opening my lipstick. I'm not sure what he expects to find. Maybe a James Bond style remote control missile launcher? He opens my New Zealand passport and waves it triumphantly under Henry's disbelieving nose. He asks something in a curt tone.

The translator, a slight man with an even slighter mustache, mimics his pitch exactly and says, "Still say she's one of yours?"

Henry recovers from the surprise. "I trust if you open her wallet, you'll find all the contents belong to Ms. Lena Mancuso."

The translator conveys this message and the army man rifles through my wallet. He says something.

We all look at the translator.

"This proves nothing," he says flatly.

Henry turns on his heels and grumbles that he doesn't have time for this. He marches away, mumbling under his breath about this ridiculous display of Russian incompetence. The soldiers resume their bickering and their superior officer looks me up and down. One of the soldiers squeezes my left arm so hard it hurts.

Then, all at once, the security men fall silent. Henry's back. He's flanked by the President of the United States, who's toting a skewer of some kind of sauce-laden mystery meat.

Shock sweeps in to replace my panic. I will my mouth to close. The president tells the translator, who's trying unsuccessfully to appear nonchalant about his newest client, to tell the Russians to unhand his agent.

The order isn't even fully translated when the soldiers release me. One of them hands back my purse with a little bow. They salute and scurry away, obviously eager to distance themselves from any potential fallout. Their commander tells the translator to assure Mr. President that he will deal with his men harshly. Henry grumbles something about how it's typically Russian to push the blame on the most junior person available.

I wonder why he calls this a Russian trait. It sounds like every day in my life at R&S.

Henry thanks the president for his intervention. I stand, rooted to the floor, in stunned silence.

The POTUS, bizarrely unfazed by the unexpected drama, takes a large bite from his miniature shish kebab. He chews noisily and then, with his mouth almost empty, asks me, "So you're the young lady who didn't want a photo with me this morning, aren't you?"

I look at my feet and feel my ears start to burn. I mumble something along the lines of, "Well, better late than never." I can't believe I can't offer a more intelligent remark.

Henry explains, very suavely, "We decided a photo opportunity could compromise her identity as a covert operative. I advised against doing it."

The president congratulates Henry on his dedication and good thinking. He excuses himself and waddles back towards the food.

"At least he's not a drunk," Henry says, as he takes my arm and hustles me to the edge of the room. Miraculously, most people have stopped staring at us. They're busy jockeying for proximity to the presidents.

We reach a relatively quiet corner and before Henry can demand an explanation, I shove the now-crumpled letter at him. "From Mikhail. It's about the arms smuggling. He said to consider it an incentive to pay him the balance."

Henry regards me with suspicion. "Does this mean he's reneging on his contract to deliver the flash drives?"

"Not at all," I insist. "I have the key." I stop short of telling Henry it's stashed in my bra and it feels like it's carving a hole in my breast. That seems like too much information.

I wonder why I'm so sure the Swiss vault will yield the promised goods. That's if the key and code work at all. For all we know, Mikhail and Korov could have played the FBI for five million dollars, and now they're using this tip to make it ten. That would explain why Mikhail is still breathing.

Henry tears the envelope open.

He reads the note and whispers something into the microphone on his cufflink. He cocks his head, as if that amplifies the reply through his earpiece, then raises his wrist to say, "Roger that."

Seconds later, the President of the United States is being hustled towards us. He's flanked by several aides and a Secret Service detail of six agents. I scan their faces. None of them even remotely resemble the men in Max's pictures.

Henry whisks us into an adjacent sitting room, lavishly appointed with antiques and wallpapered in that strange color the Crayola people would label sea foam.

Henry says, "Sir, we need a helicopter to take us to the airport and then we'll need a plane to St. Petersburg and a helicopter transfer to the Vladimir Ilyich Shipyard, which is thirty kilometers north of the city. How soon can I have that?"

The president looks to his security personnel. The man who's evidently highest in rank replies, "We could have a chopper ready to take you off the roof in ten minutes. But what's the mission? Why weren't we given advance notice?"

"I'm afraid that's classified. Patriot Act, Section 431," Henry explains, with a wry smile and a subtle wink my way.

I'd bet any amount of money he made that up.

The agents, caught off guard, and not wishing to admit ignorance of the laws they're sworn to enforce, look to their Commander in Chief.

The president says, "Give the FBI whatever they need."

"Thank you, sir," Henry says. He presses his lips together to make a stern, resolute face, but it's obvious something's troubling him. He scrutinizes the Secret Service men out of the corner of one eye. That's the problem. Henry wants to get to the helicopter, but he doesn't know what to do about protecting the president.

"If you'll all excuse me, I have a reception to attend," the president says.

He retreats, his entourage swirling around him, before anyone can muster the gumption to object. One fortyish man with a bald spot and oversized eyeglasses stays behind. I don't immediately pin him as American, probably because the tuxedos go a long way to cancel out the obvious hallmarks of nationality. But when he opens his mouth to speak, he leaves no doubt. "Who's she?" he demands of Henry, while pointing, rather rudely, at me.

"My section 204 agent."

Brownell begins blinking rapidly, as if Henry's answer has actually short circuited some critical wiring in his brain. "But why is she here? Section 204 clearly states that—"

Henry cuts him off, "Section 204 (g) (41)(ix). Special circumstances. Her name's Lena. Lena, this is Martin Brownell, the Bureau's newly appointed legal attaché for Moscow."

I attempt to smile politely.

Brownell scowls. "You know this is against the rules. I need to make sure procedures are followed, particularly where relations with an important partner like Russia are concerned. I'm afraid we'll have to hold everyone here for a moment while I finesse some details."

Henry raises his voice and cuts Brownell off. "And I'm afraid I'm your boss. Right now I need to pursue a key development. As you know from this morning's briefing, I have a detail inside this building, investigating a possible plot to harm the president. Since the president has repeatedly refused to cancel or even curtail his summit activities, we have a delicate situation. I need you to stay here and take charge of protecting him. Do you think you can handle that?"

Max is going to love answering to this guy.

Brownell stands up a bit taller and practically flutters with delight. "Yes, sir. Absolutely, sir. You can count on me, sir."

"Good," Henry says. "Now get back in there."

Brownell trips over his own feet in his haste to re-join the important people. As he dashes out, he slams right into one of the agents from before, who's come to tell Henry his chopper is ready and waiting.

I stand rooted to the floor for a second, unsure whether I should follow Henry or not, when he says, "Come on. We're going to the airport."

We're following the agent through a main hallway when Max comes running towards us at breakneck speed.

"Where the fuck is Brownell? I've been trying to reach him, or you, for ten minutes. Mikhail has our suspects at bay in the freezer. He flashed his FSB credentials to enlist a couple of chefs to help stand guard."

"You're sure you have them secured?" Henry barks. I realize the question he wants to ask is, "Why on earth aren't they dead?"

"They're secure. Or they were two and a half minutes ago. I need Brownell to ask the Moscow police commandant for permission to arrest them. We caught them red-handed. U.S. Secret Service men, poised to lace the entire first tray of champagne glasses with diarsenic pentoxide."

"That's what they put in Charlie's coffee," I hear myself gasp. The leader of the free world would undoubtedly be served from the first tray. I wonder how many people would have become collateral damage, if Max hadn't intervened in time?

"That's true," Henry says to me, ignoring his legat, who is rambling about the proper paperwork to file a warrant request. Henry scratches his chin and adjusts his glasses, the rimless ones I like. He asks Max, "How do you know it was arsenic?"

"Chemical label. They were stupid, or cocky, enough to carry the crystals in original packaging."

Henry rolls his eyes before taking charge. He flings off his tuxedo jacket, loosens his bowtie and starts shouting commands. "Von Buren, get back down there on the double." I still can't believe Henry regularly employs that phrase, and evidently neither can Max. He gives a facetious mini-salute, spins on his heels and takes off at a run in the direction from which he came.

"Martin, you get the nearest available police officer, parking officer or truant officer to arrest those traitorous bastards."

Brownell's face contorts with indecision.

"Do it now!"

Brownell whips out his cell phone and starts issuing orders in English and fluent-sounding Russian, with an air of the smugness that often results from a sudden increase in authority.

Henry waylays a waiter. "Do you speak English?"

"Yes, a little." He sounds indifferent to the urgency in Henry's voice.

"Good. FBI. Deputy Director Henry Redwell. Take me to your kitchen."

The waiter abandons his sulky tone as well as his tray of canapés, and hustles us out of the ballroom and down a huge marble staircase. He does it on the double, without even being asked.

34

We sound like an advancing army as we storm down the steps, which Henry takes two at a time. The waiter screeches to a halt in front of swinging double doors.

Henry pulls out his gun and motions for me to step behind him. The waiter, delirious with the excitement of the most interesting episode of his working life, crowds in close behind me.

Henry flings the doors open and we burst into a nearly empty kitchen. Duran Duran, which I recognize because I grew up hanging around Diana's older sister, blares over the sound system.

"Over here!" Max's familiar baritone calls from one of the prep rooms.

The kitchen staff parts for Henry. The room isn't a true freezer. It's more like a chilled storage area. Salads and cheeses lie strewn in a mess on the floor. In the back corner sit the two agents from Max's photos, tied back to back, with what looks like hundreds of yards of cooking string. The head chef brandishes the biggest cleaver I've ever seen in my life, right under the prisoners' noses. Max keeps his handgun aimed at the larger man's head.

Henry surveys the scene and asks what I want to know first, too. "Where in damnation is Mikhail?"

"Gone," Max says. "The head chef speaks some English. He said the FSB man told him to keep watching these men and use the knife, but only if absolutely necessary."

Henry and I look to the head chef for confirmation.

He nods emphatically. His white hat, which is taller than those worn by his staff, flops up and down on his head. "*Da, da.* Yes, yes. He did say this thing but is not, how do you say? Is not in my job." For all the flourish with which he wields his knife, the old man is clearly eager to be relieved of his present responsibility.

"You can stand down," Henry says. He trains his own Glock on the captives.

The chef, visibly relieved, takes a few steps back. His knife falls out of his shaking hands to the floor. Everyone near him jumps back and one of his young female assistants eases him onto the only available seat, a step ladder.

Henry barks, "Where the hell did Mikhail – I mean, the FSB man – where did he go?"

"He did not say," stammers the chef. "Just said wait for FBI."

I wonder why Mikhail would want to disappear after helping to deliver the culprits. The waiter who led our charge down the stairs pushes against me to get a closer look at the scene.

Max never looks up from his prisoners, not even to address Henry. A bruise has started to form under his left eye and a long trickle of sweat rolls down the side of his face. He doesn't move his hand to wipe it away. It winds its way down to his chin and drips onto his collar.

It's not hot in here. Actually, I would guess it's a damp fifty degrees Fahrenheit.

Martin Brownell, still wearing his tuxedo jacket and twitching with excitement, bursts into the room waving his badge as if anyone cares. He ushers in a team of Russian police, decked out in riot gear.

Two of the Russian cops clear the room of wait staff, kitchen staff and non-essential persons such as myself. They herd us back into the main kitchen. Like everyone else, I hover by the door and watch. They pull the prisoners to their feet, handcuff them, shackle them in leg irons and untie the makeshift restraints.

The staff parts to form a column and the Russian police march the arrested men through. Henry grabs my arm as he follows the procession. Max starts to debrief his boss, but Brownell interrupts. "The Russians will let us repatriate them if you agree to transfer them out of Russia immediately. Do you want to accompany the suspects?"

"Yes, of course," Henry says. "So they won't require us to file extradition papers?" He looks disbelieving.

"The Russian authorities will allow our agents to take custody, so long as the men are transferred to the airport and out of Russian territory without delay. I've filed all the necessary paperwork to circumvent the normal proceedings."

I wonder whether he's a lawyer. He must be. Nobody else talks like that.

"All they want in return is full credit for the arrests," he adds.

Henry nods. "I'll take it from here."

"I don't even get a thank you, for pulling off a bureaucratic miracle?" Brownell practically whines.

"Henry doesn't believe in thanking his staff for doing their jobs." Max says nastily.

"That's right." Henry turns to Max. "Go with them to the helipad. Get the suspects ready to board. I'll meet you on the roof as soon as I finish down here."

Max runs to catch up with the Russian police. A few yards down the hall, they shove their captives into an elevator and disappear.

Feeling useless, or perhaps even like an impediment, I summon the courage to ask Henry what I should be doing.

He considers for a moment, adjusts his glasses without slowing his stride and says, "You stay with me. If you can access that vault I don't want you out of my sight."

Of course. I quicken my pace to keep up with Henry.

Martin trots along half a step behind us. "What vault?" he brays. "I need to alert the local authorities to any developments and we've asked a lot of our Russian hosts already today."

Henry stops short, turns to face his legal attaché and demands, "Do you ever stop talking? Just *shut up*. For Christ's sake. *None* of this concerns you."

Brownell deflates and excuses himself to make a phone call. Henry and I hustle back to the reception, where they're in full swing, oblivious to the drama unfolding under their feet.

Henry pushes us through the crowd towards POTUS, who's regaling a portly man with a football story while not so surreptitiously spitting olive pits into his cocktail napkin. After every three or four pits, one of his aides swaps him a fresh napkin.

A Secret Service agent moves to stop us, but the president waves at Henry. He even berates his guards for failing to recognize such a high-level appointee. Henry whispers something into the president's ear. The president nods and furrows his brow, but doesn't stop chewing the wad of olives in his mouth. He swallows, and as if able to focus at last on the imminent danger, the leader of the free world starts to shake with rage. Henry urges him in a not-so-hushed tone to keep it together, as cameras are flashing. He suggests they adjourn to the ballroom's annex.

As they begin to move towards the door, POTUS focuses on me and asks why I'm still here. Henry says it will all be in his report and that my continued presence is crucial to the investigation. Despite his valiant and obvious attempts to maintain a stoic facade, even I can see the president is nearly frantic with concern for his personal safety.

As we make our way across the room, the president stares at his Secret Service detail, no doubt wondering if he can trust any of them. A legitimate concern. If two were corrupted, might not some others have known? Turned a blind eye? I've heard it's a pretty tight fraternity.

But wouldn't sedition go beyond the pale of what any decent agent could tolerate, even if he counted the conspirators as friends?

The orchestra has started *Eine Kleine Nachtmusik* when guests at the opposite end of the room start screaming. A half-dozen soldiers appear, seemingly out of nowhere. Metal gates crash down to seal the room. The orchestra stops playing. They spring from their chairs and join the panicked mob in its frantic swarm around a disturbance I can't see.

Word spreads immediately that Russia's president has been shot in the head. Perayev lies on the ground, bleeding and unconscious. Several people yell for a doctor. Apparently nobody knows where the bullet came from. Perayev's bodyguards seal the room.

I look to Henry for answers but he's as stunned as everyone else. POTUS has gone white and his Secret Service agents have closed ranks around him. One of them is yelling at the Russian soldier nearest the closest exit that they need to evacuate him. Now.

After a tense exchange the sentry reluctantly complies, on the condition that nobody leaves the building until his section chief gives the all clear. He speaks much better English than his comrades who tackled me earlier.

The metal gates swing open long enough for us to pass into an adjacent sitting room. A Russian guard flips a switch on a wall panel and an armoire opens to reveal a series of surveillance videos. He adjusts the settings to follow developments in the ballroom. A doctor has arrived, and he's supervising the evacuation of President Perayev on a stretcher. We can't tell from the grainy video feed, whether he's regained consciousness.

POTUS has recovered from his initial shock. He barks at his security detail that he needs to go out and make a statement, to reassure people. By hiding in this annex, he looks likes he's cowering.

The senior Secret Service man shakes his head. "We can't allow that." When the president glowers at him, he adds under his breath, "It's not like you're ever running for office again."

I hold my breath and brace for a tirade. I glance at Henry. He's taken aback as well, but the president surprises us both. Instead of losing his temper, he plops himself into a leather wing chair, which groans under his weight, and agrees to wait.

The agent who'd spoken so rudely a second ago adopts a business-like tone and says, "Mr. President, our men in the room tell us Mr. President Perayev has been evacuated by air. The medical team is assessing the extent of his injuries. The palace guards and presidential protection force have secured the area, and they're conducting a systematic search of every individual on the premises. So far, they've found no trace of a gun. The FSB and their forensics team will arrive within minutes. They should be able to give us more complete information, sir."

POTUS nods and mumbles his thanks. His numerous chins flap over his bowtie. He looks frustrated to be stuck here, sidelined.

Henry clears his throat. "We need to look at the big picture, Mr. President, and I'm afraid you haven't heard the worst of it. Sir, we got the tip on your agents from Abdul bin Aziz. He was correct about them and my men apprehended them red handed. The good news, if I may call it that, is that the tip implicated only your advance team. Not your personal detail." Henry shoots an approving glance at the president's senior bodyguard. "The unfortunate wrinkle is that Mr. Aziz's information leads us to believe the agents were acting on orders—and with financial incentives—from Jack Prescott."

"No," is all the leader of the free world can manage to say. He looks like he's been hit with a taser.

"I'm afraid that's how the evidence looks, Mr. President. Of course we shouldn't jump to conclusions. But sir, do you know where your vice president is? I think it would be best if he not leave the States until we conclude our investigation."

The president lunges out of his chair. "That bastard! I ought to—" He's getting red in the face and the vein above his left temple has bulged to such extreme proportions I think it will burst. His hands clench into fists and he blows air from his nostrils like a winded racehorse, before regaining his composure and adopting a more presidential tone. "Are you sure?" he asks Henry. "Are you absolutely certain about the quality of your intelligence?"

"As sure as I can be without interviewing the principals directly, sir."

POTUS springs into action. Within moments, one of the Secret Service men has Jack Prescott's head secretary on the line. He passes her to the president, who demands to be connected to Jack. I'm standing close enough that I hear her say he's on his way to Andrews Air Force Base. The president demands to know where his vice president is flying.

Henry whispers, "Mr. President, could you indulge me and put her on speaker?"

The president nods, but needs assistance from one of his aides to switch the setting on the phone.

The secretary says, "He's heading to the ranch in Texas, Mr. President. It's his mother's eighty-fifth birthday celebration, sir."

"Thank you," the president says. He sounds remarkably calm and self-possessed, considering he looked like he was going to succumb to shock moments ago.

We hear typing on the other end of the line.

"Sir, please wait just a second." More typing. "Sir, this is highly unusual. The pilot of Air Force Two filed a change in flight plan."

She pauses. The president starts to lose patience. "Well, where the hell are they flying?"

"That's the strange thing. My screen says details not immediately available. Sir, this is most unusual, if you'll give me one moment, I'm sure I can sort this out. I apologize for taking your time this way, Mr. President."

POTUS hangs up and bellows, "Get me the highest ranking man at Andrews. Now!"

The Secret Service men fall all over each other in their attempts to be the first to connect their boss to Andrews Air Force Base. A blond man who looks younger than the rest holds his phone out. "Colonel McCarty's office, sir. She's advised her boss to hold for the President of the United States."

The president grabs the phone and rams it against his ear. "Colonel? I don't have time to discuss how I am... I'm pissed off, if you must know... Colonel, I need you to ground all traffic in and out of Andrews, effective immediately... Yes, of course I know Jack is scheduled to depart momentarily... I want you to detain him there until further notice... Yes, that's an order... And not a word to the press. Take their cell phones before you tell the vice president." The president pauses, presumably waiting for confirmation he's made himself clear, and slams the phone down on a marble end table. He throws his weight into it and the phone smashes to smithereens under the force of the blow.

On the video screens, the crew of soldiers pats down the reception guests, none of whom appear accustomed to such treatment. The ranking Secret Service man cocks his head. He listens to his earpiece and says, "Roger that," into his sleeve. "We've secured the building for you to fly out, Mr. President." He turns to Henry. "Mr. Redwell, your helicopter will re-land as soon as the president's clears the pad."

One of the agents checks the hallway and gives the all clear. The security detail surrounds POTUS and whisks him out of the room. Henry and I follow. One of the Russian soldiers ushers the president's group into a back passageway, like the one Max and I traveled through earlier. They disappear into the wall.

One of the English-speaking palace guards informs Henry that his prisoners have been transferred to the helipad, and that he can head on up. Henry asks if we can have a quick look around the reception room first. The soldier agrees, but says he'll need to accompany us. Most of the people have cleared out. Uniformed and undercover Russian agents are interviewing the stragglers and combing for clues.

Henry scans the scene and says to me, "Clearly a professional hit. I might even venture this was an inside job. If that's the case, they'll never solve it."

I don't know what to say. I have my suspicions, but I keep them to myself. It's not like I have proof.

Henry says, "I'm sorry I can't be two places at once. I'd love to delve into this." He scrutinizes the room. His eyes pan the paintings. Maybe Henry thinks the gunman fired through a hole in one of them.

He's saying we need to leave when my eyes settle on the profile of a tall, lithe man standing twenty yards from us. His hair's slicked back in a completely new style, but there's no question it's him. The duffel bag is gone, replaced by a slightly smaller leather messenger bag, worn slung across his chest. Henry, who's busy scouring the intricate wallpaper for a gun barrel sized slot, hasn't noticed him yet.

Mikhail's talking to two of the guards who were on duty at the time of the incident. They're the same guys who tackled me. One of them catches my eye and looks at me, as if questioning what I'm still doing here.

His confused gaze attracts Mikhail's attention. Not only are his hair and luggage different; he's ditched his cat burglar clothes in favor of a suit.

Mikhail's eyes register recognition for half a second. Then he makes his face as neutral as possible, excuses himself from his conversation and strides over to us.

"Max was wondering where you went off to!"

"He had the situation downstairs under control and the FSB needed me here."

Henry's eyes narrow. He's not convinced this is the whole truth. Neither am I, to be honest. It seems awfully odd that Mikhail swoops down to help Max save POTUS from poisoning and then disappears.

Only to materialize again in the immediate aftermath of a possibly successful attempt on President Perayev's life. Mikhail's eyes challenge anyone to speak against him. They say, *Yeah, I know you have your suspicions but you can't do anything about them.*

Henry asks, "Is that so?"

"It is." Mikhail stands up as straight as possible, and looks Henry in the eye. "I need you to give me a lift."

"We're not driving. We're going by chopper. In mere minutes."

"I know that."

Henry takes off his eye glasses and pulls a handkerchief out of his breast pocket. He starts to clean the lenses slowly, methodically.

Mikhail tires of waiting for the older man to respond. "You take me to the airport and I give Lena the code." He steals a glance my way and gives me the slightest smile. His eyes implore me to play along.

I don't know whether I will or not. Mikhail's starting to make me very uneasy.

Henry holds his glasses up to the light, inspects them and says, "Why her?"

I'm wondering the same thing.

"Because it's my vault and I set the terms. And I'll only give her the code if you take me to the airport first."

Henry considers. Mikhail leans in and whispers, "I know you haven't made up your mind about me, and even if you have, an old school man like yourself won't have trouble making a deal with someone with a less than immaculate record."

Henry restores his spectacles to his face. "What's your point?"

"My point is simple. I stand a better chance of staying alive if I fly off the roof with you, rather than giving you everything you want right here."

"Fine," Henry says. "Let's go."

35

The palace helipad is a big painted circle staffed by a couple of kids in army uniforms.

Max rushes over to us and makes no effort to disguise his displeasure at seeing Mikhail. "What the hell is *he* doing here?"

"We give him a lift and he gives Lena the bank code," Henry says, in a tone that discourages discussion. Max starts to object, but Henry cuts him off. "I've made an executive decision and it's final."

Max shakes his head in disbelief, turns away from his boss and asks me, "Are you alright?"

"I'm fine." I've cycled through bewildered, terrified and exhausted. Adrenalin surges through my body, jolting my mind into overdrive. *Mikhail shot President Perayev.* That's what he meant when he told me he was keeping his end of the bargain with Korov. What I can't figure out is how he pulled it off.

Max decides to challenge Henry. Maybe he's overtired, overworked and over-extended. Or perhaps he no longer cares whether he gets himself exiled to North Dakota, to patrol border crossings used mainly by grizzly bears. "She's a fucking *civilian*, Henry. Or have you forgotten that inconvenient detail? We've put her in enough danger. She needs to go home. Now."

"For all intents and purposes, she's acting as an agent. And I don't appreciate your tone."

"I don't give a damn if you appreciate my tone. She's an informant who got dragged in over her head, Henry. Not an agent. Not even close. You know that. For Christ sakes, we didn't even teach her to protect herself. And your precious Bureau is going to look awfully bad, no, not bad, *incompetent*, if we don't return her safely back to American soil."

"I have every intention of doing that after she opens the bank box for us." Henry spits every word at Max. "We're so close. Think about it. We're going to nail Prescott, and Acheson and, if we can get him back on U.S. territory, Korov. Your career will skyrocket, if you don't fall apart in the home stretch."

Max considers but doesn't back down. "We could be paying ten million dollars for a fake code. Or better yet, it's the real code, but the vault contains a Cracker Jack prize. Has that even crossed your mind?"

Mikhail says to Max, "Don't blame me if you're second-guessing your own judgment."

Henry ignores Mikhail. "Of course the possibility of an empty vault has occurred to me. It's a calculated risk. The payoff could far exceed our gamble, agreed?"

The helicopter's blades spin to life with a deafening roar that gives Henry the last word.

One of the soldiers passes out earphones with little microphones, which we all clamp on our heads. He makes a cursory check that we did this correctly – not that it was difficult – and herds us on board. I remember hearing that helicopter travel is incredibly risky. Damien wanted to take a helicopter safari when we were in Hawaii last year, but he couldn't persuade me. If he could see me now.

Two big men wearing similar headsets are already strapped into seats. They're handcuffed and hobbled by leg irons, and though they never set out to hurt me, their mere proximity makes me uneasy. Strange that I have no such reservations about Mikhail. He strides on board and belts himself in next to me, carrying himself as if he owns the helicopter.

We lift off the roof with a gentle push that accelerates into a stomach-dropping ascent. I send up a silent prayer that I won't need the prominently positioned airsickness bags. The sound of Henry's voice crackles through my headset. He asks the two captives whether they've decided to cooperate. One of them answers that they want to speak to their attorneys.

Max says, "Lena's a lawyer. I hear she's pretty good. She works for a big fancy firm."

"Fuck yourself," comes the reply. I can't say I entirely disagree with the sentiment.

We ride in silence. I muster the courage to look out the window at the lights of Moscow glittering below. By the time I've acclimated to the helicopter's unusual motion and decided that I won't embarrass myself by puking, we've started to descend. Max, seated across from me and closest to the captives, stares straight ahead, jaw clenched, immersed in his thoughts. A landing pad comes into view.

The pilot sets us down softly. Henry removes his headset and motions for us to do the same. The blades slow. A team of eight men storms the passenger compartment.

The senior guy identifies himself to Henry as an FBI special agent based in Kiev. He's got a junior agent with him, along with two Russian police, two FSB men and two military policemen from the U.S. Air Force.

The FBI agent explains that he and his partner will fly back to Andrews with the prisoners and the MP's. "We're fueled up and ready to go," he says. "We have clearance from the tower and can be wheels up in ten minutes, barring any unexpected delays." He shoots a sidelong glance at the FSB men.

Henry nods his approval and hands some paperwork to the older FSB agent. He stamps it twice with a rubberstamp produced from his pocket and hands it back to his American counterpart. He appears disinclined to cause any of the delays the FBI man warned about.

Mikhail avoids meeting anyone's gaze. He stares out the window, as if fascinated by the scene on the tarmac. None of the agents pay any attention to him.

The shackled Secret Service men stare at their shoes as the MP's and Russian police shove them onto their feet and out the door. The younger FBI man steals a long, questioning look at me on his way out, but says nothing. They vanish down the tarmac on two of those modified golf carts used by airport staff.

A security guard meets us as we step out of the chopper. "Mr. Redwell?" he asks.

Henry says yes and flashes his badge.

"This way, please. Your plane is ready."

It's our turn to pile into one of the golf carts. They seat six, including the driver, so with him and the airport security guy, we're loaded to capacity. Henry sits up front. I end up sandwiched between Max and Mikhail. Not knowing what to do with myself, I adjust my purse in my lap and check for the hundredth time that Korov's tape is still there. The key in my bra has gone from uncomfortable to outright painful, stabbing into my skin.

The driver takes a corner too sharply and we all list to the left. Mikhail takes the opportunity to squeeze my leg, but the electric charge I felt when he touched me before is gone. It's been replaced by a brewing anxiety over what he's really up to and what kind of deal he's made with his devils. We come to a screeching halt under the wing of a flashy private jet, probably a Lear or a Gulfstream.

Henry launches himself out of the golf cart, says a cursory thank you to our escorts and barks at us to hurry.

"You go ahead. I want a word with Lena," says Mikhail.

"You're not coming?" I ask.

"This is where I go my own way." He says it quietly but his expression is determined. He turns to Henry. "I keep my promises. You'll have your safe deposit box and the containers."

Max scowls. "We'll see if all this lives up to the hype."

Henry jumps in. "As you wish, young man. Von Buren, let's move." He gestures towards the airplane's stairs and says to Mikhail, "Five minutes. We come down for her in five minutes."

Henry's tone sends a shiver down my spine. Does he know some sinister specifics about Mikhail? Max jogs up the steps two at a time. Henry follows at a more stately pace. The security guard, who's standing back with the cart driver, looks relieved that his charges are about to be airborne. He frowns when he notices that Mikhail and I aren't boarding.

As Henry disappears inside the plane, Mikhail says, "Over here." We step further under the wing, close to the fuselage. "They can't see us—or shoot me—here," he adds wryly.

I smooth my hair nervously. I already have the bank code. I wonder what he wants from me now.

"Do you remember the code?"

I rattle it off effortlessly, as if reciting my childhood phone number.

"Good. Your government will be more than pleased with its purchase and I have something for you as well."

He reaches into the outside pocket of his messenger bag and pulls out a scrap of paper. "It's an account number in the same bank. Use the same access code. There's five hundred thousand dollars for you. Buy yourself something nice. You deserve it." He smiles, and his dimple makes a fleeting appearance. His resemblance to Damien is haunting. It's not that they look alike, but their facial expressions strike me as eerily similar.

I'm speechless. I should say I can't accept so much cash, but instead I blink at him like an idiot. "But why?" I finally stammer. Half a million dollars is a lot of money to get for nothing.

"Because I want you to have it. And if you don't collect it, nobody else will."

I nod, unsure of what to think or say.

"I'm going to disappear for a while. I can't tell you where. Please, don't try to find me." He looks spent and resigned, almost like he's aged five years in two days.

"Is this part of your deal with Korov?"

"Would you believe me if I denied it?"

I shake my head no. I open my mouth to ask whether he shot President Perayev. I stop the question on my tongue, because I suspect I already know the answer.

Mikhail says, "He gave me a ticket, wherever I wanted to go."

I wonder where he chose. I know better than to ask, but I bet he picked someplace populous.

He leans closer to me. Sometime between the time I left him in the kitchen with Max and now, he's applied the same cologne he was wearing when we met. I breathe in its familiar scent. "I have to go," he whispers. His lips graze my ear.

I don't know what to say and he doesn't wait for my response. Instead, he takes his hands, the ones that presumably shot at least two men in two days, and turns my face up to his. He leans down and kisses me hard, but without the same passion as the other night. Maybe that's my fault. I'm not sure what I feel. A strange sense of loss creeps over me and I will it to subside. It disregards my orders utterly.

Mikhail pulls his head back and stares at me, as if committing my face to memory. "I have to go, and so do you. Good luck, Lena."

"Good luck to you, too," I mutter, because I can't think of anything else to say. I turn for the plane. By the time I'm on the stairs, Mikhail's climbed into the golf cart for transport to some faraway destination. Away from Korov. Away from the FBI and the FSB. And away from everything familiar. He could be jetting off to Tahiti tonight, but I don't envy him at all.

I force myself not to look back as I climb the last steps. Max meets me in the doorway. "It took him long enough to tell you a simple bank code," he says accusingly.

I shrug. His eyebrow raises in skepticism, but he doesn't push for details.

Onboard the jet, the mood is surprisingly celebratory.

"Drink, my dear?" Henry calls in way of greeting. He's brandishing a scotch.

My eyes scan the luxuriously appointed cabin and settle on the nearest telephone. "Actually, I'd love to call home. Just for a moment. To let my family know I'm okay."

"I'm sorry. I can't allow that at this juncture." Henry frowns, visibly unhappy to give such an unwelcome edict.

"I'll take two minutes. Less than that. Half a minute."

"The answer is no." He must see my eyes start to well up, because he apologizes for having to enforce such a draconian policy.

Max has a half-empty beer in his hand. "A toast!" he announces, and his voice sounds more awake than he looks.

Henry raises his glass gamely. He must have forgotten his annoyance with his subordinate.

"To success, and to being rid of that Russian creep!" Max takes a hearty swig of his Beck's. I roll my eyes.

Henry lowers his glass. "He's proven very useful, von Buren, and I daresay today would have been much bloodier without his help. I rather liked the chap. Pity he's not American. He'd make an excellent CIA man."

"Takes one to know one." Max changes the subject. "Have a beer with me, Lena."

"I wouldn't mind one, actually." I'm pleasantly surprised that the Beck's is cold. I sink into the big leather seat opposite Max and take a long drink. Henry excuses himself to use the washroom before takeoff.

Max stares out the window and says, "Don't let this go to your head, but I feel like Laszlow to your Russian's Rick. I was almost certain you'd disappear on us again."

"He's not *my* Russian. I doubt I'll ever see him again. And he looks nothing like Humphrey Bogart."

As soon as we're airborne, Henry dials a number into the black device on the table in front of him. A man's voice answers almost immediately, and the screen on the wall blinks to life. It's an amazingly clear picture, considering we're at forty-one thousand feet. A balding man in a blue suit and striped tie blinks back at us.

Henry says, "Von Buren, you know Ron Goldstein, my assistant deputy director. Goldstein, this is Lena Mancuso, our key informant in this case."

Agent Goldstein says a quick hello, but even through the video, it's obvious he's bursting with excitement. "Have you heard the news, boss?" he asks.

I glance at Max. He looks perturbed at the introduction of another level of middle management.

"We finished the data recovery from the computer system at Rutledge & Smerth. You'll never believe what we found," Goldstein says.

I glance over at Henry. He's taken off his glasses and he's spinning them in a circle by the ear piece, sort of like a lifeguard would twirl a whistle. Maybe he's trying to keep his hands busy to pace his scotch consumption. The corners of his mouth turn up slightly, suggesting he knows where Goldstein is going. The suspense must be for Max's benefit.

Goldstein continues, "It turns out that Evelyn Peabody, who went on every news show on television and wrung her hands about the *tragedy*, tried to purge some very interesting items from the law firm's computer system."

"Such as?" Henry asks. He restores his glasses to his face and takes a sip of scotch.

"She did extensive research on various poisons. She created an email account under an alias and ordered enough diarsenic pentoxide to kill off half her staff. She had it mailed from Canada, to a P.O. box in Capitol Heights. She thought if she cleared her browser, the trail would disappear forever. Silly woman."

I'm stunned. So, judging by the fact that his mouth is hanging open and his eyes look like they're about to pop out of his skull, is Max.

"I hope you can tell me she's in custody," Henry says.

"Yes, sir, boss. She turned herself in. She broke down completely. Told us everything. Never once even asked for a lawyer."

Max finds his voice. "But what the hell was her motive? Are you absolutely sure she wasn't framed?"

"A hundred per cent. When we confronted her with the evidence, she sang like a Viennese choir boy."

Even after all that's happened, this seems unfathomable to me. My head actually hurts from the strain of trying to process it.

Goldstein says, "Why, indeed? She gave us our answer about five seconds after we threatened her with federal murder charges. I don't know if we could even get her on federal capital murder. If it's a garden variety homicide, the D.C. system will want jurisdiction."

"Goldstein, old chap, you're digressing a wee bit, aren't you?" Henry asks, although it's obvious he enjoys the theatrics.

"It was blind ambition, boss, pure and simple. Acheson gave her a kickback with each Congressional bribe he passed through the firm. That bought her silence for years, but when he was indicted, she panicked and threatened to go to the authorities."

"So why didn't she? She could have saved us countless man hours," says Max. He's reaching for a third beer. Henry shakes his head sternly. Max frowns but doesn't argue. I can sympathize. It might feel nice to get obliterated. I try to nurse my beer as it's surely the only drink I'll be offered.

"That Acheson devil's a Goddamned genius. He knew if his old firm turned on him, he'd get forty years, and not at a Club Fed, either. So he had Prescott go to Evelyn Peabody and pay her an enormous retainer, in exchange for representation should the inquiry into his role in Clearwater Partners heat up. That meant anything they discussed would be protected by attorney-client privilege and inadmissible against *either* Acheson or Prescott. Then they made a huge gamble."

"I'm not following," complains Max.

"They said if she helped them make Jack Prescott president, Prescott would appoint her to the U.S Supreme Court."

Ambition, indeed. Evelyn would certainly be qualified, but she's never been enough of a political operator to make the short lists. And with one justice suffering from lung cancer and two others pushing ninety, it's nearly impossible that a vacancy or two won't open very soon. *Of course, if they open too soon, the current president would fill them and Evelyn would miss her window.*

Henry clears his throat, "So where are we?"

"The U.S. Attorney offered her a deal. No more than twenty years, at a medium security women's prison, in exchange for her full cooperation against Acheson and Prescott. She'll be arraigned later this afternoon. I'm tempted to do a perp walk for the media, if it's alright with you, boss."

"Use your discretion."

Twenty years sounds like a life sentence to me, but it must sound better than capital murder, especially when you're the person sitting under the bare light bulb in handcuffs. Still, I'm shocked at Evelyn. I can't believe she had it in her.

Henry signs off the video conference and swivels his chair to face us. "Now if we could find Acheson, my day would be perfect. Like this Mac 15." He smiles at his glass. "Any bright ideas?"

"He could be anywhere by now. I'd guess Switzerland or some other country with a high standard of living and no pesky extradition treaties," Max says.

"He was in Moscow last night," I say. "He and Korov broke into Mikhail's apartment."

Both men look at me quizzically. Max's eyebrows shoot up.

Henry asks, "Are you sure?"

"Absolutely, positively sure. I was hiding under the floor boards. I'd recognize his voice anywhere."

They regard me with rapt attention. I straighten in my chair some more. It feels good to feel useful again.

"You were hiding under the floor boards?" repeats Max. He's shaking his head and smiling in spite of himself. "You're pluckier than I thought." He smiles a little wider and I think, for the thousandth time, that he's wasting his time and energy with the FBI. He and his unnaturally perfect teeth could make a much easier living endorsing toothpaste.

Henry mumbles, "But we thought Acheson and Korov had a falling out."

"Who told you that?" I ask.

"Damn it," says Max, and the smile vanishes. "We got that bad tip from your jailbird former boss lady." He shakes his head in disgust.

Between Casper and Katya, or whatever her name is, and now Evelyn, the FBI's not exactly batting a thousand with their choices of informants.

Max gets up from his seat and paces the narrow aisle. "We've lost Acheson for sure." He pulls at his hair in frustration.

Henry says, "I think you're losing sight of the fact that we hope to indict the Vice President of the United States before the week is out. That's a coup, by anyone's standards. Don't be so hard on yourself, young man."

By the time the pilot announces our descent into St. Petersburg, Henry's eyes are dancing. He looks almost spring-loaded and giddy with anticipation. Max looks sullen.

I swallow hard to keep my ears from popping and try to make sense of everything. I can't imagine what my family must be thinking. I bet they're glued to the news, wondering how I ever got wrapped up in such a cataclysmic chain of events. They must have been so relieved to see me free and headed home this morning. By now they must be panicking all over again, since I haven't managed to get in touch. The jet's wheels hit the ground. Henry launches out of his seat and yells at us to hurry.

36

A four seat helicopter delivers Henry, Max and me to the Vladimir Ilyich Shipyard, a vast and seedy establishment that smells like an unsavory mix of trash and ocean. The night air is heavy with bone chilling fog.

We land in an empty parking lot. Endless rows and stacks of giant containers sprawl in every direction like a city constructed from oversized toy blocks. The lighting is far from adequate and gets no better as we look downhill at the docks, where a bedraggled crew works to unload an enormous freighter with an equally enormous crane.

Henry announces that we need to find the foreman. He stops abruptly behind a random blue container and draws his gun. Max does the same.

"Are you expecting a shoot out?" I hiss. I naively imagined they'd march up to the man in charge, confiscate some containers and that would be that. Is this some kind of karmic payback for my stunt at the palace? I should fish the key from my bra, rattle off the bank code and hightail it out of here. The code is on the tip of my tongue when I remember I have no money, no transportation besides the helicopter—whose pilot presumably answers only to Henry—and no Russian beyond *hello*, *thank you* and *I'm a spy*.

"We're expecting no such thing, my dear," Henry assures me. "We're merely following standard protocol for exploring an unknown site in the dark."

"Shouldn't we be heading for the bank vault? And then home?" I ask hopefully. "Don't you have special forces people to raid shipyards? Do the shooting, if shooting is necessary?"

"No time," Henry says.

I don't believe him. Max grabs my arm, pulls me close and barely whispers into my ear. "This investigation is personal to Henry.

He's been trying to blow the world's largest arms smuggling ring wide open for over a decade. Ever since one of BXE's people blew his cover and he had to retire from the CIA. Reinforcements are on their way, probably only minutes out. But Henry wants to make the arrest."

My eyes widen. "Titan is the world's largest arms smuggling ring?"

"Ever since Acheson brought Korov and Clearwater together. Did you really think anyone would pay all those millions of dollars to send farming equipment all over the globe?"

Before I have time to answer, Max tells me to stay close, and not to worry.

Easy for him to say.

Our quarry is a ruddy-faced, heavy set man, with shoulders that run into his head without a neck. He's easily identifiable as the boss, since he's the only person not kitted out for manual labor. He holds a clipboard and wears a quilted yellow vest over his button-down shirt.

Henry says to Max, "Let's see whether the taxpayers got their money's worth from that two-month language boot camp you attended."

The foreman looks understandably surprised to have visitors. Max approaches him with a freakishly broad smile that does nothing to neutralize the fact that he's brandishing a handgun. He introduces us in what even I can tell is severely limited Russian. The foreman looks puzzled by, but not overtly hostile to, our presence. He leads us to a construction trailer.

A space heater blasts us with dusty air as we step inside the cluttered space. The office smells like a locker room. The foreman motions us to a ripped up sofa, settles himself behind a giant metal desk that dominates the room, and lights a hand-rolled cigarette. He takes a long drag as the three of us wedge ourselves onto the couch. If the foreman's concerned about the agents' Glocks, he hasn't let on. He's acting as if armed men in formal wear show up at his place of business on a routine basis.

Max launches into a speech in halting Russian. When he pauses, the foreman swings his feet on the desk and makes a big show of considering whatever Max is proposing.

Max says something else. The foreman leans further back in his seat and closes the blinds on the trailer's lone window. Dust billows. I stifle a cough as Henry produces a substantial stack of crisp hundred dollar bills. He hands them to our host without counting them out. The foreman's eyes bulge and he practically drools as he counts them carefully, once, twice, three times. If all those bills are hundreds, he's just enhanced his net worth by ten thousand dollars.

Evidently satisfied with his accounting, the foreman lights a new cigarette with the smoldering stump of its predecessor. He addresses Max in a more indulgent tone. It appears we have some kind of deal. Max makes a new request in hesitant Russian.

The foreman grunts his assent, swings his feet down from the desk and motions for us to follow him.

We walk back outside into the shipyard, to the closest ship on the dock. The foreman says something to one of his employees, a wiry man who looks over sixty but probably isn't. A short negotiation ensues. A fistful of hundreds pass from Henry to the recalcitrant longshoreman, whose face lights up with a nearly toothless grin as he counts the bills. He checks to make sure none of his co-workers are watching too closely, and launches into an animated narrative. He points towards a group of blue containers further down the pier. I think I catch the word Helsinki.

Max repeats it back, to make sure he understood, before turning to Henry and me. "Those are the containers shipped by Titan for the Burtonhall Corporation. They're scheduled to go by rail in a few hours, down to the Dagestan frontier, and then onward by truck. He thinks their ultimate destination is Syria, but it could be Iran or Saudi Arabia. He says that's where all Titan's containers go, and they always travel some crazy route."

The longshoreman looks on as Max takes his best stab at translating.

"Circumstantial, but good enough," says Henry, when Max pauses for air. "Can we open them?"

"Yes," Max answers. "But there's another thing. The longshoreman says an American man came through tonight, asked about these same containers, and then asked to get on a ship out of here as soon as possible. They stashed him on a boat that leaves for Helsinki in a couple of hours."

I knew I heard Helsinki. "Acheson!" I gasp.

"It would have to be. No one else makes sense," says Max.

"How much did he pay?" asks Henry.

"Evidently not enough to keep the men quiet. He must be getting cheap in his old age."

Henry tells Max to have the foreman summon the port's head customs official. Max translates, looking apprehensive, as if Henry's made a request that surpasses his linguistic capabilities. The foreman understands and shakes his head no.

Max says, "He says he's asleep."

Henry pats his gun. He addresses the foreman directly. "FBI. Wake the customs man up."

It's a bold move by Henry, since the customs man should understand that the FBI has no law enforcement powers in Russia. Evidently the foreman neither knows nor cares about such fine points of law. He gets on his phone and has an agitated conversation. We wait, and watch the cranes move container after container.

Finally, a man about Henry's age appears, speeding towards us on a golf cart. He screeches to a stop and jumps out waving his own badge. In passable English, he says, "This better be important."

Henry explains, very matter-of-factly, that he is the second highest ranking man at the FBI, and a reliable source tells him these containers contain weapons that are being smuggled to Islamic terrorists by a criminal gang.

The customs man looks unsure, not to mention sleep-deprived, mildly intoxicated and more than a little annoyed. Henry tries again. The man looks like he's on the fence, like he might humor Henry, or decide to go back to bed. It seems odd that Henry summoned him at all. Since he seems so amenable to bribing people, couldn't he pay someone to pry open the containers? He's so close. Why slow down now?

A spark of inspiration hits me. "What he means is, the guns are going to *Chechen* terrorists," I say to the recalcitrant customs man.

Who cares if this isn't likely to be true? It does the trick. The customs man begins ranting about Mother Russia. Within minutes, he's ordered the workers to crack open the first of the containers.

Max winks at me.

Henry says, "Brilliant. Truly brilliant."

The container is not only *not* half-empty. It's not even half full of agricultural equipment.

Instead, it's filled to capacity with machine guns, shoulder fire missiles, rounds of ammunition, grenades, night vision goggles, body armor and lots of other scary things I can't identify.

The customs man wastes no time getting on the phone. His men, who must have been on duty elsewhere in the shipyard, start to appear out of nowhere.

"Who's he calling?" I ask Max, who's visibly straining to understand.

"I think his bosses. And the press."

"Mission accomplished," says Henry. He asks the customs man for a copy of all documents pertaining to this particular shipment. The foreman dispatches a younger worker to make them. He returns at a run and hands Henry a sheaf of papers, which he folds and pockets.

Max snaps several photos of the container's contents.

The first wave of FSB men arrive within ten minutes to supervise the handling of the evidence. Henry looks on with approval, but not for long.

I muster the gumption to ask, "Why did you call in Russian customs and police?"

"Because we don't have the manpower, or authority, to seize the shipment, and because I can't take the time to go through that idiot Brownell. I want to find the elusive Mr. Acheson before he slips through our fingers for good."

37

Max produces Acheson's photograph and shoves it under the previously helpful longshoreman's puffy red nose, along with a small wad of hundreds. I expect him to demand more money before surrendering any further nuggets of intelligence. Maybe it's the excitement of the arms seizure, or maybe he thinks he's extorted as much as he can, but he nods and says, "*Da*. Helsinki."

"Where's the Helsinki-bound ship?" Henry demands.

Max starts to translate, but the longshoreman must understand the gist of the question because he points down the docks.

"*Bolshoi spaseba!*" Henry says, and sets off at a run. I've never seen him move so fast. Max and I rush to follow.

The foreman, swept up in the excitement of a huge illegal arms cache in his shipyard, doesn't bother to have one of his men accompany us. Henry and Max draw their guns as we hustle up a rickety, rusty gangplank. The ship's so enormous that it doesn't rock with the light motion of the water, but it still creaks and groans. Its decks are lit up, but the indoor lights are dimmed.

Henry stops us on the main deck, under an awning. "Let's find a crew member."

Max looks less than optimistic. "They have a few hours before departure. I bet the crew went into town to tie one on."

I tend to agree. Henry, in his eagerness to apprehend Acheson, has overlooked this rather obvious possibility.

"Fine," Henry says. "We'll search the quarters ourselves. It might be better if the sailors aren't around to interfere. If we come up empty and need to get into the hold, then we'll wait for the crew."

Henry steps aside and lets Max push through the metal doors to enter a stairwell. He hesitates. Henry says, "Down. The bunks would be below decks."

We march down one flight of metal steps and make such a racket that I imagine the workers on the docks can hear us. We arrive at the first landing and Max tries the door.

"Locked," he says.

Henry says to go down another flight.

An identical metal door, one flight down, opens with a creak and we find ourselves in a narrow passageway lined with doors, most of which are propped open. Only every third or fourth light bulb is burning. Dark shadows impede our line of sight. But it's only when Henry whispers to me to hang back with him while Max takes an initial sweep of the corridor that my heart starts pounding madly.

We stay several paces behind Max as he makes his way, gun drawn, down the hall for a cursory inspection of the cabins, which are really just glorified bunks. Each contains two narrow beds and a couple of footlockers, which don't look large enough to contain Acheson. Many of the bunks have been decorated, if you can call it that, mostly with posters of topless girls.

The hallway intersects another. As Max rounds the turn a few paces ahead of Henry and me, he walks smack into a night watchman. He's a square-shaped man with a stained shirt. He wears a belt under his beer gut, weighted down by a nightstick, a flashlight and a revolver that looks like a prop from a school play. He grips an almost empty bottle of clear liquid with both hands. He's so drunk, it's amazing he's upright.

Max and Henry lower their guns. The watchman looks more bewildered than alarmed. He rambles something. When Max appears confused, he repeats the same jumble of words again and holds up the vodka for emphasis.

Understanding lights up Max's face. "I think he's explaining that he's been consoling himself. He drew the short straw and had to stay behind while his shipmates went into St. Petersburg."

Henry's expression registers only annoyance. He tells Max to get to the point. Max asks the watchman something in halting Russian. He sounds unsure of himself and has to repeat his request several times. I can't tell whether Max is outside his depth, or whether the watchman is so far in the bag that he can't understand his mother tongue.

After several moments the watchman grins with comprehension and flashes us a mouthful of rotting teeth. He explains something else in Russian, and it sounds like he's not slurring as badly as he was a minute ago.

Max translates, "He knows where our man is, but he wants money."

"How much?" Henry makes a face as if he's reluctantly launching into a negotiation with a child over an allowance.

"Two thousand, U.S.," Max says.

The watchman nods emphatically and sticks out a grubby hand.

"Fine." Henry looks satisfied, as if he expected to pay more.

Max produces a thick envelope from his pocket. He counts the bills and passes them into the waiting hands of the watchman, who gleefully re-counts his take before stashing it in the inside pocket of his trousers.

"You have your money. Let's go," Max says, first in English and then in halting Russian.

The watchman explains something else and gestures down another, darker hallway.

Max turns to Henry and says, "He'll take us to Acheson's cabin."

"Excellent," Henry says. "Now we're getting somewhere. I think Lena should wait here. It's much safer in the event shots are fired. Tell him."

I don't like the idea of being left behind, and judging by the look on his face, Max isn't a fan of the suggestion, either. He waits to see if I'll speak up, but my mouth feels paralyzed. If Henry, with his lifetime of field experience, believes I'm safer here, maybe I am. At least I tell myself so. When I don't object, Max puts Henry's request to the watchman. He waves at three open doors.

"Pick one," Max translates.

I step towards the closest bunk. Max flips on the lights and looks under the beds. He tries to open the foot lockers, but they're locked.

"We'll be back in mere minutes, my dear," says Henry. He has a grim look in his eyes. Maybe the bad lighting magnifies it, but there's a sober resolve. "You're safer hanging back here. Max, give her a gun."

Max lifts his pant leg and removes a handgun from a holster on his ankle. "Glock 23. No safety. You just aim and pull the trigger. It has a hell of a kick for a weapon of its size." He passes me the gun. I send up a silent prayer that I won't need to use it.

I watch them walk away down the corridor, weapons drawn, two paces behind the watchman who's so unsteady that he must be exaggerating his inebriation for the fun of it.

A metal door clangs shut after they round the corner out of my sight. I try to combat my rising panic by counting the squares on the cabin's checkered carpet, but I can't help feeling like one of those girls in a B horror film. The naïve ones who wander off alone and get hacked to pieces by the hatchet wielding serial killer.

I'm focused on keeping my imagination in check when a male voice from the hall says, "You're much more tenacious than I thought."

Acheson, looking gaunt and exhausted, but somehow hardened, steps out of the shadows and into the doorway. I scream at the top of my lungs. He must not have expected that, because he rushes inside the cabin and slams the door shut behind him.

I grip Max's gun with both hands and squeeze the trigger with both index fingers. I'm not sure how many bullets fire – more than one – and miss their mark, flying over Acheson's head into the cabin's metal door with a deafening series of cracks not unlike fireworks exploding at close range.

Acheson tucks and rushes toward me. I try to duck clear of his reach, but I have no place to go. I hear myself yell for help as he tackles me by my hips and sends me crashing into the back wall of the cabin.

I manage to fire again as his free hand scrambles to close around my wrist. I scrunch my eyes shut, hold my breath and squeeze the trigger one last time before Acheson wrests Max's Glock from my grasp. I hope the bullet will pierce his heart.

38

My shot hits Acheson in the leg. He yowls in pain, but doesn't release his grip on Max's gun. Maybe I only managed to graze him. There's a negligible amount of blood, and he seems to be bearing weight on the injured leg. Damn it.

When I scramble back to my feet, Acheson leans in so close that I can smell his breath, which is sour, like bad milk. I try to push away from him, but there's nowhere to go. I've cornered myself against the back wall.

His upper lip curls like a rabid dog's. At the height of his career, Acheson always looked slick, polished and most of all, charming. His current expression is anything but. He snarls, "Did you really think I would let that blundering fool stumble around and rat me out to anyone who wandered onboard?"

I stare at him with what I'd like to think is disbelief, but it all makes sense. The watchman was paid by Acheson to play the drunken buffoon for us. Of course. My hands curl into fists and my nails dig into my palms. I consider punching him, but I doubt I could swing hard enough to do anything but piss him off. And he'd retaliate, gun in hand.

"I figured that fat fuck of a foreman might give me away. So I made a larger investment in onboard security."

I find my tongue. "You're not going to get away with this. Jack Prescott's already in custody. Maybe you should turn yourself in." It comes out in a meeker tone than I intended.

Acheson forces a laugh. "That's a pity about Jack, but I have no intention of doing any such thing. Now I hope you understand that what I need to do here is regrettable, but you've meddled far too much in my affairs."

He grabs my right arm and raises Max's gun with his free hand. I feel my whole body flush with panic. I open my mouth and sink my teeth into his hand like some kind of possessed demon. Blood spurts into my mouth, nauseating me, but I bite down even harder, trying to inflict maximum damage. Acheson releases his grip on my arm and jams his fist into my forehead. My neck wrenches back, and I feel something pop. My hands fly up to protect my throat.

Acheson tucks the gun into his waistband. I regroup and kick him in the groin as hard as I can. He yowls, stumbles forward, but recovers before I have any chance of pushing past him and out the door.

When he stands back up, he's brandishing a knife. "On second thought, a gunshot would be too kind." His eyes dance and in that split second I understand just how much he's enjoying this. Screw him. I'll be damned if I make this easy.

I lunge at his face. I aim my fingernails at his eyes, but only manage to scratch his cheeks, though badly enough to draw blood. I stomp down on his toes, but he hardly notices. He grabs my right hand with the hand holding the knife. I kick him in the shins. He manages to wrangle both my wrists into his free hand. He shoves me back against the wall with a thud and positions the point of his knife under my chin. A calendar of Baltic ports crashes down onto the bed below.

I've never believed people who claim their lives have flashed before their eyes, but now it happens to me. It's the most bizarre experience, because a thousand different pictures race through my brain in a millisecond, but somehow each one lingers long enough to register.

I see myself as a little girl, picking strawberries in my grandmother's garden and riding my bike in the driveway with my dad. Sledding on the hill in Diana's backyard. Reading Dr. Seuss on my mother's lap. Baking Christmas cookies and caroling in the old folks' home where Nana had to move after she set her house on fire. Waving to my mother from the bus on the very first day of school. Winning the eighth grade spelling bee. Losing the high school tennis championship. Countless family vacations. The first day of college, and the last. Spring break in Mexico with Diana and Hannah. My first date with Damien. My first day at the law firm. Moving into the T Street apartment with Damien. Walking down the aisle at St. Peter's by the Sea on my father's arm. Dancing at the reception with

Damien. Lying on the couch with Damien, watching stupid movies during last winter's blizzard. Burying Damien.

And countless other images, all fleeting and oddly chronological, yet all crystal clear. I feel the point of Acheson's blade skirt down my throat and the scenes from my past vanish. This cannot be happening. I was so close to going home. The case was solved. I got the tape, which will now languish unwatched in the helicopter, where I foolishly stashed my bag for safe keeping. I turn my head gingerly, taking care not to move too quickly or to apply more pressure to the knife. I look Acheson in the eye. "Just tell me! Was it you?" For a moment indecision flashes across his face, and I shriek again, "Was it? Did you break into my apartment that night? Are you the one who ruined my life?"

His eyes start to bulge, as if in awe of my capacity for hysterics. A persistent thumping noise comes from outside.

Acheson's head cocks at the sound of footsteps running down the hall. The color drains from his face.

The door swings open, but Acheson recovers his wits and reels us both around to face the exit, the knife still at my neck. The chilly metal presses hard against my windpipe. A new, breath-taking horror seizes me as I realize I'd rather die from a slashed jugular vein than a stabbed throat.

Less agony.

Probably.

Max bursts through the doorway, gun drawn. His eyes flash white with anger, or adrenalin, or both. He stops in his tracks, less than seven feet away from me.

"Drop the gun," Acheson says.

My knees knock together. Acheson's shaking, too. The blade bobs unsteadily on my skin, not cutting me, but scraping over my throat. I hold my breath.

Max takes his left hand off his gun and holds it up in a gesture of acquiescence. "Okay, okay," he says, and starts to lower his weapon slowly. Acheson readjusts his grip on the knife handle just as Max shoots his hand back up and fires. It happens in a split second, and the sound could wake the dead.

At first I think he's hit me, because I crash to the floor, but then I realize I'm alright. Acheson pulled me down when he fell. I disentangle myself. Max rushes to my side and extends a hand to help me up. He looks almost as shaken as I feel. "Are you hurt?"

"No." I fight back tears. I swear I felt the bullet whiz past my cheek. I feel my face, to check for injury, but find none.

Max crouches next to Acheson. "Dead," he pronounces, as Henry comes charging in from the hallway.

Henry is huffing and blowing like he just completed the Boston Marathon. He hunches forward slightly, catches his breath enough to speak and starts, to my surprise, apologizing. "I should have known something wasn't right. We shouldn't have left you. When the watchman sent us down another flight and we split up, I got a premonition of sorts, you see. It appears that Max had the same feeling."

"I didn't have any feeling, Henry. I heard shots."

Henry stoops down by Acheson's inert form, places his hands on his neck and says, "Definitely deceased. Well done, von Buren."

Blood the deep red color of brick seeps onto the carpet under the dead man's head. I turn away.

Max says nothing. Maybe there's no way to accept a compliment for being a deadly shot. Instead he goes to work patting down Acheson's corpse and emptying his pockets. He dumps keys and several wads of cash on the floor. He rips open Acheson's shirt and I hear the scratchy sound of tape ripping. "What the hell?"

Max holds a laminated index card up to the light and squints at the tiny print. "It looks like a schedule. In Russian."

Without thinking, I grab the card from Max's grasp. I can't be positive, but it looks an awful lot like the paper Charlie turned up in Acheson's files. The one we shrugged off that day we had lunch and speculated about the map. I remember that one started with 9:15, because that's the embarrassingly late time I normally roll into work. The schedule on Acheson's card runs from 9:15 to 23:22.

"Go always with your God," Max whispers over my shoulder.

"Excuse me?" I look from Max to Henry. A smile plays on the deputy director's lips.

"It's not a schedule, or meeting minutes. It's a code. Some kind of Bible code," Max says. "The numbers don't represent times of day. They're chapters and verses. Go always with your God. Whose God? Henry, which Bible did Casper give you?"

"The Russian Synodal." Henry grabs the card from me and squints at the Cyrillic text as if expecting to see the key to the code if he stares hard enough. That's the same version the nun gave me on the side of the highway. It must be somewhat common. My head reels. Have I been unwittingly carrying around a key piece of the puzzle for two days?

Henry pushes himself to his feet and pulls out his phone. "Brilliant!" he says, in an inordinately bright tone, considering we're standing around a bloody corpse. "The blasted thing gets reception."

"Excuse me, Henry," I say. He waves me off with his hand and turns away to make his call.

Henry gets his deputy, Ron Goldstein, on the line and tells him to page the elite cryptography unit.

I start to ease myself towards the door. I'm uncomfortable, at best, with my proximity to Acheson's body. They maybe trained for this, but I'm not. My crazy, self-inflicted crash course hasn't made the violence any easier to take.

Henry barks into the phone. "Get me the CIA's Moscow station chief...Yes, I realize it's late...I don't care if he's at his Black Sea *dacha*...wake him up and get him on the bloody line...no, I don't want to be transferred to that useless twit Brownell..."

Once he's on hold, he says to us, "I'll clean up here. You two go. Take the helicopter back to the airport and the Lear to Zurich. Get yourselves on the first flight back to Washington—as soon as you empty the vault."

"Henry?" I say again.

"What?"

"Mikhail removed a Russian Bible from Casper's body."

Both agents speak in unison. "Which edition?"

"I don't know, but it had the same red leather binding with gold trim as the one he gave you in Cleveland Park."

39

Less than an hour later, the Lear takes off. Max and I haven't exchanged more than a couple of words. I can't speak for him, but in my case, it's because I'm too stunned. When the pilot announces we've reached our cruising altitude, I break the silence. "Now that Henry's not here, can I please call home?"

He opens the armrest and retrieves an in-flight telephone.

"No details. Say you're okay, you're not a hostage and you'll be on this afternoon's Swiss Air flight from Zurich to Dulles."

I have a brief conversation with my emotionally fried mom, who answers on the first ring. She passes the phone to my dad. We go through the same things and when he asks where I am, I hesitate for a second before deciding there's no harm in telling him that I'm on a plane to Zurich. My father, whose ability to shift psychological gears in an instant will never cease to amaze me, marvels at the quality of the connection.

My mother pries the phone from him and demands to know what's really happening. She says she deserves to know when her only child is in danger. Now that the crisis has passed, she's pissed off and growing shriller. Max can obviously hear every word. He squelches a smile. I assure my mother that I'll fill her in as much as possible by the end of the day. I tell her I can't wait to see her. This placates her enough to end the call.

"Thanks," I say to Max once we've hung up.

He shrugs. "Don't mention it." He gets out of his seat and crosses to the bar by the galley. He holds up one of Henry's preferred bottles, the Macallan 15. "How about a drink? We deserve one." He pours and raises his glass. "To never having an assignment like this again."

I'll gladly drink to that. The cool, velvety liquor tempers my adrenalin. HIgh over Eastern Europe, we speculate about what will happen to Katya once they find her stuffed in a kitchen cabinet in the palace, and about how Henry plans to explain a dead, indicted American lobbyist to authorities from both sides of the pond. We wonder if Aziz will still receive immunity and agree that the Russians will finally have to arrest Korov, if they can locate him within their borders.

The only person neither of us mentions is Mikhail. I'm convinced he shot President Perayev. The security team found no other plausible suspects in the room.

And I'm fairly certain he did it through a hole in the ceiling. He spent a long time studying the palace's air ducts and crawlspaces. The one above the ballroom would've been tight, but Mikhail was probably agile enough to maneuver up there. And I wouldn't be surprised if he left the duffel bag and his black burglar clothes right above all our heads.

By the time the Alps come into view, Max has nodded off with his head against the window. He naps until the wheels hit the ground.

Actually, he sleeps until the plane comes to a halt and the copilot opens the door. I nudge him awake. He lurches up, embarrassed, and checks that he hasn't drooled on himself.

The Swiss officials barely glance at the New Zealand credentials Mikhail procured for me, although Max raises his eyebrows and mutters that I can explain later. We rush from the private flights terminal to the main concourse, where the shops are starting to open. Everything is literally sparkling clean.

Max makes a beeline to the Swiss Air desk. He buys two first class tickets for this afternoon's flight to Dulles from a fresh-faced girl with French braids and bright eyes. She's wearing the airline's red uniform with the scarf tied jauntily around her neck. "Your tax dollars at work," he says, as he hands over his AmEx.

"You know where we're going, right?" he asks, when we step away from the counter.

"The main branch of the United Bank of Switzerland. On Bahnhofstrasse."

"Excellent." Max consults his watch. "Let's go. They should open soon."

"*Guten tag.*" A well dressed, large boned and bald taxi driver studies us while he holds the car door. "Baggage?" he asks, as I slide across the seat of his black Mercedes. A fair question, since we certainly don't look sharp enough to be here for the day on business. Max looks like he slept in his suit several nights running and I resemble a grad student on holiday. Max ignores the question. "UBS, on Bahnhofstrasse."

The driver nods knowingly, as if this explains everything. We wind our way out of the airport and speed down a highway flanked on both sides by immaculately groomed gardens and trees. The rush hour traffic proceeds in an orderly fashion, with the left lane reserved only for passing. It's the exact opposite of Russia, where drivers apparently believe they get extra points for intimidating fellow motorists.

We cross a river so clean it gleams almost Carribbean blue, and enter the city center. We come to a major square flanked by two giant cathedrals, one gothic and somber, the other more whimsical and fairy-tale-like. My heart pounds with anticipation, but not in the frightened way that's become all too familiar. This time I feel like I can see the finish line.

The driver pulls up in front of a large stone building with an understated brass plaque that announces, U.B.S. The neighboring stone buildings bear similar brass plaques engraved with the familiar names of other giants of world commerce. It's five to eight in the morning. Our driver explains, "They'll open. Five minutes."

We wait on the steps for less than two minutes before we hear the electronic locks click.

A series of glass doors admits us to an enormous marble lobby. Trees reach up to an atrium flooded by brilliant sunlight. There's a huge marble staircase, with an imposing equestrian statue at the top.

A few other customers come in right behind us and head for various counters. Obviously these Armani-clad patrons know what they're doing. I feel out of place as I point out the desk that reads, Safety Deposit Accounts, in five languages.

A well-dressed forty-ish woman, whose name plate identifies her as Madame LeBlanc, gets up from behind the desk as we approach. She extends a hand in polite greeting. Her thick legs taper down into Chanel pumps and her muted pink suit sets off her coloring to maximum advantage. I catch her looking us up and down.

Max notices, too. "Don't worry. They get all sorts," he whispers to me, but the woman overhears and smiles primly before asking if she can help us, in perfect English.

Max starts to introduce himself. Her eyebrows elevate ever so slightly and he realizes that's not a necessary part of the protocol.

I say, "We'd like to access a safety deposit box."

"Of course. Please step this way, madam." Madame LeBlanc ushers us back through the lobby into an elevator bank.

She holds the doors for us and presses the lowest button. We drop down what feels like multiple flights and the doors open into a well appointed sitting room. My breath catches as I realize the décor reminds me of Korov's Moscow house. It's similarly furnished with high-end antiques. A sideboard offers an array of beverages.

It's all very nice, but I don't see the safe. I glance at Max, but he looks clueless, too. Madame LeBlanc doesn't wait for us to inquire. "It's quite simple, really," she explains, as she enters a code on a wall keypad and places her palm on an adjacent screen. The doors, which look wood paneled, but turn out to be fashioned from steel slabs, two feet thick, swing open.

She ushers us through into an ordinary bank vault, not nearly as elaborate as depictions of Swiss banking in the movies. "Your key has a number. I'll escort you to your box and leave you for as long as you like."

Madame LeBlanc clears her throat, daintily. "Madam, may I have the box number on your key? The number alone cannot compromise your privacy."

That's not why I'm hesitating.

"Um, uh, excuse me, just a second." I turn my back to them and fish the key from under my shirt.

Madame LeBlanc politely pretends not to notice me digging around in my undergarments. Max stifles a laugh by turning it into a snort.

I wipe the key on my shirt to remove any traces of sweat before holding it up for inspection. Madame LeBlanc consults the number on the stem and marches down the row of boxes inside the vault. She stops and points out the correct one. "I'll leave you now. When you're finished, simply replace the box in the vault and close the door."

She bows slightly, which seems absurd, before disappearing up the elevator. My hand shakes with excitement as I insert the metal key into the slot next to the box's keypad.

The screen flashes to life and asks for the pass code. I key it in, carefully, pausing between each digit. 3-3-0-2-8-7-4-4-9-1.

Nothing happens. Max and I look at each other. I might be about to see a grown man cry. Then, the screen flashes green and says, in five languages, *access approved*. A mechanism inside unlatches the door, which reveals a plain black box with handles and a lid.

Max says, "May I?"

It's funny he's asking. The FBI paid a hefty sum for whatever Mikhail stashed here.

He grabs the black container and carries it out to the sitting area by the elevators. The lid pops right off. There's nothing inside except ten flash drives. Max's face breaks into a grin. I'm still holding my breath. What if they're blank? What if they harbor a virus?

I can't stand the anticipation.

Max whips out his laptop and pops in the first memory stick. The computer whirs, acknowledging the new arrival. He opens a series of scanned documents. Max smiles wider, then frowns.

"What?"

I'm reading over his shoulder. It looks, at a glance, pretty good to me. There's every type of document Mikhail pointed out in his apartment, before it burned. Wire transfers. Bribes. Money laundering. False shipping orders. And much more.

Max shakes his head. "That bastard."

"What?"

"This will be enough to secure a warrant to seize Clearwater's computers and back up files. We can nail Prescott for sure, and Aziz, if we can find him. His half-brother will strip him of his diplomatic status so fast it'll make his head spin. We could have put away Acheson for the rest of his natural life, too."

I'm confused. Max should sound happier. He motions for me to look closely.

Names are blacked out all over the page. Max scrolls through the document. Redactions everywhere. "No mention of Korov," he says, shaking his head. "Damn."

I bet Mikhail let Korov off the hook when his wife got sick, well before it occurred to him to sell his stash to the FBI.

And Korov had no idea.

"Three out of four isn't bad," I say, because I feel a need to break the stunned silence.

We spend about an hour in the vault, reviewing the files and backing them up on Max's computer. As Madame LeBlanc promised, nobody disturbs us. Mikhail delivered the goods. He merely failed to inform the FBI of certain editorial decisions.

Anyone familiar with the case could easily conclude the blacked out name is Korov's and the blacked out company is the Victory Group. But courts at home thankfully don't accept mere assumptions. At least I don't think they do.

Max looks at his watch and says, "Even with the redactions, this is a gold mine. But we need to move if we want to catch our flight."

He packs up the spoils of the vault and his computer. We replace the lid on the now empty black box and return it to its rightful place. I stow the key in my purse, since Max doesn't ask for it.

Max slings his bag over his shoulder and we march out of the bank, with a lighter step than we had on our way in, and dive into a cab for the trip to the airport.

Two hours later, I sink into the first class seat assigned to Ms. Anne Lewis of Christchurch and fall asleep before the attendants pass out the pre-flight champagne.

MAY

40

No bride could wish for a more perfect day. It's a beautiful late spring afternoon. Everything about Hannah and John's reception at her grandparents' estate overlooking Charleston's harbor is gorgeous. Everything, that is, except for the yellow bridesmaid's dress I'm wearing. It's a flattering style, but the color doesn't look good on anyone but Diana, whose deeper skin tone helps her carry it off.

The cocktail reception is in full swing, with white-gloved waiters passing elaborate hors d'oeuvres and a steel drum band playing upbeat standards. I watch Hannah making her rounds, pulling her new husband along by the arm, glowing.

I had worried that today might be tough, that the wedding festivities would bring back all kinds of sad memories. But instead I feel hopeful, and full of happiness for one of my two best friends in the world. My date's gone off to search for the men's room and I find myself alone for the first time all day. I take my champagne glass and stroll down from the terrace into the gardens.

It's been over two months since my family and a small army of federal prosecutors met Max and me at Dulles Airport. In some ways it feels like it all happened yesterday, but at other times, recent events feel like hazy memories from a lifetime ago.

The U.S. Attorney and his underlings whisked away Max, the flash drives from the vault and Korov's video. It took a week for an FBI lab to authenticate the tape. One of the prosecutors called to ask me whether I wanted to watch it.

It took me four double-length sessions with a psychiatrist in as many days to decide I did not.

The prosecutor came to see me. She sat me down and told me bluntly, that the tape clearly implicated Acheson and another man, identified by Agent Max von Buren as a now-deceased Russian criminal known to us only as Casper. Evidently Casper was the trigger man, but Acheson talked their way into the apartment. Poor laid-back, trusting Damien. Though I imagine they would have knocked the door down if he'd refused to let them in. Emotionlessly, the junior prosecutor described how they tied him up, posed him with the pizza box and shot him dead, before undoing the ropes and leaving the gun to make it look like a self-inflicted death. There's no struggle on the soundless tape. Damien had a gun pointed to his head from the moment he opened the door to his killers.

They have no idea who served as the cameraman. The prosecutor, a swine-faced woman decked out in an ill-fitting navy blue suit, offered no theories. She editorialized only about the ropes, remarking that it was ingenious to pad them so the forensics team wouldn't see signs of strain.

People always talk about closure, but I don't feel any relief from learning these details.

Nor do I get much comfort from the knowledge that the perpetrators died violent deaths themselves. The prosecutor suggested that the silver lining, if she could call it that, was that I would be spared the heart wrenching ordeal of a trial. I told her that wasn't a silver lining and calmly asked her to leave. She did so after mumbling her condolences.

I stayed in bed for a week. On the eighth morning Diana and Hannah said they'd force me up if they had to. They said Damien would hate my sulking. So I reluctantly hoisted myself out of the bedroom to get on with my life. Amazingly, it gets easier with every new morning.

My parents are lobbying hard for me to move home to Rhode Island, but I plan to stay in Washington. Even though my life will never be as it was, my closest friends and best career prospects are here.

The venerable 150-year-old firm of Rutledge & Smerth imploded shortly after Evelyn's arrest. Its lawyers scattered to competitors around the city. Henry asked me whether I would consider a career with the Bureau. Out of the question. I've seen firsthand that spy games aren't nearly as glamorous as they look on screen and I've witnessed enough violence for a hundred lifetimes.

Right before the visit from the prosecutor, I withdrew $30,000 from Mikhail's Swiss account, to reimburse Diana and Tobey for the plane tickets I never used. Incidentally, those two are still going strong. I bet she makes a dash for the bouquet tonight.

I feel strange about spending the rest of Mikhail's cash. On one hand, it's a substantial sum that would buy me some time to consider my next steps. On the other hand, it feels like blood money. While I can't blame Mikhail for making a deal with Korov to save his own neck, I can fault him for it, if that makes sense. Still, I mostly hope he got away someplace nice. He was something of an enigma, and I can't believe he was all bad.

Speaking of Korov, he emerged from the scandal without suffering the slightest repercussions for his role in the largest money laundering, terror financing and arms smuggling ring in recorded history. His star has risen faster than anyone could have predicted. President Perayev did not die of his wounds, but remains in a persistent vegetative state in a Moscow hospital. The Russian Parliament called a special election a mere four weeks after the shooting. Korov won in a landslide, after his only serious challenger was gunned down on his front stoop two days before the vote.

Armed with head of state immunity, Korov won't face charges for his role in what the press has dubbed the K Street Affair.

In one of his first official presidential acts, Korov announced a new cooperative venture with the Saudi oil company headed up by Crown Prince Muhammed bin Aziz. The talking heads on television say that if the two sides can manage to agree on terms, the alliance will exercise unprecedented influence over oil and gas prices on the world markets.

In another of his initial executive acts, Korov pardoned former FSB operative Irina Sluvanskaya, alias Katya, for her role in a series of criminal acts, which were not enumerated to the public. Why he did this remains a mystery. Maybe she was working for him the whole time. The only condition for her release from the grim women's prison where she'd been awaiting trial was that she leave Russia.

I heard through the grapevine (alright, I heard from the new CIA Chief, Henry Redwell) that Katya flew to Geneva to shack up with Abdul bin Aziz. Henry believes she somehow spirited Abdul out of Moscow right under the noses of the FBI and various other authorities, but I'm not supposed to tell anyone that. Switzerland doesn't extradite, so apparently, the only price he'll play for his role in the affair is that he won't become king of Saudi Arabia. I'd still like to ask Korov why he told me the video would implicate Aziz, but it's unlikely I'll have that chance any time soon.

The President of the United States, once he returned home and replaced Jack Prescott with a squeaky clean self-made junior Congressman from Ohio, used a significant amount of political capital to push his surprise nominee for CIA chief through the Senate. Henry's in his glory at the job of his dreams. Right after the president swore him in, Henry gave a joint press conference with the U.S. Attorney to announce a freeze of all Clearwater Partners' assets, which effectively shuts down BXE and the Burtonhall Corporation. At least for now.

Based on evidence seized from files at Clearwater Partners, the FBI has arrested eight senators and forty-six congressmen who took money from Acheson in return for favorable votes on a host of bills supported by Clearwater and its subsidiaries. The press has hailed the unraveling of the K Street Affair as a shutdown of one of the largest highways for illegal weaponry on the planet.

Max, on the other hand, is thrilled to be back to his routine caseload, where he can toil without his boss breathing down his neck. The case he built against Jack Prescott catapulted his career. He can go wherever he wants in the Bureau now. He's also received more than a few offers from those big law firms he used to deride.

Rumor has it that Prescott will plead guilty, to spare the nation the spectacle of his trial, and to spare himself the death penalty. The two Secret Service agents he hired to kill the Commander in Chief will be tried separately, probably early next year. BXE's chairman, Royce Prescott, was arrested at his hunting cabin in Tennessee, transported to a lock up in West Virginia, and indicted on a list of federal charges so extensive that the major papers printed up a special section to enumerate them. They included over five hundred counts of murder for the hotel explosion in Abu Dhabi that was designed to look like an attempt on the vice president's life. Royce hung himself in his jail cell the day after the grand jury issued its ruling.

That leaves William Acheson, the man I was paid to defend at the firm and persuaded to investigate at the FBI. Strangely enough, Henry was on the scene when an FSB dive team pulled Acheson's swollen, waterlogged body out of a canal in the middle of downtown

St. Petersburg, two days after Max and I arrived back home. The case was closed as a Russian mafia hit. Max worried that the autopsy Acheson's widow demanded would turn up the bullet from his Glock. The corpse, however, was inexplicably misplaced by the FSB. I read the other day that Mrs. Acheson pulled her kids out of their school in McLean, moved to Connecticut and resumed her maiden name, in an attempt to escape the media glare.

It took the FBI's cryptography team a week to decipher the coded message found on Acheson's person. Max told me that the information was encoded using the Russian Synodal Bible as a key. Just like Henry and Max suspected at first glance.

The resulting message steered an international team of agents to the location of Casper's nuclear arms auction, a cellar hidden behind the wall of another cellar, underneath a grain silo in Kazakhstan. The special forces stormed the site and found nothing. Max confided that Henry's sources suggest the nukes are still out there and their owners will regroup before trying to reschedule a sale. Hopefully, armed with the clues and information from Mikhail's vault, the CIA will manage to get one step ahead of the traffickers.

I will kick myself until the day I die for not copying the supposed minutes Charlie placed under my nose in the sushi restaurant. I photographed hundreds of worthless pages of Acheson's papers. Why didn't I grab the one that mattered most? Had Henry seen that page in the wake of the bombing, he might have picked up on the Bible verse connection when Casper told him to go with his God, at the end of that bizarre meeting in Cleveland Park.

Henry assured me I exceeded his expectations exponentially. I helped break up a massive crime ring, and I should hold my head high. "You slay one serpent and another appears to take its place, my dear," he said at our formal debriefing. "Look at what you've helped us accomplish. Acheson, dead. Smerth, dead. Clearwater, trading at pennies on the share. Titan, shut down. Lotus Group, shut down. BXE, disemboweled, emasculated and under federal oversight for the next hundred years. Prescott in prison. His no-good cousin, dead. Two bad agents, going away for life, if they're lucky. *And* you avenged your husband. I'd say, good show. A very good show indeed."

I try to believe he's right. One thing I've learned is that the successes and failures of law enforcement turn as much on luck and circumstance as on expertise and intellect. I tell myself I gain nothing by obsessing over missed chances. The same day I read that Mrs. Acheson was packing up her children and leaving Washington, Special Agent Max von Buren received a package sent from the UBS branch in Zurich, which contained the recording in which Acheson admitted his role in January's attacks on the metro. He sent it to the same FBI lab that reviewed the videotape of Damien's murder. If the tape is real, Mrs. Acheson will need to move her family further than Connecticut to shield her children from the press frenzy. Maybe I should have a little sympathy for her, but I don't. She must have had some inkling that her husband was a bad apple.

We should know for sure within a week, but I would bet all the money in my Swiss account that the recording is authentic. I'd love to know how Mikhail carried it out of the Bucharest Hotel. I didn't notice him remove anything from his computer before he sent it flying out the window.

As my heels sink into damper ground, I realize that I've been wandering by myself for longer than a bridesmaid should be absent. I extract my shoes from the lawn and head back up to the party. The wedding coordinator, a perky woman with angular features and a headset clamped onto her over-shellacked chignon, announces that dinner is served.

The night starts to speed by and I catch myself having *fun* for the first time since I can remember. We dance all night. Hannah's parents have hired an eighteen-piece orchestra and everyone's on their feet as soon as the waiters clear the plates. My date, my only straight single guy friend, turns out to be a decent dancer, which I wouldn't have guessed. I've settled into what my shrink calls "healthy widow behavior." I haven't been a shut-in, but I'm taking it slow.

My date surprised me by agreeing to come here for a whole long weekend, since I was clear we'd have two hotel rooms, and not only for appearances. He's been clear that he hopes we can become more than friends, but he's sweet and understands I'm not ready. And not because I'm concerned about what people think, especially since I've been widowed for almost as long as I was married.

He says I'm his first widow love interest so he has nobody with whom to compare me. I hate that label, but I'm getting used to it. It's an indelible part of my persona now and I'm realizing that despite what our parents, teachers and commencement speakers tell us, we don't always get to choose who we are.

The lead singer calls Hannah up for the bouquet toss and a small swarm of eligible ladies gathers on the dance floor. I hang back, unsure, behind the rest of the single girls. I suppose I'm one of them, but I'm not. I decide against joining the group. Hannah, though given the chance to single out evaders with the microphone, exchanges glances with me and understands. I stand in the front row of the assembled audience, with a few of the bride's camera-toting, chiffon-wearing aunties.

Hannah turns, covers her sparkling blue eyes for added drama and lets the flowers fly. The bundle of peonies and roses soars over the squealing mass of girls and lands right in my arms. Everyone applauds as Hannah turns to see who got it. Her face breaks into a huge smile. I scan the crowd for my date, thinking he'll feign horror, but he looks content, even happy, sitting with Tobey and a few of John's college friends, drinking Stellas and watching the proceedings from our table.

The happy crowd of wedding guests parts so Hannah can make her way over to me. She slings her arm around my shoulders for the obligatory bouquet pitcher and catcher shot. While the photographer refocuses, she whispers in my ear, "Look over there." She motions to my date, who's smiling broadly.

He raises his drink to us. I smile back, but then lower my eyelids and glance away. Hannah says, "You know, you're right. He really could do toothpaste commercials with that smile. When you feel up to it, you should give him a chance."

"I probably will," I assure Hannah, though I'm not as certain as my happy expression suggests.

What Hannah doesn't know, what no other soul knows, as far as I can tell, is that when I checked into the inn two nights ago, the concierge sent up a sealed envelope. It was handwritten in black ink on heavy, cream colored paper, folded over, and sealed with old fashioned wax. No return address. Sent airmail from Johannesburg, inside another envelope addressed to the hotel. The typed instructions, which the concierge also passed along for my examination, simply asked the hotel to hold the enclosed correspondence for me until I arrived for the Smith-Lorenzano wedding.

The card inside, the one I'm struggling to put out of my head with no success, even though I burned it to ashes in the hotel sink, proved maddeningly brief. The elegant cursive I first saw on the files in Mikhail's hiding place under the floor boards presented a straightforward invitation.

Lobby bar, Pera Palace Hotel, Istanbul. 7p.m. June 30.

AUTHOR'S NOTE

Although *The K Street Affair* is a work of fiction, I consulted several sources to get the details right when I first conceived of the idea for this book in 2005. At that time, I was convinced whatever my imagination could concoct risked sounding far fetched next to real world events. My views on that subject have evolved, and I'm afraid the writing process has left me less optimistic about the motivations of many prominent men who seek to rule the world. In drafts as recent as six months prior to my final edit, I never imagined I'd be writing about a pretend politician, Vice President Jack Prescott, who laundered his fortune offshore, hid his assets in blocker companies and made hundreds of millions without paying the IRS, while a real politician stands credibly suspected of doing precisely the same thing.

As long as countless politicians are owned by multinational corporate interests, as long as they can flout the rules they make for the masses, as long as they shroud their financial actions and motives in secretive corporations (like my fictitious Lotus Group in Bermuda, or like William Acheson's fictitious private bank in Palau), as long as they have vested interests in prolonging violence (as in Acheson's and Prescott's interests in the fictitious war mongering security firm BXE, a subsidiary of the massive, though thankfully fictitious, multinational called Clearwater) we will never be sure that those leaders will act in the best interests of the people they purport to serve.

Perhaps Lee Raymond, the chairman of Exxon/Mobil said it all, when asked about building oil refineries in the United States, because doing so would be good for the American economy: "Why would I want to do that? I'm not a U.S. company and I don't make decisions based on what's good for the U.S."

Among the most valuable and eye opening references I consulted were Craig Unger's critically acclaimed *House of Bush, House of Saud: The Secret Relationship Between the World's Two Most Powerful Dynasties*; *Merchant of Death: Money, Guns, Planes and the Man Who Makes War Possible*, by Stephen Braun and Douglas Farah; *The Halliburton Agenda: The Politics of Oil and Money*, by Dan Briody; and the excellent documentary film *The Corporation*, written by Joel Bakan and directed by Mark Achbar and Jennifer Abbott. Much, much later in the game, indeed during my last re-writes, I came across the February 2012 issue of *Vanity Fair*, which included a piece called "The Meaning of Mitt," an adaptation from the book *The Real Romney*, by Michael Kranish and Scott Helman.

I owe a huge thank you to Sean Gordon, for his insights into law enforcement, his willingness to listen to my endless barrage of questions and his good humor when I said I might need to take a bit of poetic license from time to time (mainly in the interest of keeping Lena alive and adventuring).

I am also grateful to the private equity executive who first floated the phrase "offshore money laundering" my way, and who for obvious reasons will remain anonymous.

Thank you to my tireless editor, Jennifer Fisher, whose enthusiasm for this novel inspired me to take it out of my desk drawer and finish it after a long hiatus. I'm grateful to April Fulton for her editorial vision and her encouragement to go big, and to Dawn Tringas, for her invaluable blue comments.

To my uncomplaining earliest readers, Annette Widener Stafford and Lisa Mogan: I am deeply grateful for your enthusiasm, honesty and support over many months and several re-writes.

Thank you to Regina Starace for another unbelievable cover.

Thank you also to those who read various versions of this book as a work in progress and encouraged me to keep going: Monique Appleton, Matt Bialer, Jennifer Rose Cramer, Valerie Friedholm, Rick Howes, Hank Phillippi Ryan, Vicky Crawshaw Scanlon, Wendy Walker, Heidi Wolmuth, and various people who share the name Passananti: Riitta, Vincent, Mikko, Sara and Anja.

Mari Passananti, Boston, July, 2012.

Made in the USA
Lexington, KY
07 January 2013